CW01512309

THE SECRET OF GIZA

THE KWAN THRILLERS
BOOK 1

KEN WARNER

VIBRANT CIRCLE BOOKS LLC

Copyright © 2021 by Kenneth H Warner, II
All rights reserved

Cover Design by Broken Candle Book Designs

For Jeff, the best alpha reader an author could want.

CONTENTS

THE SECRET OF GIZA

PROLOGUE

Egypt, seventeen years ago

D r. Stephen Kwan gazed out the window of the limousine. The Great Pyramid loomed in the distance, lit up against the night sky. He'd always wanted to visit Egypt, but had imagined *vacationing* here. Never did he expect to travel to the country on business.

The information he'd received only two days earlier seemed impossible; it flew in the face of common sense. He was no Egyptologist, but nothing in Dr. Kwan's experience could explain this startling discovery.

"You still don't know the woman's identity?" he asked, turning to the man sitting adjacent to him. "The one who tipped you off?"

"No," replied Jacques Moreau. He was a short, scruffy-looking man. Dirt seemed permanently etched into his skin.

"Nor do I understand how she could have known about the chamber. We'd long suspected other rooms might exist within the structure, but radar analysis always came back negative. Yet somehow, this woman was able to give us the exact coordinates."

Dr. Kwan stared out the window, shaking his head. He didn't like mysteries.

They drove past the Great Sphinx a few minutes later. A sudden sense of foreboding overcame Dr. Kwan. The impressive statue looked like it was guarding the necropolis. Dr. Kwan couldn't help but wonder if the secrets it protected were better left undisturbed.

The car continued past the southern edge of the Great Pyramid. They turned a corner and stopped near the southwestern tip of the structure. Dr. Kwan and Jacques Moreau exited the limousine. Moreau led the way, walking by the pyramid's southern face.

"What are those?" Dr. Kwan asked, gesturing toward the low, rectangular structures to their right.

"Mastabas," Moreau replied. "Tombs," he added in response to Dr. Kwan's blank stare.

Near the center of the pyramid, they came to an enormous tent. Moreau pulled open a flap and motioned Dr. Kwan inside. Heavy machinery filled the space—digging equipment and winches. In the middle, a vast hole plunged into the earth. Moreau moved to the gap and stepped onto a ladder.

"I don't understand," Dr. Kwan said apprehensively. "I thought the entrance was in the north face?"

"It is," Moreau replied. "But you can't get where we're

going from there. The entrance to the hidden chamber is buried in the bedrock. Follow me!"

Moreau disappeared down the ladder; Dr. Kwan took a deep breath and followed. They descended for several minutes. Thick cables and hoses ran down the wall on either side of the ladder. Sweating now, Dr. Kwan wished he'd worn something other than a suit.

Finally, they emerged into a cavernous space, illuminated by floodlights. Dr. Kwan followed Moreau to an opening in the rock wall. Hieroglyphs adorned the stone on either side.

"It is highly likely that this chamber has sat undisturbed for over four thousand years," Moreau said, turning on a flashlight and leading the way into the tunnel. "Centuries of grave robbers plundered the rest of the pyramid. And various research teams have drilled and excavated over the years, looking for hidden rooms. But *this* chamber shows no evidence of previous entry."

They walked on level ground for a minute, until they reached a steep incline. Dr. Kwan walked carefully up the slope; it felt like his shoes would lose traction against the smooth stone.

There was a faint scent in the air—sulfur, maybe. Dr. Kwan guessed there wouldn't be much air circulation in a chamber that had been buried for four millennia. Whatever he was smelling had probably been floating around that entire time. He thought of the various chemicals that would escape a decomposing body. A shiver ran down his spine.

After several minutes, the shaft leveled out again. They

came to a small room, not much bigger than a closet, with a narrow opening in the far wall.

"This is it," Moreau said, excitement in his voice. "We are almost as high as the Queen's Chamber, but many meters to the south."

He walked through the opening. Dr. Kwan followed.

"Welcome to the hidden chamber," Moreau said. The beam of his flashlight revealed white walls, much smoother than the stone in the tunnel. "This room must have been very special. It is constructed of white limestone, meticulously crafted—much like the casing stones that originally covered the exterior of the pyramid. We have touched nothing; you are seeing everything exactly as we found it."

The room was empty except for a square, stone structure in the exact center that rose only waist-high. Dr. Kwan moved toward it. The top was open; he peered inside and gasped.

"This cannot be…"

1

HORROR

Marlton, Maryland, present day

Malia Kwan opened her eyes. She'd fallen to the floor, crashing through the end table. The lamp had landed on top of her. She pushed it away and sat up—and gasped, inhaling a mouthful of dust. Coughing, she looked around in horror. What used to be her living room was now destroyed. The front wall of the house was gone, blown out by the force of the explosion. Only a handful of wooden beams remained.

Most of the room's contents—including the sofa, television, and bookcase—were now strewn across the front lawn. The lights from the police cars in the driveway continued to flash, casting shadows through the dusty air. The officers lay motionless in the yard.

Malia spotted her mother. She was splayed out, face down

in the hallway. Malia ran to her side, tripping over the rubble, and dropped to her knees.

"Mom…" she cried. Melissa Kwan didn't move. She wasn't breathing. Malia noticed a dark pool on the floor beneath her. She touched it with a finger and held her hand up to the light. It was blood.

"Mom!" she yelled, shaking her.

"Malia—we have to get out of here!"

She turned—Jaden was standing over her, his face mirroring her despair. But there was something else written in her twin's features—a look of determination that Malia didn't share. She felt only anguish.

"She's… dead," she told her brother between sobs.

Turning back to her mother, Malia saw something by the overturned recliner. Stephen Kwan's legs were sticking out from behind the chair, the rest of his body hidden from view. Malia stood up, stepping toward her father. She was terrified of what she was going to see, but she had to go to him. Maybe by some miracle, he was still alive.

But Jaden grabbed her by the arm. "No—we have to go. Now!" Sirens blared in the distance.

In some deep recess of her brain, Malia knew her brother was right. She surrendered, allowing him to pull her through the house. They went out the back door and ran into the darkness. Malia followed Jaden into the woods, no idea where to go or what to do, as the sirens grew louder.

2

NEAR-DEATH EXPERIENCE

Seven hours earlier

Jaden Kwan had always looked forward to high school. He knew the classes would be harder, and had no doubt there would be much more homework. But along with the academics came broadened social horizons. He'd eagerly anticipated the dances and football games and parties—and girls. Older girls with boobs and driver's licenses. The increased workload was a small price to pay.

But there was one thing Jaden hadn't considered: Freshman Friday. It was the day before homecoming and the opening game of the football season. School tradition called for a certain amount of hazing of the incoming freshman class.

"I can't believe they allow this," said Seth Bowman, Jaden's best friend since the second grade. They were making their way through a crowded hallway to their sixth-period classes. "It's criminal! Have they done anything to you yet?"

"Jaden's got nothing to worry about," Malia declared before Jaden could reply. "They don't bother the football players—only the *geeks*," she added, staring pointedly at Seth.

"Not true! They stuffed Derek Flint into a locker on the third floor! I saw it right after the pep rally this morning."

"You're full of crap. Derek's a lineman—he's too big to fit in a locker," Jaden retorted.

"Oh, he fits," Seth insisted. "It took three kids to squeeze him in, but they did it. I guess it's a good thing you're a receiver—at least you can outrun them."

"Yeah, whatever," Jaden replied, doing his best to sound unconcerned. "This is Cafferty's room, isn't it?"

"What?" said Seth, looking around in surprise. "Oh, right. I'm still not used to this place. See ya!"

Seth ducked into the classroom. Jaden hoisted his backpack higher on his shoulder and continued toward the stairwell with Malia; their next class was downstairs. But before they reached the end of the corridor, Jaden stopped in his tracks.

"Uh-oh," he muttered.

Marcus Crouch had just descended from the third floor with two of his friends. He was a second-time junior whose favorite sport was bullying freshmen. And he was as big as a house.

"Let's go the other way," Jaden suggested.

"What? Why?" Malia asked, confused.

"Crouch," Jaden said.

Malia rolled her eyes. "Don't be silly. We'll be late if we go around—just ignore him."

Jaden suspected this would be easier said than done, but followed her anyway. They entered the stairwell, and he did his best to avoid making eye contact with Crouch. But as they went by, Crouch bumped into him, pushing him into another student and the huge trash bin holding the door open.

"Watch it, douche bag," said Crouch.

"Sorry," Jaden muttered, trying to get past him to the stairs. But one of Crouch's friends blocked his way.

"Hey—it's that Kwan kid," the boy announced. "He's on the freshman football team."

Jaden recognized him. It was Andrew Pinski, who lived three doors down from the Kwans.

Crouch's eyes lit up. "Yes! Grab him!"

Pinski reached for him; Jaden dodged out of the way. He darted up the stairs, but Pinski grabbed him by one foot. Jaden fell. He thrashed and squirmed, trying to free his ankle and regain his feet. But it was no use.

Crouch picked him up, turning him upside down. Jaden's backpack fell to the stairs.

"Put him down!" Malia shouted.

Crouch carried him to the trash bin. He tried to stuff him in, but Jaden braced himself against the top of it with both hands. Crouch kept trying to push him in. Jaden's iPhone fell out of his pocket and clattered to the floor.

Suddenly Crouch pulled Jaden away from the bin. Jaden didn't know what he was doing at first, but quickly realized he was attempting to pin his arms to his sides.

"Hey Crouch, listen to this," Pinski said gleefully. "'I love your braids, Jaden. They're so *sexy!*'"

Jaden groaned. Pinski was reading his text messages.

"Who wrote that?" Crouch asked, successfully squeezing Jaden's arms against his ribs.

"Caitlin Rudolph," Pinski replied. "She's a junior—why's she talking to *him*?"

Crouch grunted and resumed his effort to stuff Jaden into the trash bin. Jaden managed to free one arm, but Crouch still had the other one pinned. This made it much harder to resist.

"*Leave him alone!*" Malia screamed.

"Make me, you little bitch," Crouch taunted.

"I don't believe it," said Pinski. "Caitlin's going with him to *homecoming!*"

"She must've been desperate after Barbieri turned her down," Crouch replied.

"I know why you're picking on the football team," Malia said. Jaden recognized the superior tone of voice she always used when she knew something he didn't.

"And why's that?" Crouch asked, lifting Jaden a little higher, then pushing him down again.

"To get revenge for last week," she said.

"Malia—shut up!" said Jaden. Crouch had lost a fight to Vinnie Barbieri several days earlier; Vinnie was a varsity lineman.

"I'll go get him if you want," Malia continued. "He's in the classroom right there."

Crouch pushed Jaden even more forcefully. "Malia—*shut up!*" Jaden yelled. He figured Malia's theory was probably correct, but at the moment, it was doing him more harm than good.

Suddenly Pinski burst out laughing. "You're gonna love this one! 'You're a good kisser, Jaden. I've never made out with a Black boy before.'"

Jaden groaned again; Crouch chuckled. "Was that Caitlin again?"

"No—Elise Smith," said Pinski.

"*Elise Smith*?!" Malia repeated. "You did *not*!"

"Malia—SHUT UP!"

Elise was Malia's best friend. Jaden had arranged to meet her the previous night. They'd agreed to keep the encounter a secret from Malia.

At that moment, the bell rang. Crouch had had enough. He punched Jaden in the ribs. Jaden's arms contracted reflexively as the air vacated his lungs, and he landed on his head in a pile of garbage.

But in the same instant, there was a crashing noise. Someone shouted. Jaden couldn't see a thing from inside the bin. He kicked his legs violently and managed to tip the garbage can over. He got to his feet in time to see Crouch and his cronies running down the hallway.

Before disappearing around the corner, Crouch stared back at him. He was bleeding from the forehead, and he looked *scared*.

Jaden collected his backpack and his iPhone, which Pinski had dropped on the floor. He and Malia ran downstairs to their history class. Luckily, Mr. Slater was nice: he didn't give them a detention for being late.

Jaden took a seat in the back of the classroom next to his sister.

"What happened back there?" he whispered. "What was that noise?"

Malia shushed him and moved one seat farther away. Jaden knew she was probably angry about Elise. He pulled out his binder and started taking notes as Mr. Slater droned on about the ancient Egyptians.

"The Great Pyramid is the oldest and largest of the Giza complex. It was built over a period of twenty years, ending in 2560 B.C. to serve as a tomb for the pharaoh Khufu.

"The pyramid is remarkable for a number of reasons. For 3,800 years, it was the tallest manmade structure in the world. It weighs almost *six million* tons. Each side of the base measures 756 feet in length. And yet despite its colossal size, the length of each side is accurate to within fifty-eight millimeters, and the base is almost perfectly flat, with an error of only twenty-one millimeters. Furthermore, the structure is precisely aligned along the points of the compass, and the ratio of the height of the pyramid to the length of each side of its base equals exactly one half of pi.

"But incredibly, the ancient Egyptians achieved these feats of engineering centuries before the invention of the compass or the wheel. It is believed that it took nearly 100,000 men to drag the various..."

Fascinating though this was, Jaden had more pressing matters on his mind. He tried texting his sister, demanding to know why Crouch had looked so scared. But she didn't even look at her phone. He'd have to apologize about Elise repeatedly, that much was certain. But even then, Malia probably wouldn't talk to him for a few days. She was way too moody. He wanted to know about Crouch *immediately.*

He would have spent the entire class thinking about this, but then the text messages started.

"Dude, I heard you beat up Crouch. Is that true?" wrote Seth.

Elise said, "You pushed Crouch down a flight of stairs?!"

"You kicked Crouch in the head?" asked Derek Flint, the boy who'd been stuffed in the locker.

"Where did you hear that?" Jaden typed back.

"From Vinnie Barbieri," Derek replied. "He heard it from Pinski."

Several more messages followed; Jaden didn't understand what was going on. He texted Malia again. "What the hell happened to Crouch?"

He knew it was futile. Even if she weren't angry, Malia never sent text messages during class. She didn't like breaking the rules.

"I didn't beat him up," Jaden typed back to Seth. "He stuffed me in the stupid garbage can and then there was this crashing sound. By the time I got out of the garbage, Crouch was down the hall. He had a cut on his forehead and he looked scared."

"You mean you didn't touch him?" asked Seth.

"No."

"Maybe Malia beat him up."

"Miss prim and proper? I don't think so," wrote Jaden.

He realized it didn't matter what happened with Crouch.

Everyone believed he'd beaten him up, regardless of the truth. And as nobody liked Crouch, it might gain him some popularity—and "cool points" with the girls.

And besides, Malia wouldn't stay angry at him *forever*. She'd tell him what happened eventually.

His phone buzzed. It was Seth again.

"Dude, Crouch says you're dead after this period."

"What?!"

"Flint told me. He's coming to your classroom when the bell rings to kick your ass."

"Now what am I gonna do?" Jaden asked.

"Run for it," Seth replied. "Get to Ferrell's class ASAP. Crouch'll never catch you and he's not gonna pick a fight in front of a teacher."

Jaden knew he was right. If he moved quickly, there was no way Crouch could get here in time.

Derek Flint texted him next.

"Jaden, you're screwed. Crouch is pissed. I think he might actually kill you."

Jaden refused to panic. He was nervous, but he had a plan. As the end of the period neared, he kept his eyes on the clock. The moment the bell rang, he'd be out the door.

Finally, the time came. Jaden stood up before the bell had even sounded. He tore out of the room at top speed, crashing through the door.

He bounded up the stairs and dashed into the corridor. Classroom doors opened as he ran, students pouring into the hallway. Jaden looked back as he rounded the corner—there was no sign of Crouch.

But an instant later, someone grabbed him around the waist and pulled him into a stairwell. It was Pinski.

Jaden struggled to free himself, but Pinski was bigger and stronger. He hauled him up the stairs as passing students pointed and laughed. But they didn't stop at the third floor; Pinski took him all the way to the roof.

"What the hell are you doing?" Jaden demanded. "Let me go!"

Pinski threw him down. Jaden scrambled to his feet in time to see Crouch emerging from another stairwell. He tried to dart around Pinski back to the stairs, but Pinski grabbed him again. He dragged him, kicking and screaming across the roof. They met Crouch at the edge of the building over-looking the courtyard. Pinski took Jaden's backpack away and handed him over.

Crouch grabbed him in a headlock and held him over the edge. Jaden screamed.

"That's right, go ahead and scream, you little girl," Crouch taunted him. "You told the whole school that you beat me up, didn't you? But now they'll see you're nothing but a little bitch."

"I didn't say *anything*!"

"Tell me how you did it, and I'll let you go," said Crouch.

"How I did *what*?!"

Jaden stared down at the ground three stories below, and tears welled up in his eyes. There was nothing but concrete to break his fall.

"You shoved me into the door, and I smashed my head.

But when I turned around, you were still in the garbage. So how'd you do it, Houdini? Was it like magic or something?"

"I DIDN'T DO ANYTHING! I DIDN'T TOUCH YOU!"

Crouch loosened his grip, and Jaden felt like he was about to fall. He screamed again, clutching Crouch's arm.

"Keep screaming, but if you don't tell me how you did it, I'm gonna let go!"

At that moment, there was a noise—someone had opened the door to one of the stairways.

"JADEN!" a voice shouted. It sounded like Seth.

Crouch turned to see who was there and lost his grip. Screaming, Jaden dropped several inches. He clung desperately to Crouch's arm. To his surprise, Crouch tried to help. But Jaden slipped out of his hands and plummeted toward the ground.

He squeezed his eyes shut, trying to protect his head with his arms. But suddenly he felt himself stop moving. Jaden opened his eyes. To his shock, he was floating several inches above the concrete.

3

MYSTERY

Jaden remained utterly still for several moments, hardly breathing. Finally, he reached out with one hand, touching the concrete—and promptly fell to the ground. He shouted in surprise, scrambling to his feet.

Looking up, he saw Crouch, Pinski, and Seth staring down at him from the roof. Crouch and Pinski turned to run; Seth didn't move.

Jaden gazed around the courtyard. Students crowded the windows of several different classrooms, watching him in stunned silence. Suddenly self-conscious, Jaden headed back inside. But something on the ground caught his eye. It was his iPhone. He squatted down to retrieve it, noticing only then that the face was shattered. He pushed the button to turn it on, but nothing happened. Pocketing the useless gadget, he ran inside.

A minute later, he reached his geometry class. Seth ran up the hallway behind him and handed him his backpack.

"Dude..."

Jaden ignored him and went through the door at the back of the classroom. Mr. Ferrell was writing notes on the chalkboard; Jaden tried to sneak to an empty desk unnoticed. Seth took the seat directly in front of him. The rest of the class paid them no mind—this room didn't have a view of the courtyard, so nobody would have seen what had just happened.

"Bowman and Kwan, why are you late?" Ferrell asked without turning around.

"Sorry, Mr. Ferrell," said Seth, "but it's not our fault—we were—"

"*Shut up*," Jaden hissed, smacking him in the back of the head. "We got lost," he said to Mr. Ferrell. Several students sniggered.

"Next time, it's detention," said Mr. Ferrell.

Jaden looked around the classroom and spotted Crouch sitting by the windows. He looked away the moment Jaden made eye contact.

A few minutes later, there was a knock at the door. A student came in and told Mr. Ferrell he was sent to bring Crouch to the principal's office. Crouch collected his things and left the room.

Jaden paid no attention to the lesson. He couldn't stop thinking about what had happened outside. How had he survived that fall, totally unscathed? It wasn't possible—gravity didn't shut off like that. What unseen force had stopped his descent? Had *he* done something to cause it? If he had, it was unintentional.

But the notion was ridiculous—what could he have possibly done to stop himself from falling? He started to wonder if he was crazy. Maybe he'd hallucinated the whole thing. By the time the bell rang, he'd convinced himself that he should see the school nurse. But Seth's outburst as they left the classroom made it clear he hadn't imagined anything.

"Dude! What the hell happened out there?! How did you not die? That must have been like a hundred-foot drop—and you just… *walked away*! It was incredible!"

Jaden walked in silence as Seth suggested any number of possible explanations, from voodoo to a sudden suspension of the laws of physics. None of it sounded plausible.

They entered their English classroom. It was around the corner from geometry, so they arrived before anyone else. Dropping their backpacks, they took two seats at the back of the room. Elise ran in a second later. Her eyes went wide when she saw Jaden; she dashed over to him.

"Oh my God!" she screeched, grabbing him in a hug before taking the seat next to his. "I saw you fall! You're not… hurt?"

Jaden shook his head.

"How? I thought you were *dead*! You hit the ground, and you didn't move—"

"I *didn't* hit the ground," he corrected her. "I stopped… somehow, a few inches above the concrete."

"But that's impossible," Elise said, looking at him as if he were insane. "You must have landed just right—I read about something like this once. This guy survived a skydiving accident. His chute didn't open, but he only had a couple of broken bones."

"Wait—you *didn't* hit the concrete?" asked Seth.

"No," said Jaden. "You saw me…"

"Nah, man, it looked like you hit from where I was standing. This is even weirder than I thought… You levitated!"

Elise snorted. "You're an idiot. I'm telling you, he must've landed in exactly the right position, so the force was spread out—"

"Look, let's drop it," said Jaden, uncomfortable with the speculation. He was sure Elise was wrong—he *didn't* impact the concrete. But nothing else made sense either.

"Wait a minute," said Seth. "If you saw it from your classroom, why didn't the teacher do anything?"

"She didn't see it," Elise replied with a shrug. "Malia and I only noticed Jaden right before Crouch dropped him—nobody else was looking out the window. I screamed when he fell, and everyone ran over. But by the time the teacher looked, there was nothing to see. Jaden was just standing there."

Malia walked into the room at that moment, stopping in her tracks when she saw Jaden. She opened her mouth to say something, but turned away and sat down at a desk near the front instead. Elise went to sit with her.

The rest of the students filed into the room. A few came over to talk to Jaden; others simply stared at him in awe. From the numerous conversations he overheard, Jaden could tell news of his incident was spreading.

But Mrs. Sheehan walked in a minute later, and the classroom grew quiet.

"Jaden and Malia," she said, "Principal McLaren would like to see you in his office. Now."

Malia looked back at Jaden for a moment before packing up her things, her face full of worry. Jaden slung his backpack over his shoulder and followed her into the hallway. They walked through the corridors in silence, each lost in thought.

One of the secretaries looked up when they entered the main office.

"Ah—have a seat, and Principal McLaren will be right with you."

They sat down in the chairs outside McLaren's office.

"What do you think McLaren wants?" Jaden asked.

Malia didn't respond.

"He probably heard about what happened," Jaden continued. "I don't understand it—I was falling, and I just *stopped*. You saw it, right?"

Malia said nothing.

"Look—I'm sorry about Elise, okay? I know I shouldn't—"

"I don't care about that. I'd *rather* see you with her—that Caitlin girl is a tramp."

Jaden was stunned. "Then why haven't you talked to me all day?"

Malia frowned, shaking her head.

Jaden sat quietly, adding Malia's strange mood to the list of the day's mysteries. If she wasn't upset about Elise, what was bothering her?

He didn't have long to contemplate these matters; Principal McLaren opened the door a minute later and ushered them inside his office. He took a seat behind his desk, Jaden and Malia across from him.

"It's come to my attention that the two of you have been involved in a couple of altercations with Marcus Crouch today. I'd like to hear your version of these events."

"It was just me," said Jaden, staring at his knees. "Malia wasn't part of it."

McLaren nodded. "Is it true that Mr. Crouch stuffed you in a garbage can this morning?"

Jaden felt reluctant to answer this truthfully. If word got around that he'd ratted someone out—even Crouch—the social ramifications would be severe. But he didn't see what choice he had. Lying wouldn't help—McLaren had obviously heard the story already.

"He did, but only because it's Freshman Friday. Someone else stuffed Flint in a locker—that's what people *do* today. He didn't hurt me or anything."

"And did you kick him in the head in retaliation?"

"I guess," said Jaden, thinking fast. "I didn't mean to—I was upside down in the garbage can, and I was kicking my legs trying to get out. My foot must have hit him by accident."

"That's not true," said Malia. "Crouch tripped over his own feet. Nobody touched him."

McLaren regarded them quietly for a moment. Jaden couldn't tell what he was thinking.

"It wasn't a big deal," he said. "It was just a joke—this happens every year, right?"

"What about this afternoon?" asked McLaren. "If the rumors are true, Mr. Crouch threw you off the roof. Although I'm finding that difficult to believe—you appear uninjured," he added with a smile.

Jaden saw an out. McLaren would never believe that Jaden had fallen three stories completely unscathed. This time lying would definitely help him avoid being labeled a rat. But Malia spoke before he could open his mouth.

"It's true," she said. "I watched the whole thing. Crouch held him over the edge, and then he lost his grip. Jaden fell."

"Malia—shut up!"

McLaren looked confused. "Where did this happen? Was it the roof of the annex? That's not *too* high, which would explain—"

"No, sir," said Malia. "Crouch dropped him from the top of the east wing, right into the courtyard."

McLaren stared in disbelief for a moment. "But that's impossible—there's nothing but solid concrete there. A fall like that would…"

"I know it should've killed him," said Malia, looking at Jaden for the first time, tears welling up in her eyes. "But that's what happened."

"This is a grave accusation," said McLaren. "I assumed the stories were blown out of proportion—and Mr. Crouch was unwilling to tell me anything. But what you're describing here is a serious crime—"

"He didn't drop me on purpose!" said Jaden. "He tried to

help when I started to slip! He was just trying to scare me—he didn't mean for anything bad to happen!"

McLaren shook his head. "He never should have taken you to the roof in the first place—"

"He didn't—Pinski did," Jaden said without thinking.

"Andrew Pinski?" McLaren asked, picking up his pen and scribbling on a legal pad.

"They didn't mean to drop me! Please, Mr. McLaren, don't give them detention or anything—"

"I'm afraid this incident warrants far more than *detention*," said McLaren. "If they took you to the roof and dangled you over the edge, I'm going to have to call the police."

"The police—no!" yelled Malia, jumping to her feet.

Jaden stared at her in utter disbelief.

"Malia, these boys committed a very serious crime. Your brother could have been killed."

"I know, but he *wasn't*! He's fine! Mr. McLaren, please don't bring the police into this!"

Jaden couldn't believe his ears. He would have expected the exact *opposite* reaction from his twin.

"I'm sorry, I'm left with no choice. If you two could please excuse me for a moment, I'm going to call your parents. Would they be home now?"

"My mom probably is," said Jaden, getting to his feet.

"Very well, have a seat in the main office, and I'll be with you in a moment."

Jaden and Malia left the room, closing the door behind them. They retook the same seats they'd occupied before the meeting.

"I can't believe this," said Jaden. He noticed Malia was crying. "Why are *you* so upset? I'm the one who's gonna be a social outcast once people hear about this."

Malia didn't reply.

Jaden sat alone with his thoughts for several minutes. It was hard to believe that he'd started the morning with nothing but excitement for the following day's football game and homecoming dance. Things had changed radically in a few short hours.

Mr. McLaren emerged from his office. "I wasn't able to reach your parents, but I left a message. I also contacted the Marlton police department. The matter is in their hands now —I'm sure they'll contact your parents directly.

"You did the right thing telling me the truth. I know it wasn't easy. But what these boys did was very serious. They'll face the consequences and hopefully, think twice before they ever pull another stunt like this again."

He looked at his watch. "Well, the period's almost over. You two can wait here and go home when the bell rings."

"Yeah, okay," said Malia.

He gave them one last worried glance before returning to his office.

"*Why* did he have to go to the police with this?" she said once McLaren's door had closed behind him.

"What are you *thinking*? Why don't you want him going to the cops?"

"Oh please," she replied impatiently. "You mean, you *do*?"

"Of course not—but it's *you* we're talking about!"

Malia glared at him for a second before turning away.

"This is gonna be awful. When people hear I ratted on Crouch..." Jaden shook his head. "And how the hell did I survive that fall? McLaren's right—that should've killed me."

Malia didn't reply.

"Tell me exactly what happened with Crouch this morning. When I was in the garbage can."

She sat in total silence.

"Will you please talk to me? Crouch did *not* trip over his own feet. I wanna know what *really* happened."

Malia sniffled.

Jaden stared at her. "Fine. You're not gonna talk to me? Two can play at this game."

He shifted in his chair to face away from her. Five minutes later, the bell rang. Jaden hoisted his backpack over his shoulder and headed out the door, not bothering to wait for Malia.

The main corridor quickly became crowded and noisy. Jaden weaved his way through the chaos, keeping an eye out for Crouch the whole time. He reached the stairwell and left the building through a side exit.

The high school was located in a residential neighborhood; the Kwans lived only a few blocks away, so Jaden and Malia walked to and from school every day. Jaden set a brisk pace along the sidewalk. Within minutes, he heard footsteps running behind him. He looked over his shoulder—as expected, Malia was racing to catch up. He knew she hated walking home alone.

She fell into step beside him without saying a word. They turned the corner onto Menlo Drive. Jaden knew she'd talk if he gave her the cold shoulder for a while. She couldn't stand being ignored.

Sure enough, as they turned onto their street five minutes later, Malia stopped in her tracks, grabbing him by the shoulder.

"Will you please talk to me!" she demanded.

He rounded on her. "Oh, *now* you wanna talk? Great! Why don't you start by telling me what the *hell* happened to Crouch when I was in that stupid garbage can?!"

Malia stared at him, fear in her eyes. "I don't know… he punched you and…"

"And *what*?"

"It was weird. He turned to walk away, and it was like someone pushed him. He flew into the door and smashed his head."

"And *you* didn't touch him?" Malia shook her head. Jaden believed her; pushing someone like that would be totally out of character. He started walking again. "Maybe he *did* trip over his own feet."

"No. Something pushed him—hard," Malia insisted. "You didn't see it—"

"Obviously. So what are you saying? It was like a ghost or something?"

"There's no such thing as ghosts."

"Then what pushed him?"

"I…" She hesitated. "I don't know."

"Yes, you do—what were you about to say?"

"Nothing."

"Bullshit—you were about to say something. What do you think pushed him?"

"Just forget it," she said, walking faster. "And watch your language."

Jaden tried to get her to tell him more for the rest of the walk home, but it was futile. The house was empty when they arrived—which wasn't too unusual. Jaden figured his mom was probably out running errands or something. She used to be a doctor, like their father but decided she wanted to spend more time with her children. She was always finding ways to keep herself busy since she'd stopped working—typically gardening or home improvement projects. Jaden tried his best to avoid being roped into such activities but was often unsuccessful. He'd spent much of the previous weekend helping plant trees in the backyard.

Jaden went straight to his room, dropped his backpack on the floor, and plopped down on his bed. He pulled his iPhone out of his pocket to text Seth—he'd forgotten it was broken. He stared at the shattered screen, hopelessly pressing the home button.

A minute later, he heard his mom's SUV pulling into the driveway. Jaden slid out of bed and headed downstairs. He'd have to tell her what had happened at school, and figured it would be best to do it before the police contacted her.

He found Malia already downstairs, heading out the front door; he followed her.

"Oh good—you two are home," said Melissa Kwan from the back of the SUV. "You can help me take in the groceries."

Jaden groaned, reluctantly taking a heavy paper bag from his mother.

Five minutes later, all the groceries inside, he sat at the island in the kitchen with his sister as Melissa bustled around, putting everything away. She was chattering about some new vegetables she wanted to plant in the garden over the weekend. Jaden wasn't listening. He was trying to decide how to tell her what had happened. But he wasn't sure what to say. The words, "I fell off the roof, but floated a few inches above the concrete and didn't get hurt," sounded crazy. The distressed look on Malia's face told him she was also struggling with how to explain the day's events.

"I'm talking to you!" Melissa was staring at the two of them expectantly, her hands on her hips.

"Oh—huh?" said Jaden.

"What's *wrong* with the two of you? You haven't said one word since I got home—did something happen at school today?"

"Uh…" Jaden replied.

Malia turned to look at the counter. Jaden and Melissa both followed her gaze. Melissa's phone had flashed a notification—she had a voicemail.

Melissa looked back at her daughter for a moment before moving to the counter. She tapped her phone to play the message.

"Hello, Mrs. Kwan, this is Oliver McLaren from Marlton High School," the voice said. "I wanted to talk to you about an incident that took place with your children today. Everything's fine now, and they're both perfectly okay. But I am going to need to contact the police. They will probably be in touch with you at some point as well."

Melissa listened to the rest of the message, staring intently at Jaden and Malia the whole time.

"The *police*?" she asked, folding her arms across her chest and looking stern. "Explain."

Jaden and Malia glanced at each other before promptly looking away again, staring at the floor.

"I'm waiting."

"We didn't do anything," said Jaden. "We're not the ones who are in trouble."

Melissa's expression softened, turning slowly to worry. "Then… what happened?"

"Marcus Crouch dropped Jaden off the roof of the building," Malia blurted out.

It took several seconds for the shock to register on Melissa's face. "He did *what*?!" She rushed over to Jaden, taking his head in her hands and staring at him as if examining his skull for signs of damage.

"Mom, I'm fine—I didn't get hurt," he said, squirming out of her grasp.

She backed away a step, eying him from head to toe. "Tell me everything," she said, sitting across the island from them.

Jaden took a deep breath. He still wasn't sure how to begin. He started out explaining Freshman Friday, and the incident with Crouch and the garbage can. Once he got going, he found it easier to continue. By the time he reached the drop from the roof, the words were pouring out of him. Malia sat in silence, contributing nothing.

He finished the story, wondering anew how he'd survived the fall. Melissa stared at him quietly for nearly a full minute. Did she think he was lying? The story did sound ridiculous.

"What did you do?" she asked finally.

"Huh?"

"How did you stop yourself? Before you hit the ground?"

At first, he felt only relief that she believed him. But then he realized that she seemed almost *excited* to hear his reply. He didn't understand her reaction.

"Mom, I didn't *do* anything! I can't explain it—I thought I was dead. But then… I just *stopped*."

Melissa nodded slowly, rising from her chair. Her expression was unreadable. "We'll discuss this when your father gets home."

Jaden decided to go visit Seth. He walked out the back door, across the yard and into the woods. He followed a narrow, winding path. His mother's reaction baffled him: how could he have done *anything* to stop himself from falling? Of course, nothing about the incident made sense. But she hadn't appeared fazed by the fact that he'd dropped three stories, completely uninjured, asking only *how he'd done it*.

He came to a broader trail and turned north. Usually, he'd text Seth before turning up at his house, but his broken iPhone made that impossible. He followed the path until he reached a rocky escarpment. After clambering up its face, he found Seth waiting for him at the top.

"Hey, I texted you, but you didn't answer. I figured I'd come over," Seth explained. Jaden pulled his iPhone from his pocket, showing him the broken glass. "Oh… right."

They sat down on a fallen tree trunk.

"Dude, *everyone's* talking about your little stunt today."

"Great," Jaden replied, rolling his eyes.

"There's already two fan pages about it on Facebook. One's called *Jaden Kwan is Superman*. It's got like 150 people already. The other one's *Can Jaden Kwan Levitate?* Or something like that—that one's got over 200 people!"

"Maybe my mom should look at those. She asked me how I did it."

"Really? Well, Elise was probably right. You must have hit the ground exactly right. Nothing else makes sense when you think about it."

Jaden didn't want to remind him that he *hadn't hit the ground*. He was quickly coming to the conclusion that he'd never know what had really happened. Elise's explanation was the only plausible one—even if he knew it to be incorrect. But at least it would stop the speculation about other possibilities—like levitation—that made him extremely uncomfortable. If something like that were true, it would make him some sort of freak.

"This sucks," he said. "Now, everyone's going to be talking about me at homecoming."

"Oh—homecoming!" Seth replied. "Is Malia still going?"

"Yeah, she bought a dress and everything."

"Good—maybe it's not too late… Did someone else ask her to go yet?"

"Nah, she's going with like Sara and Ashley… I think. But I'm telling you, she doesn't *like* you."

"Yeah, but she will if she goes with me to homecoming," said Seth. "I'll win her heart."

Jaden laughed at him. "You're an idiot."

"Dude, shut up. I'm gonna ask her. She's the hottest girl in the whole school—it's the whole half-Black, half-Asian thing…"

"Seth, shut the hell up."

"No, really—your sister's freakin' gorgeous, dude! But… she doesn't look *too* Asian. It's just her eyes…"

"Yeah, cuz my dad's only like one-quarter Korean, you moron. Now shut up about my sister!"

"You wanna ask her for me?"

"You want *me* to ask *my sister* to go to homecoming—with *you*?!" Seth nodded hopefully. "Forget it. *You* ask her. Her phone still works. But I'm telling you, she's gonna say no. You'll embarrass yourself."

They talked for a while longer. Seth failed to work up the nerve to call Malia. Jaden was grateful when the conversation shifted to the upcoming football game. Marlton was expected to win—Jaden couldn't wait to watch it.

Eventually, he decided to return home. But as he emerged from the woods, he spotted a car at the end of the driveway. The police were there.

4

EXPLOSION

Jaden entered through the kitchen door, as quietly as possible. He crept down the hallway, edging along the wall of the staircase until his sister came into view. She was sitting on the sofa, next to their mother. Tears were streaming down her face.

"You have nothing to worry about, Malia," said a female voice Jaden didn't recognize. It must have been the police officer. "You've done nothing wrong—we're just gathering information."

"I know," Malia replied with a sniffle.

"Jaden!" It was his mother—she'd spotted him. "Get in here—I've been calling you, why didn't you answer your phone?"

"It's broken," said Jaden, walking into the living room and taking a seat next to his mother.

"Hello, Jaden," said the officer. She was sitting in the

recliner in the corner. "I'm Detective Murphy. I understand you had some trouble today with a boy named Marcus Crouch?"

Jaden nodded.

"I've talked to your sister already, but do you think you can tell me what happened?"

Jaden told the whole story, again starting with the garbage can episode.

"But Crouch didn't mean to throw me off the roof," he concluded. "He tried to grab me when I started to fall."

"It doesn't make any difference," said the detective, shaking her head. "He acted recklessly in a manner that could have caused you extreme harm. That makes what he did a crime."

"Are you gonna arrest him?"

"Most likely," she said. "I'll bring him in for questioning, at least. And I believe we have sufficient evidence at this point to make the arrest."

"Will he go to jail?" asked Malia.

"That's up for the court to decide. It'll depend on the charges. If the DA goes for attempted murder—"

"*Murder*?!" said Jaden. "But, I'm *fine!*"

"Jaden, why are you trying to defend this boy?" Melissa demanded. "He dropped you off the top of a three-story building!"

"Yeah, but..."

"Your mother's right, Jaden," said the detective. "And you have nothing to fear—with Crouch in prison, he won't be able to harm you."

"But he wasn't trying to *kill me*!" Jaden insisted. "Why should he go to *jail*?!"

"Well, he may be convicted on some lesser charge. But frankly, you're lucky to be alive. I don't understand how you weren't hurt very badly. If it weren't for all the witness testimony I've collected, I wouldn't believe it!"

"Oh… well, I heard about this skydiver who fell… and his chute didn't open," Jaden stammered, suddenly alarmed. The last thing he wanted was the police investigating *him*. "And… he lived, cuz I guess he landed just right… and the force of the fall was spread out or something…"

Detective Murphy chuckled. "I guess that makes sense. One thing's certain, though: you are extremely lucky!" She rose to her feet; Melissa did the same. "I think I'm done here. Thank you for your time, and someone will be in touch with you soon."

Melissa shook her hand and walked her to the door. But at that moment, Stephen Kwan walked in, looking distressed.

"What's going on—why are the police here?" he asked. "Oh—hello," he added to Detective Murphy. Melissa introduced them.

"We need to talk," she said to her husband once the detective had left. She glanced at Jaden and Malia, still sitting on the couch. "*Privately.*"

Stephen greeted his children, still looking very worried, before following Melissa upstairs.

Jaden and Malia waited on the couch until they heard the door to their parents' bedroom close. Then they hurried quietly up the stairs into Malia's room. Jaden followed his sister into her closet. There, they each took a seat, pressing an ear against the back wall. They'd figured out long ago that they could eavesdrop on their parents' private conversations this way.

At first, Jaden couldn't hear anything. But as he listened more intently, he could make out a soft humming sound—his mother was whispering. He looked inquiringly at Malia. She shook her head—she couldn't discern what Melissa was saying either. Unfortunately, their mother had once discovered them listening in on their father's private phone conversation. After that, she'd always been careful to keep her voice down.

"That's incredible." It was their father's voice.

Their mother's soft humming resumed for a couple of minutes.

"We have to tell them the truth." It was their father again. Malia looked sharply at Jaden.

"Quiet down," their mother said. She said something more, but Jaden couldn't tell what it was.

"They're not children anymore," their father said. "They're in high school—it's time to…"

"Would you *please* lower your voice!"

Stephen kept talking, but Jaden could hear nothing more than a low rumble.

"Damn!" he said. Malia shushed him.

They listened for several more minutes but were unable to glean anything else. When they heard the bedroom door open, they scrambled out of the closet. Malia jumped into her bed, and Jaden sat on the floor next to her desk. Their parents went downstairs.

"What was *that* all about?" Malia whispered.

"I don't know," said Jaden. "But I'm gonna ask Dad as soon as Mom goes to sleep tonight."

Melissa always fell asleep watching television long before Stephen went to bed. It sounded like their father *wanted* to tell them something. Jaden would get it out of him.

But he wondered what it could be. Clearly, his mother had told his father what had happened at school. And upon hearing that his son had survived a three-story fall, Stephen Kwan had decided there was something—some information —that he wanted to tell his children. Was it possible that he had an explanation for what had taken place that day? Jaden could only wonder.

He went to his room and sat down at the computer. He logged into Facebook and found the pages Seth had mentioned. Each now had over 300 people. He wanted to chat with Seth, but he wasn't signed in. Instead he went on Elise's page and browsed through her pictures. She'd added an entire album from her trip to the beach the previous week-end; her bikini was very revealing. Jaden found himself wishing he'd asked *her* to homecoming instead of Caitlin— especially after Malia's revelation that she'd prefer to see him with Elise.

"If only I'd known," he muttered to himself.

Thirty minutes later, Malia barged into his room. Jaden closed the browser before she could see what he was looking at. She threw her phone down on the carpet and jumped into his bed, lying flat on her back.

"UGH!" she yelled.

"What's up?"

"Seth!"

Jaden chuckled. "He asked you to homecoming?"

Malia sat up. "You *knew*? And you didn't warn me?"

"I didn't believe he'd actually do it. He thinks you're hot, but I didn't think he had the balls to ask you. I'm impressed."

"Ugh!" she said again. "He's *gross*."

"So, did you say yes?" Jaden said, knowing very well she hadn't.

Malia glared at him.

"I wish I'd known you'd be cool with Elise and me," he told her.

"Why? What difference does that make?"

"Cuz, then I coulda asked her to homecoming instead of Caitlin," he said, thinking of her Facebook pictures.

Malia giggled. "Wouldn't have mattered. She's already going with Derek Flint."

At that moment, their mother called them down to dinner. But as Malia jumped off the bed, her phone buzzed from the floor. She headed out of the room.

"Aren't you going to see who that is?" asked Jaden.

"I don't have to. It's Seth. I don't want to talk to him," she replied without stopping.

Jaden picked up the phone. Sure enough, it was a text message from Seth, begging Malia to go to homecoming with him.

"He *really* wants you to go to the dance with him," Jaden yelled.

"UGH!" she called back.

Chuckling, Jaden dropped the phone on his bed and went downstairs.

Malia was already sitting at the table in the dining room, next to their father. Jaden sat across from her. Melissa Kwan walked into the room a few seconds later, setting down a platter of grilled chicken breast. Nobody said a word.

Everyone served themselves and started eating. Jaden looked at Malia; she shrugged. It was unusual for a meal in their family to be so quiet. Jaden guessed that his parents had yet to resolve their disagreement. He could feel the tension in the air.

Jaden ate quickly, hoping to escape to his room as soon as possible. But when he finished and pushed his chair back from the table, his father spoke.

"I need to talk to the two of you, so don't disappear."

Melissa had been taking a sip of water, but she slammed her glass down on the table. Jaden froze. "Stephen, no."

"I'm sorry. This won't wait any longer." He got to his feet and moved into the living room.

Melissa sat quietly for a few seconds, then took her plate—her food hardly touched—and walked into the kitchen, leaving Jaden and Malia alone. They stared at each other for a moment before following their father into the living room.

Stephen was sitting in the recliner, leaning forward with his forearms on his knees, his fingers laced together. Jaden had never seen him look so serious. He and Malia sat down on the couch.

Several minutes went by. Stephen opened his mouth to speak a few times but instead repositioned himself in the chair without uttering a word. Jaden could hear his mother in the kitchen, loading the plates into the dishwasher.

Finally, Stephen took a deep breath. "There are some things I need to explain to you. I wanted to wait until you were older... Well, I guess you *are* older now. And it's not right to keep this from you. You wouldn't have understood when you were younger—and your mother still thinks you won't. She doesn't want me to discuss this with you. But we always agreed—"

"Dad, spit it out already!" said Jaden.

Stephen looked at him and grinned. "Okay. You're right. It's um... I've never really told the two of you what I do for work, have I?"

Jaden rolled his eyes. "You work in a government lab. What else is there to know?"

Malia gasped. Jaden turned to look at her; her eyes had gone wide.

Stephen laughed. "What if I told you I work at a *top-secret* government lab?"

"Yeah, right," said Jaden. "You're always complaining about how *boring* your job is."

"Usually, it *is* pretty boring. Breakthroughs are few and far between—but *those* days are quite exciting. Today is one of those days." He paused, looking back and forth from Jaden to Malia. "It all started at work. Everything."

"*What* did?" asked Jaden.

"How much do you know about the ancient Egyptians?"

"We're learning about them at school," said Jaden. "What's this got to do with anything?"

"Tell me what you know," Stephen insisted.

"Uh… they were really smart," said Jaden. "They built the pyramids, and those are bigger than almost anything we can build today…"

Malia sighed in exasperation. "Their understanding of mathematics and astronomy went far beyond anything Western culture would achieve for millennia. They built the pyramids with a level of precision that wouldn't seem possible without modern tools."

"That's correct," Stephen said with a nod. "And it was always a mystery—how exactly had they achieved such knowledge and skill?"

"I don't understand what this has got to do with *anything*," said Jaden. "They were geniuses—so what? That was thousands of years ago."

"A discovery was made," Stephen told them. "About seventeen years ago. Evidence that the ancient Egyptians possessed technology far beyond anything we'd previously suspected."

"What do you mean by *technology*?" Malia asked. "You make it sound like they had computers or something."

"After what I've seen, anything is possible," Stephen replied.

"*What*?!" said Jaden. "*Computers* four thousand years ago? You're joking—"

"Nobody's found any ancient computers, no," said Stephen. "But a kind of technology was discovered, incredibly advanced even by today's standards. In fact, it took a long time to fully understand what it was.

"Archaeologists found a chamber, previously hidden, underneath the Great Pyramid—"

"We learned about this at school," said Malia. "That chamber was never finished."

"No," said Stephen. "The one you're referring to has been well-documented for centuries. But there was another. Deep in the bedrock. From it, a tunnel led into the structure, to another room at roughly the same level as the Queen's Chamber."

"We didn't hear anything about this in world history," said Malia.

"No, you wouldn't have. Its existence has been kept a secret."

"But they scanned the whole pyramid with radar, and there *weren't* any other rooms," Malia insisted.

"Indeed. Scientists searched for years and found nothing. But this room was encased in an unusual metal alloy that rendered it invisible to radar."

This was too much for Jaden to believe. The idea was ludicrous—like something from a science fiction movie. "That's crazy!" he said. "The ancient Egyptians could block *radar*? But... radar wasn't invented yet! I don't get it..."

"I know it sounds incredible," said Stephen. "It took me a long time to accept the truth."

"Was *that* the discovery? The metal alloy, or whatever?" asked Jaden.

"No. The important discovery was what they found *inside* the chamber. And *that* is what I've been working on at my boring job," he said with a grin.

"So what is it?" asked Malia. "What did they find?"

"Yeah—and what's it got to do with us?" asked Jaden.

Stephen started to reply, but there was a knock at the door. "Hold on," he said, walking to the hallway.

Jaden noticed flashing lights coming from outside. He turned, pulling the curtains away from the window. The sun had set, and it was dark outside. Several police cars were parked in their driveway. He heard his father open the front door and looked to see who was there.

"Chris—what are you doing here? What's going on?" asked Stephen, backing away as the man entered the house, followed by the female detective who'd visited earlier and three uniformed officers.

Melissa came running from the dining room. At the sight of the visitors, she stopped, taking her position at the end of the couch, as if to protect Jaden and Malia. "Stephen—what are they doing here?"

"Melissa, this is Officer Christopher Babcock with the CIA," said Stephen.

"CIA…" Melissa whispered. "Detective Murphy, you said you'd be in touch, but I didn't expect anything like this!"

"I'm sorry, Mrs. Kwan…" Murphy moved into the living room. "I had nothing to do with this."

"Chris, what's happening here?" asked Stephen.

"I spoke with McLaren today," Officer Babcock replied. "It's time that we take over the project."

"I *knew* something like this would happen!" said Melissa. "I told you, Stephen—"

"What do you mean, *take over*?" Stephen demanded. "The CIA has no jurisdiction—my work is funded by the NIH."

"I'm sorry, Stephen," said Babcock. Jaden didn't believe him—he had the air of someone who'd eagerly awaited an opportunity to do what he was doing. "Your *work* presents a critical threat to national security should it fall into the wrong hands."

"That's absurd—what reason is there to believe it would fall into *anyone's* hands?"

Babcock ignored him, pushing past him into the living room. The uniformed officers followed, guns drawn and spread out around the room.

Melissa grabbed Jaden and Malia, pulling them to their feet, and pushed them into the far corner of the room, shielding them with her own body.

"Get out of my house," she ordered. "You have *no right* to invade my home like this."

"Mrs. Kwan, it's important that we keep calm," said Detective Murphy, moving toward her. "The moment I caught wind of this, I informed Officer Babcock that he'd need to get a warrant to enter the premises—"

"And as I told you outside, I don't need a warrant," said Babcock. "The project is government property."

"How dare you point those guns at my family!" Melissa yelled.

"Officer Babcock has convinced these men that this operation might prove dangerous," said Murphy. "He gave the order to enter with weapons drawn."

"You have no idea," said Babcock. He nodded to one of the officers.

The man approached Melissa, gun in one hand, reaching toward her with the other. "You'll need to come with me, Mrs. Kwan."

"Mom, no!" Malia yelled from behind her. "Don't go with him!"

"I'm not going *anywhere*!"

The officer grabbed Melissa's arm. She jerked it away and shoved him in the chest, knocking him back.

"Mom—no!" Jaden pleaded. "He's got a *gun*! Just chill!"

"Mrs. Kwan, please!" said Murphy, holding the officer back as he tried to grab Melissa again. But he pushed through, grasping Melissa's forearm.

"I said *NO*!" Melissa yelled, attempting to wrench herself free. Murphy tried to pull the officer away. And in the confusion, his gun discharged. Melissa staggered backward, slamming into the wall. The officer stared at her in shock.

"MOM!" Jaden yelled. Malia screamed. Melissa looked down at her abdomen in surprise; she was bleeding.

"*What did you do*?!" Stephen yelled. He tried to move across the room, but Officer Babcock held him back. Stephen broke free, but before he'd taken two steps, one of the other officers shouted at him.

"Don't move! Put your hands on top of your head!" He was pointing his gun at Stephen.

"You shot my wife! You bastards!" Stephen stepped forward, but Babcock grabbed him again.

"Stephen, no—we'll call an ambulance. Stop this craziness now before someone else gets hurt."

"Let me go!" Stephen yelled, shoving Babcock away from him. He tried again to get to his wife, but the officer fired his gun. Stephen fell backward over the recliner and onto the floor.

"DAD!" Jaden yelled. He and Malia charged across the room. An officer grabbed Malia; Jaden darted around him.

But at that moment there was an explosion. The force of it threw Jaden into Babcock. The two of them flew into the hallway. Babcock smashed his head against the wall and fell to the floor, on top of Jaden.

Jaden struggled out from underneath the man. Regaining his feet, he ran to his father—but stopped at the sight before him.

His living room was destroyed. Jaden didn't understand what had caused the explosion, but it had blown a hole in the front of the house, opening it to the outside. Only some of the wooden beams were left standing. Most of the furniture had landed on the front lawn, along with the uniformed officers and Detective Murphy.

Jaden dropped to his knees behind the upended recliner. His father was flat on his back, not moving. His chest was covered in blood.

"Dad!" Jaden yelled. He fell on top of him, sobbing. "Dad…"

But suddenly he heard a noise. It was Babcock. He'd grunted, and was stirring.

Jaden pulled himself together—they had to escape. Where was Malia?

He stood up and scanned the area. It was difficult to see through all the dust and the flashing lights. He moved across the room, careful to avoid tripping over the rubble—part of the ceiling had collapsed.

He found Malia. She was on her knees in the small hallway that led to the dining room, bent over their mother.

Jaden rushed over to them. Melissa wasn't moving.

"Mom!" Malia yelled, shaking her.

"Malia—we have to get out of here!"

She looked up, startled; Jaden saw his own despair and horror written on her features. She was sobbing.

"She's… dead," she told him.

Malia turned and stared across the room. Jaden followed her gaze. His father's legs were sticking out from behind the recliner.

Malia rose, stepping toward their father.

Jaden grabbed her. "No—we have to go. Now!"

He tried to pull her away. She resisted for a moment, but then she moved, letting him guide her through the dining room. Jaden led her out of the kitchen door. They crossed the backyard and entered the woods as sirens blared in the distance.

5

NIGHTMARE

Far away from Marlton, Maryland, Nadia Bashandi sat in front of a computer at the observatory where she worked. She'd spent many long years on her research but had so far come up empty-handed. Her shift was nearly over, and she felt exhausted.

She'd done enough for one day, she decided. After initiating the software that would analyze all the data she'd collected during her shift—a process that would take several hours—she closed up shop.

Twenty minutes later, she was at home, lying in bed. She stared at the ceiling, wondering like she did every night if tomorrow would be the day. Maybe the stars she'd scanned tonight would finally yield the clues for which she was searching. Despite years of failure, she had to believe she'd find what she was looking for eventually.

Nadia rolled over and closed her eyes, wishing her

partner were beside her where he belonged. But his job kept him away tonight.

She fell asleep within minutes but didn't rest well. Horrible visions invaded her dreams.

She saw a young girl, strikingly beautiful. But the girl was terrified: there were men with guns. One of them shot the girl's mother. Her father tried to get to her, but another man shot him in the chest.

The girl screamed. And suddenly there was an explosion. The vision changed. Nadia was staring at a woman's dead body—it was the girl's mother. Nadia saw the girl again. She looked vaguely familiar, but Nadia couldn't place it.

Nadia woke with a start, sitting bolt upright. She knew she'd been dreaming, and tried to remember what she'd seen as the visions fled her consciousness.

With a gasp, she remembered.

Who was that girl? Where had she seen her before? Nadia wondered what it all meant as she drifted back to sleep.

6

ESCAPE

Jaden ran blindly through the trees, pulling Malia along, not bothering to follow the path. His only thought was to put as much distance behind them as possible. He couldn't think of the horror they fled— not yet. They had to get to safety.

It was dark out and hard to see where they were going. They both tripped over rocks and branches. But within minutes, they reached the broader trail.

"This way!" Jaden said, running full speed now.

He stopped at the rocky escarpment where he'd met Seth earlier, and started climbing.

"Jaden, wait!" Malia yelled. "I can't get up that!"

"Sure, you can! Let's go!"

"No—I *can't*!"

He heard the panic in her voice and jumped back down to the trail.

"You can do this. I'll help you."

He started again, giving her a hand and helping her up the slope. The going was slow, but they made it to the top.

Jaden looked back the way they'd come, across the woods. He could still see the flashing lights of the police cars through the trees.

"Come on!" He set out at a run again. Malia followed.

"Where are we going?" she asked.

"I don't know yet."

They ran for five more minutes, deeper into the woods. Jaden needed time to think. But he wanted to get far away from the house before he stopped.

Finally, they came to a pond. Jaden paced back and forth along the water's edge, trying to catch his breath.

Malia sat down on a big rock. She was winded too.

"Do you have your phone?" he asked.

Malia reached into her pocket, then looked surprised. "No—I left it in your room. Why, who are you gonna call?"

"I don't know."

"We can't call the police—"

"Obviously."

Malia started sobbing. "What… are we gonna do?! Mom and Dad…"

"I know," said Jaden, sitting down next to her. He pulled her into a hug, and she cried and sobbed on his shoulder. Several minutes went by. Jaden rocked her slowly back and forth.

Memories flooded in. He could see his dad lying on the

floor with the wound in his chest, his mom in a pool of blood. Jaden cried too.

After everything else that had happened that day, a span of maybe ten minutes had shattered his entire life. What were they going to do now? He and Malia were alone, and it was only a matter of time before his parents' killers came looking for them.

Malia started to calm down. Jaden took a deep breath and said, "It's me."

"What?" she asked, pulling away from him.

"They came for me," he said. "I must be the project."

"Jaden, no—"

"Wait—hear me out. First, all that weird stuff happened at school. Somehow *I* must have pushed Crouch into the door, even though I didn't touch him. And then I stopped myself from falling. I don't know *how* I did any of it, but what other explanation is there?

"And now we find out Dad works at a *top-secret lab*?! He's a *doctor*! They must have done some sort of experiments on me or something—that gave me… powers. I don't know."

Malia was staring at him as if worried about his sanity.

"I know it sounds crazy. But you heard that Babcock guy —he talked to Principal McLaren! McLaren must have told him about everything that happened, and that's when Babcock decided to come for me.

"But Mom wasn't gonna let him—she must have known about the experiment. That's why she asked me how I did it! Remember? When we first got home… She didn't seem surprised at all—she was excited! She must've known that I could do it. And she said she knew the police would come for me—when the cops first showed up, remember? She said she knew this would happen!

"The only thing I can't figure out… is *when*."

"When *what*?" asked Malia.

"When they did it to me. I've never been to Dad's lab… Unless maybe he did it at home. He could've given me like… shots or something while I was asleep…"

Malia was shaking her head slowly.

"What?" he asked.

"You've got it all wrong."

"What do you mean?"

"It's not you. It's *me*."

Jaden stared at her. "You? But you're not the one who fell—"

"No, but I'm the one who stopped you."

"What are you talking about?"

"I saw Crouch holding you over the edge. And when he dropped you, I made you stop."

"How?"

"I don't know. But I knew I could do it."

"What? How..?"

"Because *I'm* the one who pushed Crouch in the stairway."

Jaden opened his mouth to reply, but no words would come out. His head hurt; he rubbed his eyes with the heels of his palms. "That's what you were gonna say before—when we were walking home. I asked you if it was a ghost, and you started to say something, but then you wouldn't tell me."

"I was afraid you'd think I was crazy," she said. "But I'm certain it was me."

"Did anything like this ever happen before?"

"No. The first time was Crouch in the stairway—and that was by accident. I was scared and upset because I *knew* I'd done it and I didn't understand. I tried some other stuff after that."

"Like what?"

"I pushed my notebook across the desk just by thinking about it," she said. "And then I made it float. I tried pushing someone again, and that worked too."

"Who?"

"I don't know—some kid in the hallway. He thought the boy behind him did it! But it was me… So when you fell, I *knew* I could stop you."

Jaden stared at her in awe. "You caused the explosion."

Malia nodded. "That was an accident, too. When they… when Dad… and that officer grabbed me, I lost it. I didn't know I could do anything that big. I tried to make Mom's car move earlier, and I couldn't—it was too heavy. But when the explosion happened… I was just thinking about making them all go away."

Jaden considered this for a minute. "How does it work? How are you able to do it?"

"I don't know. I think about what I want to do… and it happens."

"Can you do something now?" Malia nodded. "Well… do it." She pointed over his shoulder. Jaden turned—there was a rock floating right behind his head. He passed his hand above and beneath it, unable to believe that nothing was supporting it. "This is cool," he said with a grin. "Can you lift me?"

Malia concentrated. The rock fell to the ground, and suddenly, Jaden found himself floating a few inches in the air.

"Whoa!"

But a second later, he landed hard, back where he'd started.

"It's harder with heavier things," she observed.

Jaden stared at a rock on the ground. He focused with all his might on making it float the way Malia had done. Nothing happened.

"Why can't I do it?"

"I don't know… but do you really think Dad would do experiments on us—on his own kids?"

"No… that does seem a little creepy," said Jaden.

"And *neither* of us has ever been to his lab. It doesn't make any sense—if he *were* doing experiments on us, he'd *have* to take us there. Do you think the government would let one of its employees take a top-secret project *home*?"

"But whatever's going on *must* have something to do with us," said Jaden. "Babcock said he talked to McLaren, and that's when he decided to take over the project—whatever it is. Why else would a CIA agent talk to a high school principal?"

"Yeah…"

"And how do you explain what you can do? It's like tele… telepath…"

"Telekinesis."

"Right, that! People can't just do that—it's not natural.

That's *gotta* be the project! Dad found a way to give you telekinesis!"

"You know, I read about something like this once," said Malia. "It was in the 1950s, I think… and the CIA did experiments with psychics and stuff to try to use them to spy on other countries."

"*See*?! Babcock was from the CIA—there's got to be…"

At that moment, there was a noise out in the trees—a crashing sound. Malia gasped. Jaden jumped to his feet, peering into the woods. He thought he saw a light flicker in the distance. And then he heard voices.

"They're coming—let's go!"

Jaden led the way around the pond. They came to a narrow stream and jumped across it. The voices grew louder —someone was definitely following them.

They ran along a path adjacent to the stream. Suddenly the voices behind them stopped—the forest was silent. Jaden could hear only their own footfalls on the ground.

"I hear them—this way!" someone shouted.

"Jaden—wait!" Malia yelled.

Jaden skidded to a stop. Malia was pointing into the trees. There was a fallen tree trunk surrounded by dense under-brush. Jaden nodded. They left the path, jumped over the tree, and ducked, hiding in the bushes.

Only seconds later, two men with flashlights ran up the path. They were uniformed police officers.

Jaden waited until they were out of earshot before leading Malia back to the path. They returned to the pond.

"This is nuts," said Jaden. "We've gotta get out of the woods and find help."

"Where can we go?" asked Malia. "It's the *police*. They'll find us no matter where we go."

"We can try Seth's house," Jaden suggested. "His parents will know what to do."

Malia cringed at the thought. "I guess it'd be better than running around the forest all night."

They set out again, back to the pond and down another trail. But moments later, they heard noises behind them again.

Jaden ran as fast as he could, Malia right behind him. They climbed a hill and came to a rock wall that rose fifteen feet above the path.

"Can you do your thing and get us to the top of this?" Jaden asked.

Malia looked up doubtfully. "I can try…"

Jaden could hear the officers behind them. He spotted the beams of their flashlights approaching the hill.

"You go first—hurry!"

Malia looked scared—she'd seen them too. She concentrated for a few seconds before suddenly shooting to the top of the rock wall. She lost her footing and fell over, out of Jaden's view.

"Malia!" he hissed.

Suddenly he saw her peering over the edge.

"Quick—bring me up!"

Malia focused again. And an instant later, Jaden rose from the ground, landing right next to his sister.

"Get down!" he told her.

They dropped, pressing themselves flat against the ground. Peering over the edge, Jaden watched the two officers run into view, and right past them. But they stopped twenty feet up the trail.

"Quiet," one of them said to the other. The men listened for several seconds. Jaden held his breath.

"I don't hear anything," the other officer said. "They must have stopped again."

One retraced his steps back down the trail, passing directly under Jaden and Malia again. The other continued farther up the path. They both searched the underbrush on the other side of the trail.

Finding nothing, they returned to the path. Jaden worried they'd look for them up here—it was the only obvious hiding place on the open trail. Sure enough, one looked up, pointing to a spot only a few feet away from Jaden and Malia. "Up there," he whispered.

Malia backed away—knocking debris over the edge as she moved.

"There they are!" one of the officers yelled.

Jaden jumped to his feet, dragging Malia along with him. They ran off the trail. There was no clear path, but the trees weren't too dense—Jaden ran blind, away from the noise of the officers behind them.

But suddenly Malia fell, letting out a little scream as she hit the ground. Jaden ran back to her, helping her to her feet. They took off again, but Malia was limping. The officers were right behind them.

"Faster!" Jaden yelled.

"I can't—I twisted my ankle!"

It was too late; the officers had caught up to them. One grabbed Jaden as the other held Malia.

"Come along quietly, and nobody will get hurt," said the officer holding Jaden. He pulled a pair of handcuffs from his belt.

"No!" Malia yelled. The officer flew through the air. He smashed into a tree; his head snapped back, hitting the trunk, and he fell to the ground.

The other officer released Malia. He drew his gun and pointed it at them, backing away. "Hold it right there!" he yelled, looking as scared as Jaden felt. "Don't move!" He pulled his radio from his belt.

But suddenly, the gun flew out of his hand. Malia focused; an unseen force slammed into the man's chest, throwing him through the air, over the edge of the ravine and out of sight.

"Damn, that's cool!" said Jaden. "But we gotta go—how's your ankle?"

"It hurts," Malia replied, moving it gingerly from side to side.

"Well, it's not that far to Seth's house—but we should hurry before anyone else finds us."

They set out, Malia limping along behind Jaden. He was careful not to get too far ahead. He listened intently for any sound of pursuit. If anyone else came, they'd have to hide— Malia couldn't run anymore.

For ten minutes, they hobbled through the woods, their pace limited by Malia's ankle. Jaden found the trail that led to

Seth's house. He halted their progress at the slightest noise, always keeping a lookout for somewhere to hide should it become necessary. But the only sounds they heard were crickets and small animals scurrying through the underbrush.

They were only minutes from Seth's house when something went horribly wrong. Jaden heard a loud noise and froze. Turning, he saw lights—many of them—pursuing them up the trail. And he heard voices shouting—and dogs barking.

"Crap!"

He moved off the path, making sure Malia could keep up. They had little time. He spotted a thick tree growing right next to an outcropping of rock and guided them to it as quickly as possible. First helping Malia sit behind the tree, Jaden ducked out of sight, crouching behind the rock. Seconds later, half a dozen police officers ran into view.

The dogs stopped several feet beyond the point where Jaden and Malia had left the trail. Noses to the ground, they tried to pick up their scent again. Jaden panicked—now what?

Malia peered out from behind the tree. Suddenly there was a crashing noise far across the trail.

"This way! They're in here!" one of the officers shouted, pointing the wrong way. He strode into the trees, his comrades—and the dogs—close behind.

"Let's go," Jaden whispered.

They emerged from their cover and moved silently along the path—the men weren't too far away. But before they'd gone ten feet, an officer appeared on the trail, stepping out from behind a tree.

"Hold it right there!" he shouted, pointing his gun at them. "Hands up where I can see them!"

"HEY! I've got them—OVER HERE!" he shouted to the others.

Malia concentrated. The gun flew into the trees, and the officer sailed through the air, crashing into a tree. Jaden and Malia tried to get away, but it was no use. The other officers came running back to the path, guns drawn.

Jaden and Malia put their hands on top of their heads. The officers closed in quickly. Jaden didn't see how they were going to escape this time—there were at least six men.

But before he knew what was happening, violent ripping sounds erupted from both sides of the trail. Two giant trees were being pulled out of the ground by some unseen force.

"What the hell!" one officer shouted.

Another screamed as the uprooted trees crashed down across the path, landing on the men. Two of them managed to get out of the way. They looked back and forth from Jaden and Malia to the fallen trees before turning and running up the trail. The dogs followed, yelping the entire way.

Jaden stared at Malia in awe, but she was shaking with fear.

"Right, let's get out of here," he said. "Seth's house isn't far now."

"No."

"What do you mean, *no*?"

Malia walked toward the fallen trees.

"What the hell are you doing?! We've gotta get outta here!"

She kept going, one step at a time, favoring her injured leg. Jaden grabbed her by the arm. Malia turned to face him, a look of absolute resolve showing through her fear.

"I have to make sure they're okay!" She wrenched her arm free and continued toward the trees.

"They killed Mom and Dad! Who cares if they're okay?!"

She paid him no heed; Jaden followed her. They had a hard time moving through the leaves and branches, but they found the four officers. Two were unconscious but breathing. One was awake and seemed perfectly healthy except for the fact that he was trapped beneath the trunk. A look of sheer horror came over his face as they approached.

The last one was injured; he too was pinned under a thick branch. He was holding his leg and groaning. But he was alive.

"Satisfied?" Jaden demanded.

Malia only nodded.

They negotiated their way out of the trees and moved as fast as they could—which was little better than a snail's pace with Malia's injured ankle. Jaden reflected on his sister's newfound abilities. They would have been captured, were it not for her. But wielding that power seemed to terrify her.

And it was clear that she was much stronger under pressure than she was otherwise. She could barely lift *him* back at the pond. But when surrounded by enemies, she'd been able to rip two enormous trees right out of the ground.

Jaden wished he possessed that power, too. Next to Malia, he felt helpless.

They arrived at Seth's house. The path from the woods came out in a far corner of the backyard. Jaden stopped at the tree line: something was wrong. There was a car in the driveway he didn't recognize. Someone was sitting in the driver's seat.

"Damn," he whispered.

"What's wrong?" Malia asked.

"The cops are here," he told her. "In an unmarked car. We're gonna have to go somewhere else. But for now, let's go back in the woods before he sees us."

They crept back along the path, far enough to avoid being seen. Malia sat down on the ground, massaging her injured ankle. Jaden leaned against a tree.

"Now what?" she asked.

"We gotta find *somewhere* to go. They must know I'm friends with Seth, that's why they're watching his house. They figured we might show up here."

"So Elise's house is out of the question."

Jaden nodded in agreement. "This sucks. We can't go to a friend's house, because they'll probably be waiting for us. But if we show up on some random person's doorstep, they'll just call the cops."

They sat in silence for a few minutes, each privately contemplating their predicament.

"What about Sydney?" Malia finally suggested.

"Hastings?" said Jaden. "That's not a bad idea... Mom used to be best friends with her."

"But they don't talk anymore," said Malia. "Mom hasn't seen her since she stopped working! Jaden, this could be perfect—the cops would have no reason to be watching *her* house!"

"Yeah… the only trouble is, she lives pretty far from the woods. We're gonna have to walk in the open to get there—you *know* they're patrolling the streets."

"What choice do we have?"

"None, I guess," said Jaden.

"What are we going to tell her?"

"What do you mean?"

"I don't think we should show up and announce that I might be part of a secret government experiment, I'm telekinetic, and the CIA is after us!" Malia said sarcastically.

"Good point… But we're gonna *have* to tell her that the cops are after us. And that…"

"They killed our parents," she finished for him.

"Yeah… cuz otherwise she might *call* the cops."

"We shouldn't tell her the rest," said Malia. "She might think we're crazy."

"Right—and if she knows the CIA's involved, she might decide it's too much trouble and just turn us in… But what can she do? I mean, we can't hide at her house forever."

"Let's worry about that when we get there," Malia suggested.

In the end, they decided to try to get to Sydney Hastings' house. They waited a few more minutes so Malia could rest her ankle, then they set out.

After moving a little farther through the woods behind Seth's street, they emerged in someone's backyard. They dashed across the lawn and crept along the edge of the house.

Jaden peered around the corner—he could see the police car still sitting in Seth's driveway.

They returned to the rear corner of the house and cut across the yard into the neighbor's property. There was a fence at the edge of the next lot, and Jaden had to help Malia go over the top of it. She fell when she landed, trying to avoid putting any weight on her bad ankle. But before long, they'd made it to the end of Seth's street.

They had to move into the open to get to the other side of the road. So they hid behind a parked van as several cars went by. They were about to move when Jaden noticed a police cruiser turning onto the street. It went by very slowly; Jaden's heart hammered in his chest.

The car moved on, and the coast was clear. They crossed the street and made their way from one backyard to the next. Occasionally they had to climb a fence or hide when someone came outside. But they encountered no more trouble until they reached the end of the residential neighborhood.

"Here comes the hard part," Jaden said as they crouched behind someone's garage. "There's no way to get to Sydney's house without going through the center of town. There's gonna be a lot more people around. If anyone sees us, you might have to... you know, do your thing again."

Malia took a deep breath and nodded. "I'm ready."

They crossed the main road and walked along the back of a parking lot. Jaden knew the restaurants along this road represented the most significant threat. Most of the other businesses were closed at this hour.

At the edge of the parking lot, they ran into a problem. A

high brick wall separated the lot from the adjacent property. Only a narrow alley ran between the rear of that building and the pizza place next door. If they went around the front of the pizza shop, they'd have to walk along the main street. And the back door of the restaurant was open.

"Damn," said Jaden. "Well, let's go through the alley."

They crept along as quietly as possible. As they approached the open door, Jaden could hear a newscast. Peering around the edge of a dumpster, he could see the television and someone watching it. As he inched forward to see if the person had a view out the door, the newscast caught his eye.

"Authorities say these two teens are armed and dangerous. *Do not approach them!* If you see either one of them, call the police immediately."

School pictures of Jaden and Malia accompanied this report. Jaden couldn't believe it—*armed and dangerous*?!

He turned to see if Malia had seen the newscast too. She had, judging by the horrified look on her face.

Suddenly the man watching the television got to his feet. He picked up two giant bags of garbage and headed out the door.

Jaden and Malia scurried away, crouching down against the wall on the opposite side of the dumpster. They heard the man grunt as he lifted the lid and threw the bags inside. Jaden flinched when the top of the dumpster crashed closed again, but a few seconds later, they heard the door to the building slam shut.

They crept along the alley to the edge of the building.

"We're in big trouble," said Malia.

"Gee, really? I hadn't noticed," Jaden replied.

"No, seriously—no matter where we go now, people are going to recognize us! It's not only the police we need to hide from! And what if Sydney's watched this report? We haven't seen her in years—how do we know what she's going to think? What if she turns us in?!"

"Where else can we go?" asked Jaden.

They looked at each other for a moment. Jaden saw his own feeling of helplessness mirrored in Malia's face.

Malia sighed. "There is nowhere else," she said. "Sydney's our only hope—we should try to talk to her, and… see what happens, I guess."

The two of them continued along the alleys and parking lots behind the various businesses. Eventually, they entered another residential neighborhood. The houses were closer to each other here than they had been on Seth's street. It felt safer to creep along against the backs of these homes than it had to run across open stretches of lawn.

Within minutes, they arrived at Sydney Hastings' house. They tiptoed up the stairs of the back porch. Gazing inside a window, Jaden saw the flicker of a television screen in an adjacent room. He knocked on the door. There was no answer. He knocked a little harder, but still, nothing happened.

Malia rang the doorbell. Jaden cringed at the noise, clearly audible from the outside, but still, nobody stirred. Finally, Jaden tried the door. It was unlocked.

Jaden and Malia crept inside.

7

CAPTURED

The house was dark and quiet except for the television in the front room. Jaden walked softly through the kitchen, Malia right behind him. A floorboard creaked when he reached the hallway. Something brushed up against his ankle, and he froze, his heart pounding.

It was just a cat.

They moved into the living room and found Sydney sprawled out on her couch, sound asleep.

"Whoa," whispered Jaden.

"What?" Malia hissed.

"She's *hot*!"

Malia rolled her eyes.

Sydney was lying on her back, her long blond hair spread out on the pillow, one arm dangling off the couch. She'd dropped the remote on the floor. She was wearing shorts and a cutoff T-shirt that left her midriff exposed. It looked like she'd just come from the gym.

"I do *not* remember her looking this good," Jaden observed.

"Of course not—you were like eight the last time we saw her," said Malia. "Wake her up!"

"Me?! You do it!"

"Fine." Malia approached the couch and gently shook Sydney's arm. "Sydney?"

The woman didn't stir. Malia grasped her shoulder, shaking her a little more forcefully. "Sydney, wake up!"

She groaned and turned her head, but didn't wake up.

Suddenly the cat jumped onto the couch. Malia gasped, backing away in surprise.

"What?" Sydney asked without opening her eyes. "I fed you already." She scratched the cat on the head with one hand. The cat meowed. "Let me sleep."

The cat walked across Sydney's chest and touched its nose to hers.

"Ugh!" Sydney opened her eyes, grabbed the animal with two hands, and held it up in the air. "*Why* can't you let me sleep?!" She sat up and placed the cat on the couch next to her. Stretching out both arms, she opened her mouth and yawned.

"Hi, Sydney," said Malia.

Sydney jumped to her feet and screamed. The cat hissed, diving off the couch and scurrying away. Sydney moved toward the hallway, spotted Jaden, and screamed again.

"Don't scream—someone's gonna hear you!" said Jaden.

"It's just us—Malia and Jaden," Malia told her.

Sydney stood there for a few seconds, half-crouched as if preparing to run, looking frantically back and forth at the two of them. Finally, recognition replaced panic.

"Wha—what are you two doing here?"

"We had nowhere else to go," Malia said apologetically.

"The cops are after us," Jaden explained. "We need your help."

Sydney shook her head. "Wait a minute—what? What do the police want with you? Where are your parents?"

Malia looked stunned as if someone had slapped her in the face.

"They're… our mom and dad…" Jaden stammered. "Well, they're dead." It hurt him to utter these words. His throat burned, and he fought back tears.

Sydney's jaw dropped. She stared at him as if he'd said something incomprehensible.

"What are you talking about? They can't be—tell me what's going on!"

But suddenly, Malia began sobbing. Jaden and Sydney both turned to look at her. Malia wilted to the floor, shaking with grief. Sydney ran over and sat down next to her, pulling her into a hug, a look of shock and disbelief on her face.

"Hush, child," she said quietly. "Tell me what happened," she added to Jaden.

Jaden sat on the couch, staring at the television. There was a commercial for a local car dealership. He collected his thoughts, trying to decide where to start, and taking several deep breaths. It was difficult to remain composed.

Looking at Sydney reminded him of the close friendship she used to share with his mother. He could remember spending a lot of time with this woman when he was younger. The memories were comforting.

"Everything happened so fast," he said. "I don't know…"

"Take your time," she replied.

Jaden nodded. His primary concern was to tell the story without the more extraordinary elements. "I guess it started at school. It's Freshman Friday—that's where everyone else gets to pick on the incoming class. This kid named Crouch stuffed me in a garbage can… and then we got in a fight later. He… uh… did some other stuff too, and me and Malia got called to the office to talk to the principal about it.

"Crouch was in big trouble, so McLaren—that's the principal—had to call the police about everything, so later on a cop showed up at our house. She questioned us about Crouch. But after that, the police came back. And there was a big argument, and… they shot my mom and dad…"

Sydney looked horrified. "But I don't understand—why did they shoot?"

Jaden could hold back the tears no longer. He tried to talk but sobbed instead.

"Come here, sweetheart," she said.

Jaden slid off the couch and crawled over to her. She pulled him tight with one arm, still holding Malia with the other. Jaden cried into her shoulder, finally releasing the anguish that had been pent up inside of him. The years of separation melted away, and Jaden felt the same closeness to her he'd known before.

"How did you end up here?" Sydney asked once he'd calmed down. Malia was still sobbing.

"We ran away," he said. "We had to find somewhere to hide. We tried to go to my friend's house, but the cops were watching the place."

"But why?" she asked. "We should call the police so they can sort this out—"

"NO!" said Jaden, pulling away from her. He knew he had to offer some sort of explanation, but worried about what she would think. They were fugitives now, and harboring them could get Sydney in trouble. He didn't want to tell her *too* much, but needed to convey the true nature of the situation— and why they had to avoid the authorities at all costs. "They're after us! They said something about taking over some project my dad was working on—and this guy from the CIA was there. What was his name… oh yeah, Babcock. The cops chased us through the woods and—"

But at that moment, the newscast started on the television. The pictures of Jaden and Malia flashed on the screen.

"Breaking news tonight. Authorities in Marlton are looking for these two teenagers, accused of killing their parents. They are considered armed and dangerous. Do not approach them—if you spot either one of them, police urge you to call 911 immediately…"

"That's a lie," Jaden said, pointing at the television. "We didn't kill our parents—*they did.*"

Sydney stared at the screen, watching the rest of the story. Then, as if to punctuate the report, flashing lights suddenly flooded the living room. Jaden scrambled to the window.

Parting the curtains, he saw a police cruiser making its way slowly down the street.

Jaden returned to Sydney, sitting on the floor in front of her. "I swear it wasn't us. We didn't do anything."

She looked at him blankly for a moment, processing the information. Jaden held his breath.

"They really are after you," she said finally. "We have to get you out of here!"

Jaden heaved a sigh of relief.

"Where can we go?" Malia asked, speaking for the first time.

"Your uncle's," Sydney said without hesitation.

"*Uncle Brian*?!" Malia and Jaden said in unison.

"He's the only uncle you've got, isn't he?" asked Sydney.

"Yeah, but he's crazy," said Jaden. "No way are we going there."

For as long as he could remember, Brian had eschewed almost all contact with the family. He'd come to the house for Christmas one time when Jaden was very little. But he hadn't stayed long and spent most of the time searching the house for something. He'd gone through the kitchen cabinets and every closet in the house, even checking behind the television and underneath the lamps in the living room. Jaden recalled wondering if he was looking for hidden presents. After that incident, they'd seen him only a handful of times, always at random restaurants miles from home where they'd meet for dinner.

"He's also filthy rich and has connections in the government. If anyone can get you out of this mess, it's him. Your mom always said he was your next of kin if something ever happened to her and your dad," Sydney explained. "Now that I think about it, it's almost like she expected something like this… Weird. She told me more times than I can remember that Brian had to be the one to take care of you if… well, if something should happen."

"Where does he even live?" asked Jaden, realizing he had no idea.

"North Carolina," said Sydney. "He's got a big ranch down there. Wait here—I've got his info upstairs."

Sydney ran upstairs. Malia and Jaden relocated to the couch.

"I missed her," Malia said with a smile.

"I wonder what ever happened with her and Mom," said Jaden.

"I don't know," Malia replied. "I asked once, but Mom said they just lost touch."

Sydney returned a minute later with a page ripped from a legal pad. "I've got his number," she said, grabbing her iPhone from the end table and sitting in a chair in the corner. She tapped in the number and held the phone to her ear.

"Out of service," she said a few seconds later. "Hmm…" She tapped something else into her phone. "His new number's not published, but the address I have is still correct."

"So… now, what?" asked Jaden.

Sydney shrugged. "I guess we drive to North Carolina."

Malia rushed over and grabbed Sydney in a big hug. "Thank you so much."

Sydney ran upstairs again to change her clothes and pack a bag. She returned five minutes later wearing jeans, a backpack slung over her shoulder.

"Let's go," she said.

But as Malia and Jaden walked into the kitchen, Sydney noticed Malia's limp.

"Are you hurt?" she asked.

"It's just my ankle," said Malia. "I twisted it or something when we were running in the woods."

"Let me take a look," said Sydney.

They returned to the living room. Malia sat on the couch, and Sydney dropped to her knees in front of her. She moved Malia's foot gently from side to side.

"Does that hurt?"

"A little," said Malia, wincing.

"Well, there's no swelling," Sydney told her, "and I don't think it's broken. But we should wrap it before we go. It'll be easier to walk."

She ran upstairs again and came back with an Ace bandage. Once she'd wrapped the ankle, Jaden and Malia followed her out to the attached garage. An old Ford Explorer was parked there. Sydney opened the back door for them. The inside was a mess—clothes and boxes of paper were strewn everywhere.

"You two should hide," she said. "See if you can fit under the back seat."

They had to move some of the clutter out of the way before getting into the truck. But with some effort, they managed to squeeze themselves underneath the seat. Their legs were sticking out, but Sydney covered them with a pile of clothes.

"Stay down until I tell you to come out," she said. "No matter what. Promise?"

"We promise," they replied.

With that, Sydney closed the door and climbed into the driver's seat. Jaden could see her through a small opening in the clutter. The engine roared to life, and Jaden felt the vehicle backing out of the garage. Sydney cut the wheel, and they moved forward.

They drove for a few minutes in silence. But suddenly Sydney said, "Stay down—there's a cop car up ahead."

Seconds later, Jaden could see red and blue lights flashing on the interior of the truck.

"We're clear," Sydney informed them. "He drove right by us."

Several minutes passed. Jaden felt the truck turn a couple of corners. It was extremely uncomfortable squished underneath the seat, and he was growing hot.

"Can we come out now?" he asked.

"Not till we get on the highway," said Sydney. "We're almost there—hang on."

But less than a minute later, she said, "Oh no—oh crap! This isn't good!"

"What is it?" asked Malia. "What's wrong?"

Jaden felt the truck slow to a stop.

"There's a roadblock up ahead," Sydney told them.

"Turn around!" said Jaden. "Get us out of here!"

"I can't," she replied. "There's only a short line of cars in front of us. If I turn around now, it'll look suspicious. And besides, they've probably blocked every route out of Marlton."

"What are we going to do?" asked Malia, fear in her voice.

"Nothing—sit tight," said Sydney. "Don't move and don't make a sound. They're not searching the cars—we'll get through this."

Jaden's heart was beating a mile a minute. If the police found them now, there would be no escape.

The truck moved forward a minute later.

"Two more cars, then it's our turn," said Sydney.

The minutes seemed to fly by. Before he knew it, Sydney said, "Here we go." Jaden heard her window opening.

"License and registration," a voice said. Jaden couldn't see the officer, only the back of Sydney's head.

"Hang on, my wallet's in the back seat," she said.

"Go ahead," the voice replied.

Sydney reached behind her and grabbed her backpack from the seat above Jaden. She rummaged around inside of it and handed the officer her license. Then she leaned across the front seat and pulled some papers out of her glove box.

"What's going on?" she asked, handing him the registration.

"We're on the lookout for a couple of fugitives," the voice replied. "Where are you headed tonight?"

"Work," said Sydney. "I'm a nurse at Sibley Memorial."

"Is there anyone in the car with you?"

Sydney laughed nervously. "Does it look like I could fit anyone back there with all that crap?"

Suddenly the beam of a flashlight fell across the floor of the truck. It moved right across Jaden's face but kept going.

The officer chuckled. "You're probably right—but I'm going to have to search the vehicle."

"*What*?" demanded Sydney. "Look—I'm running late—"

"I'm sorry ma'am, can you please step out of the car?"

Jaden felt a wave of panic hit his body. How could they possibly get out of this?

"You've got to be kidding me," said Sydney. "I need to get to the hospital—they just called me in! There was a huge pileup on the Beltway, and there have already been two fatalities. You've gotta let me through!"

"Ma'am…"

"We're wasting time!" Sydney insisted, a hysterical edge to her voice. "People are dying—I don't have time for this!"

"Okay, okay—look, can you just show me your ID tag for the hospital?"

"Yes, I can," she said, digging through the backpack again. "Here."

"Looks good," said the officer. "Sorry for the holdup, you can go on your way."

"Thank you," she said, taking back her ID, license, and registration. She stuffed everything in the backpack, tossed it into the back seat, and sped off.

"Damn, that was close," Jaden yelled.

"I thought we were *screwed*!" Sydney called back, laughing with relief. "I lied my ass off!"

"Can we come out now?" asked Malia.

"Yeah," said Jaden. "It sucks under here."

"Not yet—let's make sure there aren't any more road-blocks first."

They drove for a few more minutes until Jaden felt the truck accelerate hard.

"We're getting on the highway," said Sydney. "No trouble yet—but let's wait a little longer just in case."

"*Longer*," Jaden groaned. "I'm dying down here! How much longer do we have to wait?"

"We're on the Beltway now," said Sydney. "Let me get us to I-66, and then you can come out. As long as they're not stopping traffic between here and there, we should be home free."

Jaden stayed where he was for what felt like an eternity. He was cramped, and his right side, pressed against the floor, began to go numb. His neck ached from holding his head in such an awkward position.

Finally, he felt the truck slow, go around a long curve, and pick up speed again.

"Are we there yet?!" he demanded.

"Yes," Sydney replied. "You can come out now."

"Thank God!" said Jaden, digging himself out. He had clambered into the front seat before Malia managed to get free. She sat behind Sydney, clearing herself an empty spot.

Jaden picked up Sydney's iPhone from the center console. "I've missed this," he said, scrolling through each page of applications. "My phone broke. Oh—you have Facebook. Do you mind if I log in?"

"That's not a good idea," Sydney said with a frown. "They might be able to track you that way."

"Can I text my friend—"

"No, Jaden! No texting, no Facebook—and definitely don't call anyone! You two are in hiding now. Any contact you have with the outside world can be used to find you. But you want to be a big help?"

"Sure, how?"

"Go into Google maps and tell me where we're going."

"Uh, how am I supposed to figure *that* out?" he asked, tapping the icon.

"I already put the directions in there. Just look at the blue dot—that's where we are—and tell me what's next."

"Oh… uh, we're on I-66 now. We have to stay on this till I-81."

"Got it," said Sydney. "Now, give me that!" She snatched the phone away from Jaden.

"Hey! I won't go on Facebook or anything, I promise! Can I just play games and stuff?"

Sydney smiled at him. "Yeah, I guess," she said, handing him the phone back. "Knock yourself out."

For the first time since leaving his house, Jaden felt safe. He knew they weren't out of danger yet—he had no idea if they ever truly would be. And he wouldn't allow himself to think about his parents. The events of the evening were like a black cloud hanging over his thoughts, but he forced himself not to focus on them. He knew he'd only fall apart if he did.

But being with Sydney reminded him of the good times they'd shared. She used to babysit for him and Malia and came to visit so often it was as if she'd been part of the family. It had been years, but she was a constant presence in the background of his memory. He knew that she'd do whatever it took to protect him and Malia. They weren't alone anymore.

An hour later, they came to I-81 and headed south. Soon after that, Sydney stopped at a rest area to refuel.

"Can we go inside and use the bathroom and stuff?" asked Jaden.

"I don't think so," said Sydney. "Someone might recognize you—we're not that far from Marlton yet."

"But I gotta *pee*!" said Malia from the back seat. "And I'm hungry."

"Let me get gas, and I'll go inside and get us something to eat—*my* picture's not all over the airwaves. Once we get moving again, I'll pull over, and you two can relieve yourselves somewhere."

She got out of the car.

"Are we supposed to go to the bathroom on the side of the road or something?" asked Jaden.

"We can go in the woods," suggested Malia. "But it's not fair—that's way easier for *you*!"

Jaden laughed at her.

Once she'd filled up the tank, Sydney drove to a spot far from the building and parked. She made them promise to stay put and ran inside to buy food.

"I love McDonald's," said Jaden when she returned five minutes later. He scarfed down two double cheeseburgers and an order of fries. They threw away their garbage and hit the road again.

A few miles farther down the road, Sydney pulled over.

Jaden and Malia took turns running into the woods to go to the bathroom.

"That was gross," Malia announced as she climbed back into the truck. "I almost peed on my foot. Hopefully next time we can find an actual toilet somewhere."

They resumed their journey. Within minutes, Jaden fell asleep. He woke once or twice, but it was dark out, and Sydney was still driving, so he went back to sleep.

He woke again to find the sky growing light; Sydney was pulling over at another rest area. Jaden sat up and stretched. Malia was still asleep.

"Where are we?" he asked as she parked at the gas station.

"See for yourself," she said, handing him her iPhone. She'd plugged it into the cigarette lighter to charge.

Jaden looked at the map. "Wow, we're almost there!"

"Another ninety minutes or so," she confirmed.

"So… since we're so far away from home now, do you think we can go inside?" he asked. "I gotta use the bathroom again, and this time I'm gonna kinda need to sit down on a toilet."

Sydney giggled. "Maybe. Let me see the phone for a second."

He handed it to her and watched what she was doing. She opened the CNN application and entered his name in the search box.

"Hmm… Nothing's coming up. This probably means they haven't expanded the search beyond Marlton yet. If they had, the news networks would've picked up the story by now."

"So, we can go inside?" Jaden asked hopefully.

She looked at him gravely for a moment before finally cracking a smile and saying, "Sure, I guess we'll give it a shot."

"Yes!"

"But first," she added, dialing a number on her phone, "I need to call out sick." She held the phone to her ear. "Hi Liz—this is Sydney. Listen, I'm really sick. I think I have the flu or something... Yeah, it's awful... Uh-huh... Well, maybe you'd better count me out for the whole weekend... Sure... No problem, I'll give you a call tomorrow night. Bye."

"I'm sorry you gotta miss work for us," said Jaden once she'd ended the call.

"No worries," said Sydney. "I hate working weekends anyway."

Once she'd filled the tank, they parked in the lot. They woke Malia, who was ecstatic at the chance to use a real bathroom, and headed inside.

"In and out," Sydney told them as they walked toward the building. "Do what you need to do, then go straight back to the truck. And don't talk to anyone. I'll get us some breakfast and meet you back outside."

"Got it," Jaden agreed.

They walked inside and looked for the bathrooms. The place was crowded. Malia spotted a sign at one end of the large room pointing down a hallway. As they started walking, Jaden crashed right into someone, bounced off, and fell over backward.

"Sorry, kid," said an enormous man with a shaggy beard. He held out his hand to help him up.

But Jaden's heart almost stopped: it was a security guard.

He let the man pull him to his feet, keeping an eye on his face the whole time. But the guard only glanced at him and showed no sign of recognition. His attention was focused across the room; Jaden followed his gaze. A man and a woman were shouting at each other. Passersby gave them a wide berth.

"You okay?" the guard asked, looking directly at Jaden.

"Yeah, I'm good. Sorry about that!"

The guard nodded and ran off.

Jaden looked at Malia and Sydney, both of whom were staring at him with their mouths wide open.

"That was *way* too close for comfort!" said Sydney. "Now, let's go so we can get out of here as quickly as possible!"

Sydney and Malia ducked into the women's room. Jaden continued down the hall to the men's room. It was busy, and he had to wait a few minutes to get a stall. He felt nervous after the encounter with the guard. Maybe coming inside was a mistake—there were a *lot* of people here. Any one of them might recognize Jaden or Malia, even if the story hadn't spread this far yet. People in Washington had likely seen their faces on television, and plenty of them probably traveled down this highway.

Jaden washed his hands when he was done and met Malia and Sydney in the hallway.

"Get outside and wait for me in the truck," she reminded them. "I'll be right out."

Jaden didn't need to be told twice. He and Malia headed for the exit.

But no sooner had they crossed the threshold than someone grabbed Jaden from behind.

"Gotcha!" a man yelled in his ear, holding him in a bear hug. The guard he'd run into before had snatched Malia the same way and was now holding her off her feet.

"Let… me… GO!" Malia shouted as she struggled to free herself.

But the guards trotted toward the hallway with them. The crowd parted to let them pass. Many people took pictures as they went by. Jaden spotted Sydney across the room, looking horrified. She was trying to squeeze through the crowd to get to them. Jaden didn't see what she'd be able to do now.

A third guard was waiting for them at the end of the hallway. He was holding open a door beyond the bathrooms. The guards threw Jaden and Malia into the room, and the door slammed behind them.

Jaden heard the lock click. He turned the handle and threw his whole body into the door, but it was no use. They were trapped.

8

DESERTED

"Settle down in there," a voice yelled from outside the door. "You ain't goin' nowhere."

"I *knew* I recognized that kid when I knocked him over," another voice said.

"Little hard to believe, isn't it? They seem like a couple of harmless kids."

"*Harmless*? According to the APB, those two killed their own parents."

"Don't matter what they done. FBI said to hold them here till they arrive, that's what we're gonna do. Harold, you stay here and watch the door. They didn't drive themselves here—whoever's with them might try a rescue."

Jaden heard footsteps walking away up the hall. He looked around, taking in his surroundings for the first time. They were in a storage room, lined with shelves from floor to ceiling.

"Why didn't you do something when they grabbed us?" he asked.

"I couldn't," Malia said with a shrug.

"Why not? Did you lose your powers or something?"

She raised one eyebrow at him. Suddenly, Jaden found himself floating a foot off the ground.

"Okay, okay—put me down!" His feet hit the floor. "So why couldn't you do something before?"

"I tried," she said. "But the guard was behind me, and I couldn't see him."

"So?"

"I don't know—I guess I have to see what I'm doing to make anything happen."

Jaden pointed at the door. "Can you open that?"

"And what if I can? The guard's standing right there!"

"We'll deal with that when you open the door," he said. "He's by himself—just make him fly or something, and we'll run."

Malia focused. The door rattled hard against the frame but didn't open.

"Cut that out!" the guard yelled from outside. "We'll let you out as soon as the FBI gets here."

"Try the lock," suggested Jaden.

Malia examined the space between the door and the frame, running her fingers up and down along the edge. She focused for a minute before saying, "It isn't working. I can't see what I'm trying to move to make the lock work."

"Damn!" he shouted.

"It's not my fault, Jaden," she said pleadingly.

"We gotta find a way out of here." He scanned the nearest shelf. It was piled with cleaning supplies. "This isn't gonna help… Look for a crowbar or something we can use to pry the door open."

They spent the next few minutes searching the room. Jaden failed to find anything useful.

"Hey, come here—look at this!" Malia said. He found her in the back of the room, gazing up at the top of the shelves against the wall.

"What?" he asked, following her gaze, but seeing nothing unusual.

"There's a window up there," she said, pointing. "You can see the frame above the top shelf."

Malia was a few inches taller than Jaden. He had to jump to see it. But she was right: there was a window.

He moved to the end of the shelves. "We're gonna have to get this out of the way," he said doubtfully. It was loaded with large boxes. He grasped the metal frame with both hands and tried to slide it away from the wall. "No way. This is too heavy. But maybe we can knock it over," he suggested.

"Imagine all the noise it's going to make when it crashes into the other shelves," said Malia. "The guard's going to know we're up to something. Don't be stupid. And anyway… I can do it."

"You sure?" He recalled the trees she'd ripped out of the ground in the forest but also knew she wasn't under imme-diate duress at the moment.

"Move," she commanded. Jaden backed away. The shelves rose several inches above the floor, creaking and groaning under the strain. They moved a few feet away from the wall before coming to rest again.

"That was hard," Malia said with a sigh.

"Now we have to get through *that*," Jaden observed. The window was small—barely big enough for them to squeeze through. It was also near the ceiling, well out of reach.

"And it's locked," said Malia. "But I can do this."

The lock was only a simple latch in the center of the window. As Jaden watched, it slid open.

"Great," he said. "Now, lift me so I can get out."

Malia nodded. Slowly, Jaden floated up to the ceiling. He pulled the window open—the bottom edge lifted out away from the wall. He clambered through with difficulty, holding on to the casing as he pulled his legs out. Looking down, he dropped to the ground.

Several tense moments went by as he waited for Malia. He was behind the building and worried that the guards would come running around the corner at any moment.

But suddenly, Malia's hands reached out through the window, followed by her head.

"How am I supposed to do this without landing on my head?" she asked.

Jaden started explaining that she had to pull her torso out first when Malia slid entirely out of the opening, floating gracefully down to the ground.

"That works too," he said. "Come on—we gotta find Sydney!"

They ran along the back of the building toward the parking lot. They stopped at the end, and Jaden peered around the corner. Someone was right there—she almost ran into Jaden. Malia screamed. They ran back the way they'd come.

"Jaden! Malia—wait!"

It was Sydney.

"Thank God!" said Malia, grabbing her in a hug.

"I thought we were screwed," Jaden said with a grin.

"I saw them lock you in that room," said Sydney. "They left one of the guards at the door—I was about to look for another way inside. How did you get out?"

"We crawled through a window," Malia replied.

"Good thinking," she said with a nod. "But we're not out of the woods yet. They're going to come looking for you as soon as they realize you're gone. You two wait here. I'll go get the truck, and I'll be right back."

Jaden and Malia waited for what felt like an eternity. But finally, Sydney pulled up right next to the building. Jaden opened the front door, but Sydney said, "No—both of you get in the back. Sit on the floor and keep your heads down."

"Here we go again," he muttered, climbing under the back seat.

"Don't worry—there shouldn't be any roadblocks this time," said Malia.

"Let's hope not," Sydney agreed.

Sydney drove through the parking lot. Jaden felt them accelerate as she merged onto the highway.

"The coast is clear, you can get up now," she told them.

Malia tried to climb into the front seat, but Jaden beat her to it.

"We're in big trouble now," he said.

"You mean more than before?" Sydney asked sarcastically.

"Yeah—seriously," he insisted. "We heard the guards talking. The FBI is looking for us. Now they're gonna know for sure we're not in Marlton anymore—and they know we're not alone because we're not old enough to drive."

"True, but they don't know about me. Take this," said Sydney, handing him her iPhone. "Go into maps and navigate for me. I know we need to get off the next exit—good thing since they'll probably be watching for us on the highway now. But I don't know where to go once we get off."

"Got it," he said, opening the application. "You're gonna turn left at the end of the ramp."

They left the highway a minute later. Sydney followed Jaden's directions. They crossed the line into North Carolina, and within the first fifteen minutes, made several turns on various state roads. Jaden felt more confident with every passing mile that the authorities would be hard-pressed to find them.

"I'm a little worried about our plan," Malia said from the back seat.

"Why, what's wrong?" asked Sydney.

"Well… don't you think the FBI might guess we're going to our uncle's?"

Jaden felt his heart drop into his stomach. "Oh, crap! She's right! As soon as they found out we were at that rest area, they probably started looking for places we might be going!"

"Damn," said Sydney. They sat in silence for a few

minutes. Jaden waited expectantly for Sydney to say something more; she seemed lost in thought.

"I don't see what else we can do," she said finally. "I don't know where else to go. Your mom was always adamant that you had to go to Brian's if anything ever happened. And you don't have any other family, do you?"

"No," Jaden confirmed.

"It's got to be him," she said. "He'll be able to find a way out of this mess. We'll just have to be careful. Remember, they don't know about me—they won't be looking for my car or anything. So… we'll just drive by the place and see what there is to see. If the cops are there, we'll keep going."

"I guess," said Jaden.

But now, instead of feeling safer, his anxiety increased as they drew closer to his uncle's ranch. What would they do if the FBI was already there, waiting for them? Where else could they go?

They drove for another hour, making several more turns. Finally, they came to their uncle's road. Sydney drove a little under the speed limit as Jaden kept an eye on the map.

"We're almost there," he said. "It should be coming up on the left."

"Okay," said Sydney, "I'm going to drive by the place, and I want you two to see if any cars are there."

A few seconds later, they found it. A high brick wall marked the edge of the property. There was an iron gate, which was open at the end of the driveway. A carved wooden sign read, "Liberty Ranch."

"This is it," said Sydney as they drove by.

Jaden had a clear view of the house as they went past. He couldn't see a single car. Sydney continued almost a quarter of a mile down the road before turning around.

"Nobody's there, and we're not being followed," she said. "Let's pay your Uncle Brian a visit, shall we?"

Jaden felt nervous but excited. He wondered if perhaps the police were waiting for them *behind* the house and out of view.

As they entered the driveway and passed the iron gates, Jaden noticed a security camera mounted atop the wall. And a moment later, the gates closed ominously behind them.

"Uh-oh," said Malia. "I hope this isn't a trap."

"I don't think so," said Sydney, without offering any explanation.

They pulled up at the end of the driveway next to the house. The place was enormous. A porch spanned the entire front of the structure.

Sydney cut the engine, and they got out of the car. As they walked around the front of the sprawling home, Jaden realized the front door was open. They climbed the steps onto the porch. Jaden knocked on the door, peering inside.

"Hello?" he called. "Uncle Brian?"

There was no response.

Malia walked inside; Jaden and Sydney followed.

"This is weird," said Malia.

They walked from the entrance hall into a cavernous living room with cathedral ceilings and a giant fireplace.

"Uncle Brian?" Jaden called again.

"Let's take a look around the house," Sydney suggested. "He must be here—that gate didn't close of its own will."

But as they headed out of the living room, a phone rang. Jaden followed the noise and found a den behind the living room. There was a desk in the corner, which hosted a cordless phone.

"He'd answer it if he were here, wouldn't he?" asked Malia. The phone kept ringing.

Jaden shrugged.

Finally, an answering machine picked up. There was silence for several seconds as the outgoing message played.

"Who the hell has an answering machine anymore?" Jaden asked. "That thing must be ancient."

"Jaden, Malia—pick up the phone. It's me. Uncle Brian," his voice said from the machine.

Jaden dashed across the den and picked up the phone.

"Uncle Brian!"

"Jaden, is that you? Are you and Malia okay?"

"Yeah, we're fine—where are you?"

"I'll explain everything in due time," he said. "But not right now and *not* on this phone. I need you to go upstairs."

"Uh… upstairs, right," said Jaden. Malia eyed him inquisitively; he shrugged in response. "Where's the stairway?"

"Go back through the living room, past the front door, and turn left. The stairs are at the end of the hall."

"Got it," said Jaden. Malia and Sydney followed him out of the room.

They climbed the stairs, and Jaden said, "Now what?"

"There's a door to your left," said Brian. "Go through that into the master bedroom."

"Okay…" Jaden opened the door and walked in. The room was enormous. Sunlight flooded the space through giant skylights in the ceiling.

"Go to the chest of drawers in the far corner. Open the bottom drawer. There's a satellite phone in there. Turn it on."

Jaden walked across the room. He found the satellite phone and pressed the power button.

"Um… it's on," he said.

"Good, I'll call you right back," said Brian. The line went dead.

"Hello?" said Jaden. His uncle was gone.

"What's going on?" asked Malia.

"I don't know," he replied.

Sydney looked concerned. But a second later, the satellite phone rang. Jaden pressed the large green button and held the phone to his ear.

"Uncle Brian?"

"Hello again," said Brian. "Sorry about that—the land line's been tapped. By now, the FBI knows you're at the ranch. So we need to get you out of there as quickly as possible."

"Oh no!" said Jaden.

"What?!" asked Malia, alarmed.

"The FBI is coming," he told her and Sydney. "We wondered if they'd look for us here," he said into the phone.

"They've already been there, looking for me," said Brian.

"But I was one step ahead of them. I left, and they followed, leaving the house safe for your arrival."

"You knew we were coming?!" said Jaden.

"I hoped you would be. Rescuing you from the FBI would have been difficult. But once you escaped them at the rest stop, I was certain you were on your way."

"How did you know about that?!" asked Jaden.

"I'll explain everything later. Right now, I need you to go outside and get back in Sydney's Explorer."

"We have to go," Jaden said to the other two. They walked out of the bedroom. "How'd you know she's got an Explorer?" he asked Brian.

"I watched you pull into my driveway."

"Oh—on the camera, you mean? You closed the gates behind us?"

"I did, but I don't expect that to keep the FBI at bay for very long. You need to hurry."

They ran downstairs and outside to the truck. Jaden jumped into the front seat again.

"We're in the truck, now what?" he asked as Sydney started the engine.

"Drive around behind the house. Go across the yard. There's a trail leading into the woods. Follow that."

Jaden relayed the instructions to Sydney.

"So tell me how you knew the FBI was coming for you," said Jaden as Sydney drove across the yard.

"It was inevitable once you'd fled your parents' house," said Brian. "They tapped my phone immediately in case you called."

"We didn't have the number!"

"I know, and I apologize for that," he replied. "But it worked out for the best—they didn't know for sure that you were coming here until you showed up at the rest stop. That's when they came to the ranch."

"Yeah, but how'd you know they were coming?" Jaden asked again.

"I have access to their computer network," he said.

"You hacked the FBI computers?!"

"My company designed their network security," Brian explained. "I have superuser privileges—unbeknownst to them."

"What does that mean?"

Brian chuckled. "It means I can do whatever I want on their computer system."

"Whoa..."

"What now?" asked Sydney. They'd crossed the yard, and she was now driving up the trail. The SUV rocked back and forth on the uneven ground.

"We're on the trail," Jaden said into the phone. "What do we do now?"

"You're going to come to an open field. There's a dirt road around its perimeter. Turn right and stick to that until you come to the road. You're going to need to get to Interstate 26 and drive south. To Miami."

"*Miami*?!"

"Yes. I'll meet you there. You're going to have to get directions..."

"Sydney's got an iPhone. I can use that."

"Good. I'm going to give you the address of a hotel in Miami Beach. I want you to check in there. I'll call you when you arrive."

Jaden grabbed Sydney's phone and opened the notes application. Brian gave him the address, and he typed it into the phone. Sydney reached the end of the trail and turned onto the dirt road.

"Jaden, I need you to listen to me very carefully. You and Malia *must not* use your own cell phones—"

"We can't—mine broke anyway, and Malia forgot hers at home."

"Good. But you must not make any calls or send any text messages or use any social networks from Sydney's phone either. The FBI can use any contact you have with the outside world to trace your location."

"We figured," said Jaden.

"And don't go out in public again! You must make sure that nobody sees you. Sydney should be safe. They don't know she's involved. But please ask her to limit her contact with people as much as possible."

"I will."

The line was silent for a moment.

"Uncle Brian?"

"I'm here, Jaden. I want you to know I'm very proud of you and your sister. You've been through hell and acted very bravely. I'm sorry I wasn't there to help."

"We're all right," Jaden assured him. "Sydney's taking good care of us."

"I'm sure she is. I'll see you in Miami. Oh—and make sure

you keep the satellite phone turned on. It will go into standby mode automatically, so the battery should last the whole trip. But don't use it to call anyone!"

"We won't, I promise. See you in Miami."

Jaden pressed the big red button to end the call.

"We're going to Miami, I take it?" asked Sydney.

"Yeah, Brian's gonna meet us there," said Jaden. "I'm really sorry about this—I know you probably thought you'd be done with us by now."

Sydney smiled at him. "It's not a problem. I'm just going to have to call out of work a little longer."

Jaden copied the hotel address into the maps application as Sydney continued along the dirt road.

"Oh damn," he said. "Miami's almost fourteen hours away!"

"That's farther than I thought," said Sydney. "Is your uncle expecting us there at any certain time?"

"No. He said he'd call us when we get to the hotel."

"Good, because I'm not going to make it all the way there without some sleep," said Sydney.

"Oh no," said Malia from the back seat. "That's right—you drove all night. You haven't slept at all!"

At that moment, the satellite phone rang.

Jaden stared at it in surprise for a moment before answering.

"Hello?"

"Jaden—you have to get off that dirt road!" It was Brian.

"What—why? I thought we were going to take this to—"

"Stop the truck!"

"Stop!" Jaden yelled to Sydney. She slammed on the brakes, halting the vehicle.

"Tell her to back up about fifty feet, and turn onto the trail to the right."

Jaden told Sydney this. She threw the truck into reverse.

"Wait—how'd you know where we were?"

"The camera at the front gate is not the only one on my property," said Brian.

"I haven't seen any other cameras," said Jaden. Sydney hit the brakes again, shifted into drive, and turned up the trail.

"Of course not," replied Brian. "Tell Sydney to step on it!"

"He says go faster!" said Jaden.

Sydney gunned the engine; the truck bounced around violently. They followed the trail along a sweeping curve.

"That's far enough," said Brian. "Stop where you are and kill the engine."

"Stop here and shut the car off," said Jaden.

"Shut it off? Why?" asked Sydney as she came to a stop.

"Why are we shutting it off?" Jaden asked his uncle.

"To make sure they don't hear you—and tell Sydney to make sure she keeps her foot off the pedals. We don't want them seeing the brake lights either."

Jaden relayed the message.

He, Malia, and Sydney turned in their seats, staring out the back of the truck. Seconds later, they spotted an unmarked police car speeding along the dirt road.

"Crap!" said Sydney. "I hope they don't see us!"

"Be ready, Malia," said Jaden.

She turned to him and nodded. He saw the fear in her eyes, but there was determination too.

"Ready for what?" asked Sydney. But two more cars drove by before Jaden could reply. "Oh, damn!"

They waited another minute, watching for any more vehicles.

"You should be clear now," Brian said.

"Three cars went by," Jaden told him. "Nobody else is coming?"

"Not yet," said Brian. "But they'll be back once they realize the house is empty. You need to hurry. Get to the road as quickly as possible."

Sydney had no room to turn around, so she put the truck in reverse and backed down the trail. Once out of the woods, she floored the accelerator, spraying dirt everywhere, and raced down the road.

"That was close," said Brian. "But you should be safe now. They won't have any way of knowing where you're headed next. Get to I-26, and I'll see you in Miami."

Jaden ended the call and set the satellite phone down on the floor. He looked at the map on Sydney's iPhone again.

"We're almost up to the main road," he said. "You're gonna turn right."

Sydney drove faster than usual. Jaden and Malia both kept looking out the back of the car. But fifteen minutes later, they merged onto the highway with no pursuit in sight.

9

DISCOVERY

Nadia Bashandi sat in front of her computer at the observatory, strumming her fingers impatiently against the top of her desk. The machine was old, the software out of date. This was taking forever. But she felt an inexplicable certainty about what she was about to find.

There was a knock on her office door.

"Come in," she yelled.

The door opened, and Awan Busiri let himself inside.

"It's about time you rolled out of bed," Nadia teased.

"After a twelve-hour shift, I earned the rest. So what's up —what's your big news?"

Nadia had told him most of it already, as she got ready for work. But he'd been only semiconscious at the time. She was mildly surprised he remembered *anything* about the conversation.

"I found a planet," she said.

"Yeah, that's what you do," he responded sarcastically, sitting across from her in the only other chair in the small room.

"No—you don't understand. This could be *it*. At first, the star was only one of dozens that had the telltale wobble—"

"You've told me about this. When the star wobbles, it means there's a planet orbiting it. Right?"

"Yes, exactly," said Nadia. "The planet's gravity tugs the star back and forth as it revolves, causing a slight oscillation in the star's position over time. But after running the numbers and calculating the mass and orbital radius… Awan, this is a rocky planet and it's in the star's habitable zone."

Awan scrunched his eyebrows in concentration. Clearly, he knew this was supposed to signify something important. "And that means…"

Nadia sighed. She'd explained this to him at least a hundred times. "Most planets we can detect are gas giants because those have more mass and cause bigger wobbles in the star's position."

"And gas giants do us no good because they wouldn't support life," said Awan.

"Precisely. But this planet is tiny compared to a gas giant. *And* it's the right distance from the star for life to evolve."

"Oh, right—now, I remember. If the planet's too close to the star, it would be too hot. Too far away, and it would be frozen. So this one's in the habitable zone?"

"That's what I said!" Nadia told him, throwing her hands in the air in exasperation. But at that moment, her computer beeped.

She turned to the display. At first, she could only stare at the blinking message: Positive Identification. But after a few seconds, she scanned through the report to see the numbers for herself.

"I knew it! I don't believe it... but I knew this would be it!"

"What is it?" Awan asked, pulling his chair over to her desk.

"The spectroscopy is positive. This planet has an oxygen-nitrogen atmosphere—and *water*!"

"So, it could support life?" Awan asked.

"Support it? Yes—and with this chemical makeup, life is probably already there!"

10

FALLING OUT

"I'm hungry," Malia announced from the back seat. "We never actually had breakfast."

"Yeah, me too," Jaden agreed.

"We'll stop soon," said Sydney. "But I want to get some miles behind us first."

They'd crossed the line into South Carolina before Sydney was satisfied that they'd gone far enough. There were no rest stops here, so she pulled off the highway. Once she'd filled the tank at a gas station, they found a Burger King. Breakfast hours were over, so Sydney went inside to buy them lunch while Malia and Jaden waited in the car.

She returned a few minutes later. Jaden became so engrossed in eating that he failed to notice Sydney dozing off in the driver's seat, her food untouched—until she started snoring.

"I feel so bad for her," said Malia. "She hasn't slept. We should stop somewhere so she can get some rest."

Malia shook her awake and suggested that they find a hotel somewhere.

"Not yet," said Sydney. "I'll be good for a few more hours. I want to get as far away from your uncle's ranch as possible. The farther we go, the harder it'll be for them to find us again."

Once she'd finished eating, she threw away the garbage, and they resumed their journey. Sydney asked them to keep talking to her to help her stay awake and alert. So they told stories and reminisced about times from their childhood when Sydney and their mom had still been close.

But by late afternoon, Sydney could go no farther without rest. They pulled off the highway in Georgia, only a few miles away from the Florida state line. Malia spotted a big hotel almost immediately.

"We should look for a motel instead," Sydney suggested. "The type of place where the doors to the rooms open to the parking lot."

"What difference does it make?" asked Jaden.

"In a *hotel*, you and I would have to walk through the building, and people would see us," said Malia. "But at a *motel*, we can go directly from the truck into our room."

"Exactly," said Sydney. "Jaden, take a look on the phone and see if you can find us something."

But it ended up not being necessary. They drove up to a motor lodge before Jaden had found anything.

Sydney parked the truck near the office and ran inside.

She returned a minute later and moved the truck to the very end of the building, right in front of the door to the last room.

"Nobody's around," said Sydney. "Let's get inside."

It was only twenty feet from the Explorer to the door of their room, but Jaden couldn't help feeling nervous. He looked around the parking lot, afraid that someone would see them and report to the police. But the area was deserted. Sydney opened the door, and they hurried inside.

Sydney collapsed on the first bed.

"I'm *exhausted*!"

"I'm hungry!" said Jaden. "Can we get a pizza or something?"

Malia glared at him.

"You're so selfish! Sydney hasn't slept in days—your stomach can wait!"

"It's not a problem," said Sydney, sitting up. "I'm pretty hungry myself—and pizza sounds great. I can stay awake long enough to eat; I just couldn't drive anymore."

She searched on her phone and found a place right up the street. They decided what they wanted, and Sydney called in the order. She left fifteen minutes later to pick it up.

"I've been thinking," said Malia once Sydney had left, "and we should probably tell her everything."

"What do you mean, *everything*?" asked Jaden.

"You know. What I can do. And the fact that Dad's project had something to do with me, and I'm the real reason they're after us."

"I don't know," he replied. "You don't think it'd freak her out?"

"More than being chased by the FBI? She's risked everything for us—she deserves to know the whole truth."

"Yeah, I guess you're right," said Jaden. "And this way, if you end up having to do something, she won't be all surprised."

"Exactly—like what almost happened when we were leaving the ranch, and we hid from those cars. And besides, Sydney might know something. She and Mom were best friends for *years*. Maybe Mom told her something about Dad's project at work."

"That's true," replied Jaden. "And maybe she knows more about Brian, too—I realized I have no idea what he does for work or anything. But satellite phones and hidden cameras all over the place—and breaking into the FBI computer?! Must be something cool."

Sydney returned a few minutes later with a large pizza and a two-liter bottle of Coke. She set the box down on the desk while Malia retrieved three glasses from the bathroom sink. Jaden sat at the desk and started eating.

"You're such a slob," Malia chided him, handing him a napkin. She poured Coke for the three of them before grabbing a slice of pizza herself and sitting on the edge of one of the beds.

"Sydney, what does our Uncle Brian do for work?" asked Jaden.

"What *doesn't* he do," she said, sitting next to Malia with her pizza in hand. "His background is in computer science—that's what he went to school for. But he owns a company that designs everything from computer security software to surveillance equipment to guidance systems for missiles and stuff."

"Oh, wow," said Jaden.

"We haven't seen him in years," Malia observed. "And Mom and Dad hardly ever talked about him."

"Mmm," said Sydney. "He and your dad had a falling out several years ago."

"Over what?" asked Malia.

"I'm not sure," said Sydney. "But it had something to do with your dad's job." Jaden looked meaningfully at Malia. "You know he worked for a government lab, right?"

"Yeah, we know," said Jaden. "What did that have to do with Brian?"

"Your uncle was always very distrustful of the government," said Sydney. "From what your mom told me, he tried to convince your dad to quit his job and seek private funding for his research."

"But Brian said his company designed the computer system for the FBI," said Jaden. "He worked for the government too!"

"That doesn't mean he trusts them," Sydney replied. "And he never worked for them directly—the government hired his company. They've had a lot of government contracts over the years, and they do a lot of work in the private sector, too. But Brian owns the company, and that means he calls the shots—he's in control. Your dad's situation was different. He was an employee of the National Institutes of Health, so *they* had control of his research."

"Why did Brian try to convince him to quit?" asked Malia.

"I don't know the details," said Sydney. "But according to your mom, Brian found out that the government planned to use your father's work for military purposes. Your dad didn't believe it. He thought Brian was just paranoid."

"I don't get it," said Jaden. "So, Brian didn't want my dad to work for the government anymore. Why'd they stop talking to each other?"

Sydney smiled at him. "Sometimes, it's hard for people to put their differences aside. Brian believed very strongly that your dad was wrong to allow the NIH to keep control of his work. And your dad felt differently. They argued about it very passionately, and I guess after a while, it drove them apart."

"What happened with you and Mom?" asked Malia. "You guys used to be so close."

Sydney looked sad. "She never told you?"

"No," said Malia. "I asked, but she said you just went your separate ways. She never said why."

"It's a little more complicated than that," said Sydney, taking a deep breath. "And I've regretted it very much. Your mom was the best friend I ever had." Tears welled up in her eyes at these words. "We used to work together at the NIH research hospital in Bethesda—that's where we met."

"I knew Mom was a doctor, but she never told us she worked for the NIH," said Jaden. "Did she work with our dad?"

"No, but your dad's lab was in the same building. In fact, that's where your parents met, too—but that was before I started working there.

"Anyway, one time about six years ago now, I was working the night shift. It was almost two in the morning, and I had to go up to another floor to get something. And... I found your mom there, at the nurse's station."

"What was she doing there at two in the morning?" asked Malia. "I don't remember her ever working the night shift."

"She didn't," said Sydney. "So I was pretty surprised to see her there myself. She was sitting at one of the computers, and she closed the window she was working in the moment she saw me. But it looked like she was in a restricted area of the NIH network. Now, I was only a floor nurse, and your mom was a research physician, so it seemed reasonable to me that she'd have access to information that I wouldn't."

"But it's still a little strange that she was there in the dead of night," said Malia.

"Yeah, exactly," said Sydney. "And it gets stranger. A couple of months went by, and I'd pretty much forgotten about that incident. But the hospital issued a security alert. Apparently, someone had been illegally accessing top-secret information on the computer system. Some of the NIH projects were tied to the Department of Defense, so this was a pretty big deal. And the worst was, whoever was doing it logged in from somewhere *inside* the hospital."

Malia gasped.

"Was it our mom?" asked Jaden.

"I think so," said Sydney. "And that would explain why she used a computer at the nurse's station—they could have tracked her if she'd used her own. They interviewed everyone privately to find out if we'd seen anything suspicious. I didn't tell them about your mom at first. I talked to her directly and asked her what she was doing at the hospital that night. But she wouldn't tell me.

"Now, we'd been best friends for years at that point, so I couldn't understand why she wouldn't tell me. And I begged her to give me some clue as to what she was up to. I promised that if she had a good reason for what she was doing, I'd keep my mouth shut. But she refused to discuss it."

"You ratted her out?!" said Jaden, seeing her in a different light for the first time. Maybe they'd been wrong to place so much trust in her. "You were her best friend, but you turned her in, didn't you?"

"I had no choice!" Sydney pleaded. "You have to understand, after 9/11, everything was different! Nobody ever would have believed that a group of people could devastate our country like that—until it happened. And working at the NIH, with some of the research that was going on there, was very stressful. What if some terrorist group had found a way to blackmail your mom somehow? I didn't want to believe it; I *begged* her to tell me what she was doing. And if she'd given me *any* hint that there was a legitimate purpose for her actions, I wouldn't have said a word.

"But she wouldn't tell me anything—she refused to talk about it. And she seemed *scared*. I was worried that someone had manipulated her somehow into giving them classified information. And who knows what could have happened. Imagine if some group had used NIH research to create some sort of biological weapon! I couldn't let that happen!"

"It did happen once," said Malia. "I read about the anthrax attacks that took place right after 9/11."

"Yes, and you can't imagine the horror people felt," said Sydney. "The man who did it worked for the biodefense labs at Fort Detrick—right in Maryland. So it wasn't so hard to believe that someone would compromise an NIH doctor to gain access to their computer systems."

"But it was our mom!" yelled Jaden. "How could you do that to her?"

"Jaden, she's right," said Malia. "What if a terrorist had threatened to do something to us if Mom didn't do what he wanted?"

"That's precisely what I feared," said Sydney. "I told your mom I was going to turn her in. She begged me not to do it— but she still refused to explain her actions. They never proved that she was the one who'd infiltrated the network, but they forced her to resign. Your mom never spoke to me again."

"Yeah, and I don't blame her," said Jaden. He may have been reluctant to rat out Crouch, but he'd *never* turn in *his* best friend—under any circumstances.

"You're being ridiculous," Malia told him.

"I am not. She even said she regretted it."

"I regret losing your mom's friendship," Sydney corrected him. "But I'd do what I did again, no question. It wasn't right for her to expect me to cover for her without providing *any* explanation.

"But now I have a question for the two of you," she added, looking from Jaden to Malia.

"I'm not telling you anything," said Jaden.

Malia glared at him. "*I will.* What do you want to know?"

"What was your dad working on?"

Malia opened her mouth to reply.

"Malia—no!" yelled Jaden, getting to his feet. "Don't you dare tell her a *thing*! She turned Mom in—how do you know she won't do the same thing to us?"

"How can you say that after everything she's done for us?" Malia demanded.

"It's all right, Malia," said Sydney. "I understand your brother's distrust. But the truth is I had good reason to suspect your mom was doing something that could have put our whole country in danger. And that's not the case here—in fact, it's quite the opposite this time."

"What's that supposed to mean?" Jaden demanded.

"I think that your dad's project had something to do with the two of you," she said.

Malia stared at her wide-eyed.

"You don't know that," said Jaden. But he was scared—what reason could she have for suspecting it?

"No, I don't," Sydney agreed. "But the evidence certainly points in that direction. Whatever your dad was working on, Brian believed the government would take it over and use it as a weapon. And you said yourself that someone from the CIA showed up at your house to take over your dad's project. Yet now that Melissa and Stephen are dead, the FBI is pursuing *you*.

"I never put it together before, but after what's happened, I think your mom believed Brian—she feared the government was going to militarize your father's work. She knew the project involved her children, and probably thought the two of you were in danger. That's why she accessed those restricted documents—and that's why she refused to tell me what was going on. She was only trying to protect *you*."

"It's me," said Malia before Jaden could stop her. "*I'm* the project."

"Shut up, Malia!"

"Honey, what do you mean?" asked Sydney, confused.

Malia stared at her hard, furrowing her brow. Suddenly every piece of furniture in the room—including the bed upon which she and Sydney were sitting—rose several inches in the air.

Sydney gasped. She jumped off the bed, staring around the room in complete surprise.

"Malia, stop it!" said Jaden.

She returned everything to the floor.

"*You* did that?" asked Sydney, backing away from Malia. "How?"

"I don't know," said Malia. "I think about it, and it happens."

"Can you do it too?" Sydney asked Jaden.

He stared at her for a moment before shaking his head. "Only Malia."

"But we think you're right—somehow, my dad's project gave me this power. And that's why they're after us."

"This certainly wasn't what I was expecting," said Sydney, standing still now. "Well, I don't know *what* I was expecting…"

"You're not going to turn us in, are you?" asked Jaden.

"No, of course not! And if your mom had only told me that she was trying to protect you, I never would have turned her in either! Why didn't she just tell me..." Tears streamed down her cheeks.

Jaden believed her.

"She must not have wanted you to get involved," said Malia. "You probably would've gotten in big trouble if you knew about any of this but didn't report it."

Sydney nodded. "When did you find out?"

"What?" asked Malia.

"That you were the project—that you had these powers?"

"We don't *know* that I'm the project—Dad sat us down for a big talk right before the police showed up. He was going to tell us something but never had the chance. And I found out about my powers by accident. This boy was picking on Jaden, and I pushed him into a door without touching him. And after that, he dropped Jaden off the roof, and I stopped him from falling... just by thinking about it."

"Yeah, and the principal at our school told Babcock—the CIA guy—about everything that happened on Friday," said Jaden. "I wonder how McLaren knew Babcock?"

Sydney shrugged, shaking her head.

"Do you know if the ancient pyramids in Egypt have anything to do with all of this?" asked Malia. "With my dad's work?"

"Not that I know of," said Sydney. "Why?"

"Yeah, I almost forgot about that," said Jaden. "Dad started talking about the pyramids—he said everything started at work, and he asked us what we knew about ancient Egypt."

"He said they discovered some kind of technology in a hidden chamber inside the Great Pyramid," Malia added.

"Wait—*technology* in ancient Egypt?" Sydney asked. Malia nodded. "I've never heard anything like that. But your mom never discussed your father's work. I knew he ran a top-secret lab, but I had no idea what he was researching.

"I know one thing for sure though: your Uncle Brian has the answers. He knew what your dad was working on, and it's clear now that he was right to fear government involvement. What you can do, Malia would certainly make you a very dangerous weapon."

Jaden looked at his sister with newfound respect. He'd seen what she could do but hadn't begun to consider the ramifications. He imagined her on a battlefield, singlehandedly destroying an enemy army. Or using her power to take down hostile aircraft or missiles. He understood a little better now why Babcock had come for them and instructed the police to enter their home with guns drawn.

Sydney went to sleep a few minutes later. Jaden and Malia sat up in the other bed for a long time watching television. They discovered very quickly that a nationwide manhunt was now underway to locate them—their faces were plastered all over every channel. But this time, a third picture was included in the report.

"It's Uncle Brian!" said Malia.

He looked precisely like Jaden remembered him, with his dark, wavy hair and glasses. His smile reminded Jaden painfully of his father. But then he realized this picture was probably quite old.

"Authorities say the teens may now be traveling with this man, Brian Kwan," said the reporter. "He is their uncle and the brother of their murdered father. We're getting some reports tonight that Brian Kwan is now a suspect in the homicides, and may have *kidnapped* the teens. Police are investigating a reported sighting of the trio in Little Rock, Arkansas."

"Arkansas?" said Malia. "They're way off."

Jaden flipped through the channels for a few more minutes, but there was nothing on. They watched the pay-per-view movie service instead.

Eventually, they decided to turn off the television and go to sleep. Malia drifted off rather quickly. But Jaden lay awake for a long time, listening to her deep breathing. Why hadn't their mom and dad ever told them about their dad's work? And why, even in the end, was Melissa against Stephen revealing the secret to them?

Jaden couldn't believe they were gone. He tried to think about how they'd been in life—his mom planting trees in the backyard, his dad watching football. But he couldn't stop himself from recalling how they'd died. The image of his dad lying there with a bullet wound in his chest and his mom's lifeless body kept surfacing in his mind's eye, no matter how hard he tried to shake them.

Jaden cried for hours before finally falling asleep.

When he woke up in the morning, he found Malia and Sydney sitting on the other bed, eating breakfast.

"Good morning," Sydney said cheerfully. "I hope you like pancakes."

Jaden sat up and stretched.

"What time is it?" he asked.

"Nine thirty," said Sydney. "So get up and eat. I want to hit the road as soon as possible."

Jaden rolled out of bed. He sat at the desk and wolfed down his pancakes. Sydney had bought them toothbrushes, too. Once Malia and Jaden had each had a turn to brush their teeth and shower, they got ready to leave.

Sydney opened the door and checked to make sure nobody was around. She beckoned to them, and they ran outside and jumped into the truck—this time Malia claiming the front seat.

"We need to buy some clothes at some point," said Jaden, sniffing his shirt. "These smell."

Sydney giggled as she pulled out of the parking space. "We can stop somewhere. You'll have to let me know your sizes, though, because there's no way you're coming inside to try anything on."

They ended up stopping only for food and gas. Malia used Sydney's iPhone to navigate, but it was a straight shot down Interstate 95 to Miami. They arrived in the city a little before five o'clock. Sydney took the exit for Interstate 195, and they drove over a causeway to Miami Beach, across the bay from the city proper. Within minutes they found the address Brian had given them. It was a rundown resort.

Sydney was parking at the far end of the lot when the satellite phone rang.

"Hello?" said Jaden, holding the phone to his ear.

"Did you encounter any trouble?" Brian asked right away. He sounded nervous.

"No, none," said Jaden.

"Good. Stay in the truck. Tell Sydney to turn it around, so she's facing out, and keep the motor running. I'll call you back in five minutes."

"Okay—"

The line went dead.

Jaden told Sydney what Brian had said. She turned the truck around.

"I wonder what's going on," said Malia.

"Who knows," said Jaden. "He always was weird."

"Yeah, but now it makes sense, doesn't it?" she said. "That time he searched our house, he was probably looking for cameras or microphones. He probably figured the government was spying on Mom and Dad at home."

"I never thought of that," said Jaden.

A few minutes later, the phone rang again.

"Hello?"

"Tell Sydney to go inside and check in—for one night only. I'll call back when she returns to the truck."

Brian hung up again. Jaden relayed the message.

"Should I keep the engine running this time?" she asked bemusedly.

"Uh... I don't know. He didn't say," he told her.

Sydney went inside—and kept the car running.

"What the hell is going on?" Jaden asked. Malia only shrugged.

Five minutes later, Sydney returned. No sooner had she closed the door than the phone rang a third time. Jaden answered it.

"Good, you're not being followed. I want you to look on the map on Sydney's iPhone."

"I need the phone," said Jaden, reaching into the front seat. Malia handed it to him.

"Got it," he said to Brian.

"Look to the south of Miami Beach and find Key Biscayne. It's an island."

Jaden scrolled down on the map. "I see it!"

"Good. Now zoom in on the southern tip of the island and find the lighthouse."

"Uh… I don't see it. Everything's green."

"Switch to satellite view," said Brian.

Jaden did as he said.

"I still don't see it."

"Zoom in more."

Jaden double-tapped the very southern tip of the island. He still couldn't find a lighthouse. He double-tapped again, and then he spotted it.

"Yeah—there it is!"

"Go directly to the west, to the next building you find."

"I see it," said Jaden.

"That's a diner. I want you to drive there and park in the lot. Then walk along the footpath through the woods and meet me at the lighthouse."

Jaden started to reply, but Brian hung up again.

"Why did I check in to the hotel if we're going to the light-house?" Sydney asked once Jaden had told her everything.

"Not a clue," said Jaden.

He plotted the directions and handed the phone back to Malia. They had to drive back to the mainland, farther south on Interstate 95, and across another causeway to Key Biscayne. But thirty minutes later, they parked at the diner. Sydney locked the truck, and they walked into the woods, following the footpath to the lighthouse.

They walked around the perimeter of the structure. It was much broader up close than it had appeared from afar. There was only one door, facing away from the ocean.

"Now what?" asked Jaden.

Malia rolled her eyes and knocked on the door. There was a buzzing sound, and the door opened of its own accord.

11

LIGHTHOUSE

Malia walked inside. Sydney and Jaden followed; Malia closed the door behind them. Jaden was surprised—it looked like they'd walked into someone's apartment. There was a sofa, recliner, and loveseat oriented around a television mounted on the wall. The other side of the room hosted a stove, refrigerator, and kitchen table.

Jaden heard footsteps. Directly across from the front door was a metal staircase that wound along the curved wall, disappeared into the ceiling. Suddenly someone descended into view. The man had long graying hair, pulled into a wild ponytail, and wore crooked wire-rimmed glasses.

"Uncle Brian!" said Malia, running over to him. At that moment, Jaden recognized him. He joined Malia as Brian gathered them into a hug.

"I'm so glad you're safe. I worried you wouldn't make it."

"They think we're in Arkansas," Malia told him, "and that you kidnapped us. At least that's what it said on the news last night."

"Yes, I heard that report, too," said Brian. He walked over to Sydney and shook her hand. "It's good to see you again—it's been too long, Sydney."

"It has," Sydney agreed. "I wish it could be under happier circumstances."

"Indeed," he muttered. "Indeed... Well, make yourselves at home, and I'll get us something to drink."

Jaden sat next to Malia on the sofa, and Sydney positioned herself on the loveseat directly adjacent to them. Brian joined them a minute later with a tray containing a pitcher of lemonade and several glasses. He poured them each a drink and sat down in the recliner.

Jaden took a sip of lemonade and realized that he was starving. They hadn't eaten since lunch.

"What was up with all the weird stuff back at the hotel?" asked Jaden.

"What do you mean?" said Brian.

"Making us wait with the engine running, and then having Sydney check us in..."

"Ah," he said with a nod. "I logged into the hotel's security system. They have cameras in the lobby, as well as the parking lot. I watched every car that pulled in while you were waiting to see if anyone had followed you. And I wanted Sydney to go inside to make sure nobody followed her on foot."

"So is this where you live... when you're not at the

ranch?" asked Malia.

"Sometimes," said Brian. "The lighthouse was situated near one of my larger ventures, so I purchased the place some years ago."

"It's lovely inside," Sydney observed, looking around. "I never would have imagined."

"I did some renovations, mostly restoring it to its original condition. Lighthouse keepers of old typically lived where they worked, you know."

"It's not a functioning lighthouse anymore?" asked Malia.

"It hasn't been in years. With modern GPS and radar, lighthouses are largely obsolete. But we have weightier matters to discuss."

"Yeah, like how'd you know we were coming to the ranch?" said Jaden. "I know you said you could go on the FBI computers and stuff, but… how'd you know to look in the first place? We were only on the local news in Maryland when they caught us at that rest stop, so you couldn't have heard about it in North Carolina yet."

"I long expected the day would come when the government would try to take over your father's project," said Brian.

"That's what Sydney told us," Malia noted.

Brian nodded. "Well, that prompted me to take certain precautions. I installed a program that would notify me any time the name Stephen Kwan turned up on FBI computers. I was alerted after they raided your house two nights ago."

"Why *after*?" asked Malia. "Wouldn't he have been in the system ahead of time? You could have warned us…"

"I had no warning," said Brian. "And I'm not certain why.

But as the FBI was operating at the behest of the CIA, the case information may not have been entered into the FBI computers ahead of time. In any event, once you two escaped, it turned into a manhunt with serious national security ramifications. At that point, the case *did* show up on the FBI's network, triggering my program."

"Yeah—it *was* the CIA," said Jaden. "That Babcock guy was in charge, and he said he was from the CIA."

"Wait, I thought it was illegal for the CIA to operate domestically," said Sydney.

"It is," Brian confirmed. "And that's why they needed the assistance of the FBI, as well as local and state police forces. The CIA planned to take over Stephen's project for use in covert military operations overseas—which falls perfectly within its jurisdiction. But to physically remove the project from Stephen's control, they had to bring in domestic law enforcement agencies. And of course, once this turned into a manhunt—especially one that crossed state lines—it was an FBI matter.

"But make no mistake, it's Babcock calling the shots. The FBI is working to deliver the project to *him*. And speaking of the project... your powers have finally manifested, I assume?"

Malia choked, nearly spitting out her lemonade.

"How'd you know about that?" asked Jaden.

"If your father's little experiment was successful, you two should have developed telekinesis and telepathy sometime soon after the onset of puberty."

"I have telekinesis," Malia said quietly.

"I don't, though," added Jaden. "I'm supposed to?"

"Neither of us has telepathy," said Malia.

"How interesting," Brian observed. "How much do you know?"

"About what?" asked Jaden.

"The experiment, of course."

"Nothing," said Malia. "Dad was about to tell us something when the police showed up. He never had a chance."

"He did start talking about the ancient Egyptians, but I have no idea what they have to do with anything," said Jaden.

Brian laughed. "The Great Pyramid is indeed where everything began. But you're going to find all of this a little difficult to believe."

"Try us," said Jaden. "We have a right to know what the hell is going on."

"I agree," said Brian. "It started when a woman contacted an Egyptologist by the name of Moreau. She had information about a hidden chamber inside the Great Pyramid. Now, the structure had been searched countless times with ground-penetrating radar. Nothing was ever found—no hidden rooms. But this woman also told Moreau the location of the secret entrance, buried deep in the bedrock. Nobody had ever scanned that area below the pyramid before.

"So Moreau brought in the radar, and sure enough, they discovered an underground tunnel, exactly where the woman said it would be. The excavation project alone took three months. Once they had uncovered the entrance, they followed the tunnel to a chamber deep inside the structure. It had never shown up on radar—"

"Dad told us about this," said Malia. "He said there was some sort of metal surrounding the chamber that deflected radiation."

"That's correct," replied Brian. "But it also resisted cutting and drilling. Moreau's team couldn't get inside. That's when he finally contacted your father."

"Why Dad?" asked Malia. "He was a doctor."

"Indeed. But the woman who told Moreau about the chamber also insisted that he bring your father into the investigation. He saw no reason to do so and didn't bother at first. But when they discovered they couldn't gain access to the chamber, Moreau decided to abide by the woman's wishes.

"Of course, your father was completely stymied. He knew nothing that could help them. But he did contact me, and I put Moreau in touch with a mechanical engineering company. Conventional methods would have required blasting a hole in the wall of the chamber. But the power required would have taken out half of the pyramid.

"The engineers ended up using a laser to cut their way inside the chamber. Once they figured out the correct frequency, they sliced through the material like a hot knife through butter.

"What they found inside that chamber represented a technology far more advanced than anything else produced by ancient Egypt. It took months to understand it fully. But your dad was the one who finally pieced it together. He wanted to use the technology, experiment with it, but we lacked the resources to fund such a project. This was years before my company contracted with the government; otherwise, I would have funded the research myself. Much to my dismay, Stephen sought government funding. And he found it."

"Now wait a minute," said Jaden. "Here we go with this ancient technology crap again—*they didn't have technology*! They built the pyramids four thousand years ago. That's impressive and everything, but they *dragged the stones*! If they had technology, why didn't they use it to build the pyramids?"

"No, Jaden, the pyramids were not built four thousand years ago," said Brian.

"It was between 2580 and 2560 B.C., so it was more like forty-five hundred years ago," Malia told him.

"Oh, whatever—four thousand, forty-five hundred—close enough," Jaden said impatiently. "My point is—"

"No, Malia, I'm afraid that's not correct either," said Brian. "The actual date was closer to 10,000 B.C."

Jaden, Malia, and Sydney stared at him, their mouths wide open.

"I'm sorry, what?" said Sydney. "That's impossible. There were no civilizations in 10,000 B.C. Wasn't it more like 5000 B.C. when the first civilizations came into existence?"

"Let me show you something," said Brian, without answering Sydney's question. He picked up an iPad from the table. A few seconds later, he handed it to Jaden, who held it so Malia and Sydney could see it too.

"It's the Great Sphinx," said Malia.

"Yes. Now swipe to the next picture." Jaden dragged his

finger across the touchscreen. "That is the body of the Sphinx before the modern restoration efforts began. What do you see?"

Sydney gasped. "It looks like… water erosion."

Malia leaned in to examine the picture more closely. "But there's no water there—that had to be caused by blowing sand."

"No," said Brian. "First of all, wind erosion would cause horizontal markings. That pattern is vertical. Furthermore, the body of the Sphinx spent most of its history buried in sand, which would have protected it from any sort of wind erosion."

"But there's no water in the desert," said Jaden.

"Yes, exactly," said Brian. "Go to the next image."

Jaden swiped the screen again. It was an aerial photo of the three Great Pyramids of Giza.

"So?" he asked.

"Look familiar?" asked Brian.

"Of course it does," said Jaden impatiently. "It's the pyramids. We were just talking about them."

"Next picture," Brian told him.

Jaden moved to the next image; it showed three stars in the night sky. Malia gasped.

"Orion's belt," Brian said, grinning at Malia.

"Wait—I don't get it," said Jaden. Brian made a swiping gesture with one finger. Jaden swiped the screen. The next image showed the stars overlaid on top of the aerial photo of the pyramids. They lined up precisely.

"You see, the third, dimmer star is offset slightly," Brian

pointed out. "It's not quite on the same line as the two brighter stars. The same holds for the pyramids. The third, somewhat smaller structure doesn't exactly line up with the two larger pyramids."

"Did they build them that way on purpose?" asked Jaden.

Brian gestured at the iPad again. "You tell me."

Jaden scrolled to the next picture. It was the same as the previous one, but this time included a wider area of the sky. Malia gasped again.

"What do you see?" asked Brian.

"The Milky Way lines up precisely with the Nile!"

"Indeed it does," Brian said, smiling broadly. "The pyramids are oriented with the river the same way the stars of Orion's belt line up with the plane of our galaxy, seen as a milky river of stars in the night sky."

"Now hold on," said Sydney. "I'll admit this is fascinating, but it's still true today. Orion lines up with the Milky Way this way *now*. How does that prove the pyramids were built in 10,000 B.C.?"

"I'm glad you asked," said Brian, gesturing to the iPad.

Jaden swiped the screen. The next image showed two images, one above the other. The top image showed the stars and the Milky Way, with an arrow pointing to the north. The bottom image showed the pyramids and the Nile again, also with an arrow to the north. The angles were different.

"But that's all wrong," said Malia.

"Yes," Brian agreed. "But watch this. Jaden?" Jaden moved to the next image, but it was a video instead. Brian nodded to him. Jaden tapped the icon in the middle of the screen to play the clip.

It was the same two images from the previous frame. But the one with the stars and the Milky Way was slowly changing. The stars were rotating in the sky as a timer across the top counted down from A.D. 2000. When the counter reached 10,000 B.C., the stars in the top part of the image formed the same angle to the north as the pyramids in the bottom picture.

"I don't understand," said Sydney. "You mean the position of the stars in the sky changes over time?"

"It's called precession," Brian told them. "You know, of course, that the Earth's axis is tilted?"

Malia nodded. "That's why we have seasons. We experience summer when the Earth's axis points toward the Sun, giving the northern hemisphere more direct sunlight. In the winter, the Earth is on the other side of the Sun, so the axis points away from it. The southern hemisphere gets the direct sunlight instead—that's why it's summer there when it's winter here."

"Very good," said Brian. "Well, it turns out that the Earth's axis hasn't always pointed in the same direction. You see, the planet wobbles, very slightly. The north pole moves about in a circle every 26,000 years. Thus the position of the stars in the sky changes very slowly over time. And in 10,000 B.C., the stars of Orion's belt formed the same angle with the North Pole as the pyramids on the Giza plain.

"And you remember the water erosion we discussed?"

Sydney, Malia, and Jaden nodded in unison.

"There was an ice age that finished up right around 10,000 B.C. Europe was still under ice, but Egypt was covered in lush vegetation, and enjoyed plentiful rainfall. And *that* is what caused the water erosion on the walls of the Great Sphinx."

The three of them sat in silence for a minute, struggling to take everything in.

"Okay, wait," Jaden said finally. "So what if all that crap was built in 10,000 B.C. Who cares? It's even crazier to think they'd have technology *that* early!"

"On the contrary! It makes much more sense because this places the building of the pyramids *before* the downfall of the great progenitor civilization."

"The *what*?" asked Malia.

"Have you ever heard of Atlantis?" asked Brian.

"Sure," said Malia. "It was supposed to be an incredibly advanced civilization on an island in the Atlantic Ocean that sank into the sea thousands of years ago. But that's only a myth."

"Not according to Plato," said Brian.

"He was an ancient Greek philosopher," Malia said to Jaden.

"I know that!" said Jaden, glaring at her. In truth, he hadn't been sure.

"Plato described Atlantis as a great naval power and a 'perfect society,' advanced both technologically as well as culturally—until it suffered a great cataclysm in 9600 B.C.

"In any event, I believe the ancient Atlantians *must* have been the ones who designed the technology we discovered in the hidden chamber inside the Great Pyramid. It's the only explanation for how something so advanced could have existed so long ago."

Sydney opened her mouth to say something, but no words came out. Malia looked confused. But Jaden was irritated.

"This is insane," he said, getting to his feet. "Nuts! People didn't have *technology* 10,000 years ago, or 2,500 years ago, I don't care if they were Egyptians, Atlantians or *Martians*! You've lost your mind if—"

"Jaden, *you* are the proof," said Brian. "You and Malia. We found a tissue sample inside that hidden chamber. Whether it was genetically engineered, or the DNA of actual Atlantians, I cannot say. But only a highly advanced society could have produced such a sample."

Before Jaden could respond, Brian stood up and took the iPad from him. He scrolled to another picture and handed it back to him.

"Look. When they entered the hidden chamber, they found a stone enclosure in the middle. After removing the lid, they found this metal canister inside."

Jaden looked at the picture. There were hieroglyphs etched into the metal.

"So what?" he demanded.

"Let me see," said Malia, taking the iPad from him. She and Sydney examined the image.

"No way," said Malia.

"What?" asked Jaden, sitting next to her to look again.

"Look at that," she said, pointing to a larger symbol in the middle of the others.

"It's a double helix," said Sydney.

"Precisely," said Brian. "The double helix of DNA, the molecule common to all life, which provides the genetic blueprint for every species on Earth—and which modern science didn't discover until the nineteenth century.

"Your father was part of the team that mapped the human genome at the dawn of the twenty-first century. Undoubtedly that's why the anonymous source insisted that Moreau contact *him*.

"Your father studied the DNA samples found in the pyramid for over a year. His team concluded that it contained extra chromosomes. With those genes, these samples would produce human beings with seemingly supernatural powers."

Malia's eyes suddenly went wide as she stared at her uncle. "Like telekinesis and telepathy," she said quietly.

"Quite right," Brian confirmed. "Your father's team produced two viable eggs from the Giza sample—twins, one male, and one female," he said, indicating Jaden and Malia.

"Wait—you're saying that Dad made Malia and me in a lab or something?"

"From DNA discovered inside the Great Pyramid," said Malia. "It's almost like cloning, isn't it?"

"Yes," said Brian. "DNA is the basic building block of all life. It's the genetic code that makes you who you are—biologically, at least. But in the case of cloning, you'd take the DNA from one person, and create a copy of him or her. Your father didn't start with a person—he used the samples found inside the pyramid. But the process is quite similar. He infused the Giza DNA—exactly how he found it—into human egg cells. The two of you are a direct product of that DNA. A surrogate mother was found to bring you to term. Of course, she had no idea that you weren't perfectly normal human children."

"So our mom and dad weren't our real parents," Malia observed.

"They certainly were your *real* parents, in every way that matters," said Brian. "But not biologically."

"Your father spent the rest of his career trying to develop a way to duplicate the extra chromosomes from the Giza sample and combine them with regular human DNA. But six years ago, he reached a critical impasse. He discovered that it might not be possible with current technology. Soon after that, I learned that the CIA was planning to take over the project—in other words, kidnap the two of you— because your father was unable to produce more specimens."

"Specimens?" asked Malia. "You mean people. He couldn't engineer more people with... the powers that I have?"

"That's correct," said Brian. "You and your brother are the only people in the whole world who possess such abilities."

"But couldn't they create more eggs from the original sample?" asked Malia.

"No," said Brian. "There was only enough genetic material for *two* eggs. You and Jaden."

"But I don't have any powers," Jaden reminded him. "I can't do anything."

"You will," said Brian. "And the CIA knows it. I'm sure Babcock spoke to McLaren before you two ever set foot in the high school. He probably warned McLaren to contact him immediately if either of you ever did anything… *strange*. No doubt, he had a similar conversation with your middle school principal as well."

"But why?" asked Malia.

"Because the moment one of you manifested your powers, they'd want to put you to work, conducting experiments to see exactly what you could do—and to decide how they could put those powers to work for the military."

"This explains everything," said Sydney. "When I found Melissa looking at the restricted documents…"

"She was searching for information about her children," Brian finished for her. "Yes. I went to Stephen and Melissa immediately when I discovered the CIA's plans to abduct the children. Stephen didn't believe me—I had no proof, you see. I begged him to seek private funding—by that time, I possessed the resources to fund his research myself. But he refused. He insisted that he'd lose everything if he left the NIH, and would have to start over from scratch.

"My concern was for the children. I wanted Stephen to move away, to go into hiding, to prevent the CIA from abducting them. But the naïve fool trusted the government. He didn't believe they'd ever do such a thing. Eventually, it drove us apart.

"But Melissa, on the other hand, believed me. She'd been

leery of government involvement from the very beginning. She understood that Jaden and Malia wouldn't merely be science experiments—they'd be her *children*.

"When I told her what I'd found out about the CIA, she wanted evidence, proof that what I was saying was accurate. That's why she searched the secure network at the NIH."

"Did she ever find it?" asked Sydney.

"No," said Brian. "But I daresay the proof came the moment Babcock showed up on her doorstep."

Brian retook his seat, and the four of them sat in silence for several minutes. Jaden couldn't believe it—any of it. It was as if they'd left the rational universe when they walked into the lighthouse and entered some sort of alternate reality where nothing made sense.

"None of this is possible," he said. "The pyramids, Atlantis, the DNA—*none* of it!"

Suddenly Jaden found himself, the entire couch upon which he was sitting, and the rest of the contents of the room —including the stove, the refrigerator, and his Uncle Brian— floating two feet in the air.

"Then explain *this*," said Malia, holding out both hands. "This shouldn't be possible either—normal people certainly can't do it!"

"Remarkable," said Brian, gazing around the room in awe.

"Dammit Malia, stop showing off," said Jaden. "Put us down."

She complied. Brian almost looked disappointed.

"You're telling me you believe all of this crap?" Jaden demanded.

"I don't know *what* to believe," said Malia. "But there's got to be some explanation for what I can do, for what happened to Mom and Dad. And nothing else makes any sense."

"You require further proof?" Brian asked Jaden.

Jaden jumped to his feet. "Proof? *Proof*?! You can't prove anything because what you're saying is CRAZY!"

Brian rose to his feet. "Come with me," he said.

"What, there's more?" asked Sydney.

"This is only the tip of the iceberg, I'm afraid," Brian replied, heading out the door.

12

PYRAMID

Sydney got up and followed him. Jaden looked at Malia; she shrugged. He rolled his eyes, and the two of them went out the door after them.

Outside, Brian led them around the lighthouse to a short pier. The sun had set, and it was dark out. A boat was tied to the end of the dock.

"Whoa—you own a yacht, too?" asked Jaden.

"I do, but this isn't it," said Brian. "This is just a small cabin cruiser I use to run back and forth to my island. The yacht's currently tied up in Rhode Island."

Jaden stared at him in awe for a moment before following him onto the boat. Brian untied them, and a few minutes later, they were racing across the open ocean.

"Where are we going?" Malia yelled over the sound of the motor and the crashing sea.

"You'll see," said Brian.

For twenty minutes they continued directly away from land, the boat rising and falling with the waves. It was completely dark outside; Jaden assumed Brian was navigating by the instruments on his console.

Finally, Jaden discerned a faint pinprick of light straight ahead of them. As they drew closer, he saw that there was a small island. The light was coming from a lone lamppost at the end of a pier. Brian pulled the boat alongside the landing, then jumped out and tied it up.

"Let's go," he called to them. He helped them disembark and led them down the pier.

The island was small and rocky. Jaden could make out most of its surface by the light of the lamppost. A rocky crest rose in the very middle of the landmass; that's where Brian was headed.

When they arrived, Jaden realized there was a heavy metal door with rounded corners in the rock face, like something from a submarine. Brian entered a series of numbers on a keypad next to the door. Suddenly the door's lever popped open, and there was a sound of rushing air. Brian pulled the door open. Within was a narrow shaft with a metal ladder descending into the ground.

"Climb in," said Brian, "but be careful. It's a long drop. I'll close the door behind us."

Sydney went first, followed by Jaden and Malia. Jaden heard a clang as Brian shut the door before following Malia down the ladder.

Down and down, they climbed, their way illuminated by small lights embedded in the wall. The air grew warmer as they descended. Jaden started sweating. But five minutes later, they reached the bottom.

Jaden jumped down from the ladder to find himself in a circular chamber roughly carved out of the rock. A long tunnel extended away from them, dimly lit.

"Lead the way," Brian said to Jaden, extending one hand toward the end of the tunnel.

"Where the hell are we going?" Jaden demanded, not moving.

"Indulge me only a few minutes longer, and everything will become clear," said Brian.

Jaden rolled his eyes and set out down the tunnel. He was convinced his uncle was insane. The entire story he'd told them at the lighthouse contradicted Jaden's sense of reality. And now he'd taken them out to sea, to some sort of subterranean maze deep below the ocean. What could this possibly have to do with ancient Egyptians, Atlantis, or genetic engineering?

After what felt like a mile, the tunnel made a sharp turn to the left. Jaden stopped dead in his tracks at the sight before him, his eyes wide.

They were standing on a ledge overlooking a cavernous chamber. Stone steps seemingly carved out of the rock wall, led down at least forty feet to the floor of the enormous space. Computers and scientific equipment filled half of the area. But the structure that dominated the rest of the chamber had captured Jaden's attention.

It was a gigantic black pyramid. Its polished surfaces were

smooth as glass, almost mirror-like. Fine threads of electricity danced along its edges.

"*What* is that?" asked Malia.

"That's going to take a little explaining," said Brian. "Come with me."

He jogged down the steps; the others followed. As they approached the pyramid, Jaden realized that the rear third of it was embedded in the stone wall.

Brian walked over to a computer terminal and sat down. Jaden, Malia, and Sydney gathered around behind him.

"Do you know where we are?" he asked.

"Off the coast of Miami," said Sydney sardonically.

"Yes, but what does legend say about this area?" He brought up an image on the screen as he spoke. It was a map. Jaden could see Miami clearly labeled, along with Bermuda and someplace named San Juan on an island in the Caribbean. Red lines connected the three points, creating a triangle.

"You've got to be kidding me," said Malia.

"What?" asked Jaden.

"The *Bermuda Triangle*?" said Malia. "That's just a myth."

"What's the Bermuda Triangle?" asked Jaden. He felt like he'd heard about this before, but couldn't place it.

"It's an area of the Atlantic Ocean, bounded by Miami, Florida, San Juan, Puerto Rico, and Bermuda, that's seen an inordinate number of shipwrecks and plane crashes over the years, many under mysterious circumstances. In some cases, vessels and aircraft have simply vanished without a trace. "

"Wasn't there some movie that tried to claim aliens were abducting people from the area?" asked Malia.

Brian chuckled. "Yes, some have postulated that. But it's not true. *That* is the cause of the strangeness," he said, pointing at the pyramid.

"How?" asked Sydney.

"When Stephen first took the Giza samples to his lab, he found a map etched into the interior of the canister," said Brian. "The map pointed to these coordinates, right where you're standing. Stephen told me about the map, and I convinced him to share the information with nobody. We had the surface of the canister ground to remove the markings.

"I set out to explore the area and see what might be hidden here. The task was daunting. At first, we could find nothing—only an underground air pocket, which turned out to be the very chamber in which you're standing."

"So you didn't build this?" asked Sydney.

"Not this room," said Brian. "It was already here. But there was no way to get to it. The existence of the map convinced me there had to be something important here. And our experience at the Great Pyramid taught us that whatever it was could be hidden from radar.

"I spent a fortune, not to mention years of my life, to find a way to reach this chamber. We had to be very careful to avoid flooding it. In the beginning, we created only a small access hole and sent in a remote-controlled robot. It sent back pictures of the pyramid.

"I had to know what that was. So I had the tunnel and the

entrance on the island constructed. My team has been studying the pyramid ever since."

"So... what is it?" asked Jaden.

"And what's it got to do with the Bermuda Triangle?" added Malia.

Brian took a deep breath. "In short, it's a power plant. And it's got *everything* to do with the Triangle.

"Atlantis existed somewhere in the Atlantic before its demise. And if it truly was an advanced civilization, with all the technological trappings that go along with it, it would have required vast amounts of power, much like a modern city."

"Wait—you're telling me they had *electricity* ten thousand years ago?" Jaden asked skeptically.

"Actually, this chamber—and thus, in all likelihood that pyramid—was built closer to 40,000 years B.C."

"And how on Earth can you determine that?" asked Sydney.

"Not easily," Brian said with a frown, "nor with much certainty. There were no fossil remains anywhere inside the chamber, so carbon dating was not an option. However, this space was carved out of the rock using some sort of high-energy radiation beam."

"You mean a laser," said Malia.

"Yes," Brian agreed, "or something similar to it. The laser was so hot that it melted the rock. And in places where the magma cooled and was not shaved away from the wall, we were able to use radiometric dating to determine the age of this chamber."

"Radiometric dating?" asked Sydney.

"It's the same process used to date volcanic rock," said Brian. "Radioactive isotopes decay at a constant, known rate. By comparing the ratios of these isotopes in a rock sample, one can determine how long ago the rock formed.

"The trouble is we achieved different results depending on what section of the chamber we analyzed. But the oldest samples were formed roughly 42,000 years ago. Thus it's reasonable to conclude that construction of this station began no later than 40,000 B.C. And this would indicate that the civilization of Atlantis thrived for at least thirty millennia, ending in roughly 10,000 B.C."

"And what does any of this have to do with the Bermuda Triangle?" asked Malia.

"Ah, yes. The pyramid acts as a control center. It's linked to thousands of channels that run beneath the ocean floor. They collect geothermal energy—heat, essentially—and with the aid of various chemical reactions, turn that heat into electromagnetic energy.

"This process, in turn, yields an abundance of methane hydrates. When those chemicals are released into the ocean, they reduce the buoyancy of the water—making it almost impossible for anything to float.

"The station was mostly dormant when we found it. Periodically it would run a test cycle, and that's what caused the methane emissions. We lost a couple of boats before we figured that out. But we timed the cycles, and began limiting watercraft activity to the dormant periods."

"So that explains the shipwrecks in the Triangle," said Sydney. "What about the plane crashes?"

"In part, it's the same cause," said Brian. "Methane hydrates are a form of natural gas. As such, they rise to the surface of the ocean as tiny bubbles. But they don't stop there. Once above water, they continue to rise through the atmosphere. And with a sufficiently high concentration, that kind of gas can rob a plane's engines of the air they need for internal combustion. The engines stall, and the plane crashes. The gas can also ignite, causing the aircraft to explode. Furthermore, methane is about half as dense as air. So the sudden drop in air pressure as an aircraft travels through a gas pocket drastically reduces the lift it needs to stay airborne.

"But the pyramid also generates a strong magnetic field inside the Bermuda Triangle. For many years, pilots have reported inaccurate compass readings when navigating the airspace in the area. In some cases, this has caused planes to go off course, get lost, and run out of fuel. This is less of an issue today with modern GPS equipment. But at times, the magnetic field becomes strong enough to bring a plane down."

"So that pyramid generated electricity for Atlantis," Malia said tentatively, "but why is it still here if Atlantis is gone?"

"I don't know," Brian replied with a shrug. "We have no idea what destroyed Atlantis. Plato describes a great cataclysm—some sort of natural disaster that sunk the island into the sea. Other stories from ancient Greece tell how Athens destroyed Atlantis in battle. But for whatever reason, this pyramid survived the tragedy."

"Are there others?" asked Sydney.

"Other pyramids?" said Brian. Sydney nodded. "I don't know. We only found this one because of the map that came with the Giza samples."

"And it's still… working?" asked Jaden. "That's why the weird stuff happens in the Bermuda Triangle—because that thing's still producing electricity?"

"Indeed," said Brian. He opened a drawer and pulled out a flashlight. Opening the shaft, he removed the batteries. He screwed the head back on and said, "Come with me."

Jaden, Malia, and Sydney followed him to the pyramid. He handed the flashlight to Jaden and said, "Turn it on."

Jaden rolled his eyes. "You took out the batteries!" Brian waited patiently, saying nothing. "Fine." Jaden pressed the button. The light turned on. He nearly dropped it in his surprise.

"What the hell?" asked Sydney.

"It's no cause for alarm," said Brian. "It's not terribly surprising—it simply shows that the pyramid is still generating electricity. There's a powerful electric field in this chamber, that's why the flashlight works without batteries."

Jaden moved closer to the pyramid. Up close, he could see the tiny threads of electricity dancing over the entire surface of the structure. They appeared to be originating somewhere inside the pyramid. He held out his hand to touch it.

"Jaden—no!" said Malia, grabbing his wrist.

"It's quite harmless," said Brian, running his hand along the smooth face. "Go ahead."

Jaden touched it with only a fingertip at first—he half-expected to be electrocuted. But then he pressed his palm against it. The material felt strange—almost like it was wet. But an instant later, something weird happened.

The entire pyramid lit up, glowing from within. Characters and symbols appeared on the surface, as if on a computer screen. The icons moved about, rearranging themselves, but it was no language that Jaden recognized. At the same time, there was a noise. It sounded like a human voice, only it wasn't uttering words. Instead, it made sounds that were similar to the chirping and whistling of birds.

"What did I do?" Jaden asked, backing away from the pyramid.

"I have no idea," said Brian, looking scared. "This has never happened before." He ran back to the computer terminal.

"I *told* you not to touch it," Malia said as they joined Brian.

He was working frantically, opening different windows, and typing commands. Every few seconds, he'd turn to look at the pyramid. Nothing changed.

"I should have guessed," he muttered.

"Guessed what?" asked Sydney.

"That the children could activate the pyramid's control systems," he said. "It makes sense. They probably designed it to detect the DNA of the user, thus preventing non-Atlantians from accessing the system. That's why none of us ever caused… this. But Jaden's DNA is different, and the pyramid must have recognized that."

"So what's it doing?" asked Malia.

"I wish I knew," said Brian, turning back to the computer.

But in that instant, something changed. The characters disappeared from the pyramid's surface, and a bright red glow formed somewhere deep inside the structure. Suddenly, a light emanated from the pyramid's core, like a laser, extending through its apex and into the stone above.

"Uh-oh," said Brian. He opened a window on the screen and stared. A variety of graphs were displayed, all hitting giant peaks. "Carl was right. This is bad—we need to get out of here! Let's go!"

Without another word, he dashed around the front of the pyramid and up the stairs. Jaden, Malia, and Sydney ran after him.

"What's wrong?" asked Jaden. "What's happening?"

"No time to explain," Brian yelled back. "We need to hurry."

They reached the top of the steps and sprinted down the tunnel. Jaden had broken a sweat by the time they reached the end. Malia was breathing heavily, and Sydney had fallen behind.

Brian had Jaden and Malia precede him up the ladder. "Be careful, but go quickly."

Minutes later, Jaden reached the top. He pulled on the heavy lever, and the door opened. Running toward the pier, he looked over his shoulder to make sure the others were coming. But he froze in his tracks.

Out beyond the island, a plume of water rose from the ocean like a fountain. A red beam of light shot from its center, piercing the night sky as high as the eye could see. It must have been coming from the pyramid—that had seemed farther away underground, but from this vantage point, it appeared to be very close to the island.

Malia, Sydney, and Brian caught up to Jaden. Malia and Sydney failed to notice what Jaden was staring at.

"What's the problem, Uncle Brian?" asked Malia, catching her breath. "Why are we running?"

"You see that?" he asked, pointing to the beam. "So does the rest of North America. The FBI is going to come knocking, and we need to get you out of here before they arrive!"

They raced down the pier to the boat. Brian untied it while the others boarded. Seconds later they were speeding toward shore, going significantly faster than they had on the way out. It was a much bumpier ride.

They reached the lighthouse. Brian docked hurriedly, bumping the boat hard against the landing.

"Sydney, give me your phone," he said as they ran up the pier.

They stopped at the lighthouse. Brian typed something into the iPhone and handed it back to Sydney.

"That's where you can find my friend, Carl Sanders. That beam changes everything—there's no time to explain. But find Carl and describe what happened here—and tell him I sent you! You need to get out of here—NOW! Hurry!"

"But what about you?" asked Malia.

"I'm staying here," he said. She began to protest, but he

talked over her. "They're going to trace that island to me very quickly, and when they do, they'll stop at nothing to find me. They'll close the city of Miami, or the entire state of Florida if they have to. And that means you'll be trapped. I won't allow that—you *must* escape!"

"You're going to let them take you, aren't you?" asked Jaden.

"Yes—I'll tell them I haven't seen you. Hell, I'll say I told you to go to Canada! Now go, before it's too late!"

He gave Jaden and Sydney a hug, but Malia stood back, crying.

"What are they going to do to you?" she asked. "You're the only family we have left!"

"Don't worry, Malia—they won't harm me. I'll be incarcerated, I'm sure, but I can get out—I promise. Stay with Carl, and I'll meet you there. Go quickly!"

She gave him a quick hug, and they bolted into the trees, emerging a minute later in the diner parking lot where they'd left Sydney's truck. As they climbed in, Jaden heard a noise. He looked up—it was a helicopter, and it was landing at the lighthouse.

"Oh, damn!" he said.

Sydney started the car, and they drove away, merging into traffic, and hoping not to be seen.

13

COMMANDER

Nadia Bashandi sat down in her boss's office, across the desk from him. After more than twenty years of working for the man, she still found him intimidating.

Commander Anhur shuffled through a pile of papers, stopping to gaze intently at one report. After a minute, Nadia wondered if he'd forgotten about her. She cleared her throat.

"One moment, Lieutenant."

Nadia couldn't stand the suspense. She'd spent the whole day confirming the information. Only at the end of her shift did she call to inform him that she had news. He'd summoned her to his office immediately; why was he making her wait so long now?

"All right, what is it?" he asked a minute later, setting aside the report. "What've you got?"

"It's a planet," she said, handing him a folder with her findings.

He thumbed through the pages. "Summarize this for me."

Nadia bit down the retort she desperately wished to utter. If she had to report to this man, why couldn't he at least familiarize himself with the basics of exoplanetary astronomy?

"Initially, it turned up because the star exhibited the tell-tale evidence—a slight wobble, indicating a large orbiting mass. Upon further investigation, I determined that this is a rocky planet, well within the star's habitable zone."

"We've found several of these," the commander said impatiently.

"Yes, and like a few of the others, this one occults the star. I was able to get spectroscopy on the atmosphere."

"That's happened before, too," said the commander. "The others had poisonous atmospheres that wouldn't support life."

"This one will. It has water. And it's rich in oxygen and nitrogen—in fact, the ratios would seem to indicate that life could already be present!"

The commander raised one eyebrow at her. "You're sure this isn't wishful thinking?"

Nadia couldn't believe her ears. "I've triple-checked the numbers—they're right. And I went back through old data. We've observed this star for years but never looked for a wobble before. But it's there, through decades of scans."

"Rerun the entire analysis, Lieutenant." He turned back to his pile of papers.

"You want me to redo the whole thing?" she asked in dismay.

"All of it. The scans, the calculations, the spectroscopy— we have to be certain before we act."

"But I already *am* certain! Commander—"

"You have my orders," he said wearily. "You're dismissed."

She stared at him in utter disbelief for a few moments before getting up to leave. After all these years, she'd finally found it, and he didn't trust her data? The man who refused to take the time to educate himself on how science worked was ordering her to redo her work?

Nadia had to admit, scientific rigor did demand that she confirm her results. Under normal circumstances, the data would have to be independently verified by other teams in different locations. This was impossible, but she grudgingly admitted that he was right. And it would take only a couple of days to complete the work.

She arrived home ten minutes later and walked into her bedroom. Awan was lying in bed, reading a book.

"How'd it go?" he asked.

"He wants me to rerun the entire analysis."

"Figures."

"He's right, but he's such a pain in the ass. He's not even a scientist."

"It *would* be better to keep science out of the hands of the military," Awan suggested.

Nadia snorted. "Yeah, don't I wish."

She slept uneasily that night, unable to stop running

through the research in her head. One step at a time, she thought through the daunting task that lay before her. She wanted to make sure to get it right.

Strange images invaded her dreams. She saw the girl again, this time on an island in the middle of the sea. She was running away from a giant laser beam shooting up from the ocean. Nadia didn't know what it was supposed to mean.

14

DRIVE

J aden felt his heart beating very fast as they drove up the main road toward the north end of Key Biscayne —and the only exit off the island. They didn't meet any trouble, but suddenly Malia yelled "Look!" from the back seat.

Jaden turned in his seat to see where she was pointing. Out the back window, he caught sight of the helicopter lifting off from the southern tip of the island. Off the coast, the bright laser continued to pierce the night sky.

"What is it?" asked Sydney.

"Helicopter's taking off," said Jaden. "They have Brian."

His words hung ominously in the air for several moments before Sydney spoke.

"Well… let's hope they believe his story."

They reached the causeway back to the mainland several

minutes later. But Jaden saw flashing lights coming toward them.

"Quick—get down!" said Sydney. "Go in back and hide under my clothes!"

"Here we go again," Jaden muttered as he scrambled behind her. He and Malia squeezed under the seat, pulling clothes on top of themselves. Seconds later, Jaden heard the sirens as they passed the police cars going the other way.

"We're clear," Sydney told them. "You can come out now."

Jaden clambered back into the front seat as they reached the mainland.

"There were eight cop cars," said Sydney. "We're fortunate they didn't block the causeway."

"*Eight?*" said Jaden. "What for? They must have taken Brian away in the helicopter."

"They're still going to have to investigate that," said Malia, pointing out the window toward the beam of light.

"Where are we going now?" asked Jaden. Sydney had taken the ramp for I-95 north.

"I don't know yet," she said. "For now, as far away as we can get from here."

They drove for a while in silence. Every so often, they passed a police car going the other way, lights flashing and siren blaring. Jaden's heartbeat accelerated every time this happened.

"Oh crap," Sydney muttered, gazing in her rearview mirror.

Jaden turned around. This time, there were flashing lights behind them, gaining fast.

"Get down!" yelled Sydney.

There was no time to crawl into the back seat—the car was too close. Jaden dropped into the footwell, pressing his head into the front seat. It sounded like the siren had moved right next to them.

"Is he pulling us over?" asked Jaden.

"Hang on," said Sydney, sounding tense. "We're good," she added a few moments later. "He went right by us."

Jaden sat in the seat again.

"Do you think they're looking for us?" he asked.

"Not if they believed Brian's story," said Malia. "And that's the first time we saw the police headed *away* from the lighthouse. If they thought we were here, there'd probably be a *lot* more of them."

"That's a good point," said Sydney. "And there's no evidence that you two were at the lighthouse…"

"Yes, there is!" countered Jaden. "The lemonade! Brian left the glasses sitting on his table! They're gonna know *someone* else was there—we used four glasses!"

"Oh no," said Malia. "And after what Brian told us, I'm sure they have our fingerprints on file."

Jaden shook his head. He wasn't ready to accept everything Brian had told them. It still seemed implausible.

"Let's not get ahead of ourselves," said Sydney. "They've got Brian. If his story's convincing enough, maybe they won't bother searching the lighthouse. And besides, they're probably going to be pretty busy with that laser beam."

But despite her words, Sydney drove a little faster.

Once they'd gone past Boca Raton, she pulled off the highway and stopped at a gas station.

"I'll be right back," she said. "Stay put—and get down if anyone comes too close to the truck!"

Jaden looked around anxiously the whole time Sydney was pumping gas. But nobody took any notice of them. An old man pulled up to the pump behind them but didn't so much as glance at the truck. Sydney climbed back in and picked up her iPhone. She tapped a couple of buttons and held the phone to her ear.

"Who are you calling?" asked Jaden.

"Work," she replied. "Ugh, voicemail." She waited for several seconds. "Yeah, hi, Liz, this is Sydney. Well, I'm feeling a lot better, but my mom just called to say that my aunt passed away. She's taking it really hard—you know she's been alone since my dad died last year. So I have to head out to Cali for a while. I'm not sure when I'm going to be back... I'll be out this whole week for sure. I'll give you a call again as soon as I know anything more."

"I'm so sorry for your loss," Jaden told her once she'd ended the call, doing his best to suppress a grin.

Sydney smacked him in the head. She started the car, and they drove away.

"I'm *starving*," said Jaden. "Can we stop somewhere and get some food?"

They found a Subway right before the highway. Sydney pulled into the parking lot, again reminding them to avoid being seen. She returned with their sandwiches several minutes later, and they resumed their northward course.

"Here," she said, handing Jaden her iPhone. "Open the notes and see what your uncle typed. We should probably figure out where we're going."

Jaden opened the application. "Uh… What's this supposed to mean? It's a bunch of numbers."

"A phone number?" asked Sydney.

"Nah, definitely not. It says 37.750, and -115.874."

Sydney shrugged, shaking her head slightly. "That's a little strange."

"I'm gonna google it," said Jaden. He copied the first number and pasted it into the search box in the browser. "It says 'Map of Kentucky, 37.750N by 87.250W.' We have to go to Kentucky?!"

"Oh!" Malia called from the back seat. "They're coordinates—latitude and longitude. Type them into maps."

Jaden returned to the note, copied both numbers this time, and pasted them into the map application. Sure enough, they registered as coordinates. Jaden zoomed out and gasped. "Uh, guys… this is in Nevada."

"*Nevada*?!" said Sydney in disbelief. "Pull up the directions and see how long that's going to take from here."

Jaden plotted the route from their current location. "One day, nineteen hours."

"But that's if we drive straight through," said Malia, "which is impossible. That's going to take us at least four days."

"Right now, let's concentrate on getting out of Florida," said Sydney. "Jaden, where do we go from here?"

He looked at the directions. "We're gonna stay on 95 until the Ronald Reagan Turnpike, then take that for a while."

Sydney nodded.

"So… what do you guys think about all that crap Brian told us?" said Jaden.

"Which part?" asked Malia.

"I dunno… any of it," he replied. "According to him, Atlantis was around tens of thousands of years ago, but they had electricity and stuff, and they made these genetic samples and left them inside the Great Pyramid. Doesn't that sound a little *crazy* to you?"

Sydney opened her mouth to speak, but sighed instead, shaking her head.

"It *does* explain what I can do," said Malia. "And why the CIA wants us."

"No, the genetic engineering part of it explains *that*," said Jaden. "And that's what Dad did—he could have made our DNA. I know that's still kinda crazy, but we don't need people running around in 40,000 B.C. with electricity to explain your powers."

"No, but Dad started talking about the Great Pyramid, too. Uncle Brian might be crazy, but Dad wasn't. And besides, how do you explain that pyramid we just saw?"

"Brian's super-rich," said Jaden. "He could've built it. But you're right, Dad talked about the Egyptians too… And he did say they found some kind of technology inside the hidden chamber. But that's just so…"

"Unbelievable?" suggested Malia. Jaden nodded. "I know. I don't think I'd believe any of it if I couldn't do… you know, if I weren't telekinetic."

Jaden couldn't disagree. As far-fetched as everything seemed, he'd seen what Malia could do with his own eyes. If nothing else, he knew *that* was real. But he didn't bring up the most troubling aspect of Brian's story. Although he trusted Sydney now, this was personal. He wished to discuss it with nobody but Malia; he'd have to wait until they were alone.

"I want to know who this Carl guy is," said Sydney. "What was his last name again?"

"Sanders," said Malia.

"Yeah, that's it," said Sydney. "Put that in Google and see what you come up with."

Jaden typed in the name. "He was the governor of Georgia in the 1960s… but now he's in his 80s and still lives in Georgia."

"I don't think that's the right Carl Sanders," said Malia.

"Me neither," said Jaden. "Oh, here's another one… never mind. He's a Baptist minister in Washington state."

"Try Carl Sanders Nevada," suggested Sydney.

"Hmm… well, someone by that name was arrested in Las Vegas a few years ago," said Jaden. "But he was from Kentucky. There are a few others too… a high school football coach, and a manager of a supermarket."

"This is useless," said Malia. "It seems like he's got a fairly common name. And we know nothing about the one we're looking for, except that he knows Uncle Brian."

Jaden tried searching for his uncle's name along with Sanders' but turned up nothing that looked relevant.

"Nothing with Carl Sanders and Brian Kwan either," he said. "Why are we going to this dude? Like what's the point?"

"Do you have somewhere else in mind?" asked Sydney.

"Brian said to go there, so he must have had a good reason," said Malia.

"Yeah, but what is it?" asked Jaden. Neither of them could answer him. "I guess we'll find out when we get to Nevada."

They rode in silence for a little while, eating their sandwiches. But as they approached the Ronald Reagan Turnpike, Sydney said, "Oh no, not a chance."

"What's wrong?" asked Jaden.

"It's a toll road. I don't want to risk someone at the toll booths recognizing you two. Go into maps again—there's got to be another way."

Jaden opened the application. He zoomed out and looked around the map of Florida.

"We can just keep going on I-95," he said. "Stay on that till Jacksonville, then take I-10 west out of Florida."

"No tolls on I-10?" asked Sydney.

"I don't think so," he replied. "But it's hard to tell on here. It didn't say that turnpike had them."

Sydney went past the exit, staying on I-95.

They fell into silence again. Jaden thought through everything Brian had told them. He had to admit, Brian's argument for the Great Pyramid's age seemed convincing. The existence of Atlantis, an advanced civilization tens of thousands of years ago, was the most astonishing part of the story. He *had* seen that black pyramid himself. But how did he have any way of knowing its true origins? Brian claimed he'd dated the chamber to a time in the ancient past, but where was the proof?

His father had spoken of the pyramids, he reminded himself. If that part of Brian's story were untrue—the claim that they'd found DNA samples inside the Great Pyramid— why would his father have brought up Egypt? And as improbable as the existence of Atlantis seemed, it was still far more likely than the idea of the ancient Egyptians performing genetic engineering themselves.

Jaden grew drowsy as the miles slipped by. Eventually, he fell asleep. He woke up with an urgent need to go to the bathroom. Finding himself slumped against the door, he sat up straight and yawned. He looked at the clock on the dashboard; it was almost four in the morning.

"Where are we?"

"We'll be in Tallahassee soon," said Sydney. "We're into the panhandle, and there's been no trouble so far. I'm starting to think we might make it out of this state."

"Can we stop? I gotta pee."

Sydney pulled off the highway and found an isolated side road. Malia woke up as the truck pulled to a stop. They took turns running into the woods to relieve themselves before driving off again.

Jaden dozed off again as soon as they reached the highway. When he awoke, it was light outside.

"Where are we now?" he asked.

"Almost to the Alabama line," Sydney said with a smile. "Let's hope there aren't any roadblocks."

Jaden stayed awake, staring attentively out the windshield. What would they do if there *was* a roadblock here? But he had no reason to worry. There was nothing out of the ordinary when they reached the state line. They drove into Alabama without the slightest problem.

"Want some breakfast?" asked Sydney.

"Hell, yes," he said. But at that moment, he noticed that she looked exhausted. "We should stop somewhere so you can sleep."

"Yeah, I was thinking the same thing," she agreed. "But just for a little while. I don't want to stop for too long yet."

"Why?" asked Jaden. "We're out of Florida now—and you look terrible."

"You're such a little charmer," she said sarcastically. "No, I'll be all right. I want to put as much distance behind us as I can. Give me a catnap, and I'll be good until tonight."

They exited the highway and found a McDonald's a short distance away. Jaden woke Malia, and Sydney went inside to get them some food. A little farther up the road, they found a commuter parking lot. Sydney parked in the far corner, away from prying eyes. They ate their breakfast, and then she curled up in the passenger seat to get some sleep. Jaden climbed in back with Malia.

He looked out the window, watching the commuters emerging from their cars, waiting for the vans to take them to work. Once Sydney had nodded off, he spoke to Malia.

"How come Mom and Dad never told us?"

Malia looked at him and frowned. "I've been wondering the same thing. But it's like you said—Mom was expecting something like this when we came home from school and told her about your fall. They were probably waiting till one of us found our powers before they told us anything."

"But why? They could have warned us ahead of time."

"Well, the whole thing was a big *experiment*, right? So they probably didn't have any guarantee that we'd ever be able to do anything. Would you want to tell your kids such a messed up story if you didn't have to?"

"No, I guess not," said Jaden. "But Mom *still* didn't want to tell us. Remember? When we heard them arguing in their room? Why would she want to keep this from us, even after you developed your power?"

"Jaden, I don't know…"

"And they weren't really our parents anyway!" he added, growing angry thinking about it. "We're a couple of *lab experiments*. They should've told us way before this. We had a right to know we weren't their kids. But maybe *that's* why they didn't tell us—we were just experiments. They didn't care about us—"

"That's not true!" Malia looked stricken. "They loved us, and you know it!"

"Then why didn't they ever tell us the truth? How come Mom *still* didn't want to, even in the end?"

"Maybe *this* is why," said Malia. "She might have been afraid we wouldn't think they loved us anymore. Brian even said it—Mom knew we were her kids, not just experiments.

That's why she searched the government computer—to try to protect us!"

Jaden shook his head. "I hate this. It's like we're a couple of freaks. I didn't ask for this—I should have been at home-coming this weekend. But now nothing's ever gonna be normal again. They might not have been our *birth* parents, but they were the only ones we had—and now they're dead! What are we gonna do? How are we supposed to live?"

Malia's eyes were welling up with tears. "Brian will take care of us."

"He's in jail by now!"

"But he said he could get out. He'll find us in Nevada. It's gonna turn out okay."

Jaden wished he could believe this. But in the past three days, his entire life had been turned upside down. He didn't know what to think anymore. Everything he'd ever known was gone.

Within a few minutes, Malia dozed off too, and Jaden was left alone with his thoughts. He picked up Sydney's iPhone and started playing a game, but it failed to hold his interest. Instead, he opened the CNN application. A breaking news story was plastered across the opening screen: the beam of light now emanating from the ocean right off the coast of Miami.

Jaden scanned the article. It said nothing about the under-ground pyramid but did mention that authorities were attempting to locate the source of the beam. He wondered if they'd gained access to the tunnel yet. Perhaps they'd been unable to penetrate the steel door.

There was no mention of Jaden, Malia, or Brian. Jaden supposed this was probably a good thing. If they'd suspected their presence at the lighthouse, he figured the article would have said something about it.

He closed the phone and spent the next couple of hours gazing across the parking lot while Sydney and Malia slept. Watching the people depart to their jobs in the commuter vans, Jaden wished his own life could return to normal.

He also contemplated Malia's powers. How strong would she get? And when would he discover his own abilities? This was the first time in his life Malia had ever been able to do something he couldn't. He didn't like it much.

Sydney and Malia woke a couple of hours later, and they resumed their journey. They left the interstate when they reached Mobile and soon passed into Mississippi. They drove for hours, stopped to eat and refuel, and eventually reached Interstate 20. This led them to Louisiana. The sun set, bloody red in the western sky, and soon after, they reached Shreveport.

"Can we stop soon?" asked Malia. "I'm tired of being in this car—no offense."

Sydney chuckled. "None taken. I've had about enough for one day myself. Jaden, why don't you see if you can find a motel somewhere close to the highway."

Jaden searched on the iPhone, finding something that looked perfect. He gave Sydney the directions, and a few minutes later, they were driving up an isolated road in the middle of nowhere, directly adjacent to the highway. They passed some sort of large distribution center, its enormous parking lot full of tractor-trailers, and found the motel a little beyond it.

The place looked old and rundown; only a few cars were parked in the lot. Sydney checked them in, and they parked the truck at the end of the building, right in front of their room.

"This is ideal," Sydney told them. "There's hardly anyone here."

They made sure nobody was watching and went inside their room. Jaden flopped himself down on the bed.

"I'm hungry," said Malia. "But I can't bear to eat any more fast food. There was a supermarket a while back—they might have a salad bar."

"I'm with you," Sydney agreed. "Jaden, what do you think—something healthy for a change?"

"Sure. Why not." What he wanted was his mom's cooking. But the thought only depressed him.

Sydney left them alone to go get food. Jaden and Malia watched television until she returned. They ate in silence.

"I've got an idea," said Jaden. "We should go somewhere Malia can practice… you know, see how strong her powers can get."

"Yeah," Malia agreed. "And maybe you'll be able to do something too."

"I like the idea in principle," said Sydney. "But we need to be careful. We can't afford for anyone to see you."

"Don't worry," said Jaden. "I saw the perfect place on the way here. Remember all those big trucks?"

"At that place right next to here," said Malia. "That's a great idea! Let's go!"

Sydney went out the door first, checking to make sure nobody would see them. But the lot was empty. They didn't bother driving, instead sneaking around the back of the motel. They climbed a fence into the parking lot of the distribution center. Jaden led the way around to the rear of the building, to avoid anyone seeing them from the street.

"All right," he said. "Let's see what you can do. I know you're getting stronger, cuz you lifted a *ton* of stuff at the lighthouse."

"You're exaggerating," said Malia, gazing around apprehensively at the trailers. "That wasn't a ton."

"Yeah, but it was more than you've done before. Except when you ripped those trees out of the ground, but you were stressed out then."

"You uprooted *trees*?!" Sydney said, clearly impressed.

"Try one," Jaden encouraged her, pointing at a trailer.

Malia took a deep breath and concentrated. The trailer made a groaning sound, and Jaden saw it lift several inches off its tires. But it didn't leave the ground. Malia sighed, and the trailer sank back down again.

"I can't," she said. "It's too heavy. You try something."

Jaden focused on Malia; he imagined her rising into the air. Nothing happened. For the next several minutes, they took turns focusing on their respective targets. Not once was Jaden able to move Malia. He tried lifting pebbles and debris in the parking lot with no more success. But after several attempts, Malia did manage to raise the entire trailer a few feet up in the air.

"Damn," said Jaden, watching in awe. Malia exhaled sharply, and the trailer crashed to the ground.

At Jaden's encouragement, she repeated the feat four more times, getting the trailer higher in the air with each attempt. On her last try, she placed it back on the ground with greater control as well.

"This is tiring," she said, breathing heavily. "It feels like *physical* exercise."

"Try and lift two," said Jaden.

"At the same time?!"

"Duh."

Malia furrowed her brow in concentration. The two nearest trailers began to shake, then rose slowly. Malia's entire body tensed with the effort. After several seconds, she dropped both trailers again and nearly collapsed.

Sydney caught hold of her, helping her sit down on the ground.

"I think that's enough for now," she said. "This is clearly taking a toll."

Malia shook her head. "I'm fine. I want to do more."

"I don't want you to hurt yourself," said Sydney. "I won't lie, this is *amazing*. But it's tiring you out. You shouldn't overexert yourself."

"I'll rest for a minute, but I'm going to try again," she insisted. "If the CIA or the FBI or anyone like that catches up again, I want to know that I can take care of them."

Sydney looked worried. "Malia…"

"They killed my mom and dad," she said. "I *need* to do this."

Sydney stared at her for a moment, then nodded. Once Malia had rested for a few minutes, she stood up and tried to lift two trailers again. This time she held them both several feet in the air before returning them gently to the ground.

"Try three," said Jaden.

Malia nodded. She focused again, but nothing happened.

"What's wrong?" he asked.

"You've had enough," said Sydney. "I don't think—"

"That one's full," Malia told them, pointing to the third trailer. "It's much heavier than the other two."

"See if you can do it by itself," suggested Jaden.

"I'll try." She stared at the third trailer for several seconds. Slowly it rose into the air, at first only inches, then feet. But Malia could do no more. She fell down, and the trailer crashed to the Earth.

"Malia!" yelled Sydney, dropping to her side.

"I'll be okay," she assured her. "That was just really hard."

Jaden spent several minutes trying to move random objects again while Malia gathered her energy. He had no luck.

"You should try some different stuff," said Jaden once Malia was on her feet again.

"Like what? I don't think I can do anything heavier…"

"Nah, I'm not talking about more weight. I mean like… reaction time."

"How?"

Jaden thought about it for a minute, recalling their flight

through the forest and their capture by the guards at the rest area.

"How about this... I'm gonna try to tackle you, and you gotta stop me."

"And if I don't react fast enough, you're going to slam me into the pavement? I don't think I like this idea."

"No, I won't knock you down, I'll just grab you."

She agreed reluctantly. But the exercise turned out to be pointless. Jaden tried to tackle her a dozen times, but couldn't get anywhere near her. She stopped him every time, lifting him right off his feet on several occasions. Sydney joined the exercise too, both of them trying to get to her from opposite sides. But Malia succeeded every time.

"Good," he said. "That's awesome—as long as they don't take you by surprise. I have another idea..."

He walked away from them, moving across the parking lot.

"Where are you going?" Sydney called after him.

"Stay there—I'll be right back."

"Jaden," she yelled, concern in her voice. But he found what he was looking for at the edge of the lot. He picked up an empty Coke bottle and, holding it behind his back and out of view, walked back to them.

"Here's the deal," he said. "I'm holding something in my hand. I want you to try to take it from me using your powers."

"But I've told you, I can't do anything if I can't see what I'm working on."

"I bet you can," Jaden retorted. "You know I've got *something* in my hand, so see if you can move it."

Malia concentrated but accomplished nothing.

"Told you so."

"This doesn't make any sense. Why do you have to see it? *Pretend* that you can see something—"

"But I *can't!*"

"Use your imagination. Visualize any old thing in my hand—"

But before he'd finished his sentence, the bottle flew out of his grasp. Malia caught it.

"It worked," she said happily. "Although I imagined my phone."

They repeated the exercise a few more times, Jaden finding and hiding various objects behind his back.

"This is cool," he said. He scanned the back of the building and found a door halfway down. "Let's go see if you can unlock that," he suggested, thinking back to the time they were locked in the storage room.

"It's not going to work," said Malia.

"Just try it," Jaden insisted.

"This isn't a good idea," said Sydney. "There's probably an alarm system."

"Oh, right—good point," he replied. "Let's do it back in the room. Come on!"

They returned to the motel. Sydney went inside and locked the door, while the other two waited outside. Malia was unable to open it. But Jaden wasn't ready to give up.

"It's a deadbolt," he said once Sydney had opened the

door again. "Look at the lever and remember what it looks like."

"I'll try," Malia said skeptically.

Sydney closed the door, and Malia tried it one more time. This time the deadbolt moved, and she opened the door.

"See!" Jaden shouted triumphantly. "I knew you could do it!"

"It still wouldn't have worked back in that storage room," said Malia. "The lock was in the handle. I'd have to see the actual mechanism to make it move. Without knowing how it works, I wouldn't have anything to visualize."

"Well, this is still better than nothing," he said. "If they do catch us again, make sure you pay attention to the locks!"

Jaden was glad they'd taken the time for Malia to practice. There was no doubt she was getting stronger. And her confidence was improving too. Jaden lay awake late that night, wishing he had her power. He focused on the clock on the nightstand, desperately trying to make it move. But he couldn't do it. He fell asleep eventually and dreamed that he could make himself fly.

15

SAVANNAH

Sydney woke Jaden and Malia early the next morning. "Let's go you two; I want to cover as much ground today as possible. We've still got a *long* way to go."

She'd already gone out to buy them breakfast—pancakes and scrambled eggs from a nearby diner. They scarfed down their food and piled into the truck. Malia sat in front this time.

"We have *got* to stop and get some clothes at some point," said Jaden. "I smell."

"Yeah, you do," Malia agreed, crinkling her nose. "But so do I."

"It's too bad we're not the same size," said Sydney. "I'd let you wear some of my stuff, but it's way too big."

"That wouldn't help me anyway," Jaden replied sarcastically. "I'm not into cross-dressing."

Sydney giggled. "I'll go shopping for you soon, I promise. But not today."

They left Shreveport, and before long crossed the line into Texas. For hours and hours, they drove, stopping only for food and gas. After leaving Dallas, the country became steadily more arid. The land was flat as far as Jaden could see, and it felt almost like a desert. There was only sparse vegetation in most places. They passed through towns of varying sizes occasionally, but mostly the drive was desolate and boring.

They came to Amarillo and Interstate 40 a little before sunset, but still, Sydney pressed on. She allowed only a quick stop for dinner and fuel. But a couple of hours later, after passing into New Mexico, she finally grew tired of driving.

"Malia, see what you can find for motels," she said.

Malia searched on the phone but found only a couple of hotels.

"I guess we'll have to be extra careful," she said.

"I don't like this," Sydney replied with a frown. "It's going to be impossible to avoid people seeing you two if we're forced to go inside the building like that. Maybe there's something that doesn't register on the phone. That happens sometimes."

But after driving through a town called Tucumcari, they'd still failed to find anything.

"I've got an idea," she said, turning off the road. They drove down a long driveway, finally coming to a little house with a sign that read "Lone Star Campground."

"We're camping?" asked Jaden skeptically. "We don't have a tent or anything."

Sydney parked in front of the house. "Wait here." She got out of the car and went to knock on the door. A girl answered, maybe a year or two older than Jaden. She let Sydney inside. But a minute later, the girl came out of the house alone. She walked toward the truck.

"Damn!" said Malia. "Get down—she's gonna see us!" Malia dropped into the footwell.

But Jaden didn't move. He stared out the window. This girl was *hot*. She had long, wavy dark hair, and wore cutoff jean shorts and a bikini top. She looked right at Jaden through the window, but took no notice of him and kept walking.

"What are you thinking?!" Malia chided him, emerging from the footwell. "What if she recognized you?"

"She didn't," said Jaden, gazing out the back window to get another look at her.

"You don't know that! That was stupid!"

Jaden didn't bother to answer her. He was tired of living like a fugitive. And he decided if he had an opportunity to meet this girl, he was going to take it.

Sydney returned to the truck a few minutes later, carrying a big nylon bag.

"I got us a tent," she said. "We're staying here for the night."

"Great," Jaden replied, taking the tent from her and putting it on the seat next to him.

Malia rolled her eyes at him.

Sydney drove through the campground to a lot at the far end. Jaden saw no more than two or three occupied spaces.

"The place seems pretty empty," Malia noted.

"Yeah, the old man I talked to said business has been pretty slow," said Sydney. "That certainly works in our favor!"

Jaden hopped out once she'd parked the truck. Sydney held up a flashlight while he pulled the tent out of its bag, unfolded it and spread it out on the ground.

"Uh… this is pretty small," he said.

"We're not all going to fit in that," Malia agreed.

"Hmm… you're probably right," said Sydney. "Well, you two can take the tent if you want. I'll sleep in the truck."

A few minutes later, they had the tent set up. It quickly became apparent that it would be a squeeze even for Jaden and Malia.

"We still don't have sleeping bags," Malia observed. "This isn't going to be very comfortable."

"Let me go back and talk to Mr. Esperanza," said Sydney. "Maybe he has something we can borrow. You two wait here."

"Should we stay in the truck?" asked Malia. "So nobody sees us?"

Sydney looked around the campground, and Jaden followed her gaze. Their lot was in the back corner, surrounded by trees. The only other campers were located at the other end of the grounds, near the road. Jaden could make out a campfire, but not any people.

"I don't think I'd worry about it," said Sydney. "This place is pretty deserted."

"See if you can get some matches or something," Jaden suggested. "Maybe we can get a fire going."

She went off to the main building. Malia sat down in the opening of the tent, while Jaden walked around, collecting sticks and branches. He found a small pile of firewood that must have been left by previous campers.

Sydney returned several minutes later with a sleeping bag and a pillow.

"Just one?" asked Malia.

"He says it's all he has," Sydney replied apologetically.

She'd also procured a book of matches. Within minutes she and Jaden managed to start a fire. The three of them sat around it, staring into the flames.

"I was thinking," said Sydney. "I could use a break from all this driving. Why don't we rest here for a little while tomorrow —maybe in the morning I'll go into Tucumcari and buy you guys some clothes. Esperanza said they've got a K-mart."

"Thank you *so much*," said Malia. "I'm ready to burn these!"

"Yeah," Jaden agreed. "My jeans could probably walk around by themselves."

Sydney giggled. "We'll do some laundry too before we hit the road. They've got a washer and dryer we can use."

They went to sleep before too much longer. Sydney curled up in the front seat of the truck, and Jaden and Malia took the tent. Jaden let his sister have the sleeping bag. He used a pile of Sydney's clothes as a pillow. It was uncomfortable, with only the thin nylon of the tent floor separating him from the ground. He didn't sleep very well.

Sydney woke them in the morning.

"I'm heading out. I'll be back with two new wardrobes and some breakfast."

"Thanks, Sydney," said Jaden. "You're the best."

She drove away a minute later. Jaden got out of the tent and stretched.

"I hope she gets back soon," he said. "I'm starving."

"We should stay in the tent," Malia told him. "Somebody might see us."

"Like who?" Jaden retorted. "There's nobody here."

But at that moment, he spotted someone walking up the road from the house. It was the girl from the previous night. As she approached, Jaden noticed that she was again wearing jean shorts and a bikini top.

"Hey," she called out when she reached their lot.

"Hi," said Jaden.

"*What are you doing*?!" Malia hissed from inside the tent.

"Where'd your mom go?" the girl asked.

"Oh—that's not our mom. It's uh… you know, our aunt. She went to do some shopping in Tacmari… or whatever that place is called."

The girl giggled. "Tucumcari. Did you eat yet?"

"Nah, I'm starving, though," Jaden replied, his stomach growling.

"Come on, I'll cook you breakfast. My pappy went into

town too—he doesn't like me inviting campers inside, but he'll never know."

"Yeah—cool," said Jaden, walking toward her.

"What about your sister?" the girl asked.

"Oh, right," he said. "I guess she should come too." He went back to the tent and peered inside.

"Jaden, *no way!*" said Malia. "What if she recognizes us? Tell her *no!*"

"Forget it, Malia," he said. "I'm tired of running and hiding all the time. This girl's cute, *and* she wants to cook for us. You can stay here. I'm going."

"Sydney's bringing us breakfast—"

He walked away. Malia scampered out of the tent and followed him. He stopped and stared at her, raising one eyebrow.

"Someone's got to keep an eye on you and make sure you don't get us in any trouble," she said, walking past him.

"Hi, I'm Savannah," the girl said as Malia approached her. "But people call me Savvy."

"I'm Jaden, and that's Malia," he replied. Malia glared at him. He knew she probably wanted him to use fake names, but he didn't care.

They followed Savannah down the dirt road. Jaden had trouble keeping his eyes off of her. She had a dark tan, and her top was rather skimpy.

"Don't you go to school?" asked Malia, derision in her voice.

"I'm homeschooled," she said. "Ever since my parents died.

I've gotta stay home and look after Pappy. He's getting on in years, and he's not as spry as he used to be. Mostly I teach myself from the books. Pappy checks up on me once in a while."

"What happened to your parents?" Malia asked, her tone softer.

"Car accident. I was thirteen. A drunk driver hit them head-on. Of course, *he* walked away from the wreck."

"I'm so sorry," said Malia.

"What's your... pappy doing driving if he's so old?" Jaden asked.

Malia punched him in the arm. *"Be nice!"*

Savannah giggled. "He's not *supposed* to be driving anymore. Especially not since I got my license. But he sneaks out now and then when I'm not looking."

"You have your license?" asked Jaden. "How old are you?"

"Sixteen," she said. "I got it right after my birthday, back in May."

She led them inside the house. The place was a mess. Books filled the entire living room—the floor, tables, and half the sofa in addition to two walls of shelves. A portrait of Thomas Jefferson hung on the wall behind the couch. The caption read, "Every generation needs a new revolution."

The whole house was filled with old-looking furniture. And the large kitchen hosted numerous piles of antique china. But hanging on the wall in the hallway was an item Jaden found quite disturbing.

"What's with the Confederate flag?" he asked. He'd heard

stories of white supremacist groups using the flag as a symbol.

"Oh, Pappy's big into states' rights," Savannah said as she cleared space for them at the table. "He's not real crazy about the government. Thinks they've taken away too many of our liberties. *And* he believes all those conspiracy theories—you know, about how our government was behind the attacks on 9/11 and stuff. But don't worry, he's not racist or anything. What do you want for breakfast?"

Jaden didn't feel reassured by Savannah's explanation and hoped to avoid her grandfather. It sounded like the man might be insane. But as it turned out, Savannah was an excellent cook. She made them omelets and pancakes. Jaden stared at her the entire time; Malia sighed and rolled her eyes every time she caught him at it.

"Hey, do you guys wanna go for a swim?" Savannah asked once they'd finished eating and she'd piled the plates in the sink. "There's a lake out behind the grounds."

"Hell yes," said Jaden, getting up from the table.

"We don't have bathing suits," Malia told her. Jaden could tell from the look on her face that this was only an excuse. Malia loved to go swimming.

"I've got something you could borrow," said Savannah. "Wait here."

"This is a bad idea," Malia told him once she'd disappeared down the hallway. "What if she calls the cops on us?"

"She would've done that by now, don't you think? The girl made us breakfast; I don't think she's gonna turn us in."

"And she's acting overly friendly," she said, ignoring his response. "She's never met us—why is she being so nice?"

"People out west are just nicer," Jaden said with a shrug. "And besides, she said she's homeschooled. I bet she doesn't get to see her friends that often."

Malia opened her mouth to reply, but Savannah returned to the kitchen.

"This is too small for me anymore, but it'll probably fit you perfectly," she said, handing Malia a yellow bikini. She took it from her, eyeing it skeptically. Jaden tried to hide his amusement—he'd *never* seen her wear anything so revealing. Malia tended to dress conservatively.

"And I found these for you," Savannah added, handing Jaden a pair of shorts. "They were guy jeans originally, so they should fit you okay."

Malia protested a little more, but Jaden refused to listen. She wasn't going to let him go without her, so they took turns changing in the bathroom. Malia looked uncomfortable; Savannah handed them each a towel, and Malia covered herself immediately. They left the house, dropped their clothes off at the tent, and set out through the trees.

A few minutes later, they arrived at a small beach. The lake wasn't very big; Jaden could see houses on the opposite shore.

They set down their towels, Malia somewhat reluctantly. Savannah wriggled out of her shorts and said, "Follow me!"

She led them around the lake to a point where a ridge rose above the water. Without warning, she jumped off the edge, curled her body into a ball, and hit the water with a big splash.

"Come on!" she yelled once she'd surfaced. "It's deep here."

Jaden dove in after her. The water was surprisingly warm. Malia took some coaxing, but eventually, she joined them.

For the first time since leaving Marlton, Jaden felt like a typical teenager. Swimming, flirting with Savannah, and diving into the lake over and over again, he forgot their troubles for a while. When they returned to the beach to lay in the sun, he reflected that it was much warmer here than Maryland. And with a jolt, the memory of why they'd left home in the first place flooded his brain. Only then did he realize that he'd had his first respite in days from all the worry and stress.

"What really happened to your parents," Savannah asked as if reading Jaden's mind.

Malia stared at her in shock.

"What… what do you mean?" asked Jaden. Had she recognized them after all?

"I've seen you two on the news," Savannah explained. "I thought it was you, but I wasn't certain till breakfast. But I don't believe you killed your mom and dad."

"We didn't," Malia said, "so *please* don't turn us in or anything!"

"I would never do that," Savannah assured her. "I have to confess I've been following your story pretty closely. And I know *something* weird is going on because the reports change every day. First, they said you killed your parents; then they started saying your uncle did it—and kidnapped you two.

But last night it said they arrested *him*, and they're back to saying you two did it.

"This is exactly how it was when my parents were killed."

"How do you mean?" asked Jaden.

"The guy who hit them was a judge. At first, the cops told Pappy and me that he was drunk. They said he'd go to jail for a *long* time. But then the story changed. They told us he wasn't drunk after all, and just fell asleep at the wheel. I know they were protecting their own. By the time it went to court, they'd turned it all around and said it was my *parents'* fault! Made it out like they were the ones on the wrong side of the road. The guy got off in the end.

"Anyway, I bet the same kind of thing is happening to you. I mean, how could anyone murder their own mom and pop? I know it happens sometimes… But you'd have to be *demented* to do that. And you two seem pretty normal. I bet somebody's covering for the people who *really* killed your parents. Do you know who it might've been? Was it your uncle, after all?"

Jaden stared at Malia for a second, surprised at how close to the mark Savannah had struck. But Malia shook her head slightly—she didn't want him to say anything. And he had to agree to a point. He liked this girl a lot and didn't want to scare her off by telling her the *whole* truth.

"It was the cops," said Jaden. "They killed them. At first, they showed up because of something at our dad's work. But… it got crazy. They shot our parents, and we ran away."

Savannah nodded knowingly. "There's no justice unless you have powerful friends. It's not right."

They returned to the campground a few minutes later. But when they arrived, they found Sydney tearing the tent apart.

"Hey! What's going on?" asked Jaden.

Sydney turned at the sound of his voice, and after a moment's surprise, heaved a sigh of relief.

"Where the *hell* did you go?"

"Swimming," he told her.

"*Swimming*? Next time can you leave a note? I was terrified! I came back and found the tent empty, and *these* inside!" She was holding up Malia's underwear. "I thought the worst…"

Malia snatched her clothes away from her, looking highly embarrassed. "We're fine—we've been with Savvy all morning."

"Oh, hello," said Sydney, noticing the girl for the first time. "Would you mind giving us a few minutes alone?"

"No problem," said Savannah. "I'd better get back before Pappy gets home anyway."

Jaden and Malia handed her their towels, and she walked away.

"What are you *thinking*?" Sydney demanded once Savannah was out of earshot. "She could have recognized you!"

"She did," Jaden told her. "But it's cool; she's not going to turn us in or anything."

Sydney stared at him in disbelief. "And what if she does? We've got to get out of here…"

She ran around the site, picking everything up and throwing it inside the truck. Jaden and Malia watched her, unsure of what to do. They tried to tell her that everything was okay, but she wouldn't hear it. Finally, she ordered them into the truck—Malia still in Savannah's old bikini, and Jaden wearing her jean shorts—and they drove off.

But as they approached the house, an old man hobbled out into the road in front of them. It was Esperanza, Savannah's grandfather. He was pointing a shotgun at the truck.

"Damn!" Sydney shouted, pulling over to the edge of the road. The man motioned them out of the truck.

As they disembarked, Savannah came running out of the house.

"Pappy—no! I told you they didn't do it!"

"They're fugitives, Savvy," he told her. "You've seen the news. Now get inside, all of you!"

Sydney, Jaden, and Malia filed past him, toward the front door.

"*Do something,*" Jaden hissed at Malia. But she shook her head. He followed Savannah inside the house.

Esperanza came in last, still pointing the gun at them. He told them to sit. Only Malia and Jaden were able to fit on the couch because of the clutter. Sydney sat on the floor.

"Get me the phone, Savvy," he said. "I'm calling the cops."

"No! They're innocent. You can't—"

"*GET ME THE PHONE!*" he repeated, spittle flying from his mouth. Savannah ran out of the room.

"Please, sir," said Malia, tears streaming down her cheeks. "She's telling you the truth—we didn't murder *anyone.*"

Jaden couldn't understand why she wouldn't use her

powers to get them out of this. He didn't want to think about what would happen if Esperanza carried through on his threat to call the police.

"You may have hoodwinked my granddaughter," he said. "But I'm not so naïve. There's a nationwide manhunt for you two. You must've done something."

Savannah returned, holding a cordless phone.

"I've got the phone, Pappy, but I'm not gonna give it to you till you hear them out."

"Dammit, Savvy!"

"It's true," said Jaden. "We didn't kill our parents—*the cops did*!"

Esperanza gave a harsh laugh. "And why would they do that, huh?"

"Because the CIA tried to take over a project our dad was working on at a government lab," Jaden told him. "But the project was *us*—Malia and me. Our parents wouldn't let them take us, so they shot them."

"Hah!" said Esperanza. "Figures. Savvy would fall for a story like this with them crime shows she's always watching on television. But that's a load of crap—"

Suddenly every book in sight—the ones on the shelves as well as those stacked on the furniture—rose into the air and floated around the room.

"What the hell?!" shouted Esperanza, backing away, but still pointing the shotgun at them. Savannah dropped the phone, gazing around at the books in stunned silence.

"This is the secret project," said Malia. "I have telekinesis. The government wants to use me as a weapon, that's why the CIA came for us. Our parents died trying to protect us."

Esperanza looked around the room, a mixture of awe and fear coming over his features. "*You're* doing that?" he asked, gesturing at the books with one hand.

"Yes," said Malia, getting to her feet. "And if you call the police, they're going to take me to the CIA and use me to fight wars for them."

"But you're only a little girl…"

"They don't care," said Jaden. "These people killed our parents. You think they give a crap how old we are? Look at what she's doing! They could use her to take down airplanes and stuff. That's all they care about!"

"You don't have to tell me," said Esperanza. "Taxing us into poverty to pay for those stupid wars in other countries that nobody cares about… Makes my blood boil. I guess this *would* explain why the CIA wants you," he added, waving his hand at the books again. "But still, if you two killed your—"

"We *didn't*!" shouted Malia.

"Honestly," said Jaden, doing his best to look innocent. "Do we look like the type of kids who would murder their own parents?"

Savannah put her hand on her grandfather's shoulder. "I told you, Pappy. They didn't do it."

He stared at his granddaughter as if seeing her for the first time. Several tense moments went by as Esperanza looked back and forth between the books and Malia. Jaden didn't know if they'd convinced him, although he thought it was hard to deny the evidence: books didn't just float around in midair on their own.

But finally, Esperanza lowered his gun.

"A girl needs her parents," he said. "What they did to you is wrong."

Jaden let out a long sigh. "We're good, Malia. You can put everything down now."

The books flew back to their original locations, many of them kicking up clouds of dust. Jaden coughed, fanning the air in front of his face.

Malia's demonstration turned Esperanza into an ally. It made Jaden uncomfortable when he talked about enlisting them in a revolution, but he stocked them up with food and supplies and gave them sleeping bags and a bigger tent.

"I never loan this stuff out to campers," he told them. "But, the tent will sleep four comfortably."

He also insisted that they stay for dinner. As Sydney wasn't looking forward to more driving, they agreed.

When they had a moment away from the others, Jaden asked Malia why she'd refused to use her powers to disarm Esperanza.

"I didn't want to risk hurting him," she said with a shrug. "He's Savannah's only family, and he didn't know the truth. He thought he was doing the right thing. I just couldn't do it, Jaden."

He and Malia took turns in the shower and trying on the new clothes Sydney had bought for them. They weren't exactly stylish, Jaden decided, but he preferred them to the smelly ones he'd been wearing for days.

Savannah took care of their laundry, and that evening cooked on the grill for them—steak and barbecue chicken breast and roasted vegetables.

After dinner, Jaden and Savannah sneaked out of the house together, leaving Malia and Sydney to chat with the old man. They went to the lake for a moonlight swim. Jaden flirted with her more, and before he knew it, she kissed him. He found himself wishing they could stay here longer instead of driving off to Nevada.

But they got up at first light the next morning, and after Savannah had cooked them breakfast, hit the road once more. She gave Jaden her number, but he could only wonder how long it would be before he could use it to contact her again.

16

THE CALL

Sydney pulled onto Interstate 40, heading west. They were going to be on this road for almost the whole day.

"It's fourteen hours to these coordinates if we drive straight through," Malia announced from the front seat; she had the iPhone.

But Jaden was hardly paying attention. He was sprawled out on the back seat, staring at the paper Savannah had given him with her number on it. He missed her already. Being with her reminded him of what it was like to have a normal life; she made him think of home.

Today was Thursday. It was hard to believe that only six days ago, his biggest concerns were Freshman Friday, and regret that he hadn't asked Malia's best friend, Elise, to the homecoming dance. That life seemed like it was a million miles away.

"You all right back there?" Sydney asked, glancing at him in the rearview mirror.

"Huh?" he asked, looking up and stuffing the paper in his pocket.

"You haven't said a word since we left the campground," Sydney observed.

"He misses Savannah," Malia told her in a stage whisper.

"She was beautiful, Jaden," said Sydney. "And I did notice a sparkle in her eyes when she looked at you."

"Jaden didn't notice her eyes," Malia told her. "He was too busy staring at her *boobs*."

"Well, that's understandable," said Sydney. "She did tend to flaunt them—and they *were* ample—"

"Come on, you guys. Give me a break. I liked her. But I'm probably never going to see her again."

"Oh, you never know," said Sydney. "There's got to be an end to this madness eventually. Brian will sort everything out somehow, and life will go back to normal."

"How?" Jaden demanded. "We're a couple of freaks, and the *CIA* is after us! How is anything ever going to be normal again?"

Sydney could give him no answer.

The truth was they had no idea how their situation could *ever* be resolved. Jaden knew only that they were driving across the country to find someone named Carl, and that Brian would meet them there. But how was that going to happen if Brian was in jail?

"Can I see the phone for a second?" Jaden asked. "I want to check on something."

Malia handed it to him. He opened the CNN application. Sure enough, the top story was about the beam of light shooting out of the ocean—and Brian's arrest. The report indicated that the authorities had still not been able to penetrate the underground chamber. But this time, Jaden and Malia were also mentioned.

"I guess they bought Brian's story," said Jaden. "This says they think we fled to Canada with 'person or persons unknown.'"

"Well, that's good," Sydney replied. "Now, as long as we can avoid anyone else seeing you, we might make it to these coordinates!"

They drove for hours. The desert landscape was mostly barren, with only stunted shrubs for vegetation. They stopped for gas a little after noon. Jaden rummaged through the big cooler Esperanza had given them and handed out chicken salad sandwiches. They crossed the Arizona line soon after that.

As they penetrated deeper into Arizona, Jaden began seeing signs for the Grand Canyon.

"Maybe we can stop and check it out," he suggested.

"I don't think so," Malia said, looking at the map on the phone. "It's pretty far out of the way. I-40 doesn't go far enough north, and we have to stay on this for a while longer."

"Figures," he muttered.

After passing through Flagstaff, they came to an area that was much greener than anything else they'd seen on this leg of the journey. Pine, spruce, and fir trees grew right up to the side of the road.

"It's the Kaibab National Forest," Malia told them.

"I didn't know there *were* any forests in this state," said Jaden.

But at that moment, there was a noise like a gunshot. The truck swerved violently, and Malia screamed. Sydney managed to pull over to the side of the road without hitting anything, and Jaden heard a thumping sound.

"Crap!" yelled Sydney as they came to a stop. "Flat tire."

She jumped out of the car and walked around it, examining each of the wheels. Jaden watched her as she came to the right, rear corner of the vehicle. After squatting down for several moments, she straightened up and mashed the palm of her hand against her forehead.

Jaden got out of the car and joined her. Sure enough, the tire was completely flat. Looking closely, he spotted a large nail protruding from the tread.

"I can change a tire," he told her. "My dad taught me how."

"That would be great if I had a spare," said Sydney.

"You don't have a spare?!" Jaden's parents had always been borderline obsessive about making sure their vehicles had them.

"I used to, but the thingy that holds it onto the back of the truck broke, and I never got it fixed," she explained. "Damn!"

"So… now what do we do?"

"We're only twenty minutes away from Flagstaff. I'm sure

I can get a tow truck out here. It's just a nail—they can fix the tire easily. But the problem is—"

"Someone will recognize Malia and me," Jaden finished for her.

"Right. This sucks."

Jaden explained their dilemma to Malia while Sydney called a towing company.

"They'll be here in an hour," Sydney told them, closing her phone.

"An *hour*?" Jaden and Malia said together.

Sydney looked up and down the road nervously. There weren't many cars.

"This is a problem," she said. "There's no way I can take you two to the garage. And if we're sitting here that long, a cop's bound to show up."

"That's a big problem," Jaden agreed.

She gazed into the forest. "You're going to have to hide in the woods. Get far enough away that you're hidden from the road, but can still see the truck. I'll get this fixed, and come back for you as soon as I can. Keep an eye out for me."

"How are you going to find this spot again?" Malia asked.

"I'll bookmark it on my phone," she said. Malia looked apprehensive. "I'm really sorry, but I don't see another way. I'll try to make this fast."

She gave them both a hug, and Jaden and Malia wandered off into the woods. There was a hill not too far away. They walked to the top of it and stopped. From this vantage point, they could still make out Sydney's truck but felt pretty sure the trees would prevent anyone from spotting them from the road.

"This is great," said Jaden, plopping down on the ground. "Stuck in the middle of the woods for the day."

"I wonder how long this is going to take," said Malia, staring up at the sky. "It'll be dark in a few hours. And we should've brought food!"

"Oh crap," Jaden replied, already feeling his stomach grumbling. "Let's go back and grab the cooler."

But as they started to walk, a state trooper pulled up behind Sydney.

Malia dropped to the ground, squatting next to a tree.

"Get down!" she told him.

Jaden sat next to her but didn't feel alarmed.

"He won't see us from there. But this sucks. I hope that stupid truck gets here soon."

They had no means of telling the time, but it felt to Jaden like much more than an hour had gone by before the tow truck arrived. It was a flatbed, and it took at least another twenty minutes for the driver to load Sydney's truck onto it. But finally, it made a U-turn and drove away. The trooper resumed his course the other way.

"And now we wait," said Malia.

They sat with their backs against the tree, and the afternoon wore on. Jaden felt his hunger growing with every passing minute. The sun dropped lower and lower in the sky, and Jaden wondered if Sydney would return by nightfall.

"Do you think there are bears in these woods?" Malia asked.

Jaden hadn't thought of this. "I hope not…"

Dusk surrounded them, and soon full night fell. There was no sign of Sydney. The highway wasn't very busy. Sometimes minutes would go by without a single car going by.

One time a car pulled over near the spot where Sydney had parked earlier. Jaden couldn't tell from the headlights if it was her or not.

"What do you think?" he asked.

"I can't tell if that's her truck," said Malia. "Let's get closer."

But moments after they started walking, the vehicle pulled away again.

"Damn," said Jaden. "It was probably just someone taking a leak."

It was pitch dark out, so they didn't bother trying to walk back to where they'd been. Instead, they sat against the nearest tree. Jaden looked up at the sky and gasped.

"What's wrong?" Malia asked, sounding scared.

"Look at the stars!"

The trees were somewhat less thick here, affording them a clear view of the sky. Jaden had never seen so many stars. It was like looking closely at the sand on a beach and seeing the individual grains: they were everywhere.

"Why doesn't the sky look like this back in Maryland?" he asked.

"Too much light pollution," she said. "We're too close to Washington, so the city drowns out the starlight."

Malia pointed out the Milky Way, and more than a dozen constellations. Jaden had no idea where she'd learned any of this. But he was glad she had, as it helped pass the time.

Before long, the sky became less interesting. And it was growing cold. Malia started to shiver. Jaden pulled her into a hug to help her warm up, but he was cold, too. Where was Sydney? What was taking so long?

Suddenly there was a noise in the forest. It sounded like branches breaking. Malia gasped.

"What was that?" she whispered.

Jaden tensed, listening intently. For a minute, they heard nothing more. But then it happened again.

"It was closer that time," Malia said. "Jaden, I'm scared. It might be a bear or something..."

Jaden jumped to his feet, staring into the darkness. He couldn't see a thing. But he heard the noise again, off to the left.

"I think it's going around us," he said.

"What is it?"

"Probably just a raccoon or a fox," he told her, but only to calm her down. It sounded much bigger to him.

He heard it again, this time between them and the road. A car went by on the highway, and Jaden could make out an enormous shape against the glow of the headlights.

"Oh, crap..."

"It's huge!" Malia squealed.

Jaden shushed her. And then he heard a sound that made his blood freeze. It was a deep snarling, off to their other side. Whatever creature was out there was circling them.

"Malia, it's stalking us." She let out a little scream. "You're going to have to use your powers—it's the only way we're going to survive this."

"I can't, Jaden, I'm afraid!"

"You have to, or we're going to die!" He pulled her to her feet a little more roughly than he'd intended. "Now concentrate! Toss that thing a mile from here!"

"I can't—I can't see it!" she yelled.

"You *hear* it—just imagine there's a giant bear right at that spot and *get rid of it*!"

Malia took a deep, steadying breath and focused, staring out into the night. There was a roar, and suddenly the animal came crashing through the trees toward them.

"Malia! Do something!" Jaden shouted.

A great, dark shadow came hurtling out of the darkness. Jaden turned and cringed; Malia screamed. But nothing happened. The beast howled in rage; Jaden opened his eyes. There, only feet away, something giant was floating in midair. It writhed and turned over, all teeth and claws. A long tail whipped Jaden across the face, but that was the closest the animal came.

Jaden backed away, pulling Malia with him. She was staring directly at the beast, crying but focused.

"Make it go away," Jaden told her.

She nodded. The animal flew into the night sky and vanished, howling the whole way. Jaden heard a loud crashing sound, followed by a series of smaller noises, growing ever more distant. The creature was running away.

"That was close," said Jaden. "I think it was a mountain lion."

But Malia had fallen to the ground sobbing, her face buried in her hands.

"Hey," he said, sitting next to her and holding her. "It's okay—you did it! We're safe now!"

"Where's… Sydney..?"

"She'll be here soon," he said. But he didn't voice his concern. She'd been gone a long time now. What if something had happened to her? Or what if, somehow, the FBI had figured out they were with her? Had they detained her? Would she tell them where they were?

But Jaden's fears proved unfounded. Ten minutes later, another car pulled to a stop at the side of the road. Before they had started moving to investigate, a voice called out, "Jaden? Malia?"

It was Sydney.

Jaden and Malia ran headlong through the woods. He'd never been happier to see anyone in his entire life.

"Hey!" she said, smiling at them as they emerged from the trees. She was holding some sort of bag in her hands. "I'm so sorry that took so long; those mechanics were idiots—"

Malia grabbed her in a giant hug, sobbing uncontrollably. Sydney's expression changed to fear.

"Honey, what's wrong?"

"We're all right," Jaden told her, shivering with cold. "There was a mountain lion or something, but Malia took care of it."

Sydney's jaw dropped as she pulled Malia tighter, rocking her back and forth. Jaden realized she was holding a bag of marshmallows.

"What are you doing with those?"

"I uh… well, I thought maybe we'd make s'mores—you know, build a fire and camp in the woods for the night—"

"NO!" Malia shouted.

"Sorry," Jaden said with a shrug. "Maybe some other time?"

They calmed Malia down after a few minutes and climbed back into the truck. Jaden sat in front, and Sydney resumed their westward course. Jaden found a motor lodge in a town called Williams, only twenty minutes farther up the road.

Their room had a microwave oven, so Sydney melted the marshmallows, and they ate s'mores after all. Jaden had nearly forgotten his hunger during the scare with the mountain lion.

Sydney and Malia drifted off to sleep soon after, but Jaden lay awake. He couldn't stop thinking about the way Malia had saved them. Terrified though she was, she'd acted bravely. Jaden contemplated how dangerous a weapon she could truly become in the wrong hands.

They woke early the next morning and struck out with no delay, eating in the car as Sydney drove. Jaden sat in front and navigated. They followed the interstate to Route 93 and turned north. They passed through some of the most desolate country they'd seen yet.

Three hours after they left the motel, they crossed the line into Nevada. For better or for worse, they had almost reached their destination. They rolled through Las Vegas an hour later. At the north end of the city, Sydney stopped at a gas station. Once she'd refueled, she climbed back into the truck and took a look at the map.

"We're almost there," she told Jaden. "A few more hours, and that's it. I'm going to need you to pay close attention to the map. We'll be on 93 for a while longer, but after that, it's back roads. I don't want to get lost in the middle of the desert—"

The phone rang. Sydney stared at it as if it were the oddest thing she'd ever seen. "I don't recognize this number…"

"Hello?" she said, holding the phone to her ear. "Hello..?" Suddenly a look of shock washed over her face. "No… it can't be…" She listened for a few moments, her expression growing confused. "How do I know this isn't a trap or something… Okay, tell me which doctor I dated for exactly two weeks when we worked together." Her eyes went wide. "Melissa! It's you!"

"Melissa *who*?" Jaden asked, staring intensely at Sydney, his heart suddenly racing.

"I can't believe it," Sydney said to Jaden. "It's your mom!" She handed him the phone.

"Mom!" said Jaden, grabbing the device. "Is that you—I thought you were *dead*?!"

"It's me, Jaden," she said. He'd recognize her voice anywhere. "Is Malia with you?"

"Yeah—hold on." He held the phone in front of him and pressed the button to turn on the speaker.

"Mom?!" said Malia, leaning forward from the back seat, her eyes wide.

"Oh, Malia, are you both safe?"

"Yeah, Mom, we're good—we're with Sydney, and we're going to see Uncle Brian's friend named Carl," Jaden told her. "But what happened—how are you alive?"

"I don't remember much," said Melissa. "From what I've learned, they flew me to the NIH hospital in Bethesda, where I used to work. They performed emergency surgery, but there were complications. It took almost twelve hours, but they finally managed to patch me up.

"By the time I woke up, they had me under guard. One of the docs I used to work with came to visit. He told me what happened and helped me escape. I'm with him now."

"Which doctor?" asked Sydney.

"Baxter—I'm using his phone," said Melissa.

"I remember Baxter," Sydney said fondly. "He was a good guy."

"Sydney, I'm so glad you've got the kids. I tried getting in touch with Brian, but I didn't have any luck. So I tried calling you at work, but they said you had a family emergency… I hoped maybe they were able to get to you. Baxter told me that Stephen was dead, and the kids were missing…"

"Mom, Uncle Brian's in jail," said Malia. "We met him at this lighthouse in Miami, and he told us everything—you know, about Jaden and me and the Egyptians and Atlantis. But then there was this pyramid, and a laser shot out of it. He said we had to go to Carl, and we escaped, but they took Brian away in a helicopter!"

"He said he would meet us at Carl's," Jaden told her, "but I don't see how that's gonna happen if he's in jail."

"If I know your uncle, he's probably already got a plan in place," Melissa told them. "Don't worry about Brian, believe me."

"Mom," said Jaden tentatively, "how come you never told us the truth?" He couldn't stop the pain that had been building up inside of him from lashing out. "We had a right to know that we were only science experiments."

"Jaden, I'm sorry I didn't tell you. In hindsight, I wish I had. And it sounds like you still don't know everything..."

"I know that we're genetically engineered from 12,000-year-old DNA, and you're not our real mom. What *else* did you hide from us?"

"Jaden..." He could tell that his words had stung. And although he was disgusted with himself for it, the hurt in her voice gave him some satisfaction. "I *am* your mother, and don't you ever forget it. I hid everything from you because I wanted to protect you. I know now that it was a mistake. And I want to tell you the rest, and I will as soon as I can get to you.

"But for right now, I need you to look after your sister and go to Carl's. I'm going to talk to the people at Brian's company and see if we can get him out. Stay with Sydney. I'll call you again as soon as I can."

"I love you, Mom," said Malia, crying now.

"I love you too," Melissa replied. "And you too, Jaden."

"I'm sorry," said Jaden. "I love you."

But it was too late. The connection was dead.

17

PLANET

Far away from Nevada, Nadia Bashandi sat across the desk from Commander Anhur. She'd handed him the new report ten minutes ago. He had yet to say a word, instead taking his time to gaze at the data she knew he didn't understand.

"This confirms your preliminary analysis?" he asked finally.

"It does. This time, we were able to collect much more data for the spectroscopy. We confirmed there's an oxygen-nitrogen atmosphere on this world. And based upon the total absence of industrial pollutants, I'd guess we're looking at a planet rich in vegetation, but potentially devoid of intelligent life. There may be primitive civilizations at best, but there's no way to tell for sure."

"Unless we go there," he murmured.

"Well... yes," she confirmed.

He stared at the information for a few more moments. "Good work, Lieutenant. I'd like to—" At that moment, the console on the wall buzzed. "Excuse me one moment." He pressed a button and said, "Anhur."

"Commander, we're receiving a bizarre signal. You should probably come to see this for yourself," said a voice.

"I'll be right there," he replied. "Care to take a walk?" he asked Nadia.

"Uh, sure," she said, getting up to follow him out of his office.

He led the way down a short corridor and into the command center. Nadia stood next to him as he took a seat in the large, leather chair in the middle of the room. A dozen men and women sat at computer consoles along the back wall. Several rows of workstations occupied the floor in front of the commander. Nadia never felt comfortable here. The observatory was her domain.

"What have you got?" asked the commander.

"You're not going to believe this," said a man near the front of the room. A viewscreen activated on the front wall. Pictured in the center was a small, blue planet with a thin red beam emanating from it.

Nadia gasped. "I've seen this before," she muttered to herself.

"Explain," said Anhur.

"There's a power station there," said the officer. "It's emitting a distress call on all frequencies—including delta-shifted bands."

"Delta-shifted?" Nadia repeated. "Are you sure?"

"Yes, ma'am," he said. "It's the only way we detected it. That planet's ten light-years away."

"The power station is one of ours?" asked the commander.

"I believe so, sir," the man replied.

Nadia knew nothing could travel faster than light. But scientists on her world had discovered tens of thousands of years ago that with enough energy, local areas of space-time could be reconfigured, using the extra spatial dimensions that were usually compacted. Radiation still traveled at the speed of light, but by delta-shifting the space through which it moved, vast distances could be shortened dramatically. This technology had only been implemented for space travel within the past few centuries. The military had possessed delta-shifting telescopes for twice as long—Nadia knew they carried one on this very ship. That was the only way they could see this planet in something close to real-time—without delta-shifting, it would take ten years for the light from this world to reach them.

But delta-shifted radio transmissions had been in use for millennia. This was the method their first space travelers had used to communicate with the homeworld.

"Commander, that must be Earth," said Nadia, pointing at the screen. "Forget *my* new planet—*that's* where we need to go!"

"Easy, Lieutenant," said Anhur. "We've got enough fuel for only one delta-shift. We need more information before we make this decision. You'd better get to work."

Nadia knew he wanted her to perform the same analysis on this planet she'd done for the other. "Yes, sir," she said and left the bridge.

18

BUNKER

Jaden stared out at the barren landscape as they drove north out of Las Vegas. He was thrilled to learn that his mother was still alive. Yet, at the same time, it brought his pain into sharper focus. He couldn't understand why she'd never told him and Malia the truth. She said she'd wanted to protect them, but he thought that sounded like a lame excuse.

He thought back on his life, to his friends back home, and felt utterly disconnected from everything. Everyone he knew was normal. What was he? As a product of genetic engineering, was he still human? Or Atlantian? He didn't even know what that meant—were the Atlantians human or a totally different species? And what would his friends think of him if they found out the truth—if he ever saw them again?

Jaden wanted to see his mom again. He wanted to hug her, but at the same time, he wanted to scream at her. How could she do this? How could she pretend for his entire life that she was his birth mother and never tell him what he was?

"Jaden, I'm talking to you," said Sydney.

"Oh, sorry—what?"

"You're supposed to be navigating! Which way do I go here—we're coming up on a big intersection."

Jaden looked at the map. "Go left. In a little bit, you're gonna go left again on 375."

"Thank you," she said.

They came to the intersection, and Sydney turned left. A few minutes later, they turned onto Route 375.

"What's wrong?" asked Sydney. "You don't look like a kid who just found out his mom's still alive."

Jaden grunted.

"He's angry because she never told us any of the stuff we found out from Brian," Malia told her.

Jaden turned to look at her. "Are you reading my mind?"

"I don't have to," she said. "I'm feeling the same thing."

A few miles later, they drove by something quite unusual. There was a long, steel building to the right of the road. In front of it stood a giant, metal man.

"What the hell is that?" asked Jaden.

"The sign says 'Alien Research Center,'" noted Malia.

"And look at this," said Sydney, pointing to a road sign.

"'Welcome to the Extraterrestrial Highway,'" Jaden read. "Are you kidding me?"

"Where exactly are we going," Malia asked apprehensively.

"I don't know," said Jaden, looking at the map again. "The coordinates look like they're in the middle of the desert. I don't see any buildings or anything on the satellite view."

"This reminds me of a movie," said Sydney. "Maybe we're driving into the middle of the desert to be abducted by beings from another world."

Jaden snorted.

Almost an hour later, they passed a small settlement that consisted of only a handful of buildings.

"We're almost there," said Jaden.

They rolled past miles of desolate landscape. Fifteen minutes later, he said, "This is it—turn right!"

Sydney pulled over. "Turn right *where*?"

"Uh… here," said Jaden, pointing out the window.

"Let me see that," she said, taking the phone from him. "Huh… you're right."

But there was no road. There was a faint trail through the stunted shrubs, but no more.

"I guess we're going off-roading," said Sydney. "Hold on; this is going to get a little bumpy."

She turned off the road and drove up the trail, the three of them bouncing around in their seats.

"I don't see a trail anymore," said Sydney.

"Just keep going straight," Jaden replied, doing his best to follow their progress on the map. "We'll have to turn right eventually, but you've got a while."

Before long, Sydney veered away from the course on the map as she swerved to avoid larger shrubs. Jaden had to make repeated corrections to get her back on track. Ten minutes later, they came to a rocky hill.

"We have to go around this," he told her.

As they approached the hill, the vegetation disappeared. They drove around to the north end of the ridge and found a broad gorge in the rock, large enough for a house.

"This is it," said Jaden. "We're here. These are the coordinates."

Sydney stopped the truck. They got out and looked around.

"There's nothing here," Malia observed.

She was right, Jaden thought. Looking around, he could see nothing but desert and hills in the distance.

"Is this some kind of joke?" he asked. "Why would Brian send us out to the middle of the desert? *There's nothing here!*"

"I don't know," said Sydney, gazing around. "Maybe Carl's going to meet us here?"

"And how would he know when to expect us?" asked Jaden.

"There might be cameras here," Malia suggested, "like at that hotel. Brian could have told Carl we'd be coming…"

"I don't see any cameras," Jaden replied. "I bet the coordinates are just *wrong*."

"Well, let's have a look around. Maybe there's something we're supposed to find here," said Sydney.

She led the way to the ridge. They walked along the perimeter of the rock face, searching for any sign that they were in the right place. Jaden was ready to give up when suddenly a voice shouted "Hello!"

Startled, he looked around for the source of the sound. A man was approaching them from deeper within the gorge. He was older and walked with a slight limp. His wispy gray hair covered half of his face. And he was carrying an enormous tarp, sloppily folded up.

"The Kwan children, I presume?" he said as he drew closer.

"Are you Carl?" asked Sydney, positioning herself protectively in front of Jaden and Malia.

"At your service," the man said. "Brian told me you were coming. Thought you'd be here sooner."

"We had some difficulties on our way here," said Sydney.

"Well, let's get your truck covered up," he said. "Would you mind parking it closer to the ridge?"

Sydney ran off to her car and moved it as close as she could get to the rock wall. With her help, Carl covered the truck with the tarp. It was the same color as the ridge and did an excellent job of camouflaging the vehicle.

"That should do it," said Carl. "This material makes it invisible to night vision, and the pattern eludes satellite detection."

"So how did you talk to Brian?" asked Jaden. "Did he call you from jail?"

"No, he contacted me after he got *out* of jail," said Carl. "From what I gather, he was only there a day or two. And he didn't *call* me—Brian never *calls*. But let's get inside, and we can talk more. Follow me."

He hobbled back the way he'd come.

"Inside?" asked Jaden. "Inside *where*?"

Malia and Sydney only shrugged as they followed the man into the gorge. About a hundred feet later, they came to a fissure in the rock wall. Carl disappeared inside of it. Jaden followed him, and to his great surprise, saw a steel door embedded in the stone. Carl was holding it open, ushering them inside.

"What is this place?" asked Jaden. They were inside a long, dimly lit tunnel.

"Old army bunker," said Carl, locking the door behind them and leading the way down the tunnel. "Built to monitor the nuclear weapon tests back in the 1950s. Whole place is encased in lead and concrete to shield against radiation and fallout. A hydrogen bomb could go off right outside that door, and you'd be perfectly safe."

"Wow," Jaden replied.

"How'd you know we were here?" asked Malia.

"Cameras," said Carl. "I've got them mounted all around this hill, so I'll know when they're coming for me."

"Told you so," said Malia, punching Jaden in the shoulder.

"When *who's* coming for you?" asked Jaden.

"Them. The government. Only a matter of time before they find me. But I won't go down without a fight—not old Carl."

Jaden turned to look at Malia and Sydney, both eyebrows raised. Sydney made a cuckoo sign, circling her finger by the side of her head. Malia giggled.

"Ironic that I'm using the same shelter *they* used to protect themselves from the radiation... But they can't see inside here. Radar won't penetrate the place, the heat won't escape it—heat's just infrared radiation, after all. It's all electromagnetism—X-rays, gamma rays, UV rays, radio signals. It's all part of the electromagnetic spectrum, and none of it can get through this shielding. We're invisible here."

A minute later, they emerged into a large cavern. One side of the area hosted several computers and various electronic equipment. The other half appeared to serve as a living room of sorts, with a sofa, several folding chairs, and a big coffee table, strewn with books and magazines.

"Home sweet home," said Carl. "Have a seat—can I get you anything to eat or drink? Got enough supplies down here to last a year."

"We ate in the car," said Sydney.

"Tell us about Brian," said Malia. "How'd he get out of jail?"

"Not exactly sure," Carl replied, rubbing his chin. "Message said his company got him out. I can only imagine…"

"What message?" asked Jaden.

"The one he left for me on my computer," said Carl. "Most people would use the phone, or send an e-mail. Not Brian. He likes to show off his *hacking skills*. So he leaves me little notes on my screen. I beef up my security every time he does it, but he always finds a way in… One time—"

"Sir, what else did the message say?" asked Malia. "Is he coming to get us?"

"Oh, well, yes, he is. Said he'd be here in a few days. I'm supposed to *entertain you* till he arrives. But I've got a question for you, too. What in the hell is that beam of light coming out of the water in Florida? Brian's message said you'd be able to explain it. Teased me, he did—'I'm sure you're wondering about my light show. Have my niece and nephew tell you about it.' He said something about it being the tip of an iceberg? Care to tell me what that's supposed to mean?"

"This is kind of a long story," said Malia.

"We've got all the time in the world, young lady," Carl replied.

"Well…" Malia told him everything they'd been through, starting with Jaden's fall from the top of the high school. She recounted Babcock's visit to their house, their escape through the woods, the long drive to Miami, and everything Brian had told them about Giza, Atlantis, and the DNA samples. She finished by telling him about the subterranean pyramid, and what happened when Jaden touched it.

"Aha!" said Carl, jumping to his feet. "That explains it—I knew I was right!"

"Right about what?" asked Jaden.

"Come here, and I'll show you," he replied, limping over to the computers. "Pull up some chairs!"

Jaden, Malia, and Sydney each carried a chair over to the monitor where Carl had sat down. He opened a program and pointed at the screen.

"*That* is a spectrographic analysis of the beam emanating from the pyramid. There's some sort of coded signal being sent on hundreds of frequencies. But I still can't explain the gravitational lensing effects…"

"What's that?" asked Malia.

"How much do you know about Einstein's theory of

general relativity?" The three of them shook their heads. "Ah. Well, Einstein discovered that large masses warp space-time, causing small masses to move toward them. Imagine placing a bowling ball in the middle of a bed. The resulting depression in the surface of the mattress would cause something smaller, say a golf ball, to roll toward it. Planets and stars do the same thing to the curvature of space itself.

"One of the first proofs of the theory came in 1919 with a total eclipse of the sun. General relativity tells us that the curvature of space around the sun should cause light to bend around it. And sure enough, during that eclipse, a star whose position was directly behind the sun—which should have been blocked from view—appeared instead off to the *side* of the sun. Light can only travel in a straight line, of course, but the curvature of space caused that line to *bend*."

"That's fascinating," said Sydney, "but what's it got to do with the laser?"

"That beam is producing a similar gravitational lensing effect," Carl explained. "It's much weaker, and I almost didn't notice it. But when I aimed my telescope at the beam, the stars behind it seemed to have moved out of its way—almost like Moses parting the Red Sea!"

"So what does that mean?" asked Malia.

"I have no idea!" said Carl. "I was hoping you could tell me."

"We don't know anything about it," said Jaden. "Brian ran a program on his computer that looked a lot like yours, and he said, 'Carl was right.' What were you right about?"

"The Atlantians!"

"You already knew about them?" asked Malia.

"Your uncle and I have debated this for years. I had no idea they left behind any DNA samples... that's most intriguing. However, *I'm* the one who first told Brian about Atlantis. He didn't believe me. Thought I was crazy. But that was before he discovered that pyramid of his. Let me tell you, that made him see the light! But he still refused to believe the crucial point: the Atlantians were not of this Earth."

"What does that mean?" Sydney asked skeptically.

"They were extraterrestrials!" said Carl. "And this transmission proves it. That pyramid is sending a signal deep into space—one that can be detected for thousands of light-years in every direction! It must be contacting their homeworld..."

"That's crazy," said Jaden, thinking about the metal man they saw on the way here, and the "Extraterrestrial Highway." "There's no such thing as *aliens*."

"Hah!" Carl replied, turning in his chair to face Jaden. "Do you have any idea how many stars there are in our galaxy?"

"No..."

"Billions," said Malia.

"Billions and *billions*!" Carl agreed. "And do you know the number of galaxies in the universe?"

"Billions and billions?" asked Jaden.

"Precisely! And as we're only now discovering, *most* of those stars likely have planets! So while you believe that *there's no such thing as aliens*, the truth is that it's statistically almost an impossibility that we could be the *only* life forms in the universe!"

"But how do you know the *Atlantians* were extraterrestrials?" asked Malia.

"How could they *not* be?" countered Carl. "Plato tells us that Atlantis was a great naval power, beyond the Pillars of Hercules—that means they came from somewhere in the Atlantic. They conquered much of Western Europe and Africa ten millennia before Plato's time. But after a failed invasion of Athens, Atlantis fell into the sea, in what Plato describes as 'a single day and night of misfortune.'"

"But that doesn't mean they were *aliens*," Malia insisted.

"I'm not done yet, little girl," said Carl, wagging his finger at her. "There were engravings inside some of the ancient Egyptian tombs that depicted flying machines—remarkably similar to the airplanes of today. And in Peru, they unearthed gold trinkets shaped exactly like the drawings in Egypt—"

"Peru?" asked Jaden. "What does Peru have to do with anything?"

"That's where the ancient Andean civilization lived, eons before the Inca. You see, the Atlantians didn't interact exclusively with the Egyptians. If you look carefully enough, there are records of their existence throughout the world, in ancient America, India, Greece—you see pyramids everywhere, for example."

"Like Chichen Itza in Mexico," said Malia.

"Yes, exactly," said Carl. "And there were even some ancient Egyptian artifacts found in the Mayan pyramids. Now, how do you think those got there?"

"The Atlantians?" asked Malia.

Carl nodded, but Jaden said, "Come on, Malia—you don't believe they were *aliens*, do you?"

Malia started to reply, but Carl interrupted her.

"How else do you explain the *great leap forward*?!"

"What's that?" asked Sydney.

"You've never heard of the great leap forward?" said Carl. Sydney shook her head. "Unbelievable... Imagine what humans were like sixty thousand years ago. Primitive, yes? Not much different than other primates. Anatomically, the first *homo sapiens* evolved roughly 200,000 years ago. Yet sometime around 40,000 B.C., behavioral modernity developed in several places across the globe, seemingly spontaneously. Humans began making tools, fishing, bartering goods across vast distances, using pigment for cave paintings, playing games, and music—burying their dead. These things are all part of our collective *cultural* DNA if you will. You see these aspects of human culture everywhere you look, across every civilization throughout time.

"Most scientists attribute this development to some sort of reorganization of the human brain, or perhaps minute genetic aberrations. But how do you explain the spontaneous appearance of these traits across the entire planet—at virtually the same time? Genetic permutations would have taken tens of thousands of years to propagate that far.

"But we have the answer. Atlantis. The Atlantians essentially *awakened* entire groups of human beings."

"Yeah, but that *still* doesn't prove the Atlantians were *aliens*!" said Jaden. "How do you know the Atlantians didn't come from Earth?" He realized the irony of his statement: In arguing against the idea of the Atlantians being aliens, he was tacitly accepting the *existence* of the Atlantians. He decided not to vocalize this realization.

Carl took a deep breath and let out a long sigh. "Do you know how I met your Uncle Brian?" Jaden and Malia shook their heads. "Have you ever heard of Dreamland?" They shook their heads again. "Most people know it as Area 51."

Sydney gasped. "We're right near there, aren't we?"

"You pretty much drove by it on your way here," said Carl.

"What's Area 51?" asked Malia.

"It's a secret government base—well, it's not so secret anymore. I used to work there. And your uncle designed and installed the computer security systems they use—that's where we met. It's the place they developed many of the aircraft used in modern warfare, like spy planes and stealth bombers and fighters.

"It's also become the epicenter of UFO research in this country. Many believe that they've got aliens and extraterrestrial spacecraft locked up inside of Area 51. Some say our government has allied itself with an alien race, and the aliens are sharing technology with us. You see some weird lights in the sky at night around here. People believe it's the government testing alien craft—flying saucers and the like."

"That explains the stuff we saw on the way here," said Malia. "Like the Extraterrestrial Highway."

Carl nodded.

"Is it true?" asked Jaden. "Do they have aliens there?"

"Most of what you hear is nonsense," said Carl. "The

government *does* test its newest aircraft here—most of what they're working on the public won't find out about for another twenty years.

"And they don't have *live* aliens. But... there was a crash in Roswell, New Mexico. Back in 1947. An alien spacecraft. The aliens died—but they took the debris and the corpses to Area 51. Government tried to cover it up, of course, but information leaked out."

"I've heard about this," said Sydney. "I always thought it was an urban legend. Didn't they say it was just a weather balloon that crashed?"

"That's what they said," Carl confirmed. "But look at this."

He turned back to his computer and opened a folder full of pictures. He started a slideshow. Jaden stared in awe as the photos appeared one at a time. Some showed debris that looked like it might have been made out of tin foil. But others displayed distinctly inhuman bodies. They had large, elongated heads and big, slanted eyes.

"They're shaped like that metal man we saw," said Malia.

"Yes, these photos leaked to the public. They're part of the enormous body of UFO lore. But unlike most of the stuff that's out there, these are *real*. Those are your Atlantians," he said, pointing at the screen. "There are cave paintings in France, radiocarbon dated to nearly 40,000 years ago, of figures that look exactly like these. They came to this planet and awakened humanity. By whatever cause, their civilization of Atlantis disappeared. But they've been coming back to visit. This is what I worked on at Dreamland. The Roswell incident is the only one that went public. After that, the government was more careful. But there have been other bodies, and other ships recovered over the years. Contrary to the popular mythos, we haven't been *able* to crack their technology."

Jaden continued to stare at the pictures. And a horrible thought started to form in his mind.

"If the Atlantians were extraterrestrials... and Malia and I have Atlantian DNA..."

"Does that mean *we're* aliens?" she finished for him.

"You look perfectly human to me," said Carl. "And those creatures are very different on the inside. The organs are arranged differently; their lymphatic systems don't work the same way—and their blood is green. No, I bet the Atlantians probably engineered your genes from human DNA. They augmented it, of course, with the extra chromosomes your uncle told you about... Say, would you mind giving me a demonstration of your powers?"

Malia furrowed her brow in concentration. Suddenly Carl floated right out of his chair.

"Whoa!" he exclaimed, looking around wildly. He twisted and turned in midair, trying to see underneath himself. "This is quite amazing... Can you put me down now?"

Malia returned him to his chair.

"If those things *are* extraterrestrials," she said, nodding to the screen, "then why don't they look... more alien? They're almost like humans."

"Ah yes," said Carl, looking relieved to be back in his

chair. "It's what we call convergent evolution. You know how evolution works?"

"That's how monkeys turned into people," said Jaden.

"Not exactly," Carl replied. "The process of evolution relies on genetic accidents—random mutations. Let's say you grow up and have two children. Each has an error in his or her gene code—a mutation. In one, this error leads to radically shorter legs. In the other, the error produces stronger musculature.

"Now your short-legged offspring is not very good at running away from predators. A tiger eats him at a young age because he couldn't get away fast enough—and he never produces any children of his own. However, your Herculean child pulverizes the tiger with his bare hands and eats him for dinner—and goes on to make babies that share his particular genetic mutation. This is how a new species is born."

"You're talking about the survival of the fittest," said Malia. "We learned about this in biology class."

"Yes—and that is the mechanism by which evolution functions. It's an incredibly slow process because, of course, mutations can only happen from one generation to the next. *Your* DNA will never spontaneously mutate. However, once in a hundred generations, a chromosomal error will occur in the DNA of an offspring. And one in one thousand errors will lead to some sort of physical change in the species.

"Now, think of the qualities of humankind that have allowed us to achieve space flight. Intelligence is probably the first one that comes to mind. But there are other intelligent species on Earth—why haven't any of *them* developed the ability to travel to space?"

"Wait a minute," said Jaden. "What other intelligent species are there? I thought humans were the only ones."

"Dolphins," suggested Malia.

"Yes, indeed—dolphins are highly intelligent. So too are elephants. And studies have shown that pigeons are better than humans at solving probability puzzles. But imagine a dolphin trying to build a rocket."

"That's impossible—it doesn't have hands!" said Jaden.

"That is correct," Carl agreed. "There are certain things we can say about life, anywhere it has come to exist in the universe—and about its environment. Life cannot develop without water, for example. Nearly every process that takes place in a living organism, from single-celled bacteria to humans, depends on the presence of water. DNA is another commonality—even viruses are simply strands of rogue DNA. You cannot have life without it.

"But for a species to venture into space, other higher-level qualities become necessary. Opposable thumbs," he said, holding up both hands and wiggling his digits. "You have to be able to grasp tools if you want to build rockets. Three-dimensional vision," he added, pointing to his eyes, "requires at least two of these. Bipedal locomotion for mobility in a nonaquatic environment means a spacefaring species would have to have two legs."

"But even on Earth, there are life forms that are radically different from what we're used to seeing on a day-to-day basis," said Sydney. "I've seen shows about the strange fish that have evolved around geothermal vents."

"Yes, but have any of those species blasted off into space?" asked Carl. Sydney stared at him blankly. "Of course not. What I'm saying is that only those species that *happen* to develop eyes, hands, feet, and intelligence can *possibly* build rockets and thus visit other stars. So it's not too surprising that our friends here," he indicated the monitor, "would look somewhat like us. Life forms that evolved near underwater vents on their world wouldn't achieve spaceflight either.

"One of the best examples of this here on planet Earth is the similarity between bats and birds. They can both fly—but they do not share a common ancestry. They each developed wings completely independently of one another. But only species that develop wings can fly."

They sat in silence for a minute, taking in everything Carl had told them.

"So… all those whacky stories you hear about alien abductions, UFOs—they're all true?" asked Sydney.

"Oh, no," said Carl. "Most of them are hoaxes or have other mundane explanations. But there have been a handful of genuine visits from our Atlantian friends. It's only been scout ships until now."

"*Until now*?" asked Malia. "What does that mean?"

"I didn't tell you?" asked Carl, looking puzzled. "No, I guess I didn't. In that case, I'd better *show* you."

"Show us what?" asked Jaden as Carl leaned over to his computer.

"Just a moment," he said. "I'll need to access my account

at Western Nevada College… They give me telescope time. I've been monitoring Jupiter for years…"

"Why?" asked Malia.

"Hang on… ah, here we go. Take a look."

Jaden, Malia, and Sydney gathered closer to the screen. Jaden recognized the giant red spot on Jupiter in the image, but there was some sort of weird shadow hovering over it.

"Is that one of the moons?" asked Malia.

"No. That is an alien spacecraft. An enormous one—it's as big as a city. And it's coming this way."

19

DREAMLAND

"Wait—are you kidding me?" said Jaden. "That's an alien spaceship, and it's coming to Earth?"

"Sure is," said Carl. "No doubt it's responding to that signal you initiated at Brian's pyramid. And I'm fairly sure the boys at Dreamland have seen this thing, too. There have been some pretty magnificent light shows the past few nights —I bet they're getting ready to meet this thing with whatever they're developing over there. It'll be all over the news soon enough."

"How?" asked Sydney. "You needed your telescope to see it."

Jaden pulled out Sydney's iPhone—he'd pocketed it when they arrived at the coordinates. He opened the CNN application. Nothing happened.

"That won't work in here," Carl told him, waving his

hand around at the cavern. "The shielding stops all kinds of radiation, including cell phone signals."

Sure enough, the phone had no service. Jaden gave it back to Sydney.

"To answer your question, Sydney, any amateur astronomer with a decent telescope can see this thing right now. Most would probably mistake it for a moon as Malia did. But as it comes closer, it will become apparent that it's not in Jupiter's orbit."

"How long before it gets here?" asked Sydney.

"Hard to say for sure," said Carl. "Depends how fast it goes."

"You said that you've been watching Jupiter for years," said Malia. "Why?"

"Well, I figured that if any extraterrestrials were to visit our solar system, they'd want to use Jupiter's gravity to help slow them down from their interstellar trajectory. NASA has always done the opposite—used Jupiter to accelerate their spacecraft and slingshot them to the farther planets."

"We've sent spacecraft to Jupiter?" asked Jaden.

"Just probes," Malia told him. "Not manned ships."

"Oh, right—I knew that."

"Hey, do you guys want to go see Dreamland—Area 51, I mean?" asked Carl.

"You can take us there?" asked Malia. "I thought it was top-secret."

"We can't enter the facility, no," Carl confirmed. "And I don't like to get too close—I didn't leave under the best of circumstances, so I'm sure they'd love for me to pay them a visit. Of course, I'd never be allowed to leave again... But there's a ridge about a mile out from the actual base. It's the closest you can get without tripping their security systems. Gives you a gorgeous view of the activity."

"Yeah, let's go," said Jaden, rising from his chair.

"Oh, not now," said Carl. "At about four o'clock is when the show starts."

"Four in the *morning*?" asked Jaden.

"That's the time," said Carl. "We can hang out till then... or you can get some sleep if you want. There are bunk beds farther down the tunnel."

They talked for a while longer, and Carl made them dinner, which consisted of rice, beans, and canned fruit. He showed them pictures of some of the other alien crash scenes that had been found. In one, the spacecraft was almost entirely intact.

"It's an actual flying saucer," Jaden observed.

"Yes, the craft have been saucer-shaped every time," said Carl.

"You said the flying machines they drew in ancient Egypt looked like airplanes," said Malia. "Not saucers."

"Ah, you were paying attention," said Carl. "Very good! And you're right; these saucers look nothing like the craft that were drawn and modeled by the ancient world. I can only surmise that the Atlantians' technology has advanced in the last 40,000 years. Makes sense, wouldn't you say?"

As incredible as this whole story was, Jaden began to believe it. The more he thought about it, the more credible he found the idea that the ancient Atlantians were extraterrestrials. It seemed more likely than such an advanced civilization originating on Earth so far in the past.

"What do you think they're coming here for?" Malia asked later that night. She and Jaden were lying head to head in adjacent bunks. They were supposed to be getting some sleep before their trek out to Dreamland. Sydney was snoring away in the bunk above Malia.

"It's like Carl said. They're answering the signal."

"Yeah, but what are they going to do when they get here?"

"I don't know," said Jaden. He hadn't considered this. "If I were them, I'd probably try to find whoever sent the signal."

"Right. Exactly."

"Oh, damn! That means... they're coming for *us*!"

"What are we going to do?" asked Malia.

"I don't know... there's not much we *can* do. Wait here for Brian, I guess. Hopefully, him and Carl can figure something out."

They lay in silence for a few minutes. Jaden thought Malia had fallen asleep.

"Do you think Carl's right?" she asked. "Are you and I human?"

"We must be," said Jaden. "We don't look like those dudes on those ships."

"Yeah. That's true."

"It's gotta be like Brian told us. The Atlantians used human DNA to... make us. They just gave us extra genes."

"I guess. But I can't help wondering..."

He waited a few seconds, but she didn't say anything else. "What?"

"If we're human, how come you were able to activate the pyramid?"

"Oh…"

"Brian said people touched it before, and nothing ever happened. He told us it probably detected that your DNA was different. But… wouldn't it make sense that only an *Atlantian* would be able to do that?"

Jaden didn't know how to answer this question. He thought about it for several minutes but failed to make any sense of it.

"Do you think Mom knows the Atlantians were aliens?"

Malia didn't say anything.

"Malia?"

By the sound of Malia's breathing, he realized that she'd fallen asleep. But his mind wouldn't stop racing. Malia was right. His ability to activate the pyramid did make it seem likely that they weren't human.

"But we don't look like those aliens," he muttered to himself. They might appear *similar*, as Malia had pointed out, but they were *not human*. And besides, his blood certainly wasn't green. He *had* to be human, he decided.

Jaden drifted off eventually, but after what seemed like only a few minutes, someone shook him awake. It was Carl.

"It's time," he said, acting inordinately excited. "We have to go now if we're going to get the best seats." He sounded like someone talking about going to a movie theater, not a secret government installation.

Jaden woke his sister while Carl roused Sydney. They

followed Carl down the tunnel to the main cavern. There, Carl put on a fake beard and a baseball cap.

"What are you doing?" asked Sydney.

"I have to go in disguise," he said. "There's always a risk one of the other spectators might recognize me. Don't want that!"

"We could use a disguise, too," said Jaden.

"That's a good point," Carl agreed. "I've seen those news stories. You're both more likely to be recognized than I am! Wait here."

He disappeared down the tunnel, returning a minute later with a box of clothes, hats, sunglasses, and other random items. Jaden put on an oversized sweater, a winter hat, and sunglasses. Malia donned a sweatshirt and pulled the hood over her head, tightening the drawstrings to hide much of her face.

"Well, I don't think I'd recognize Malia," said Sydney, gazing at them appraisingly, "but the sunglasses are a little suspicious, don't you think? It's still the dead of night."

"Hmm," said Carl, rummaging through the box. He came up empty-handed. "I've got an idea." He removed his beard and handed it to Jaden. "Put that on. I'll be back in a minute."

He ran off again, and Sydney helped Jaden apply the beard. Malia giggled at him.

"Shut up, Malia."

"You look stupid. It's obviously fake."

"Yes, but it does make him hard to recognize," Sydney said, making little adjustments and tickling Jaden's neck in the process.

Carl returned, and Jaden could hardly tell it was him. He was still wearing the baseball cap and had put on a pair of sunglasses. But he'd also applied makeup; now his entire face and neck were a dark shade of brown.

"That works," said Sydney. "Although I still think the sunglasses are a little sketchy."

"It will have to do," Carl told her. "Let's go!"

They went out through the tunnel, and Carl locked the door behind them. They removed the tarp and climbed into Sydney's truck. After another bumpy ride across the open desert, they arrived back on Route 375. They went back the way they came for about forty-five minutes until Carl instructed Sydney to take a right turn onto a dirt road. Jaden noticed a lone white mailbox at the intersection.

"What's with the mailbox?" he asked.

"There used to be a black one," said Carl. "It was somewhat famous in the UFO research community as a gathering point for watching the skies around here. People said it was the mailbox for Area 51. Bunch of nonsense, of course—it belongs to a local rancher. He got tired of people going through his mail, so he put in the new one. It's bulletproof, and has a lock on it."

"Fascinating," Jaden replied sarcastically.

Fifteen minutes later, Carl said, "This is good. Park here. We'll have to walk the rest of the way."

Sydney pulled over, and they got out of the truck. They started walking up a path toward the top of a ridgeline. As they approached the peak, Jaden heard voices. They discovered a large crowd at the top of the hill, milling about and staring out into the valley below.

"This is it," said Carl, pointing off to a cluster of lights in the distance. "That's Area 51. This is the closest you can get without trespassing on government property—which I don't recommend around here. I would've brought my small telescope to give you a closer view, but truthfully there's not much to see. A bunch of hangars, a couple of buildings, and the airstrip. The real show will be up in the sky."

Jaden grew cold as they waited for something to happen. They stayed away from the other people here, but one old lady came over to talk to them. She rambled about alien abductions for a few minutes but wandered away again when she failed to get a response.

"Oh, look—out there," said Carl finally. "Keep your eyes on that blinking light moving along to the right."

Jaden watched for a minute, but nothing remarkable happened. He was about to look away when suddenly the light moved straight up into the air. Then in a flash, it streaked across the sky, right over their heads. There was a loud thud as it passed that Jaden could both feel and hear. A cheer went up from the crowd, and someone screamed.

"Whoa!" said Jaden. "That thing was *fast!*"

"Was that a sonic boom?" asked Malia.

"Sure was," said Carl. "Last I knew, they were testing aircraft here that could approach Mach eight."

"That's eight times the speed of sound?" asked Sydney.

"Yes, in fact—oh, never mind," said Carl. "Look at *that!*"

Something with several sets of blinking lights had

appeared in the same area where the first plane had launched. After moving well away from the lights of the base, it came to a stop.

"Watch carefully," said Carl. "If this is the same bird I saw a couple of nights ago, you're in for a real treat."

An instant later, the object shot straight up in the air, much more rapidly than the previous one. It hovered in place for several seconds, then raced to the west. They heard another sonic boom, and the lights stopped again, holding the same position for several more seconds. Over the next few minutes, it darted about the airspace above them, moving unimaginably fast from one location to the next—causing a sonic boom every time it accelerated. But then, without warning, it shot away to the south and didn't return.

Jaden wondered what they might see next when suddenly he heard a noise off to the east. It sounded like a motor, and it was coming closer.

"What's that?" asked Sydney.

"I don't know, but I don't like it," said Carl. "We should get out of here. Come on."

He started back down the path toward Sydney's truck, but it was too late. At that moment, several vehicles crested the hill, headlights glaring.

"Everybody stay where you are and put your hands up where we can see them," a voice called over a loudspeaker.

The crowd panicked. People screamed and shouted, and several ran. Jaden heard gunfire, and the people who ran hit the ground and didn't move. One of them had fallen right in front of Jaden. He recognized her as the old lady who'd tried to talk to them earlier.

"Stay still, and you won't be harmed," the voice boomed over the speaker.

Carl knelt next to the old lady. He rolled her over onto her back and removed something from her neck. Standing up, he showed it to Jaden, Malia, and Sydney. It was a small dart.

"Tranquilizer guns," said Carl. "We need to leave. Follow me and move very slowly."

He advanced one step at a time through the crowd. The other three followed. Most of the people were milling about to some extent, so it wasn't too hard to blend in.

But a few seconds later, men with flashlights began walking among the crowd. They wore military uniforms and carried guns—Jaden hoped they were tranquilizer guns. As they moved, they flashed their lights in people's faces.

"They're looking for someone," Carl hissed.

"You there," one of the men yelled, "with the sunglasses. Stay where you are!"

Carl stopped. Jaden heard him mutter, "Crap."

The soldier ran over to him. He grabbed him by one arm and shined the light in his face.

"Take off the sunglasses."

Carl complied. The soldier moved to Jaden, blinding him with the light. Jaden squinted and turned away.

"It's you!" the soldier bellowed, backing away and pointing his gun at Jaden. "I've got them! They're right here!" he called into the night.

"NO!" Malia shouted. Suddenly the soldier flew through the air and out of sight.

"*Run!*" yelled Carl. "Back to the truck!"

He bolted down the hill, Jaden, Malia, and Sydney right behind him. But moments later, Jaden could hear the army vehicles coming behind them.

Suddenly two Humvees passed them, one on each side. One cut in front of them, blocking the path. And within seconds, they were surrounded by several vehicles.

"Don't move!" a voice shouted. Jaden couldn't see who was there; every Humvee had a searchlight trained on them, rendering the men on board invisible.

A moment later, the trucks all rose twenty feet in the air. Jaden turned and saw the intense look of concentration on Malia's face.

"Put us down, or we'll open fire," the voice shouted. But Malia threw the Humvees away. Jaden heard gunfire and cringed, but they weren't hit. The trucks sailed over the top of the hill and disappeared.

"That's a neat trick," said Carl. "Now, let's get out of here!"

They ran back to Sydney's truck and climbed inside. She started the engine and gunned it, racing back down the dirt road.

"Where the hell am I supposed to go now?" she asked.

"That's an excellent question," said Carl. "They knew you kids were there," he added, turning to Jaden and Malia in the back seat. "I don't know how. But we're going to encounter more pursuit, I can guarantee it. Area 51 is one of the most heavily guarded installations in the world. Young lady, are you prepared to continue using your powers against this force?"

Malia nodded. Jaden thought she looked scared but determined.

"Good," said Carl, turning to face front again. "We can try to get back to the bunker. They don't know I'm hiding there, and they certainly have no way of knowing you're with me. My disguise fooled that soldier back there."

"Sounds like a plan," said Sydney.

But before they reached Route 375, a convoy of military vehicles came racing up an intersecting dirt road.

"Step on it!" yelled Carl.

Jaden felt them accelerate. He glanced at the speedometer and saw that they were going nearly eighty miles per hour.

Sydney managed to beat the convoy to the intersection. Jaden turned to look out the rear window—the trucks turned to follow them. Before long, they were gaining on them.

"You'd better do something," Jaden said to Malia.

She stared out the window with an intensity he'd never seen before. One at a time, the approaching trucks swerved violently and rolled over, crashing to either side of the road. Jaden counted eight of them.

"We're clear," he said. "No more pursuit."

"I wouldn't count on it," Carl said ominously. "Sydney, don't slow down."

A minute later, they reached Route 375. Sydney turned left and accelerated hard. They went faster on the pavement. Jaden saw the needle creeping toward 100 miles per hour.

But then he heard another sound, and he knew they were in trouble.

"Helicopter!" said Carl. "Damn!"

A few seconds later, they saw it descending in the night sky in front of them. It turned, flying sideways. A searchlight shined on them, blindingly bright.

"Pull over, or we will fire on your vehicle," someone shouted over a loudspeaker.

"Malia, honey, I could use some help here," said Sydney.

Malia leaned forward between the front seats. The helicopter rose sharply into the air. Jaden heard gunfire—it sounded like a machine gun. But it missed them, and the aircraft tumbled through the sky. It smashed into a hill to their left and exploded.

"Holy crap!" said Jaden, watching the flames out the rear window.

But he realized Malia was crying.

"What's wrong?!"

"What's wrong? *I just killed those people!*" she screamed.

"Malia," said Sydney, "they fired a machine gun at us. Think of what they'd do to you if they captured you. I know this isn't easy, but you did the right thing."

Malia started sobbing. Jaden pulled her into a hug, and she grabbed him tight.

"Oh no," said Carl.

"What is it?" asked Sydney, panic in her voice.

"There's someone on the side of the road—*STOP!*"

Jaden spotted the soldier as Sydney slammed on the brakes. There was a gunshot, followed by a familiar thudding sound. The soldier had blown out one of the tires. The truck swerved dangerously from side to side. Sydney managed to stop without flipping them over.

"Sniper," said Carl. "Nobody move."

They'd gone right by him before they stopped. Jaden stared out the window, looking for any sign of movement. But without the benefit of the headlights, it was impossible to see in the dark.

A full minute went by without a single sound. Then suddenly there was a knock on the window. Jaden jumped; Sydney screamed. A man was standing right outside the truck, pointing a rifle at them. But an instant later, the soldier was tossed into the air. Jaden heard him yelling, but the sound quickly grew fainter. Looking out the window, he saw the man's rifle lying on the road.

Carl got out of the truck, followed by the others. He picked up the gun.

"We're on foot now," he told them. "And we've got a long way to go. Sydney, why don't you use that device of yours and make sure we're going the right way. It'd be best to get off the road and cut across the desert. They've got night vision, so they'll see us if they get close to us. But it's a big desert, so hopefully, that won't be too easy. You've still got the coordinates?"

"I do," said Sydney, tapping away on her phone.

"All right, let's go. I'm going to cut straight away from the road for a while, and then we can turn toward the bunker. And we should do this as quietly as possible. They hear us talking, and we're done for."

The others nodded in agreement, and they set out into the desert. They walked in a single file, Carl first, followed by Malia and Jaden, Sydney bringing up the rear. For ten minutes, they marched in a straight line. Jaden wondered how much longer they'd go before heading toward the bunker when suddenly Carl stopped. He froze on the spot for a moment before falling to the ground, dropping the gun.

"Carl!" Sydney shouted. Squatting next to him, she reached to his neck. She stood up again and showed Jaden and Malia a small dart.

"Oh crap," said Jaden, frantically searching in every direction to try to find the shooter.

"I'm afraid," said Malia.

"Get down," Sydney told them. "You'll be harder to hit—" She slumped to the ground before she could finish her sentence.

Malia screamed.

"Do what she said," Jaden told her, grabbing her by both shoulders. He dropped to his knees and ducked low, pulling her down with him. She whimpered as she hit the dirt.

Jaden thought of grabbing Carl's rifle, but he had no idea how to work it. He'd never fired a gun before.

"We have to find the shooter so you can take care of him," he whispered. "So you look that way, I'll watch over here. But be quiet!"

She nodded and gazed out into the night. Jaden did the same. But it was useless: he couldn't see a thing. Time dragged by; Jaden felt like hours had passed, but knew it could only have been a few minutes. Nothing happened, and he could neither see nor hear a thing.

He was about to suggest that they start crawling when a bright light suddenly shone upon them. Jaden squinted into it, trying to see who was there. But whoever it was stayed behind the source of the light, effectively invisible.

"Jaden and Malia," someone cried out. "We don't want to harm you. So stand up with your backs to the light and hold your hands over your head." Jaden recognized that voice.

"Can you see anything?" he whispered to Malia.

"No," she said, holding out her hand to shield her eyes.

"Final warning," the voice announced. "Stand up now, or we'll shoot."

"Just imagine a big Humvee where that light is," Jaden told her, "and make it fly! You can do this!"

"I'll try," said Malia. "But I don't—" She gasped and went perfectly still. Jaden noticed a dart in her shoulder. He pulled it out and threw it away.

A second later, he felt something hit his shoulder. Jaden tried to grab it and pull it out but discovered that he couldn't move. He couldn't even wiggle his fingers.

"It's good to see you both again finally," the man called out. Jaden could see a figure approaching them in the light. He came closer and closer, and finally squatted down right in front of them.

"Remember me?" he asked.

It was Officer Babcock from the CIA.

"Ah, but of course you can't answer me, can you? We used tranquilizers on the others. But we weren't sure if those would work against the *wonder twins*. So instead, we concocted a special formula for the two of you. It inhibits voluntary muscle movement *and* your more unique abilities.

"I'm afraid you won't be destroying any more equipment this morning. That helicopter was quite expensive, you know."

Babcock stood up and walked away into the light. Jaden heard motors and saw headlights approaching. At least half a dozen vehicles pulled into the area. Soldiers surrounded them. One of them picked up Malia and carried her away. Another took Jaden. He watched them strap Malia into the back of a jeep. They placed him in another. He didn't know what they'd done with Sydney and Carl.

He tried as hard as he could to move or to free himself from his bonds. But his muscles refused to work. His heart was beating a mile a minute, and he could still breathe, but he had no control of his body. He couldn't even move his eyes

A few minutes later, the convoy drove off, back to the main road. As they turned a corner onto a dirt road, a lone white mailbox came into Jaden's field of vision.

They were going to Area 51.

Jaden's panic rose. Why were they taking him there? What were they going to do to him?

The vehicles climbed the same hill from which Jaden had watched the aircraft. But they kept going, descending into the valley. The eastern sky was growing lighter—it was almost dawn. Ten minutes later, they arrived at a building.

A soldier lifted Jaden out of the jeep. As they approached the building, Jaden spotted two gurneys just outside the door.

The soldier placed Jaden on one of these, flat on his back. Someone strapped down his arms and legs. His head lolled to one side, and he could see them securing Malia in the other gurney.

But a few moments later, someone wheeled him inside the building, and he lost sight of his sister. They rolled along a corridor; this place looked like a hospital. The gurney came to a stop. Someone opened a door and wheeled Jaden into a small room. They positioned the stretcher in the middle.

A woman in a camouflage uniform moved into view. She was doing something above his head; he couldn't see what. But then she moved to the side of the gurney. He felt something prick the crook of his elbow. In the corner of his vision, he could now see a tube protruding from his arm. The woman left the room, and he was alone.

Within seconds, Jaden fell unconscious.

20

DESERT

An old Ford Explorer moved along the road, the only car for miles around. It was a bright, sunny day. The woman driving the vehicle was zoned out, staring blankly out her windshield. The windows were open, and her long, blond hair whipped around in the breeze.

Abruptly, Sydney gasped, realizing that she was driving. She pulled over to the side of the road. Her head was foggy as if she'd just woken from a long nap. She rubbed her eyes, trying to remember where she was or what she was doing.

Suddenly it came back to her. They had gone to visit Area 51… the military showed up and chased them. There was a helicopter and a sniper. They'd been walking across the desert…

Where were Jaden and Malia?! She turned to look in the back seat, frantically throwing clothes out of the way. They weren't here—neither was Carl.

What had happened? Who fixed her flat tire? How had she come to be here?

Where was she?

Sydney found her iPhone in the pocket of her jeans. She pulled it out and opened the maps application. It showed her location on Route 93, headed north.

She took a deep breath, trying to clear her head. What was she supposed to do now? They'd captured the children, that much was clear. But they'd let Sydney go. Why? She supposed they had no reason to hold her.

What about Carl? Was he free, too?

She decided to go to his bunker. If they'd let him go, it would make sense for him to go there. She called up the directions on her phone. It was two and a half hours away.

Great.

She turned her truck around and sped off. By the time she reached the turn from Route 375 onto the dirt road, the sun was setting. After a bumpy ride through the desolate landscape, she arrived at the gorge. She parked the truck in the same spot she had before and ran to the entrance of the bunker.

The door was open. This was odd—it seemed like Carl always locked it. She walked slowly and quietly down the tunnel.

But when she reached the cavern, she froze in her tracks. It was empty. The computers, the furniture, everything was gone. She ran to the other chambers; the bunks had disappeared too, as well as the supplies. Nothing was left.

Now what?

In a daze, Sydney made her way out of the bunker and back to her truck. She leaned against the side of it for several moments, but then fell to her knees and broke down in tears. What was she supposed to do now? Where had they taken Jaden and Malia?

She felt utterly alone and helpless.

Suddenly there was a ringing noise. Sydney held her breath, trying to discern the source. It was coming from inside her truck.

She opened the door and listened; the sound was muffled. She climbed into the back seat and dug through her belongings. The ringing continued, but she couldn't figure out what it was.

And then she spotted it. The satellite phone was under the passenger seat, totally forgotten about since they'd left Miami. The lights on its face were blinking.

She grabbed it, pushed the green button, and held it to her ear.

"Hello?"

21

LAB WORK

Jaden's eyes fluttered open. It was too bright here; he squinted against the light. His head ached, and he felt groggy. Where was he?

Someone was there; he felt movement by his side. Looking up at her, he remembered. This was the woman who had brought him to this room; he was inside Area 51. She was drawing blood.

Jaden struggled to pull his arm away. His muscles worked now, but he was strapped to the gurney. He could move his arms and legs no more than a few inches in any direction.

"What are you doing?" he demanded. "Why am I here?"

The woman said nothing. She withdrew the needle and left the room.

Jaden watched her go, trying to see into the hallway. Only the opposite wall was visible. There was a small console on the door handle. It buzzed when the door closed, and he heard a clicking sound.

He thrashed against his bonds. *"Let me go!"* he yelled. It was no use.

Looking around, he saw the room was mostly bare. Medical supplies and instruments sat on a counter next to the door. The opposite wall hosted a large mirror. Behind him was only the pump for the IV. Beyond the foot of his bed, a flat-panel television was mounted on the wall. A lone chair sat in the corner.

A few minutes went by before the door buzzed and clicked open. Babcock walked into the room, closing the door behind him. He positioned the chair next to the bed, sat down, and crossed his legs.

"The medic tells me you're doing well," he said conversationally. "I was worried—you had it rough for the first couple of days. Some of the drugs we administered didn't agree so well with your body chemistry."

"Couple of days?" he repeated. "How long have I been here? Where's Malia?"

"Oh, don't worry about her. She's doing fine. And this is your third day in our facility."

Jaden had trouble taking this in. He'd been unconscious for two entire days?

"How did you find us?"

"Ah, yes, it was my idea that did it. You kids dropped off the grid completely after you left Brian's ranch. So, once your mother was healthy enough to move around, we paid one of the doctors to help her, you know, *escape.*"

"You mean you *let her go*?"

"Of course. We didn't know how to find you, but I was confident she'd have some ideas. And sure enough, she used Baxter's phone to call that Sydney woman. We traced the call, subpoenaed the GPS information from her cell phone, and voila. Las Vegas.

"Unfortunately, it took some time to collect the data, and by then, you'd moved. The signal vanished." Jaden thought of the shielding around Carl's bunker. "But when it reappeared, you were right in our backyard, so to speak. Quite convenient."

"What do you want with us? Where's my sister?"

"Malia's perfectly safe, I assure you," said Babcock. "Her powers have progressed significantly. But what I need right now is information, and Malia hasn't spoken a single word since her arrival. I'm hoping you might be more cooperative."

"I'm not gonna help you—let us go! You have no right—"

"We have every *right*, Jaden. The American taxpayers have spent a considerable amount of money funding your very existence. It's time they saw some return on that investment.

"Now… we've analyzed the evidence from Carl's bunker. We found his pictures of the alien mother ship passing Jupiter. Have you been in contact with them, Jaden?"

This question surprised him. Had they figured out the same thing Malia did—that the aliens were probably coming for *them*?

"I don't know anything about the aliens. I didn't even know aliens existed till we met Carl."

"I find that a little difficult to believe," Babcock replied, "considering it was your uncle who activated the beam at that pyramid. That's the signal that brought them here, but of course, you already know that. We tried shutting it off, but couldn't figure out how to work the thing. I'm sure Brian's hacking expertise helped him tremendously…

"What do they want, Jaden? Why did Brian summon them?"

Babcock didn't know it was *Jaden* who activated the pyramid. So their suspicion was correct: Babcock didn't realize he and Malia had been at the pyramid.

"I *told* you, I don't know anything about this! Carl showed us the pictures of Jupiter, and that's the first time I ever saw that spaceship."

Babcock was about to say something, but the door buzzed, and the medic walked in.

"It's time for testing," she said.

"Ah," said Babcock, rising from the chair. "Very well. I'll be back later, Jaden, and we can finish our discussion."

He left the room.

"What kind of testing?" Jaden demanded.

The medic said nothing. She inserted a needle into his IV tube.

"What is that? What are you doing..?"

Everything went black.

JADEN OPENED HIS EYES. They'd moved him; he was lying on the floor. Sitting up, he took in his new surroundings. It was an enormous room, the size of a basketball court. The walls, floor, and ceiling were black and metallic. He didn't see any doors. Several metal blocks were placed in a line across the center of the room, increasing in size.

Looking up, he saw a window high above, near the top of one wall. There were three people inside a room there; he recognized one of them as the medic. There was also a man and another woman, each wearing a white lab coat.

"Let me out of here!" Jaden shouted. His voice echoed around the room. "What do you want from me?!"

The people in the window took no notice of him. Jaden moved to the smallest block. He tried to lift it, but it was extremely heavy. Tilting it, he managed to wedge his fingers underneath. But a voice called out, "Don't touch it. Do it telekinetically."

Dropping the weight, Jaden straightened up and glared at the window. The people were watching him now.

"I can't!" he shouted.

The man in the lab coat bent over and spoke into a microphone. "Yes, you can. Start with the smallest weight, please."

Jaden stared down at the metal block, backing away from it. He imagined lifting it off the floor, and it shot into the air, slamming into the ceiling.

"Whoa!" he yelled, startled. The weight hit the floor again with a loud clang that echoed about the chamber. "How the hell did I do that?! I didn't have any powers before!"

"Proceed to the next weight," the man said.

"Did you people do something to me? Cuz, I couldn't do this until now."

"Lift the second weight."

"Yeah, all right."

Jaden focused on the next block. This time he lifted it with more control, elevating it several feet and holding it there. This was *easy*.

The man commanded him to continue to each heavier block. The last few became more difficult. Jaden could feel their weight as he lifted them but knew he could handle more.

He walked over to the heaviest one after returning it to the floor. It came up to his waist. Using his hands, he tried tilting it the way he had the lightest one. Nothing happened. He put all of his weight into it, but couldn't move it this way.

Backing away, he lifted it again telekinetically. It felt heavy, but it wasn't a strain.

Replacing the block, he glared up at the window. He focused on slamming the man's head into the window. Nothing happened.

Instead, he lifted the first weight into the air and hurled it into the window with all of his force. It bounced off the glass and clattered noisily to the floor.

"Please don't do that," the man said over the speakers.

Jaden focused on the heaviest block. He caused it to rise to the far corner near the ceiling. Then with every ounce of will he possessed, he heaved it across the room. It crashed into the glass with a noise like a gong but didn't cause so much as a scratch. The weight fell back to the floor with a deafening sound and rolled over twice before coming to rest.

Suddenly Jaden felt an electric shock. He jumped off the floor, falling on his side.

"Dammit, that hurt!" he shouted, regaining his feet.

"Don't do that again, or the current will be stronger."

Jaden was about to yell back a retort when he heard an odd noise. It sounded like an air leak. A moment later, he fell to the floor, unconscious.

HE WOKE AGAIN BACK in his gurney.

"Your test results were very encouraging."

It was Babcock. He was sitting in the chair next to the bed. Jaden focused, trying to throw the man into the wall. Nothing happened.

"Why can't I move you?"

"There's a chemical in your IV that inhibits your powers while you're in this room. It wears off immediately upon being withdrawn, however, which is why the medic has to put you under before we can move you."

"And what about the people in the control room? Why can't I do anything to them?"

"The walls in that room are shielded to dampen electromagnetic fields. Your powers cannot reach beyond those walls."

"Electromagnetic?"

"Radiation, Jaden. Your telekinetic and telepathic powers work because your brain emits a complex electromagnetic field. What you can do is a result of biochemical reactions, not magic. We've been developing the technology to counter that radiation for years—ever since you and your sister were very young."

"You knew you'd have to defend against us eventually?"

"Call it being prepared for any eventuality. We were able to accelerate your development by injecting certain hormones and enzymes into your circulatory system. I have to say that I'm quite pleased with the results so far. Malia's farther along, of course. Her powers had progressed much more dramatically before your arrival. She's done with the physical testing already—we've moved her to the electrochemical evaluations."

"I want to see her," said Jaden.

"Oh, you will, very soon," Babcock replied. "But for now, I want you to watch something."

He reached behind him and grabbed a remote control from the counter. He pressed a button, and the television turned on. It was showing CNN, but there was no audio. The video displayed what was unmistakably some sort of space-craft. It had the same shape as the image Carl had shown them—like a thick pancake. Something reddish and hazy was in the background.

"Is that Jupiter?" asked Jaden.

"No. Mars. It's getting closer," said Babcock. "That's what the public can see. Thanks to our friends at the Defense Department, I can show you some much more interesting images."

He clicked the remote. The monitor changed. Jaden guessed that it was still the spacecraft, but the picture on the screen showed only a small section of its surface in sharp detail. Jaden could make out structures of various shapes. Near the center of the image was a large, elliptical opening. Dozens of small dots contrasted against the blackness of the cavity.

"What does that look like to you?" asked Babcock.

"I dunno," said Jaden. "It's a close-up of the ship, I guess."

"Indeed." He clicked the remote again. An image appeared that seemed to be the same section of the ship but zoomed-in farther. The opening filled the screen, and the dots had shape: they were saucers. "This reminds me of an aircraft carrier. The smaller vehicles are launching from the mother ship."

"So?"

"Think, Jaden. What do we use aircraft carriers for on Earth? They certainly don't serve any friendly purpose."

"You think they're going to attack us?"

"You tell me," said Babcock. "Why else would they be here?"

"How would I know?"

"Because you've been in communication with them. Tele-pathically."

"I didn't have any powers before I came here. And Malia only had telekinesis. Neither of us could communicate with anyone."

"That's not entirely true. But perhaps by some other means then," suggested Babcock. "Carl had some pretty sophisticated equipment in that cave of his. I need to know what they've told you, Jaden. The safety of the entire world may depend on it."

"You don't know that! They might be here to explore—"

"Is that what they told you?"

"They haven't told me anything!"

"Of course. Well, regardless of whatever they've communicated to you, their intention is clear. They're not explorers. Their technology is vastly superior to our own; they're going to attack. Will you help us, Jaden?"

"I already knew that's what this was all about! You want to use Malia and me as weapons!" Jaden accused. "My dad couldn't make more… more people like us, so you planned to *take us* once we had powers and *use us*—"

"You're wrong, Jaden. It's about unlocking human potential. You and your sister represent the next step in the evolution of our species. Why wouldn't you want to give the gifts you possess to others? There may be military ramifications, yes. But the powers you possess would be used only for good.

"Tell me what you know. What have they—"

"I'm telling you, *I don't know anything!*"

Babcock stared at him for a moment.

"Fine. Continue in your stubbornness. But I promise you we will get you to talk."

He rose from his chair and strode out of the room. Jaden tried to use telekinesis to stop the door from closing but failed. He struggled against his bonds, but couldn't move more than a few inches. Focusing on the straps, he imagined them releasing him. Nothing happened.

"Dammit!"

Jaden dropped his head on the pillow. If he could pull the IV out of his arm, he'd be able to use his telekinesis to escape. But he couldn't move his arms. This was incredibly frustrating.

He'd felt so powerful in the metal room—moving those weights with only his mind was unbelievably cool. But now he was helpless.

The medic returned a few minutes later. She carried a tray of food. He thought of Malia, refusing to talk, and considered doing the same thing, and going on a hunger strike. But he was starving. He let the woman feed him chicken and potatoes.

Repeatedly, he asked her about his sister, and when they would release them. But the medic didn't reply to anything he said.

After she left, the television was his only company. The medic had turned it back to CNN—he watched the newscast, but it was mostly meaningless without the audio. Most of the time, they simply left the images of the ship on the screen. He assumed the news anchor was talking but could hear nothing.

Once in a while, there would be people on the screen, reporters interviewing various government and military personnel. At one point, they showed a man who reminded Jaden of Carl. He was wearing a cowboy hat and jeans and kept pointing up at the sky. When the camera zoomed out, Jaden gasped. The interview was taking place next to the metal man they'd seen on their way to Carl's bunker.

Hours dragged by—Jaden knew this because the broadcast displayed the time. His attention to the television faded in and out. But he focused again when a "breaking news" graphic played on the screen.

The first image Babcock had shown him flashed on the screen, followed by the more detailed one that displayed the saucers. A banner across the bottom read, "Leaked images from the Pentagon."

Jaden felt a wave of fear at the next few images. They displayed large cylindrical protrusions, whole banks of them, that he guessed were weapons of some kind. Maybe Babcock was right... this ship certainly didn't look like it was here on a peaceful mission.

More time slipped by. The medic returned to feed him dinner. Jaden tried a few more times to escape his bonds. It was futile.

He started to doze off, but the medic came in again. She inserted a needle into his IV tube, and he went under.

WHEN HE OPENED HIS EYES, he was lying in another black metal room. But this one was split into two halves by a thick glass partition. He jumped to his feet and pounded on the glass.

Malia was on the other side, wearing only her underwear. They'd strapped her to a metal table, and attached tubes and wires to various points on her body.

"Hey! Malia!" he shouted, pounding on the glass. She didn't open her eyes.

There was a window high on the wall, but he didn't see anyone inside. He tried to move the partition using telekinesis, but nothing happened. Instead, he banged on the glass again.

This time Malia opened her eyes. Barely. She turned her head slightly to look at Jaden.

"*Jaden,*" a voice said in his head. "*I'm scared.*"

"Malia!" he yelled.

"*I can't hear you. Use your mind.*"

"*Are you okay? What have they done to you?*"

"*I don't know... At first, they made me move things and deflect stuff... but then they brought me here. I think I've been here for days. Sometimes it hurts—it feels like they're shocking me or something. But then I sleep a lot... Jaden, we have to get out of here...*"

"*I know—I'm going to take those tubes and wires out of you—*"

"*You can't. Telekinesis doesn't work here.*"

Jaden ignored her, focusing on the electrodes sticking to her face and neck. He tried to rip them away, but nothing happened.

"*What the hell? How come I can't do anything?*"

"*Babcock said it's a different frequency or something. I tried it too.*"

Jaden heard the leaking-air sound again.

"NO!" he yelled out loud. "Malia..."

"*Jaden,*" she said in his head.

But Jaden hit the floor and passed out.

. . .

HE WOKE BACK in his room, strapped to the gurney, with Babcock sitting at his side.

"So. How did you enjoy your little visit with Malia?"

"You son of a bitch! Let her go! Take those tubes out of her! What the hell—"

"Tell me what I want to know, and I can arrange that."

Jaden thrashed against the restraints. He felt an urge to kill Babcock.

"Calm down before you hurt yourself. If you'll just tell me—"

"It was me!" Jaden shouted. *"I'm* the one who activated the beam, not Brian."

Babcock regarded him in stunned silence.

"I don't know how I did it. I touched the pyramid, and all this stuff showed up—these icons. They moved around, and there was a voice, but it wasn't speaking English. It was a bunch of chirping and whistling noises. Brian said other people touched it, but that never happened before. He looked on his computer monitor and said we had to run. And that's all I know! I have no idea why it happened, and I didn't know an alien ship would show up! I didn't find out about that till Carl showed it to us!

"Now, let me go! Get Malia out of that room! Hey!"

Babcock had risen from his chair without saying a word. He walked out the door, leaving Jaden alone again.

"Hey!" he shouted. "Get your ass back here! You said you'd let Malia go if I told you what I knew! AARRRGHHH!"

He screamed and shouted for a few more minutes, but

nothing happened. Eventually, he calmed down. Jaden would have watched CNN some more, but someone had turned off the television during his absence.

Defeated, he closed his eyes and drifted off to sleep.

THE MEDIC WOKE him in the morning. At least he assumed it was morning—the television was off, so he had no way of knowing for sure. She fed him breakfast.

"Hey, can you turn the TV on?" he asked as she prepared to leave. She walked out of the room without answering him.

"Great, thanks."

He lay there for some time. The image of Malia, with those tubes sticking out of her, played over and over again in his mind. Somehow, they had to escape.

The door opened; it was the medic. She put a needle into his IV.

"Where am I going now?" he asked, but slipped into unconsciousness a moment later.

WHEN HE OPENED HIS EYES, he was back in the black metal room. But this time, it was empty. Sitting up and gazing at the window high above, he saw the same people who were here before.

"What am I supposed to do?"

Something hit him on the back of the head.

"Ow!" He turned and saw a red ball bouncing away from him. "That hurt," he yelled to the window, getting to his feet.

Another ball hit him from the side.

"Stop that!"

"No, *you* stop them," said a voice over the speakers. It was the woman in the lab coat.

"Oh, I get it," he muttered.

He saw a flash of red in the corner of his eye. Reflexively he stopped the ball midflight with his mind. It floated there in front of him, slowly rotating.

"This is cool."

He turned just in time to stop another one from hitting him in the back of the head. And over the next several minutes, he continued to deflect every ball they shot at him. They fired them with increasing frequency until finally the air was so full of them no more could get through.

"Oh, you're done now?" Jaden yelled to the window he could no longer see. With one sweeping thought, he sent every one of the balls hurtling at the glass. It sounded like a hail storm for several seconds as they impacted the window and fell to the floor. Finally, Jaden herded them all telekinetically into a big heap in the corner.

"We warned you," the woman's voice said. Electricity jolted Jaden's body. He fell to the floor, and the pile of balls collapsed, washing over him.

"You wait till I get out of here," Jaden murmured.

The gas came on, and Jaden passed out.

When he awoke back in the gurney, Babcock was with him again.

"Are you ready to talk more?" he asked.

"I already told you everything," said Jaden. "Did you take Malia out of that room?"

"We've still got more tests to conduct."

"You said you'd let her go if I told you what I knew!"

"Come now, Jaden. That ship is almost here. I grow tired of your obstinacy. *Tell me everything you know about those aliens!*"

"I ALREADY HAVE! NOW LET US OUT OF HERE!"

Jaden thrashed against his bonds, focusing with all of his might on Babcock, trying to throw him into the wall. But the only thing he accomplished was nearly tipping over the gurney.

"The testing on your sister will continue," said Babcock, getting to his feet. "And you'll be next—we're almost done with your physical evaluation."

Babcock grabbed the remote control and pointed it at the television. Returning the device to the counter, he strode from the room.

"I HATE YOU!" Jaden shouted. "You're gonna pay when I get outta here!"

He watched the television once he'd calmed down. It was CNN again, video only. They were still showing the alien mother ship, and a graphic at the bottom indicated it was now almost within the orbit of the Moon.

Jaden spent the rest of the day wondering what the extraterrestrials were doing here. He was sure he wanted to know as badly as Babcock.

The medic fed him lunch and dinner. Jaden reflected again

on the irony of how powerful he felt in the test chamber compared to his helplessness here.

After she left the last time, he grew drowsy. He began dozing, but suddenly there was a deafening noise—an alarm of some kind. Was there a fire somewhere? The sound was so loud it hurt—Jaden tried desperately to raise his hands to plug his ears, but couldn't reach.

But an instant later, the siren stopped, and the power went out. He was plunged into utter darkness. After a few seconds, the emergency lights came on. Jaden figured they were battery-powered.

"Hello?" he yelled. "What's going on?"

There was a buzzing sound, and the door to his room clicked open. But nobody was there.

22

SPRING

"Hello?" he yelled. "Hey! Who's there?! What's happening?"

He heard voices somewhere down the hall outside his room, but nothing nearby. Jaden didn't know what was going on, but this was his chance to escape. If he could only get the needle out of his arm, he'd be free to use his powers.

Jaden struggled and thrashed against his bonds. They were too tight; he couldn't free his arms. He kept jerking his body around violently and finally managed to tip the gurney right over. The straps still held him, but the IV line had ripped out of his arm.

Focusing on the strap holding his right arm in place, he imagined it ripping apart. Nothing happened. He took a deep breath and concentrated as hard as he could. With a great tearing sound, the strap snapped. His hand was free.

With a thought, he released his other hand. Now lying awkwardly on the floor, his legs still bound, he focused on the straps around his ankles. They tore away. Examining the remains of his bonds, he realized they were simple Velcro. He ripped them off his ankles and wrists and moved to the door.

Cautiously at first, he peered into the hallway. It was much longer than he remembered from his arrival. He heard voices still, shouting, but saw nobody. Running down the hall, he tried opening the first door he found. It was locked. He attempted to open it using telekinesis. It rattled violently against its frame but remained closed.

This was futile. There were dozens of doors, and he had no idea where Malia might be. Abandoning caution, he ran toward the voices. If he could find a guard or someone who knew where his sister was, he'd be able to rescue her and get them out of here.

But halfway down the corridor, he skidded to a stop. A door on the left had opened. Carl emerged, escorted by a soldier.

"Hey!" yelled Jaden.

Keeping one hand on Carl's arm, the soldier pointed his gun at Jaden, yelling, "Don't move—put your hands up!"

"Hell no," Jaden muttered. Using only his mind, he wrenched the gun out of the man's hand and flung it down the hall.

The guard backed away, eyeing Jaden apprehensively. Carl moved behind Jaden, who realized his wrists were handcuffed together.

"Where's my sister?" he demanded of the soldier.

"Locked up." The look of fear on his face belied his defiant tone.

Jaden caused him to rise off the ground, floating several feet in the air.

"Where is she?" he asked again. The soldier said nothing. Jaden slammed him into the wall. "Don't make me do that again—tell me where Malia is!"

"Room thirty-seven! She's in thirty-seven—now let me go!"

Jaden threw him down the hallway. The soldier screamed as he flew.

"That's this way," said Carl. "Can you take care of these?" he asked, holding up his hands to show Jaden the handcuffs.

"I can't unlock them," he said, staring at the metal, and willing them to open. "Malia was right—without seeing how it works inside, I don't know what to do. Hold on…"

He focused instead on expanding the metal. This proved difficult, but he managed to stretch them enough for Carl to slip his hands out.

"Let's go!" he said.

They ran down the hall. Near the end, they found room thirty-seven.

"Malia!" Jaden shouted, pounding on the door. "It's me, Jaden! Are you in there?"

There was no answer. Jaden tried the handle, but it was locked. He couldn't open it telekinetically either.

"Stand back," he warned Carl, moving away from the

door himself. He focused as hard as he could. The door trembled, and a few seconds later, the entire thing, frame and all ripped out of the wall and crashed into the opposite door, spraying rubble and dust.

Jaden ran inside. This was one of the large test rooms with a big glass partition, like the one where he'd seen Malia before. And there she lay, on the other side of the glass, in only her underwear. She was unconscious and strapped to the gurney. Tubes and wires protruded from her body.

"Malia!" Jaden screamed. She didn't stir. *"Malia,"* he called to her telepathically. Nothing. He slammed his fists against the glass, accomplishing nothing.

"Tear it down," Carl suggested. "Babcock told me they've got dampening fields in these chambers, but the power's out. Your telekinesis will work here."

"Yeah, it's the only way," Jaden agreed. "But, I don't want to hurt Malia if it shatters."

"Can you punch a hole in it?"

"I can try." Jaden focused on a spot at the far end of the room. He curled his hand into a fist, and punched the air, imagining his fist extending through the glass. It worked—a hole as big as a basketball ruptured the partition. He did it three more times, enlarging the opening enough to climb through.

Jaden charged through the hole and ran to Malia, Carl right behind him. He haphazardly pulled tubes out of her arms and removed electrodes from her face and torso.

Malia's eyes fluttered open. *"Jaden,"* she said to him telepathically. *"What's going on?"*

"I don't know," he replied out loud. "The power went out. We're escaping—can you walk?"

"I think so," she said, sitting up. Slowly, she swung her legs off the gurney. With Jaden's help, she stood up, shaky at first. "I feel weak, but I'll be all right."

Together, they followed Carl, climbing back out the hole in the glass and emerging in the hallway.

"The exit's this way," said Carl, leading the way down the corridor.

"Wait," said Malia. "I need my clothes! I'm not running outside in my underwear!"

"Forget it," said Jaden. "We've gotta get out of here! Who the hell knows where they put your stuff."

At that moment, a voice shouted, "Hold it—don't move!"

Jaden turned. Three soldiers were running toward them, guns drawn. Before he could act, Malia stopped them, dangling them several feet in the air. Jaden focused, and the guns flew out of their hands, landing at his feet.

"Those are tranquilizer guns," said Carl, picking one up. "Hold them still—I've got an idea." He walked around to each of the soldiers, firing a dart into each man's neck. Once they'd gone unconscious, Malia put them down.

"Let's get out of here!" said Jaden.

"Hang on," said Carl. "We've solved your problem, young lady," he added, gesturing toward the soldiers. Malia nodded and moved to one of the men—he was smaller than the other two. She started undressing him.

"What the hell are you doing?!" Jaden demanded.

"I am *not* going outside naked!"

Jaden rolled his eyes, but Malia kept going. She removed the soldier's shirt and pants, putting them on herself. They were too big for her, but she rolled up the pants, and they took off down the hall.

They reached the exit with no further resistance. But the doors were locked. Malia blasted a hole in the wall, and they left the building. It was nighttime. Only a handful of emergency lights provided illumination, casting long shadows across the base.

"Now what?" asked Jaden.

"We need transportation," said Carl, gazing around at their surroundings. "Follow me."

They crept along the side of the building. At the far end, they saw an airplane hangar across a large open area. There was activity inside. Jaden saw a few people running toward another building behind the hangar. A jeep came racing up the road, stopping in front of the far building.

"Do you know how to fly a plane?" asked Malia.

"No," said Carl.

Suddenly a voice called out to them. "Jaden! Malia!"

It was Brian. He was running toward them from an adjacent building.

"Uncle Brian!" Malia yelled, grabbing him in a big hug.

"Are you the one who knocked the power out?" Jaden asked.

"Yes," he said, smiling at him. "I hacked into their main computer system—I'm sorry it took so long. The security was formidable, and I needed a couple of days to figure it out. But

I was able to cut the electricity and spring the lock to your room before they caught me."

"They caught you?" asked Malia. "How'd you get away?"

Brian shook his head. "No—they caught me in their system. They closed the breach I used to penetrate the network before I could do anything else. But they know this was no malfunction. That siren warned the entire base of an attack."

"So, what's the plan?" asked Carl.

"I've got Sydney's truck," he explained. "I came as far as the ridge and used my laptop to hack their computers. Once I'd disabled their security cameras, I drove onto the base. The truck's parked on the other side of that hangar."

But as he spoke, electricity was restored. Lights came on outside the buildings, and the interior of the hangar lit up.

"Follow me," said Brian.

He retraced his steps, leading them along the side of the building, then ran between two other structures. From here, Jaden caught sight of the end of the hangar.

They ran behind one of the buildings and came to a road. They crossed it cautiously, hurrying past the jeep Jaden had seen earlier. There were no lights here. But as they began moving along the rear of the hangar, a door opened at the far end. A soldier emerged, followed by Babcock.

They approached quickly, deep in conversation. Brian grabbed Malia by one arm, pulling her back around the corner of the hangar. But Jaden strode forward. The sight of Babcock had filled him with rage.

"Jaden no," hissed Carl.

It was too late. Babcock had spotted them.

"It's the Kwan boy!" he yelled. "Quick—shoot him!"

Jaden guessed the soldier's weapon must have been a tranquilizer gun. Using telekinesis, he slammed the man into the wall of the hangar repeatedly, knocking him out before he had a chance to fire his weapon. The soldier fell to the ground and didn't move.

Jaden advanced on Babcock, who tried to run away. Jaden lifted him off his feet. Babcock twisted in midair to face him.

"Jaden, we have to leave," said Carl, grabbing him by the shoulder.

"No." He pulled free.

"Hurting me won't help you escape," said Babcock when Jaden reached him. "You'll never get off this base."

Jaden smashed Babcock into the wall. He pulled him away and hung him upside down.

"Stop this madness," said Brian, who had arrived with Malia.

"*Let him go,*" she told him telepathically.

"NO! He killed Dad."

"You can't bring Stephen back," said Brian. "It's time to go."

Jaden swung Babcock by his feet, around in a circle, and into the hangar. Babcock grunted as he fell to the ground in a heap. He stood up woozily and tried to run. Jaden suspended him again, right side up.

"You're going to pay for what you did," he screamed, pointing up at Babcock's face.

But suddenly, Babcock dropped to the pavement. He ran. Jaden tried to stop him again, but nothing happened.

"What the hell?!" Did they have a dampening field out here somehow?

"*I released him,*" Malia told him. "*You would've killed him.*"

"Yeah, that was the general idea!" he shouted at her. He tried again to stop Babcock, and this time it worked. Jaden hoisted him into the air just before he disappeared around the corner of the hangar. But as he pulled Babcock closer, Carl drew a gun. Jaden recognized it as one of the tranquilizer guns he'd taken from the soldiers. Before Jaden could stop him, Carl fired it. The dart hit Babcock in the neck, and his body went limp.

Brian grabbed Jaden by one arm.

"We're leaving. Now."

Jaden released Babcock, dropping him on the ground.

"Fine," he said, yanking his arm free.

They ran past the edge of the hangar and found Sydney's truck. Brian got into the driver's seat as Jaden climbed in next to him. Carl and Malia sat in the back. Brian started the engine and took off toward the hills.

"Now what?" asked Jaden, looking back at the hangar for signs of pursuit.

"If we can make it to my helicopter, we should be home free," he said.

"You have a helicopter?" asked Jaden.

"Yes. I left it in the desert outside of Carl's bunker."

Just then, Malia yelled, "Here they come!"

Jaden stared out her window and saw half a dozen vehicles approaching.

"They'll attempt to force us to stop," said Brian. "I'll try to outrun them. As long as they don't get in front of us…"

But at that moment, the vehicles swerved violently, one at a time, rolling over and coming to a stop.

"Malia took care of them," Jaden told his uncle.

"Right… good," he said. "You two keep an eye out, and do what you need to do if anyone else comes after us."

"You got it," said Jaden.

They crossed a runway and went by an enormous dry lakebed. Soon they came to a road. Brian took the turn fast, skidding around the corner. He raced toward the ridge, which Jaden could see rising against the sky.

But a minute later, they heard the sound of a helicopter. Jaden looked around everywhere, but couldn't see it. Finally, he opened the window and looked up. The aircraft was directly above them.

"*I've got this, Jaden,*" Malia whispered in his mind. Before he could do anything, she moved the chopper away from them and set it down on the ground. The rotors ripped off the top of the aircraft and tumbled away.

"Nice work," said Brian, "whoever that was."

"It was Malia, showing off again," Jaden told him.

Before long, they crested the ridge. As they drove down the other side, Jaden recognized the road from the night he'd first been caught. They reached the lone mailbox, and Brian turned onto Route 375.

"Now we just have to watch out for snipers," said Jaden. "That's how they stopped us last time."

"Well, keep an eye out for me," said Brian.

Jaden watched both sides of the road intently. But the miles slipped by, and he saw nothing. They rode for another half hour in silence, the mood tense. Jaden expected to see an ambush or hear another helicopter at any moment. But finally, Carl said, "This is it. Turn here."

Brian turned onto a dirt road that quickly melted into the open desert. The truck bounced along as he swerved around the larger shrubs. Drawing close to Carl's bunker, Jaden spotted a helicopter sitting next to the rocky hill.

As they came to a stop, a woman emerged from the helicopter. It was Sydney.

Jaden and Malia jumped out of the car and dashed over to her. She gathered them both in a hug.

"I've been *so worried*!" she said through her tears. "They let me go, and I didn't know what I was going to do… If your uncle hadn't called me—"

"That's how you found us," said Carl, wagging a finger at Brian. "Sydney told you."

"Yes, she did," Brian confirmed. "I called her on the satellite phone, and she told me what happened."

"What are we going to do now?" asked Jaden. "They're gonna keep looking for Malia and me."

"I agree," said Brian. "They won't let you go this easily. For the time being, we're going to fly to a cabin I own in the mountains. Once we get there, we can figure out a long-term plan."

Brian, Carl, Sydney, Malia, and Jaden climbed into the helicopter. Carl sat in the cockpit with Brian, and the other three sat in the main cabin, leaving one empty seat.

"Whoa—digital flight control system?" asked Carl.

"Yep," said Brian. "The computer controls everything. They call it 'fly-by-wire.'"

"I've heard of this in airplanes, but never a helicopter!" Carl replied as Brian started the engine.

"Make sure you're buckled in," Brian called back to them. "I'm going to fly low so they won't catch us on radar. It'll be a bit rough at times."

"Oh crap—Sydney, let me see your iPhone!" said Jaden.

She pulled it out of her pocket and handed it to him. Jaden opened the door of the helicopter, threw the phone outside, and closed the door again.

"What the hell?!" demanded Sydney.

"I'll explain later!"

Jaden looked down at Sydney's truck as they lifted off. He wondered if she'd grabbed their things, but then saw their bags behind the empty seat. Despite the seriousness of their situation, Jaden was relieved to know he'd have clean clothes if their escape succeeded.

Suddenly the helicopter shot forward, and Jaden was pushed back into his seat. Looking out the window, he watched the desert go by in a blur. It didn't feel like they were very high off the ground.

"Hold on!" Brian shouted over the engine. A moment later, they climbed, going over a steep ridge. They dropped again on the other side and banked hard to the left. For the next several minutes, Brian took them on a wild ride, soaring over hills and valleys.

Jaden thought they'd escaped, until Brian yelled, "We've got company!" Jaden glanced out the window in time to see something shoot past them from behind. It was still night, and he could make out only blinking lights and a dark shadow.

But Brian slowed down, hovering in place. Jaden leaned forward to stare out the cockpit window. The blinking lights were far out in front of them. But suddenly, the aircraft shot toward them. Malia screamed. Jaden gasped as the object came into view.

It was unlike anything he'd ever seen—it looked like a triangular wedge. The plane stopped right in front of them, hovering just like they were. Jaden could make out the pilot's dark helmet behind the cockpit window.

"He's signaling us to land," said Brian. "Jaden and Malia, can you get this thing out of our way?"

Jaden focused on forcing the plane onto the ground; nothing happened. He stared at Malia. *"I can't make it go down,"* he told her telepathically.

"Neither can I," she replied helplessly.

"No go," Jaden yelled to his uncle. "It must be shielded or something."

"Damn! All right, hold on back there!"

The helicopter shot straight up and over the wedge.

"What the hell is that thing?!" said Brian.

"It appears they've implemented the propulsion system from the alien saucers," Carl shouted. "Adapted it for use on a stealth fighter."

"You told me they couldn't crack alien technology!" said Brian.

"That was true when I worked there," Carl replied. "But I *told* you they were trying! You never believed any of it!"

Brian flew faster than ever, banking wildly above cliffs and canyons. Staring out the window, Jaden caught an occasional glimpse of the wedge close behind them. Brian couldn't shake it. Jaden tried again to force the craft out of the sky, but his efforts met with failure.

"Try to get underneath it," Carl yelled. "It should have vents on the bottom, and those might not be shielded. That might give Jaden and Malia a chance!"

"I'll try it!" Jaden shouted back.

Brian took them lower. They were flying over a forest now, and Jaden thought the tops of some of the trees might scrape the bottom of the helicopter. Brian slowed down. The wedge flew over them, and Jaden and Malia both had a clear view of its underside. Jaden concentrated on the vents. Suddenly the craft tumbled over sideways and disappeared behind a hill.

"It worked!" yelled Malia.

"Good job, kids!" Brian replied.

But as he flew higher, Jaden spotted the wedge again, pursuing fast.

"Damn!" yelled Carl.

Brian flew low again and came to a standstill, hovering over the trees. But the wedge didn't expose its vents again, instead flying by on the same level and coming to rest directly in front of them.

"Oh crap," shouted Brian. "He's trying to hack the control system!"

"Can that work?" asked Carl.

"Of course it can," said Brian. "We'd better keep him busy flying."

He banked hard to the right and shot off back the way they'd come. As they raced over the trees, Jaden had an idea.

"Slow down and let him get in front of us again," he shouted to his uncle.

"No way! That'll give him time to take control of our flight systems. He'll force us to land."

"Trust me!" Jaden yelled back. Malia stared at him inquisitively. *"Use the trees,"* he told her telepathically. She thought about it for a second, then nodded her understanding.

Brian brought them to rest once more, and the wedge moved in front of them. Jaden focused on the trees below them. He ripped several out of the ground and propelled them at the aircraft. Malia did the same. But the pilot realized what was happening in the nick of time and shot out of the way.

"We can't do that again," said Brian as they flew off again. "He almost gained access to the computer."

They left the forest, and the earth below turned barren again. Jaden saw the wedge closing in fast from the left. Brian hugged the landscape, flying erratically to keep the other pilot busy.

But suddenly, Jaden felt the helicopter slowing down

again. They came to a standstill next to a steep canyon wall. The wedge moved into view in front of them.

"I thought we couldn't stop again," shouted Jaden.

"It's not me," said Brian, tapping furiously on the flight console. "He's broken the security. The pilot's forcing us to land."

"Jaden," Malia said in his mind. "Landslide."

He turned to look at her, not understanding. She pointed out the window at the cliff face. Jaden nodded. He focused on the canyon wall, trying to rip the upper portion away. Together with Malia's effort, he could feel it starting to work.

An instant later, an enormous swath of the mountainside broke loose. Rocks and boulders bounded down the rock wall, some of them bouncing into the wedge. The pilot tried to fly out of the way, but one particularly large stone smashed into the edge of it. The wedge spun out of control. Suddenly the pilot ejected, shooting into the air. The craft plunged earthward as the pilot activated his parachute.

But the helicopter continued its descent.

"What's going on?" asked Jaden. "Let's get out of here!"

"I can't," Brian shouted. "He initiated a command to land, and I can't override it. We'll have to reboot the computer after we touch down."

But looking below, Jaden saw a field of jagged rock formations and a stream.

"We'll crash if we land here!" he yelled.

"I know," said Brian. "I'm trying to move us across the stream—there's flat ground over there. But the controls aren't responding."

Jaden tried to direct the helicopter to safety but was unable to affect their course. He realized he'd need to see the craft from the outside.

Suddenly Malia opened the door and jumped out of the helicopter.

"Malia!" Jaden shouted. As he watched, she landed gracefully below.

Jaden felt them moving to the other side of the water. Seeing the look of concentration on Malia's face, he knew she was doing it. A minute later, they touched down on the opposite bank.

"That was way too close," said Carl as Brian cut the engine.

"We're not out of the woods yet," said Brian, pointing out the cockpit window. "Look!" The pilot had landed close to their position. The wedge had crashed farther off, engulfed in flames. "Odds are he's got a homing beacon. If we don't get this thing off the ground soon, we'll have more company."

"We'd better take care of the pilot," said Jaden. The man was moving toward them, pointing a gun.

"You do your thing, and I'll do mine," Carl replied. He still had the tranquilizer gun.

The two of them got out of the helicopter and approached the pilot.

"Don't come any closer!" he shouted at them.

Jaden knocked the gun out of his hand telekinetically; the pilot stared at him in surprise. Carl shot him. The man pulled the dart out of his neck, but it was too late. He slumped to the ground, unconscious.

"Hope we don't need it again," said Carl, throwing the gun aside. "It's empty!"

Jaden sat on a rock, staring up at the sky. Malia jumped across the stream—clearly using her powers—and joined him. He expected to see another aircraft swoop over the canyon wall at any moment. But Brian managed to reboot the computer, and they took off again, flying into the night.

23

LAKE

They flew for hours, Brian keeping the helicopter close to the ground the entire time. Jaden frequently saw the lights of cities or towns in the distance, but they avoided flying directly over population centers. He worried Babcock would send another plane, but none came.

After what felt like an eternity, they slowed down somewhere in the mountains. Brian brought them to a hover directly above an open clearing in the trees. Looking down, Jaden spotted a log cabin. Brian set the helicopter down.

"We made it," he said happily as he cut the engine. "Home away from home."

They got out of the helicopter. Jaden helped Sydney with their bags. As they approached the house, he realized it was much bigger than any log cabin he'd ever imagined. It consisted of two stories, with an open deck spanning the front of the second floor.

Brian led them inside.

"This place is one of several hidden properties that I own," he told them. "They won't be able to track us here. It should provide a good hideout while we determine our next course of action."

"What *are* we going to do?" asked Malia through a yawn.

"I don't know," Brian said with a frown. "We've got a lot of variables to consider. But it's late; we could all use some rest. Let's sit down in the morning and figure everything out."

Carl ended up sleeping on the couch in the living room. Brian showed everyone else upstairs. He and Sydney each had a room, and Jaden and Malia shared the third bedroom.

Malia drifted off to sleep almost immediately. But Jaden lay next to her, wide awake, unable to stop thinking about everything that had happened. His life had spun completely out of control, and he couldn't see where they were supposed to go from here.

Jaden dozed off eventually but suffered horrible dreams. He found himself back in the testing chamber at Area 51, strapped to a gurney. Tubes and wires were attached to him, and he couldn't move. Babcock floated over him, pushing a scalpel toward his neck. Jaden tried to scream, but no sound came out.

He woke with a start. Sitting up, he was blinded by sunlight streaming in through the window. Malia was gone.

Jaden heard voices downstairs, and the smell of food wafted into the room. He got out of bed and trudged downstairs.

A fire was burning in the enormous fireplace in the living room. Malia, Sydney, Carl, and Brian were sitting around the table in the kitchen, feasting on French toast, bacon, and eggs. Jaden plopped down in a chair next to his sister.

"I was getting worried," Brian said with a smile. "Thought maybe they'd done something to induce hibernation back at that lab. I made enough noise down here to wake the dead."

"I told you," said Malia. "He can sleep through anything."

Jaden helped himself to the food.

"So how have you managed to keep this place a secret?" asked Carl. "I had to bribe a friend at the power company to get the electricity turned on at the bunker. But you've got heat, hot water, electricity—"

"And satellite internet and television," added Brian. "But it's *my* satellite, and it's a secure connection, so there's no way to trace it to me. This cabin is one hundred percent self-sufficient. Solar panels generate electricity, and geothermal energy provides heat and hot water. And we're sitting on over fifty acres of land that's owned by a holding company registered under a false identity."

"Where are we, exactly?" asked Malia.

"Northern California," said Brian.

"What about food and supplies?" asked Carl. "You said you haven't stayed here in months. Where'd this come from?" He waved his hand at his breakfast.

"The grocery store, Carl. Surely you have those in Nevada?"

Carl began to sputter a reply, but Sydney said, "When did you have time to go shopping? And didn't anyone recognize you? They've had your face plastered on the news."

"A woman in town works for me—although she doesn't know me by name. I called her yesterday and asked her to clean and stock the place. She's got an expense account she draws from, which is tied only to my holding company." He shrugged. "It's pretty simple."

Jaden thought it sounded far from simple.

"That sounds like a lot of trouble to go to," said Sydney, echoing Jaden's sentiments.

"My work has taught me never to trust the government," Brian replied. "I've maintained several safe houses in various places for years now, should I ever need to go into hiding. Even if one is compromised, the others remain unknown."

"You're more paranoid than I am," Carl muttered. "And that says a lot!"

Jaden chuckled but appreciated the lengths to which Brian had gone. He felt safe here. It didn't seem like Babcock would be able to find them.

"Can they hear us when we talk to each other like this?" he asked Malia. *"Or can we talk to them this way?"*

"I don't think so," she replied.

Jaden focused on Sydney.

"Hey, Sydney. Can you hear me?" She gave no reaction. *"SYDNEY! You're HOT! I love you!"*

Sydney neither said nor did anything in response. But

Malia giggled.

"What's so funny?" asked Sydney.

"So they can't hear us, but you can hear me even if I'm trying to talk to someone else," Jaden observed.

"I guess," said Malia. *"But, are you really in love with Sydney?"*

"Nah. I was just messing with her."

After breakfast, they relocated to the living room and sat around the fire.

"So," said Brian, sitting in an armchair with a great sigh, "what do we do now?"

Nobody replied.

"The situation has certainly changed," he continued. He picked up a remote control from the coffee table and turned on the large television in the corner of the room. Jaden recognized the image of the spacecraft Babcock had shown him—only now it was hovering over a city. He knew it was Miami because of the red laser beam, shooting to the sky in the background.

"Oh my God," said Sydney.

"I told you!" said Carl. "I always told you your Atlantians were extraterrestrials!"

"You were right," Brian agreed. "As much as I didn't want to believe it. And with their arrival, Babcock will want to recover the children more than ever."

"Are they a threat?" asked Sydney. "Do you think they're here to… attack?"

"There's no way of knowing," said Brian.

"What if they came for *us*?" asked Jaden. "Me and Malia?

I'm the one who activated that beam. They probably came to find out who did it, right?"

"That may well be," Brian replied, sitting back in the chair.

"What's our connection to them?" asked Jaden. "Do you think… are Malia and me *aliens*?"

"Not possible," said Carl. "I showed you the extraterrestrials. You look nothing like them."

"You're referring to the bodies recovered in Roswell?" asked Brian, looking pensive.

"Yes," said Carl. "I guess you could call them humanoid, but you can tell just from looking at them that these two aren't the same species. They're as human as you and me."

"That's not entirely true," said Brian, "but I agree Jaden and Malia are *not* extraterrestrials. Other than the extra chromosomes and some random strands of DNA that don't match the normal human genome, their genetic code is very similar to our own. An alien species would certainly exhibit more significant differences. The Atlantians must have engineered your DNA from human cells.

"This extraterrestrial connection is news to me, and as far as I'm aware, Stephen never knew anything about it either. We both believed the Atlantian civilization originated on Earth. But when I saw that beam and realized it was a signal, I knew it had to be some sort of beacon. It proved Carl was right."

As if on cue, the beam on the television suddenly changed. It turned blue and then green before disappearing altogether.

"What happened?" asked Malia. "Why'd it stop?"

"I can only guess that the aliens shut it down," said Brian. "Which would make sense—if you traveled here from another world to answer a beacon, wouldn't you turn it off when you arrived?"

"I guess…" Malia replied.

"Should we go meet these extraterrestrials?" asked Sydney. "If Jaden's right and they came here to see who activated the beam… I don't know. That ship looks pretty ominous if you ask me. But if those are the Atlantians, the people who created Jaden and Malia… What do you guys think?"

Malia shook her head. "I don't care about them. I'm human. They've got nothing to do with me—I just want to find Mom."

"Oh yeah!" said Jaden. "Have you seen her, Uncle Brian? She said she was going to go to your company and try to get you out of jail."

Brian looked from Jaden to Malia, confused. "Forgive me, but what are you talking about? Your parents were killed…"

"No—Mom's alive! That's how Babcock found us!" He realized that he hadn't told the others what he'd learned at Area 51. "Mom was hurt, but she was alive. They took her to the hospital and had to do surgery. But when she was better, *they let her go*! Babcock knew she'd try to find Malia and me. So he told one of the doctors to help her escape. She used his cell phone to call Sydney, and they found us by tracing her phone!"

"That bastard," Sydney murmured. "And now I know why you threw my phone away!"

Brian nodded to himself as he processed this information. "Smart move. Well, my company did manage to free me, but I haven't had any contact with Melissa."

"Malia's right," said Jaden. "I want to find her too. But I want to meet the aliens. They're the only ones who can explain what we are. Why'd they *engineer* us, but leave our genes sitting inside the Great Pyramid for thousands of years? I want to know."

Malia shook her head. "It doesn't matter. I don't care why they made us or any of that. This whole thing has been a nightmare, and I want it to end! Let's find Mom and… I don't know, just get away somewhere. I want my life back."

"No matter what happens with that ship," said Brian, pointing at the television, "the government will pursue the two of you. The best plan might be to disappear."

"How?" asked Malia.

"I own a home, similar to this one, deep inside the Yukon territory in Canada. We could go there. I can make sure we vanish from civilization completely. Nobody would ever find us there."

"And do what?" asked Jaden. "Chill with the polar bears for the rest of our lives? Screw that! I want to go *home*! But first, I want to talk to those aliens and get some answers."

"No matter what else we do," said Sydney, "we've got to find Melissa first. Once we've reunited her with the children, this decision belongs to her."

"Agreed," said Brian. "Let me contact my people. They'll

locate Melissa for us. But this is probably going to take a while."

Jaden and Malia spent much of the afternoon watching the television reports about the alien spacecraft. The video showed dozens of saucer-shaped objects flying to and from the mother ship. According to reporters, these saucers were flying over cities around the globe.

The military was attempting to contact the vessel with no success. And the president held a news conference, urging people to remain calm. The government did not believe the country was under attack—or so they said.

Jaden had a tough time comprehending how much his life had changed in so short a time. Regardless of what his sister said, he desperately wanted to understand the nature of his connection to these visitors.

"Have you two seen yourselves on the news?" asked Brian, coming partway down the stairs a few hours later.

"Nah," said Jaden. "They haven't shown anything but the aliens."

"Hmm," Brian replied, "I guess that makes sense."

"What does?" asked Malia.

"I just read a new report about the two of you on CNN's website. I suppose you're no longer important enough to make television, given our visitors."

"What did it say?" asked Jaden.

"Only that you were finally captured, but managed to escape again," Brian said with a grin. "You've reclaimed your positions at the top of the FBI's Most Wanted list. Babcock is using the same tactics he did before, despite the lack of success. He must figure someone will see you and call the authorities."

Brian returned upstairs. Jaden and Malia put on hooded sweatshirts Sydney had purchased for them back in New Mexico and went outside for a walk. The cabin was surrounded by an evergreen forest. A short distance away, they found a mountain spring.

"Why don't you want to meet these aliens?" Jaden asked, sitting on a rock.

"I just don't," Malia replied.

"But they've got the *answers!*"

"I don't care. Nothing they can say is going to change who I am. And besides, do you think they came here to say *hi* or something? What if they want to take us away with them?"

Jaden hadn't considered this.

"That wouldn't be cool," he said. "I want to go *home*, not to some crazy planet somewhere."

"We can't go home, Jaden. You heard Brian. The government's never going to stop searching for us."

"Yeah… that's true. Maybe we can get him to build a safe house down in New Mexico. I wouldn't mind living near Savannah."

"You're not getting it," Malia told him. "We have to go into *hiding*. We can't interact with anyone. If we do, they'll find us."

"Then maybe we *should* go with the aliens," he said sarcastically. "That'd be more fun."

"I don't care where we go as long as Mom comes with us. I miss her so much…"

They sat quietly for a few minutes, the soft tinkling of the stream the only noise.

"Hey, how were you able to put Babcock down last night? When I was holding him up in the air?"

"Cuz, I'm stronger than you," she replied with a shrug.

"You are not!"

She rolled her eyes. "Believe what you want."

Jaden got to his feet. He focused on a giant boulder on the other side of the brook, causing it to rise twenty feet in the air.

"If you're stronger, put that down," he said, pointing at the rock.

Malia took control of the boulder with a thought, slamming it into the Earth.

"Hey! I wasn't ready," Jaden protested.

"Oh, no? All right, then I'll lift it, and *you* try to put it down," she suggested.

"Fine."

The boulder shot into the air again. Malia held it still among the treetops.

Jaden concentrated but couldn't move the rock. He took a deep breath and tried again. It dropped a few feet, but he couldn't get it any farther.

"Damn!" he shouted. "Let me try again."

Malia released the boulder. Jaden caught it with his mind before it hit the ground. He moved it higher again and said, "Try it."

Jaden focused with every ounce of strength he possessed. He could feel the power of Malia's will pulling the boulder out of his control. But he concentrated even harder.

Suddenly the rock exploded under the pressure, spraying debris into the stream.

"Hah!" Jaden yelled victoriously. He knew it was a draw, but at least she hadn't beaten him. But Malia crumpled to the ground, holding her head in her hands.

"Malia! What's wrong?" he asked, dropping to his knees beside her.

"It hurts…"

"Your head? Because of the boulder breaking?" He wondered if the strain had been too much for her.

"No… it's not that," she said with a whimper.

"Let's go back inside," he suggested, afraid for her. "Come on."

With his help, she regained her feet. They walked back to the cabin, and he helped her to the sofa.

"Hey, someone help—something's wrong with Malia!" Jaden called out. Carl and Sydney came running from the kitchen.

"What is it?" asked Sydney, sitting next to Malia.

"My head…"

Jaden explained what happened with the boulder.

"That's not it," Malia insisted. "I'm seeing a lake… it's too strong… almost like when the volume's too high on your headphones, but I'm *seeing* it…"

"You see a lake?" asked Carl. "I'm not sure I understand."

"I think it's telepathic," said Malia, rubbing her temples. "Someone's trying to tell me something."

"Wait," said Jaden. "If it's telepathic, how come I don't see it too?"

She looked up at him, and suddenly he saw an image of a lake in his mind. But he knew *she* was showing him this.

"Now do you see it?" she asked.

"Yeah, but only because of you. I don't recognize this place."

"What's going on?" asked Brian, coming down the stairs.

Jaden explained the situation to him.

"Malia, can you tell *who* is communicating with you?"

She shook her head. "I'm not sure that's what's happening. This is *way* stronger than when Jaden talks to me."

"Can you describe what you're seeing?" asked Carl.

Malia tried to reply but winced in pain.

"I'll do it," said Jaden. "It's just a big lake… and the water's the deepest blue I've ever seen. There's like steep rocky walls all around the edges… and mountains in the distance."

"We're supposed to go there," said Malia.

"What? Why?" said Jaden.

"I don't know… but we have to go!"

"We don't even know where it is," said Jaden.

"Does it look like a caldera?" asked Brian.

"A what?" said Jaden.

"A basin," he replied. "It's formed when the top of a volcano collapses and fills with water."

"Yeah, that's exactly what it looks like," said Jaden.

"And is there an island?" asked Brian. "Way down at one end of the lake?"

"How'd you know?" Jaden demanded.

"Because I'm familiar with this place. It's called Crater Lake. And it's only an hour or so from here by helicopter."

"Can you take us there?" Malia asked.

"I don't know if that's wise," said Brian. "We have no way of knowing who's communicating with you."

"Wait," said Sydney. "Are you two able to talk to anyone else telepathically or only each other?"

"Only each other," said Jaden, remembering breakfast and feeling embarrassed. "Can you answer them?"

"*I'll try,*" Malia said inside his head. She closed her eyes for a few moments. But then she shook her head. "I can't. It's like trying to scream over the noise of a rock concert."

"Could it be *them*?" asked Sydney. "The aliens?"

"That's entirely possible," said Carl. "The scientists who worked on the Roswell corpses believed their brains were designed for telepathy."

"That spacecraft is hovering over Miami," said Brian. "Crater Lake is in Oregon. Why would they want her to go *there*?"

"They've got saucers going all over the planet," said Jaden. "We saw it on TV. Maybe they sent one here to find us."

Brian considered this for a moment.

"Please," said Malia. "We have to go there."

"Wait a minute," said Sydney. "Earlier, you said you didn't want anything to do with the aliens."

"I didn't," said Malia. "I don't. But I can't resist this. We've got to go to Crater Lake!"

"I don't like this," said Brian. "It could be Babcock trying to lure the two of you out of hiding. They may be able to generate a signal electronically that Malia can sense telepathically."

"I'm not sure they can do that," said Jaden. "At least they didn't do anything like that at Area 51. And they did every damn test you can think of. They made me lift stuff, and they had these rooms that shielded them from telekinesis… But they didn't do any of those other tests on me…" He glanced at his sister.

Malia shook her head. "They didn't communicate with me telepathically. Babcock told me they were using chemicals and electrical impulses to augment my powers."

"And if they *did* have some way to send a telepathic signal," said Sydney, "wouldn't they have used it before we got to Nevada? I know they lost track of us once we left your ranch, but they could have tried this then. Before we had time to get too far away."

"But neither one of us had telepathy before we got to Area 51," Jaden pointed out.

Brian nodded. "Maybe they *did* try this when you left the ranch; only it didn't work."

"Look, I don't know who's sending me this image," said Malia. "But we *have* to go! It's hurting me! If we find them, they can make it *stop*!"

"And if it *is* Babcock," Jaden added, "Me and Malia can take care of him."

Brian looked from Sydney to Carl, as if hoping for allies.

"It's their call as far as I'm concerned," said Sydney. "If they want to go, count me in."

"Sorry, Brian," said Carl. "I'm hoping it's the aliens! Let's do this!"

Outvoted, Brian gave in. Twenty minutes later, they lifted off in the helicopter again. They flew due north. After an hour had passed, the sun setting to their left, they arrived at Crater Lake.

Brian flew over the rim of the caldera, and around the edge of the lake. At the far end, they came to an island. Brian set the helicopter down on the side closest to the rim.

"Welcome to Wizard Island," he told them, shutting off the engine.

They got out of the helicopter. Jaden stared around the lake in awe. It looked like a giant had scooped out the peak of the mountain and filled it with water.

"Now what?" asked Sydney.

"This place is kind of spooky," said Jaden. "I don't like it. Maybe we should go back—I didn't see anything from the helicopter."

"We're here now," said Brian. "We might as well explore the place. But you two should keep your guard up, just in case this is an ambush."

"Yeah, definitely," said Jaden.

Brian led the way. They walked toward the peak at the center of the island. As they reached the tree line, the sun dipped below the rim of the crater, leaving them in eerie twilight.

"*I'm scared,*" Malia said telepathically to Jaden.

"*I know. Me too.*"

They reached the hill and climbed toward the top,

winding their way through the trees. But they emerged at the bald peak to find it empty.

"Nothing here," said Carl, gazing around the island and the lake beyond.

"I don't get it," said Sydney.

"Let's walk down the other side," suggested Brian. "We can circle the perimeter from there. Maybe there's something we can't see from here."

Jaden felt uneasy. He'd expected to see *something*.

They descended the far side of the hill. But as they reached the trees, a woman stepped out from behind one of the thicker trunks. Everyone froze.

"Hello," said Brian.

The woman didn't answer. She looked at each of them in turn, searching their faces. Her skin was deep brown, darker than Jaden's. She wore her long hair tied back in thick braids.

She approached them, holding one hand out in front of her, and said something. But it wasn't English. It sounded vaguely like birdsong. As she drew closer, Jaden realized there were several small objects in her hand. She reached out to Brian.

He took something from her that resembled a Bluetooth headset. The woman pointed to her ear, and Jaden realized she was wearing one herself. Brian put the device in his ear, and she handed one to each of them. They put them on.

The woman addressed Malia, and while Jaden still heard the odd whistling sound, this time, a voice in his earpiece said, "Hello. My name is Nadia. Are you Malia Kwan?"

24

NADIA

Malia was stunned. "Yes, but… I'm sorry, do I know you?"

"No," the woman said with a smile. "But I've come a long way to find you. Was it you who activated the beacon?"

"That was me," Jaden replied, raising his hand awkwardly.

"You're her brother? Jaden?" Nadia said.

"How do you know the children?" Brian asked before he could reply.

"That will take a little explaining," said Nadia. "And I'm not entirely sure myself. Will you come with me? I hope to provide us both with some answers."

"Go with you *where*?" Sydney demanded. "Brian, who is this woman? If she's with Babcock, we should get out of here…"

Brian held up his hand to quell her. "Nadia, we came here because Malia was having visions. Are you responsible for her seeing this place?"

"Yes," she replied. "That beacon drew us to this planet. I had reason to believe Malia was responsible for activating it, and that is why we summoned her here."

"So… you're not from Earth?" Brian asked skeptically.

"No. My people come from another world, which we call Othal. You know our star as Tabit."

"That's the bright star in Orion's shield," Carl said, regarding her with keen interest. "It's twenty-six light-years from here!"

"That is correct," she said. "Nobody from this planet should have been able to access the control systems on our power station. We're very curious to understand how this happened."

"I just touched it; I swear I didn't mean to fire that laser!" Jaden told her. "Ask Brian—other people touched it, and nothing like this ever happened before!"

Nadia smiled at him. "I believe you. But if you'll come with me, perhaps we can solve this mystery."

"I don't like it," Sydney said to Brian. "This could be a trap."

"Can you make these visions stop?" Malia asked Nadia. "They're hurting me."

"I'm sorry," said Nadia. "We weren't sure how strong the signal would need to be for you to sense it. Please wait." She pulled a device out of her pocket—it looked similar to a cell phone—and held it to her head. "She's here. Cut the transmission."

Almost immediately, Malia sighed with relief. "Thank you."

"I want to go with her," said Jaden. "If she is who she claims to be, maybe we can finally figure out what the hell is going on."

"I agree," said Malia. "We're here now; we might as well."

Brian considered this for a moment. "All right. Lead the way."

Nadia moved into the trees. Malia followed her with Sydney close behind. Jaden went next, but Brian held him back.

"Be ready to act," he told him. "I'm not sure if I trust this woman."

"I'm on it," Jaden assured him.

"The aliens *I've* seen certainly weren't so human-looking," said Carl.

The three of them ran to catch up with the others. The group soon emerged from the trees and walked a short distance along the beach.

"Here we are," said Nadia.

"What are you talking about?" asked Jaden. "There's nothing here."

But at that moment, a portal opened out of nowhere. It was as if someone had cut a hole in the air, that started as a crescent of light but expanded to an oval large enough to admit a person. Inside was a space as wide as a minivan.

"What is this?" asked Carl. "Some sort of extra-dimensional gateway?"

"No, nothing like that," said Nadia. "Shields render our ship invisible by redirecting all frequencies of electromagnetic radiation."

She knocked on the space next to the portal, and the air seemed to shimmer and take on shape for a moment as if there were a wall there. Jaden reached out to touch the air on the other side of the opening, and his hand met cold metal.

"This is cool," he said.

"Come with me," said Nadia, stepping inside.

Jaden followed her immediately. The space was long and cylindrical; there were three rows of seats directly behind a cockpit. A man there turned to wave his hand in greeting.

"Hi," Jaden said, waving back.

Nadia walked to an open space in the back of the craft, behind the seats. Jaden and the others joined her. The area was barely big enough for the six of them.

"This is some sort of shuttle?" asked Carl.

"Yes, exactly," Nadia confirmed.

She removed a strip of black material from an enclosure in the wall. Nadia moved to place it against Malia's forehead, saying, "I'll need to take some measurements."

The strip reminded Jaden of the electrodes they'd attached to her at Area 51.

"What are you doing?" he demanded, pulling Nadia's arm away from Malia. "What is that thing?"

"I'm not going to harm her," Nadia told him. "This device

will measure her brainwaves. It won't affect her in any way. I promise."

Jaden released her arm. Nadia placed the strip against Malia's forehead, and to Jaden's surprise, it stayed there by itself. She pulled the communication device out of her pocket again. Characters appeared on its surface, very similar to the ones Jaden had seen on the pyramid back in Miami.

"What does it say?" It was the man from the cockpit. He was standing behind Brian now. Jaden noticed that he'd closed the hatch, and felt a wave of anxiety. How would they get out if this *was* a trap?

"It's her," said Nadia. "I was right."

"But that's impossible," the man said. "We were over ten light-years away. The signal couldn't have traveled that far in real-time."

"Her brainwaves are interacting with this planet's magnetic field—Madu, it's delta-shifting them."

"Then why couldn't we detect the signal with the ship's sensors?" he asked. Jaden guessed Madu was his name.

"It's only intermittent. Her normal physiological state doesn't project sufficient energy. Heightened emotional reactions must have initiated the visions I saw."

"What are you talking about?" Malia asked, removing the material from her head.

"You're telepathic," Nadia said to her. *"You can hear my thoughts in your mind,"* she added without speaking.

Malia gasped. It was clear she was the only one besides Jaden who'd perceived the thought.

"So are you!" said Jaden. "*Can you hear me like this*?" he asked telepathically.

"*I can hear you*," she replied. "My people are not normally telepathic, but I've been able to sense thoughts and feelings from Malia for many days. We were very far from here when it occurred the first time."

"Your colleague said you were over ten light-years away," said Carl. "And that means it should have taken ten years for any sort of signal to reach you."

"Ah, this is where extra-dimensional technology comes into play," Nadia replied. "It's called delta-shifting. We live in three spatial dimensions. But there are many more that are usually curled up and inaccessible. We can move energy and matter through these extra dimensions."

"Fascinating," Carl observed. "So effectively, you're shortening distances in the normal three dimensions, rather than traveling faster than light."

"Precisely," said Nadia.

"But how can Malia be doing that?" asked Brian. "You may possess such technology, but we certainly don't."

"I needed to measure her brainwaves to confirm this," said Nadia, "but my suspicions were correct. Her brain emits a signal at a frequency that resonates with the planet's magnetic field. Once her brainwaves cross a minimum power threshold, they interact with the field and become delta-shifted.

"I had been having visions that I believed were telepathic. For example, I saw the beacon's initial activation through Malia's eyes. We didn't detect the signal for a few days, but when we did, I recognized the beam from my visions. We came here very soon after that. And once we arrived, our ship's sensors were able to detect Malia's brainwaves—nobody else on this planet emits that kind of signal. But we couldn't localize them more precisely than a few hundred kilometers.

"We decided to select a geographically unique location and send a vision of it to you. The only way to do it was with our ship's transmitters. We can reproduce a signal at a frequency you can perceive telepathically, but it was impossible to know the right amplitude. I apologize if we hurt you."

"But I'm telepathic too," said Jaden. "Why didn't I see the vision?"

"The signal we sent was tuned to match Malia's exact brainwave pattern," Nadia explained. "But that doesn't explain why I saw only her thoughts and not yours when we were still far away from here. It's possible your brainwaves aren't in the frequency range necessary for resonance with the magnetic field. Or perhaps they're simply not powerful enough."

"He's not as strong as me," said Malia. "You can probably hear him telepathically now because you're closer."

"You are *not* stronger than me!" Jaden protested. "Give me that thing!" He took the strip of black material from Malia and put it on his forehead. It tingled. "Do it. Measure me."

Nadia made a sound that might have been laughter. "If you insist." She gazed at her device again. "Your sister's right. Although your brainwaves are in the correct frequency range to be delta-shifted, Malia's are roughly eight times stronger. Yours don't emit enough energy to resonate with the magnetic field."

"Whatever," said Jaden, removing the strip from his head and handing it to Nadia. "I can still beat her in telekinesis."

Malia rolled her eyes at him.

"Jaden, when you activated the beacon, what exactly did you do?" asked Nadia.

"Nothing, really," he said. "I just touched it, and all these strange characters showed up."

"Did you touch any of those?" she asked.

"No," he replied. "There was this voice, and then the laser started. We ran away after that."

"Strange," said Nadia. "I don't understand why the beacon would have activated like that. There are still many questions… With your permission, I'd like to take you to our ship. Our commander wants to meet you. Perhaps together, we can find the answers."

"Let's do it," said Jaden.

"I agree," said Carl. "This is the opportunity of a lifetime."

"And you'll let us go when we're done?" asked Sydney.

"Of course," said Nadia. "You're free to go now if you wish. We will not take you against your will."

"I want to go, too," said Malia.

"In for a penny, in for a pound, it seems," Brian commented.

"I don't understand," said Nadia. "The translator doesn't always recognize idioms."

"Never mind," he said. "We'll go with you."

"Terrific. If you'll all take a seat, we can depart immediately."

Nadia and Madu sat down in the cockpit. Jaden took a chair in the front row, affording him the best view. There were windows both at the top and bottom of the cockpit, allowing him to see the sky as well as the ground. Seconds later, they began their ascent. Rising above the rim of the caldera, Jaden saw that the sun was only now setting below the horizon.

The craft was remarkably quiet. Jaden heard nothing more than a low humming sound coming from somewhere underneath them. Soon they surged forward, pressing him back into his seat. They climbed higher and higher, and within minutes rose above the clouds.

But they didn't stop their ascent. Before long, they were high enough to see the curvature of the Earth below.

"Aren't we going to Miami?" asked Malia.

"No," said Nadia. "Our ship is in geosynchronous orbit above the lake where we met you."

"You have more than one ship here?" asked Carl.

"The craft above Miami is not ours," she said.

"Whose is it?" asked Brian.

"This is a long story," said Nadia. "I promise I will explain everything when we meet with Commander Anhur."

Jaden didn't understand how that ship wasn't theirs. He felt more confused than ever.

A few minutes later, the sky above turned black. They had moved beyond the atmosphere into outer space. Looking down, Jaden could hardly believe his eyes. The Earth grew smaller and smaller, and he could see the entire west coast of North America. Still, they kept going.

By the time Nadia said, "We're here," they had traveled far enough that the whole planet appeared to fit within the frame of the window.

"I don't see anything," said Jaden.

"And neither does anyone else," said Nadia. "Your people don't know we're here—the shielding hides our ship from their telescopes. But watch this."

She pressed a button on the console. Suddenly, the outline of a massive object appeared in blue light directly in front of them. It looked like the hull of a giant ocean-going vessel, with great wings sweeping out to each side— nothing like the saucer-shaped object hovering over Miami.

"The shields respond to an encrypted signal allowing our viewscreen to display our own ships," Nadia told them. "This isn't visible to anyone else."

As they drifted closer, Jaden spotted a rectangular area outlined in green. They headed directly toward it.

"That's the docking port," said Nadia. "There's an opening in the physical structure of the hull, protected and shielded by an energy field."

Once they'd passed inside, Jaden could see several objects docked at regular intervals inside a cavernous space. They reminded him of thick cigars, and from the shape of their cockpit windows, he guessed the shuttle in which they were traveling looked just like these.

Madu steered them toward an empty berth. With a dull,

clanking sound, they came to rest. Jaden heard the sound of rushing air, then the hatch opened.

"Follow me," said Nadia, exiting the shuttle.

She led the way through a short corridor with a heavy metal door at the end. It swung open of its own accord when she approached it and closed again behind them once they'd passed through it.

They walked down a long, dimly lit passage. The metal walls and floor reminded Jaden of a battleship he'd once visited with his dad. People they passed looked upon them with polite interest.

Finally, Nadia stopped at one of the many doors on the right side of the corridor. She opened it and ushered them inside. It was a conference room, with a long table and chairs in the middle. Large observation windows looked out on the Earth; the view was breathtaking.

"Have a seat," said Nadia. "Commander Anhur is on his way."

Jaden and Malia went straight to the windows. It seemed incomprehensible to Jaden that they could be in space. He'd never imagined leaving the planet.

"Tell me, how do these translators work?" asked Carl.

"We've monitored your planet's communications since our arrival," said Nadia. "Our computers learned all of your languages, and we used that information to program the headsets."

Carl nodded in appreciation.

A minute later, the door opened again, and a stout, severe-looking man walked in.

"Commander," said Nadia. "These are the children, Jaden and Malia. And this is Brian, Carl, and Sydney."

He shook hands with each of them in turn.

"We never told you our names," Sydney observed.

"I know," said Nadia, looking slightly embarrassed. "Since we entered orbit, I've been able to hear many of Malia's thoughts. You're all familiar to me."

Commander Anhur sat down at the head of the table, Nadia next to him. Jaden and Malia took the chairs farthest from him, next to Sydney.

"Can you tell us more about your people?" asked Brian. "You say you come from a planet many light-years away, and yet you look surprisingly human."

"There's a good reason for that," said Nadia. "I'd better start at the beginning. Our civilization evolved much like yours. We grew from an agrarian society into an industrial one. Advances in technology allowed us to improve communication, travel, and medicine. We ventured into space, exploring our solar system with unmanned probes. Eventually, we traveled to the other planets in our system ourselves.

"But we failed to find life anywhere else. Our scientists believed it must exist elsewhere in the universe. And one day, a group of them decided to go out and find it. They intended to find a planet that supported primitive life and colonize it. They constructed a vessel that could transport them and sustain them for an interstellar journey. This was before we developed the ability to delta-shift matter—our ships could travel at only ten percent of the speed of light. Their vessel needed to be a self-sufficient ecosystem to spend years in space. They needed to grow food, and recycle one hundred percent of their water. The ship took nearly twenty years to build.

"Eighteen men and women set out more than forty thousand years ago. We had discovered thousands of other planetary systems by then, but couldn't tell if any of them hosted life. The colonists picked a trajectory that would take them close to several stars that were prime candidates for habitable planets.

"We possessed the technology to delta-shift radio signals by that time, so the colonists were able to stay in touch with our homeworld. And after journeying for over three hundred years, and discovering only barren, desolate worlds, they finally found a habitable one. This one, in fact—your world."

"They found Earth?" asked Malia.

"But surely it wouldn't have been the original colonists," said Carl. "These people must have birthed children and raised families for generations with a journey that long…"

"Not so," said Nadia. "By modifying our gene code, we learned how to eliminate aging centuries before the colonists left our planet. Our people are still vulnerable to some diseases, and injuries, of course, but those of us who opted for the gene therapy do not get old. The colonists who arrived here were the very same ones who departed from our homeworld.

"I can still remember when they left. I was only a little girl at the time. The interstellar ship was built in space, but they launched from our planet atop great rockets to dock with it."

"Wait," said Jaden. "How old are you? Didn't you say they left your planet forty thousand years ago?"

"That's correct," said Nadia. "I'm that old."

"If you've eliminated aging, do you still bear children?" asked Brian. "I would think this would lead to unsustainable population growth."

"That's a complicated question," she said. "Some segments of our society refused the cure for aging based on religious beliefs. Those communities continued to live a normal lifespan and bear children at the usual rate. You'd be surprised how many others made similar choices as the centuries went by. And of course, disease and injuries still took their toll on those who did cease aging.

"But you are correct. We took measures to reduce the birthrate to counteract the lower mortality rate."

"Tell me about your colonists," said Carl, giddy with excitement. "Did they found Atlantis?"

"Yes," said Nadia. "They arrived here to find a lush, green world. And to everyone's surprise, it was teeming with complex animal life as well. The colonists established themselves on an island in the middle of your Atlantic Ocean. They landed the interstellar ship and recycled it, scavenging its parts to build their community as well as the power stations.

"As they explored their new world, they discovered primitive humans in many pockets around the globe. The species was remarkably similar to our own but had not yet developed higher cognitive functions. Our colonists intervened."

"What does that mean?" asked Sydney. "What did they do?"

"They made small genetic modifications to select groups. This changed the species' appearance, making them less apelike—and more like us. It also altered the prefrontal cortex of the human brain in subsequent generations."

"You *did* cause the great leap forward!" said Carl. "I was right!"

Nadia smiled at him. "Yes, we did. After those initial modifications, the colonists stayed out of the way and let your species continue to develop. It wasn't long before the first civilizations began to form. Our people interacted with yours, teaching them mathematics and astronomy. For the most part, these cultures believed the colonists were simply part of a different, more advanced civilization. But the Egyptian religious leaders began to suspect they were something different. They guessed correctly that the Atlantians came from a different world."

Malia gasped. "That's why they built the pyramids that way!"

"What are you talking about?" asked Jaden.

"The layout of the pyramid complex—remember? It matches the stars of Orion's belt. They did it that way because they knew that's where the Atlantians came from!"

"That's correct, Malia," said Nadia. "They built their monuments to honor our people."

"But you come from Tabit," said Carl. "The stars of Orion's belt only appear close to Tabit from our perspective as part of the constellation. In reality, they're nowhere near each other."

"That's true," said Brian. "But the Sun Temple sat where Tabit would be on the map of Giza."

"What's the Sun Temple?" asked Jaden.

"It was the most glorious temple in the ancient world," said Brian, "although it vanished thousands of years ago. We know of its existence only from carvings on other monuments. The Egyptians built it entirely of crystal and gemstones. They dedicated it to the Sun God, Ra. But in reality, they were referring to *your* sun, not ours."

"Yes, precisely," said Nadia.

"What happened to the colony?" asked Malia. "We know Atlantis was destroyed, but how?"

"Unfortunately, not all of the ancient civilizations were as peaceful as Egypt. Athens grew very warlike. They came to envy the technology of the Atlantians, ultimately launching their ships to attack our colony. Our people were overwhelmed—eighteen colonists were ill-equipped to repel thousands of Athenian warriors. So rather than allow the Athenians to acquire our technology, they destroyed the colony, sinking the island into the sea.

"Nearly all of them were killed in the battle. Only two survived. They managed to flee to Egypt and from there to one of the power stations. Using the transmitter there, they told us about the disaster. They integrated themselves into Egyptian society and were never heard from again."

"You never sent anyone to rescue them?" asked Brian.

"No. At the time, we still lacked the technology to delta-shift matter—that breakthrough did not take place until roughly two hundred years ago. A rescue would have required constructing another interstellar ship. It would have taken decades to build and centuries to travel to Earth. We lacked sufficient political will for such an undertaking. Furthermore, the colonists did not ask to be rescued. They desired to remain on Earth.

"Given the outcome, most on our world felt it was wrong to interact or interfere with alien cultures. To do so safely would require us to exert our military might against an aggressive assault like that of the Athenians. We decided never to return to Earth. And for centuries, we did not attempt to visit any other world.

"With the advent of delta-shifting, however, we traveled to some other planets. Such expeditions were costly—the fuel we use for delta-shifting requires a lengthy and complicated refining process. In the end, we abandoned our search for habitable planets until we could improve our ground-based detection techniques. In hindsight, that may have been a mistake."

"But you decided to come to Earth when you detected the beacon," Carl observed.

"We were already on a mission to find Earth," said Nadia. "But, its exact location was lost."

"I'm confused," said Brian. "I thought you said your people decided never to return? And how was the location not known?"

"Our homeworld was destroyed eighteen years ago," said Nadia. "This ship carries the only survivors from our planet.

We have been trying to find Earth ever since. The coordinates were, of course, recorded on our planet's computer networks. But the data centers were demolished; the information was not stored on our ship's computers. With limited fuel, we couldn't afford to make more than a few delta-shifts. So we used one to get to the general vicinity of your planet, and we've been traveling under hydrogen power since then. We used the last of our fuel to get here when we detected the beacon."

"Why weren't Earth's coordinates stored on your local computers?" asked Brian. "As a vessel of exploration, you must need navigational charts."

"This is a warship," said Commander Anhur, speaking for the first time. Jaden thought his voice sounded gravelly. "We've taken significant measures to make her self-sufficient. But she wasn't designed for interstellar missions."

"A warship?" asked Sydney. "Wait a minute—how exactly was your world destroyed?"

"We were attacked," said Anhur. "By that ship that's currently inside your atmosphere."

"Wait," said Jaden. "Hold on—you mean those aliens who are sitting over Miami destroyed your planet?!"

"Yes," Nadia confirmed. "In our explorations with the first delta-shifting vessels, we discovered a planet they'd destroyed. We were able to recover data storage devices that contained records of the attack. The culture had not been sufficiently advanced to understand the aliens' technology. But the data included video, giving us some idea of how their weapons worked. That's why we built a fleet of warships in the first place. But when they came to our world, they decimated us. Our weapons were no match for theirs.

"We accessed their computer network during the attack in an attempt to disable their ship. The information we found there taught us much about their species. They call themselves the Malor. They are telepathic humanoids, physically smaller than our species, with larger skulls and big eyes. Their life spans are shorter—typically around thirty years. They function as a hive, with each individual having access to the group mind.

"Their homeworld is somewhere on the far side of the galaxy. They expended all of their natural resources, so their entire civilization now travels onboard that ship in search of more habitable planets. Once they find a suitable world, they stay there until they've depleted *its* resources as well. They always have scout ships combing nearby star systems evaluating the suitability of candidate planets for their needs. Typically they select worlds with abundant resources and intelligent species that have reached industrialization. They've journeyed in something approximating a straight line ever since leaving their homeworld, meandering from one industrialized planet to the next."

"Why target planets with civilizations?" asked Brian.

"They use existing infrastructure to process the natural resources," said the commander. "It's easier to implement tools and machines that are already there. Consuming the resources of an entire planet is no small job."

"Scout ships," said Carl. "That explains the Roswell crash. And that's why those aliens don't look like you."

"You think the Malor have been here before?" asked Nadia.

"I'm certain of it," said Carl. "A saucer crashed several decades ago. Others came later. The craft were identical to the ones emerging from that ship in Miami. Bodies were recovered that fit your description of the Malor."

"But what about those cave paintings?" asked Malia. "You said there were paintings in France from 40,000 years ago that depicted beings similar to the ones from Roswell."

"That makes sense," said Commander Anhur. "Their scout ships probably monitor candidate planets for the emergence of industrialization. They knew about this world already, and when they detected the beacon, they came to investigate. Now that they're here, your world is in trouble."

"Then what are we doing sitting here?" demanded Sydney. "We have to do something!"

"We are," Nadia assured her. "We recovered one of their saucers after the attack on our world. It allowed us to study their technology. We have a better understanding of their computer security than we did then. Our people are attempting to access their control systems as we speak. The computers on the mother ship are much more sophisticated, but we are making progress. We must be careful, however, not to give away our presence. So far, they don't know we're here."

"You can't fight them?" asked Carl.

"They wiped out our entire fleet," said Anhur. "One ship doesn't stand a chance. Their technology is superior to ours."

"But tell us your story," said Nadia. "Jaden and Malia are

the only two people on this world who possess telepathy and telekinesis. How did this come to be?"

"Their father was a doctor," said Brian. "He worked on a project that mapped the human genome. A DNA sample was discovered in a hidden chamber inside the Great Pyramid in Egypt. The room was encased in a material that deflected radar signals, allowing it to remain hidden for millennia. Through his research, Stephen deduced that the samples would produce genetically altered humans—twins, a boy, and a girl, with extra chromosomes that would give them unique powers. His team produced two human eggs that were brought to term by a surrogate mother. Stephen and his wife, Melissa, raised Jaden and Malia as their own.

"The genetic samples must have been engineered by the Atlantians. I do not believe the ancient Egyptians possessed the technology for such an endeavor. And I'm guessing the children's DNA is what allowed Jaden to activate the pyramid. This would seem to indicate that they share some elements of your species' genetic code."

"We were hoping *you* could explain… what we are," added Malia.

"I'm afraid I don't have any knowledge of this," said Nadia. "Our people made only minor modifications to the human genome when they first arrived, causing your species to awaken. But I am not aware of any genetic engineering projects."

"I've never heard of anything like this either," said Anhur. "Our people have never exhibited telepathy or telekinesis. The Malor are telepathic, but we didn't become aware of their existence until very recent times. We'd never encountered any other species with those powers. I don't understand how our colonists could have engineered those traits in the two of you."

"Hang on," said Jaden. "Nadia can hear our thoughts. So she's gotta be telepathic... right?"

"No," said Nadia. "I can communicate with the two of you that way, but nobody else."

"What about you?" Jaden asked the commander in his thoughts. "Can you hear me in your mind?"

"Yes," Anhur said out loud, looking startled. "I'm not sure I understand this..."

"Have you been able to communicate telepathically with other humans?" asked Nadia.

"No," said Malia. "But, we did try."

"Interesting," Nadia replied, sounding puzzled. "If I were to venture a guess... I'd predict that the colonists must have designed your thought patterns to be compatible with the Othali. But I still don't understand how they were able to engineer traits they'd never encountered..."

"Well, the proof is sitting right in front of you," said Carl, waving his hand at Jaden and Malia. "Someone did it— they're certainly not a product of natural selection!"

"I agree," said Nadia. "And there were two geneticists on that expedition. So it's certainly possible. It's just a little disturbing that they wouldn't have reported such an undertaking."

"Then... if *you* don't know anything about why they

created Malia and me," said Jaden, "how are we ever going to find out?"

"I'm sorry," said Nadia. "That knowledge may be lost forever. We've been unable to gain full access to the power stations remotely. But if we can defeat the Malor, I'll take you to one of them. The colonists' records should be stored there, and perhaps they will contain the answers we seek."

"It's worth investigating," said Anhur. "But don't expect too much. If they didn't report to the homeworld about this project, it's possible they didn't put it in their own files either."

At that moment, there was a buzzing noise. A voice filled the room.

"Commander Anhur, something's happening. The power output of the Malor ship just increased by a power of ten. You'd better get up here."

"I'll be right there," said the commander, getting to his feet. "Care to join me?" he asked the others.

25

RESCUE

They followed Anhur and Nadia down the corridor and up three flights of stairs. At the end of a short hallway, they came to a room that reminded Jaden of pictures he'd seen of NASA's mission control center. Computers lined the back wall, and a lone leather chair sat in the middle. In front of that were several rows of control consoles, with large monitors mounted on the front wall.

"Welcome to the bridge," said Nadia.

Anhur sat in his chair. "Activate the viewscreen, Lieutenant," he said. "Let's see what you've got."

The central monitor displayed an image of Florida. An enormous spiral storm system churned off the eastern coast.

"Zoom in on the Malor ship," said Anhur.

The image changed; Jaden recognized the giant saucer hovering over Miami. Wind and rain lashed the city. Lightning played along the surface of the ship, bolts sometimes shooting to the ground.

"Have we penetrated their network security?" asked Anhur.

"No, sir. The systems have several additional layers of protection beyond what we encountered on the scout ship. We've found a potential entry point, but can't exploit it without their detection."

"Time to discharge?"

"Thirty seconds."

"What does that mean?" asked Carl. "Time to discharge *what*?"

"They're preparing to fire their primary weapon on the city," said Nadia.

"You can stop them if you gain control of the computer system?" asked Brian.

"Yes," said Nadia. "But they'll destroy us if they detect our presence. We can't risk it."

"Then what happens to Miami?" asked Sydney.

"It will be eliminated," said Nadia.

"There are millions of people down there," said Brian. "You've got to stop them! If you can penetrate their security, do it!"

"It's one city," said Anhur. "If we expose ourselves now, they'll destroy us and continue taking over your world."

"Commander, they're opening fire," said the lieutenant.

As Jaden watched on the monitor, a thick red beam extended from the center of the saucer, hitting the middle of the city. Liquid fire poured down the beam, incinerating buildings when it reached the ground. A wave of destruction moved across Miami, radiating outward from the center.

"You have to stop them!" Sydney screamed.

"There's nothing we can do," said Nadia, placing a hand on her shoulder. "I'm sorry."

Sydney fell to her knees, holding her head in both hands. Malia turned away from the monitor, pulling Jaden into a hug and crying quietly. He couldn't bear to watch anymore either and looked away from the horror on the screen.

"Sir, our power station is activating weapon systems," said the lieutenant.

"What? How?" demanded Anhur. "I thought you told me we couldn't gain control?"

"We can't—this isn't my doing. The Malor locked us out when they shut down the beacon."

"What do they need with the station's weapons?" asked Anhur.

"It's not them, either," said the lieutenant. "Commander, the station is targeting the Malor ship!"

At that moment, a blue laser beam shot from the ocean, hitting the underside of the Malor ship. Pulses of energy moved along the beam, slamming into the vessel. The liquid fire falling from the ship faltered and died. But it was too late: the entire city lay in smoldering ruins.

Suddenly a ball of fire launched from the saucer, striking the source of the power station's laser. The blue beam disappeared.

"The power station is offline," said the lieutenant. "The Malor are heading north."

Sure enough, Jaden could see the enormous ship moving away from the city.

"Sir, a small watercraft is departing from an island next to the power station."

"Show me," said Anhur.

The image on the viewscreen changed. It showed the island Jaden remembered visiting when they went to the pyramid. A boat was headed away from the pier. It looked like the same one Brian had used to take them to the island. But it was in trouble. Rough seas were tossing the vessel about. It was hard to tell for sure, but Jaden thought the sea almost looked like it was boiling.

"The boat is sinking, sir."

"Lieutenant, I'm going to venture a guess that whoever is piloting that boat is responsible for activating the power station," said Anhur.

"You think it's one of the colonists?" asked Nadia. "Could they still be alive after all this time?"

"I don't see who else could have fired that weapon," said Anhur. "But there's only one way to find out. Lieutenant, alert shuttle command. I want a rescue team down there immediately."

"That's going to be difficult in the middle of a hurricane," said Brian.

"I agree, Commander," said the lieutenant. "Local winds are more than one hundred miles per hour. It's going to be almost impossible to maneuver a shuttle close enough for a rescue."

"Take us with you," suggested Malia. "We can help."

Anhur turned to gaze at Jaden and Malia.

"It's not a bad idea," said Nadia. "Their telekinesis may be the only way."

Anhur nodded. "Do it."

"I'm coming with them," said Sydney, standing next to Jaden and Malia protectively.

"You're all welcome to join us, but we must hurry," said Nadia.

"Commander Anhur," said Brian, "I'd like to stay behind. With your permission, I think I may be able to help your people hack into the Malor computers. I have some expertise in this area."

"You're welcome to try," said Anhur. "We need all the help we can get."

Nadia led them off the bridge. She escorted Brian to a computer lab on the same level before returning to the docking bay with the others. They boarded a shuttle that looked identical to the one they'd used earlier. Madu was their pilot.

Everyone took their seats, Madu and a co-pilot in the cockpit, and they detached from the berth. A minute later, they left the ship and headed toward Earth. But as they got closer, Jaden noticed that they were moving around the planet, away from North America.

"Why aren't we going to Miami?" asked Malia.

"The Malor would detect our entry over North America," said Madu. "Our shields cannot mask the heat and friction of a high-speed descent through the atmosphere. Don't worry; I'll get us there as fast as I can."

Sure enough, once they hit the atmosphere, flames engulfed the shuttle, blocking Jaden's view out the windows. When they reached the surface, he could see they were speeding over the open ocean. Soon daylight gave way to night, and they reached land. Still, they pressed ahead, flying unimaginably fast, the lights of cities and towns rushing by below.

As they slowed down, Jaden spotted the charred, burning remains of Miami in the distance. They flew beyond the dead city and descended toward Brian's island.

Madu turned on a floodlight, and Jaden gasped. The boat was directly below them, mostly underwater, only the bow poking out above the surface. A woman in an orange life vest was perched there, her hair whipping around in the fierce winds. The wreck bobbed up and down in the boiling sea, periodically disappearing from view entirely as giant waves threatened to swallow the vessel whole. Jaden was amazed that the woman wasn't washed away. The shuttle rocked and swayed in the wind as they drew closer to the boat.

"We can't get any closer," said Madu, emerging from the cockpit. The copilot had taken the controls. "We're locked in a hover, but the winds are buffeting us pretty severely." He moved to the rear of the shuttle, pulling a harness from a compartment in the wall. "I'm going to open the hatch—hold on tight. I'll go down and try to grab her."

"It's too dangerous," said Malia. "Let me and Jaden bring her up!"

"We're moving around too much," said Madu. "And those winds are extreme. Your control may not be precise enough—she could get hurt if she crashes into the side of the shuttle. Let me try this first. I was trained in water rescue back on Othal."

Jaden recalled the way Malia had been able to yank the boulder out of his mental grasp back at Brian's cabin. He suspected Madu was probably right—the winds here were likely strong enough to do the same thing. As they watched, the man secured the harness around himself. There was a winch system above the door. He attached the rope to his harness.

"Nadia, I've got the winch set to scroll freely. I'll wave to you once I've got her. Bring us up slowly."

She nodded, and Madu popped the hatch. Immediately the roar of the storm filled the cabin. Sydney and Carl stayed in their seats, looking out the hatch apprehensively. Heavy raindrops pelted Jaden in the face, forcing him to squint. Once the hatch had opened completely, Madu jumped into the water.

Jaden watched as he swam toward the boat. This took longer than usual with the crashing waves. When he finally reached the vessel, the woman slipped into the water. Madu grabbed her, and she held on to him. Madu waved his arms.

Nadia punched a button on the winch. The rope went taut and slowly lifted Madu and his charge out of the ocean. But seconds later, a wave washed over them. As the water fell, Jaden saw that Madu had lost the woman. She was adrift in the sea.

Madu held up both fists, pointing thumbs down. Nadia hit another button on the winch, and Madu fell back into the water. He grabbed the woman again, and they tried once more to lift her to safety. But another wave ripped her away from Madu. This time he waved his arms.

Nadia brought him back to the shuttle. With her help, he scrambled back on board.

"It's no use!" he shouted over the storm. "I'll have to go back with another harness."

"The water's too rough," said Nadia. "She'll never get it on."

"Let me try," said Jaden.

Madu regarded him skeptically for a moment before saying, "Go ahead. But be careful. Bring her up slowly."

Jaden stared down at the woman bobbing on the water's surface. He knew he was strong enough to pull her up, but Madu was right. With the waves tossing her around and the wind moving the shuttle, control was going to be difficult.

Slowly, he lifted her out of the sea. But a wave caught her once again, removing her from Jaden's grasp.

"Damn!" he shouted.

"Let me," said Malia. She focused, and moments later, the woman rose above the water. A wave crashed into her, but Malia kept hold. She brought her up almost to the level of the shuttle.

"Help me, Jaden!" she screamed. "I've got her, but I can't keep her still!"

Jaden reached out with his mind. As Malia drew the woman closer, he steadied her. Slowly they brought her to the hatch. Madu and Nadia grabbed her, pulling her inside. Madu hit a button and closed the hatch.

The woman lay on the floor on her hands and knees, coughing up water. Finally, she moved into a sitting position, looking up at them thankfully.

Jaden couldn't believe his eyes: this woman was his mother, Melissa Kwan.

But before he or Malia could say anything, Nadia gasped. "I know you! You're Tessa Gosher! You're one of the colonists!"

Sydney stared at her with her mouth wide open; Carl looked confused. Jaden looked back and forth from Nadia to his mother.

"Mom, what is she talking about?" asked Malia. Jaden could feel her shock in his mind.

"It's true," said Melissa. "I'm from the planet Othal. I came to this world more than 40,000 years ago."

"Nadia, we've got a problem," Madu yelled from the cockpit. "Engines are nonresponsive. I can't get us out of here!"

"We're going down!" said the copilot.

"It's the pyramid!" said Malia. "This is what Brian told us about—we're in the Bermuda Triangle!"

"And the station is locked at full power," said Melissa. "The alien weapon fried the control circuits. She's right. The magnetic field is probably overloading the engines. We'd be fine if we could move—the field strength reduces dramatically outside the triangle."

The storm jarred the shuttle, knocking the passengers into the walls. Jaden looked out the cockpit window and saw the waves growing closer.

He tried to use his telepathy to move the shuttle farther from the island, but nothing happened. Unable to see the craft from the outside, he found himself incapable of affecting it telekinetically. He tried to imagine what it looked like—he'd seen the others in the docking bay—and force his mental image to drift away from the island. It was futile.

Without warning, Malia punched the button to open the hatch. She jumped through the opening, plummeting to the ocean below.

"Malia—no!" Jaden shouted over the storm.

"Make the shuttle visible," Malia told him telepathically. He felt her fear as he watched her desperately tread water, trying to stay afloat.

"Turn off the shields!" Jaden yelled. "Malia has to be able to see the shuttle to move it!"

"But the Malor will see us!" said Nadia.

"I doubt it," said Madu. "They're moving on toward their next target. It's unlikely they're looking this way." He worked the controls on his console. "That should do it," he yelled. "Shields are inactive."

Suddenly they shot dozens of feet higher into the air, rising well above the waves, and moved away from the island.

"That's it!" yelled the copilot. "I've got control!"

"Come back," Jaden told his sister in his mind. *"You did it!"*

Malia rose out of the water, but a wave overcame her, and she disappeared.

"MALIA!" Jaden shouted. *"Malia!"* he called out mentally. There was no reply. He searched the water frantically, looking for any sign of her. But suddenly, she shot out of the ocean, quickly ascending to the shuttle. Jaden reached out with his mind and helped guide her to the hatch. They pulled her in, and Nadia closed the door again.

Melissa gathered Malia in her arms, holding her tight, still sitting on the floor.

"Thank you, Malia," said Madu. "We're safe now. The shields are active, and we're heading back to the ship."

Malia smiled. Melissa pulled Jaden into a hug too, sobbing quietly.

"Mom…" said Jaden, pulling away after a few minutes. "I don't understand… how can you be from another planet? Why didn't you tell us?"

Melissa let out a deep sigh, saying, "This is a long story." She, Jaden, and Malia rose from the floor, each taking a seat before she continued.

"I wasn't ready to tell you *anything* until Malia first exhibited telekinesis—when you told me you didn't stop yourself from falling off the school building, I knew it had to be her. There was no guarantee either of you would ever grow into your powers. And if you didn't, I saw no point in revealing anything that would upset your lives."

"But you still didn't want to tell us, even after my fall," said Jaden. "We heard you arguing with Dad!"

"You've got it wrong," said Melissa. "The only part of the story I wanted to keep from you at that point was where I came from. I was ready to tell you everything else."

"Dad knew you weren't from Earth?" asked Malia.

"Yes," said Melissa. "Not in the beginning. He believed I

was human when we got married. But I told him the truth before you two were born." She chuckled softly. "He was shocked, of course. But understanding."

"Why didn't you want *us* to know?" Jaden asked.

"Your father and I agreed that it was time to tell you about your powers and the nature of your DNA. And I knew that would be plenty to swallow without learning I was from another world. I would have told you eventually, but your father insisted it was time to reveal everything."

"Was it you who left their DNA inside the Great Pyramid?" asked Nadia. "How did this come to pass?"

"It was I," said Melissa. "We lived on Atlantis for millennia, interacting with various human cultures. Only the Egyptians learned the truth about our origins. They were a people hungry for knowledge. We worked much more closely with them than any of the other civilizations—too closely, perhaps.

"I fell in love with their king when the Great Pyramid was being built, more than 12,000 years ago. His name was Ashai. We had established rules governing our involvement with the natives of this world. But I broke all of them. I left Atlantis to live with Ashai in the royal palace, and I bore him two children. Twins."

"Nothing about this was ever reported to Othal," said Nadia. "You would have been severely punished."

"And that's why we didn't report it," said Melissa. "We were removed from our homeworld forever, and we knew it. The other colonists decided to keep the information from the government to protect me. I knew what I was doing was wrong. But I acted out of love.

"My mating with Ashai was the first of its kind. We had no way of knowing for certain if our species were sufficiently compatible to produce children."

"But you were," said Malia.

"Yes. But there were complications; the children aged very rapidly. By their sixth birthday, they looked like normal human teenagers. And they developed telepathy and telekinesis. These were totally unforeseen side effects of the interspecies coupling."

"The same powers Malia and I have…" said Jaden.

"Our children died before they turned ten," Melissa said sadly. "We tried to stop their aging, but nothing worked. The gene therapy we'd used on our people had no effect.

"I was devastated. I wanted desperately to give Ashai more children, but we couldn't take the risk. The odds were that any offspring of ours would age the same way.

"I returned to Atlantis. In time, I convinced our geneticists to help me. I wanted to reproduce my children, but identify and alter the genes that caused the rapid aging. It took decades, and by the time they achieved success, Ashai was an old man."

"You created *us*," said Malia.

"Yes," replied Melissa. "Using genetic samples from my first set of twins. And within the first several months after you were born, we knew for certain that you were aging normally. It only remained to be seen if you would grow into your powers."

"But… why did you hide our DNA in the Pyramid?" asked Jaden. "Why weren't we born in ancient Egypt?"

"You were going to be. I planned to conceive you myself. But the Athenians came before we were ready. Thousands of them launched an attack against Atlantis. I fled with Bomani, one of the geneticists. We took the DNA samples to Egypt for safekeeping. Our people still hoped to repel the Athenians, but I couldn't afford to take the risk of staying there.

"And as it turned out, the Athenians overwhelmed Atlantis. The others decided to destroy the colony and sink the island to prevent Athens from acquiring our technology. Bomani and I, the DNA, and one lone shuttle were all that remained of the colony.

"I explained everything to Ashai. He agreed to allow me to hide the DNA inside the Great Pyramid. I knew that I would have to wait for humanity to grow up and advance technologically before I would ever be able to bring you to life. But I also knew I might not survive long enough to make it happen myself.

"Bomani and I traveled to the power station that Brian eventually discovered. We contacted Othal and told them what happened. Then we reconfigured the control system to recognize your DNA and send a signal to our homeworld if you ever came in contact with the pyramid. I hoped that if you were born after my death, you would still be able to join my people."

"Wait," said Carl. "The power station was in an underground chamber far below the ocean floor. How did you get inside?"

"The shuttles we used were submersible. There was a docking port inside a cave underneath the pyramid. Over time, seismic activity caused the entrance to the port to collapse—Brian discovered that when he began the excavation project."

"Why didn't you ask your people to rescue you?" asked Sydney.

"I couldn't," said Melissa. "If they came here, they never would have allowed my children to be born. I wanted to go home, but I had to wait until I could bring them to life on my own, here on Earth—no matter how long that took.

"After leaving the power station, Bomani and I returned to Egypt. We scavenged the shuttle to provide the shielding for the hidden chamber. The pyramid was completed, with the DNA safely hidden inside. After Ashai's death, we blended into Egyptian society and were forgotten by the passage of time."

"What ever happened to Bomani?" asked Sydney.

"We lived together for thousands of years, traveling the globe and watching humanity grow from infancy to adulthood. After leaving Egypt, we lived in Babylon, Greece, China, and Europe. We came to North America before the colonies revolted against the British Empire. In the nineteenth century, we watched with great anticipation as industrialization took place. And by the early twentieth century, we'd relocated back to Europe.

"Unfortunately, we found ourselves trapped behind German lines when Hitler rose to power. We tried to leave but were captured. The Nazis put us in a concentration camp. Bomani died helping me escape.

"I returned to America and watched as the pace of technological growth accelerated. When the United States landed a man on the Moon, I knew my time was finally approaching.

"I had always been a doctor and kept abreast of various cultures' advancements in medicine over the eons. Until humanity developed the knowledge and the technology necessary to perform human cloning, I had no way to bring the two of you to life. And of course, without Bomani, I lacked the expertise to conduct the procedure. But when the first animal cloning experiments took place, and I heard about the project to map the human genome, I knew my time had finally arrived. After assuming an identity as a surgeon, I applied for a position at the National Institutes of Health. And that's where I met Stephen.

"Once they completed the human genome project, I contacted a renowned French Egyptologist, by the name of Moreau. I told him about the hidden chamber inside the Great Pyramid. And I insisted that he contact Stephen. By that time, I'd become romantically involved with him, and I knew he possessed the skill and knowledge to bring my children to life.

"Moreau began his excavation project to find the entrance hall to the hidden chamber. Much to my annoyance, he did not get in touch with Stephen at first. But when he finally reached the chamber, he could go no further. His team was unable to penetrate the shielding. That's when he finally abided by my instructions and contacted your father.

"Of course, Stephen had no idea why the mysterious informant had requested his involvement. But he contacted his brother, and Brian determined a way to access the chamber. Stephen was intrigued by the DNA samples. With my encouragement, he sought funding to conduct his research. And I knew Brian's company possessed the resources to reach the power station. Sure enough, when he discovered the map I'd left with the DNA sample, he found a way to visit the pyramid. And I planned to reveal my true identity to Brian once the children grew up and go to the power station to contact Othal.

"I still hoped to conceive the children myself. But Stephen would have discovered I wasn't human if his team had performed the surgery to impregnate me with the eggs he'd engineered. I was afraid of what he'd do when he learned the truth. So instead, I allowed him to select a surrogate mother.

"Once her pregnancy was established, I spoke to Stephen and told him everything. He was the only one who ever knew the whole truth. The government was aware that your DNA would produce humans with extra powers but remained ignorant of the existence of Atlantis or the Othali. And only Stephen knew that the DNA was initially created by the mating of a human with an Othali.

"After the two of you were born, Brian discovered that the government planned to take you from us and develop you as weapons. Stephen didn't want to believe it. But I made plans anyway. If the government ever tried to intervene, I was going to contact Brian. I knew he could help us contact Othal and go into hiding until they could send a rescue party.

"But I didn't know the CIA had contacted Principal McLaren at the high school. Babcock probably knew that one of you had exhibited telekinesis before I did. And once he showed up at our house, it was too late. I had no way to get you out of there or contact Brian.

"I'm so grateful that they found you, Sydney. After they shot me, I thought I was going to die. And I didn't think I'd ever know what happened to the children." She took a deep breath, fighting back tears. "Babcock was there when I woke up in the hospital. He knew by then that I wasn't human. Othali anatomy is somewhat different from humans—the internal organs are arranged differently. It caused problems for the doctors. I didn't think they'd ever let me go. But it seems everything worked out. You reached Brian and activated the beacon. Now I can finally take you home. To Othal."

Jaden stared at her, holding his breath.

"*She doesn't know,*" Malia said inside his mind, her eyes wide.

"Melissa," said Nadia. "Othal was destroyed. That ship that obliterated Miami, they're called the Malor. They came here to investigate the beacon. And now that they've found an industrialized society, they're going to take over this planet and use its infrastructure to process and consume all of its resources."

Melissa stared at her in shock. "But... you're here... You must be from Othal—you speak our language... This shuttle..."

"We escaped," Nadia told her. "One warship. Nobody else survived. We've been traveling through space for eighteen years, searching for Earth, or at least some other habitable planet."

Melissa looked from Nadia to Jaden, shaking her head in disbelief. She opened her mouth to speak but sobbed instead.

"Mom," said Jaden, reaching out to her with his mind. *"We have to stop that ship. If we can do that, we can stay here. Forever."*

"Jaden…" Her emotions crashed against his consciousness, overwhelming him with the disappointment of millennia. She'd waited tens of thousands of years to bring him and Malia to life and return home. But now her world was gone.

"Mom… is Dad really dead?" asked Malia.

Melissa sobbed before replying. "Yes. He's gone. I'm so sorry…"

Jaden moved to sit next to her, pulling her and Malia into a hug. They sat quietly for a few minutes.

"Melissa, what did you do after you called us? When we were in Nevada?" asked Sydney.

"Well, Baxter was supposed to take me back to the FBI," said Melissa. "But he was an old friend of mine. Despite what he told Babcock, he had no intention of turning me over. So he ditched his phone to prevent them from tracking us, and we went to Brian's corporate offices in Washington.

"But the place was under heavy guard. I couldn't get inside to talk to anyone. Baxter took me to his cousin's house instead and convinced him to let me take his car. That proved a little dicey, as he obviously couldn't tell his cousin the whole truth. Baxter had to agree to pay for the car if anything happened to it, but it worked out in the end.

"So I drove to Miami to see if I could access the power station. At first, it was crawling with police. But once the alien ship showed up, they abandoned it. I took Brian's boat and went to the island. They must have used explosives to get inside because the top of the hill was blown apart. The access tunnel was wide open, so I climbed down the ladder and found the pyramid.

"And I waited. I went online using one of Brian's computers and watched the news. They reported that Brian had escaped, so I could only hope that he had made it to Carl and reunited with the three of you. And then I saw the reports about the alien ship. At first, I thought it might be one of ours. I didn't recognize the design but had no way of knowing what Othali ships might look like after so much time.

"But once it entered the atmosphere, I knew it couldn't be Othali. The saucers it launched looked identical to the others that had crashed here back in the 1940s and 50s. I knew the ship belonged to some other alien civilization.

"They accessed the power station's control systems and disabled the beacon. And they tried to shut the pyramid down entirely. I was able to override their commands, but not before they partially disabled the system. I hoped they might be friendly, but I wasn't taking any chances. It took me a while, but I brought everything back online. And when they attacked Miami, I returned fire."

"What's the condition of the power station now?" asked Nadia.

"Ruined," said Melissa. "Their weapon overloaded the circuits. The reactor went into meltdown, and that's why I tried to leave. It's only a matter of time before the island sinks into the ocean.

"And I wouldn't have survived if you didn't rescue me," she concluded, hugging Jaden and Malia tighter.

The three of them sat there, huddled together for the rest of the journey. Jaden tried to wrap his mind around everything he'd learned. He'd wanted to know so badly *what he was*. But now that he knew he was half-human and half-Othali, he discovered he didn't care. The knowledge hadn't changed *who* he was. And although he'd believed otherwise ever since learning of the DNA samples inside the Great Pyramid, it had turned out his mother really was his mother after all. He found this profoundly comforting.

Once they'd docked aboard the Othali mother ship, they said goodbye to Madu, and Nadia led the group off the shuttle. But this time, dozens of people lined the corridors, cheering for them as they passed.

"What's happening?" Jaden asked Nadia telepathically.

"Your mother is a legend among our people," Nadia told him. *"We told the commander we'd found her, and he spread the word."*

But the mood was much more somber when they reached the bridge.

"Welcome back," said Anhur. "There have been developments in your absence."

"Oh?" asked Nadia.

"With Brian Kwan's help, our people have managed to crack the Malor security," said the commander. "We have some decisions to make."

26

INFILTRATE

"What kind of decisions?" asked Sydney. "Can't you just blow up their ship or something?"

"Unfortunately, it doesn't work that way," said Anhur. "Lieutenant, I've scheduled a tactical meeting in the battle room in five minutes. I'll require your presence."

"Yes, sir," said Nadia.

"Can we attend?" asked Carl.

"I don't think that would be appropriate," said the Commander.

"Sir, this situation directly concerns the Earthlings," said Nadia. "We should include them. Brian Kwan proved they can be helpful."

Anhur stared at her for a moment. "Very well."

Five minutes later, they gathered in a small room behind the bridge. Jaden and Malia walked in with

Melissa. Anhur sat at the head of the table, Brian to his left. Nadia was there along with several other Othali Jaden didn't recognize. He sat next to Carl and Sydney at the far end of the table. Malia and Melissa took the seats adjacent to him.

"Vindhu, what's the status of the Malor ship?" asked Anhur.

"Still on course," said the man sitting next to the commander. "It will arrive in the capital in two hours."

"The capital?" asked Sydney. "You mean Washington?"

"Yes," Anhur confirmed. "They'll destroy it the way they did Miami."

"You said they'd use the planet's existing infrastructure to process resources," said Brian. "If they keep destroying cities, they'll eliminate that infrastructure."

"If they follow their usual pattern," said Nadia, "they'll incapacitate the military and major governments first. This typically removes any meaningful resistance, leaving them free to harvest the planet undisturbed."

"But if you've got computer access, you can stop them," said Sydney. "Right?"

"Perhaps," said Anhur. "But the ship doesn't have a self-destruct function. So what we need to decide is how to use our access for maximum effectiveness."

"The problem is that once we do anything, the Malor will detect our presence and seal the security breach," said Brian. "We can currently monitor their systems without their knowledge. But as soon as we take action, the game is up. We'll have only one shot."

"We should take our ship into the atmosphere," suggested Nadia. "Disable their shields and open fire."

"There won't be enough time," said a man across the table from Jaden. "It won't take long for the Malor to reactivate their shields. We don't have enough firepower to destroy them that quickly."

"Who's that?" Jaden asked Nadia in his mind.

"Captain Patel," she replied. *"Second in command."*

At that moment, there was a buzzing noise. "Commander, the United States military has engaged the Malor," said a voice filling the room.

"Thank you, Lieutenant," said Anhur. "We'll watch from here."

He did something on the tabletop in front of him. It reminded Jaden of the touchscreen interface on his iPhone. Suddenly holographic images appeared above the table. Jaden recognized the Malor ship. Dozens of fighter jets were flying toward it. But Malor saucers shot beams of energy at them, knocking them out of the sky.

But then the image zoomed out. Jaden saw a wedge-shaped aircraft moving toward the Malor ship.

"What is that?" asked Anhur.

"Bomber," said Vindhu. "They're going to launch a thermonuclear weapon."

"They're going to blow up a nuke over American soil?!" Sydney said in disbelief.

"The Malor are currently over the Atlantic Ocean," said Vindhu. "The warhead isn't strong enough to penetrate their shields. But they're targeting the airspace directly over the ship for maximum impact. The shields will protect everything beneath from the blast."

"The fallout's still going to be a problem," said Brian. "Normal air currents will shower the eastern seaboard with radioactive dust everywhere north of the explosion."

As Jaden watched, the bomber fired a missile. It shot toward the ship and exploded directly above it in a blinding flash of light. Once the image had cleared, a giant mushroom cloud dominated the hologram. But the Malor ship was still there, unaffected.

"Blast yield of two megatons," said Vindhu. "Engine output of the Malor ship increased by eighty percent to counteract the force of the shockwave. They're still on course."

Anhur deactivated the hologram.

"The shockwave required that much power to overcome?" asked Carl.

"The Malor ship wasn't designed to operate inside an atmosphere," said Anhur. "From the data we recovered, we were able to determine that they've been living like this for over 200,000 years—moving from one industrialized planet to the next. Their original ships were manufactured on their homeworld. But as those succumbed to age, they built this vessel while orbiting one of the worlds they ultimately destroyed.

"They take it into a new planet's atmosphere only long enough to eliminate resistance. After that, it returns to orbit, and scout ships begin the harvesting work. When they attacked Othal, they didn't risk taking the ship inside the atmosphere at first. They sent only their saucers in the first wave until they destroyed our warships in space. But your technology isn't as advanced as ours, so they probably don't see you as a threat."

"That's one advantage we've got over them," added Vindhu. "They don't know we're here. And our ship can better handle the gravitational and environmental stress of operating inside the atmosphere."

"But your shuttles can operate underwater," said Carl. "After hundreds of thousands of years, the Malor didn't have time to build a tougher ship?"

"It's not a matter of time," said Vindhu. "All the time in the universe can't change the laws of physics. Remember, gravity decreases as the square of the distance as you move away from a massive body. That means the amount of force the Earth exerts on a spacecraft is more than twenty times greater near its surface than it is in orbit. The Malor ship has a mass equivalent to one-millionth of your moon. Operating it this close to a planet puts the superstructure under incredible stress.

"But on top of that, you've got to account for pressure. Don't forget, space is essentially a vacuum—there is no atmosphere. Air pressure brings increased stress, and water pressure is greater still. We designed our shuttles to function underwater because so much of our planet was covered in oceans. Many of our bases were on the seafloor. But there's no point in building long-range spacecraft that way. Pressure hulls can easily double the mass of a vessel, in turn requiring stronger engines and more fuel. It makes no sense for a ship that spends the vast majority of its time in space. Although

even if we wanted to, we lack the technology to make something as large as our warship submersible because of the
enormous pressure involved. And that Malor ship is about
two billion times more massive than ours."

"Wait a minute," said Sydney. "I thought you said the
Malor ship was a million times lighter than the Moon…"

"That's correct," Vindhu confirmed.

"Then how can it be two *billion* times heavier than this
ship?" asked Sydney.

"Think about it," said Vindhu. "The number one billion is
represented by the numeral one with nine zeroes after it. The
mass of your moon in kilograms is roughly equal to the
number seven, followed by *twenty-two* zeroes."

"Oh," said Sydney. "Well… I guess that explains it."

"It's almost impossible to conceive how they can generate
enough power to take such a massive ship inside an
atmosphere," said Nadia.

"Then that's the answer," said Carl. "Use your computer
access to disable their shields, and then fire on their engines.
Crash it into the ocean."

"That's problematic," said Anhur. "The engine core lies
deep within the ship. We could fire into the exhaust ports and
hope for a lucky shot. If we ignite the plasma, it may start a
chain reaction that would propagate into the core. But it
would require an *extremely* lucky shot."

"Not only that," said Vindhu, "the ports are located on the
underside of the vessel. Their position isn't very high off the
ground. We'd have to move unacceptably close to them to
achieve the right angle."

"And when we fire our weapons, they'll be able to see us," added Nadia. "From such a close range, it would take them almost no time to lock their weapons and return fire."

"A better option might be to target their primary weapon," suggested Vindhu. "The power station damaged it in the exchange. If we disable their shields, we might be able to take it out completely."

"You mean the thing they used to annihilate Miami?" asked Sydney. "If it's damaged, can they still use it on Washington?"

"They're making repairs," said Nadia. "It'll be fully functional soon."

"Taking out the primary weapon would make their job more difficult," said Anhur. "But they've still got enough firepower to eliminate every major city on this planet."

"What about these power stations?" asked Captain Patel. "Where are the others located? Their weapon systems, together with ours, may be strong enough to overcome the Malor ship."

"There are two more," said Melissa. "One off the coast of Bermuda, and the other near San Juan."

"Of course," said Brian. "The other two points of the Bermuda Triangle."

"The trouble is that the stations aren't mobile," Anhur pointed out. "And the Malor ship is out of range. We'd have to lure them to one of those locations."

"What about the children?" asked Melissa. "Their telekinesis may be strong enough to overpower their engines. Have we tried that yet?"

Jaden looked at her in surprise. "Mom, I am *not* strong enough to do anything to that ship. You've got to be kidding."

"I might be," said Malia.

"I agree," said Nadia. "Under the right conditions, her brainwaves may resonate with the planet's magnetic field the same way they did to produce the delta-shifted telepathic signals. If so, her telekinetic power output would increase exponentially."

"It's worth a shot," said Anhur. "But there's no guarantee it will work. I've got another idea.

"What if we take a shuttle *inside* the Malor ship. Enter through one of the docking bays. If we can maneuver close enough to the engine core, we might be able to destroy it. Or at least do enough damage to force them down by other means."

"That might work," said Vindhu. "But it would be difficult. We'd have to use our computer access to disable the energy field protecting the docking port. But once we're inside, they'd reactivate it. Also, the target would have to be carefully selected. The shuttle would likely get only one shot. Once it fires, they'll be able to detect its position. Every Malor saucer in the bay would return fire."

"But if they could find a way past the saucers," said Anhur, "this would work. Eliminating the energy field from *inside* the docking port wouldn't be difficult. Firing on the field generator would take care of that."

"True enough," Vindhu agreed.

"We could help," said Jaden. "Malia and I are both strong enough to knock those saucers out of the way."

Anhur stared at him intently. "Melissa? Would you allow your children to assist in such a mission?"

Melissa looked back and forth from Jaden to Malia. Tears welled up in her eyes, but she nodded slowly. "It's their choice."

"Very well," said Anhur. "Vindhu, I want you to plan this mission. Coordinate with the hackers. Analyze the engine schematics and determine the best target. And the timing of the attack will have to coincide perfectly with the deactivation of the energy field."

"Yes, sir," said Vindhu.

"Everyone regroup here in thirty minutes," said Anhur, rising from his seat. "Let's make this happen."

The meeting broke up. Jaden and Malia led Melissa down to the conference room they'd visited upon first arriving. They took seats directly in front of the observation windows and stared out at the Earth.

"It's hard to believe," said Melissa. "I've called this place home for the majority of my life. My real home's already gone, and now Earth might be next."

"Don't say that, Mom," said Jaden. "We'll stop them."

She smiled at him. "You've always been so brave."

"What was Othal like?" asked Malia.

"A lot like Earth," said Melissa. "But more water—land accounted for only fifteen percent of the surface area."

"That's half as much as our planet," Malia noted. "Thirty percent of the Earth's surface is land."

Melissa nodded. "It was warmer there, too. No icecaps. And the planet's axis was hardly tilted, so there were no seasons."

"So it was summertime all year round?" asked Jaden.

"Sure was," she confirmed.

"Why'd you leave?" asked Malia.

"For adventure," said Melissa. "Exploration. Despite the population control measures, Othal was fairly crowded. The idea of finding other worlds to settle was attractive. And I'd always been intrigued by the possibility of finding other life in the galaxy. I was a doctor, so I was curious about what alien organisms might be like."

"I wonder how many planets the Malor destroyed," said Jaden. "Do you think there are a lot of other civilizations out there?"

"I do," said Melissa. "We have direct experience with three—Othal, Earth, and the Malor..."

"Four," countered Malia. "Nadia told us they found a planet that the Malor destroyed. That's why they built their warships."

"All right, four," said Melissa. "Those four worlds existed within a tiny segment of our galaxy. Even Earth scientists have discovered *thousands* of other planetary systems. Othali astronomers found *hundreds of thousands*. It's impossible to tell across such vast distances, but I imagine many of those planets must harbor life. And given enough time, intelligent life will usually evolve."

"But the Malor have been eliminating civilizations for 200,000 years," said Jaden. "How many more can there be?"

"Well, think about humans," said Melissa. "The first *homo sapiens* evolved here at about the time the Malor set out from their home planet. It took that long for humans to achieve space flight. But in all those millennia, across the entire galaxy, I bet at least a few more civilizations have developed."

"Nadia also said they traveled in a straight line across the galaxy," noted Malia. "That leaves a *lot* of stars. There must be other people out there, *somewhere*."

They sat quietly for a few minutes. Finally, Jaden asked a question that had been bothering him since rescuing Melissa.

"Mom… Did you love Dad? Or were you only with him because he could bring us to life?"

Melissa took a deep breath, saying nothing for several seconds. Malia stared at her intensely; Jaden could tell she'd been wondering this, too.

"In my whole life, I have loved only two men. King Ashai of Egypt, and Stephen Kwan. And it happens that they are the two who gave me my children."

She pulled Jaden and Malia into a hug. But at that moment, Nadia entered the room.

"It's time for the mission briefing," she said.

Jaden, Malia, and Melissa followed her back up three decks and through the rear of the bridge to the battle room. They retook the same seats they'd occupied earlier.

"Let's hear it," said Anhur. "What've you got?"

Vindhu cleared his throat. "We'll have to start by taking this ship into the atmosphere. We can't come too close to the Malor—despite our shields, a vessel this size might be detectable. With variations in ambient temperature and pressure, the camouflaging effects wouldn't be perfect.

"But the Malor *will* be aware of our presence once we execute this mission, so there will no longer be any point in trying to hide. And we'll need to bring our full arsenal to bear on their ship as quickly as possible once we've damaged their engines.

"We'll launch two shuttles once we're in position. I'll fly lead with one copilot, and the other shuttle will carry the children. We'll stop near the Malor ship to give them a chance to try to take it down telekinetically."

"And if that works, mission accomplished," said Nadia.

"Yes, exactly," Vindhu agreed. "If not… we'll proceed to the docking bay. I'll ping our coordinates to mission command on our final approach. They'll initiate the computer attack and disable the energy field at the entrance to the port. Once inside, we'll proceed to the far side of the bay. Unfortunately, we're going to have to dock the shuttles and continue on foot."

"On foot?" said Melissa. "I thought the plan was to fire on a target from the shuttle."

Vindhu nodded. "It was. But I'm afraid that's not going to work. There's a power generator near that section, but it's too far from the port to reach with the shuttle's weapons. Hand lasers may not be strong enough, so there's a good chance we'll need the children to disable the generator."

"Will that be enough to shut down their engines?" asked Captain Patel.

"No," said Vindhu. "Four separate generators provide

power. Only one is accessible from the docking bay. But that should weaken them enough to make them vulnerable."

"Aren't we going to run into the aliens if we leave the shuttle?" asked Jaden.

"Maybe not at first," said Vindhu. "We'll be moving through service passages for the most part; they're pretty far removed from the regular operational sections of the ship. But once we take out the generator, I expect we'll meet resistance. We'll each be equipped with personal shields—those will render us invisible. But it won't prevent them from noticing us if we come in direct physical contact; shields don't stop someone from *touching* you. And if they realize there's someone there, invisible or not, they'll fire on us."

Melissa let out a soft whimper. Jaden realized she was fighting back tears. Anhur had noticed, too.

"This is going to be highly dangerous," he said to her. "If you don't want to send the children, I'll understand. We'll find another way."

"No—we want to help," said Malia.

"Yeah, you need us," Jaden added. "And besides, we can take care of those aliens—"

But Anhur held up his hand to silence them. "Melissa?"

"Jaden's right," she said, voice quavering. "You'll have a better chance of success if they go with you."

"Very well," Anhur replied. "Proceed," he added to Vindhu.

"Once we make it back to the shuttles, we should be able to return across the docking port unimpeded. I'll fire on the field generator, and we'll leave the Malor ship. We will likely encounter enemy saucers at that point, but if the children can take care of those, we should be home free.

"Once we're clear, Commander, you'll be able to do the rest from here."

"Based on observations from the thermonuclear blast," said Captain Patel, "and assuming their engine capacity is down twenty-five percent, four quantum bombs should provide sufficient explosive yield to force them down."

"I'm sorry, quantum bombs?" asked Brian.

"Similar to your nuclear weapons," said Anhur. "Instead of nuclear fusion, they use antimatter suspended in a powerful magnetic field. When the antimatter collides with normal matter, energy is released."

"But how will you get your weapons through their shields?" asked Carl.

"We won't have to," said Anhur. "The explosive yield will be equivalent to the thermonuclear warhead, without the radioactive fallout. If we're successful, the shockwave will be enough to overpower their engines and drive them into the ocean."

"The ocean water will do the rest," said Captain Patel. "It will flood their vessel and short out their shields within minutes. Moreover, operating at only seventy-five percent capacity, they have barely enough power to escape Earth's gravity. Add the weight of all that water, and they'll lack the thrust to get airborne. That ship will never fly again. We can easily finish them off at that point."

"Why not take one of these quantum bombs *inside* the Malor ship?" asked Brian. "Without the protection of their shields, surely the explosive yield would be enough to destroy them."

"It would," Anhur confirmed. "Unfortunately, we have no way to transport a missile inside the ship. They're too large to fit inside our shuttles."

"What about mounting one to the exterior of a shuttle?" Carl suggested.

"Not a good idea," said Vindhu. "Antimatter is tricky stuff. Any contact with normal electrons or protons would detonate it. The missiles are stored in a protected area of our warship—even if one explodes, the rest of the vessel is safe. But flying one of those missiles without that protection would be extremely risky for the shuttle crew—not to mention the danger of moving it to a shuttle in the first place. If it were to detonate outside the protected area, we could lose the ship."

"Could you disable the field protecting the Malor docking bay long enough to fire a missile inside of it?" asked Brian.

"Both the timing and the targeting would have to be perfect," said Vindhu. "And the hackers tell me we don't know precisely how long it will take for the command to disable the field to be processed. It would be virtually impossible to time the missile launch that accurately. And we'd get only one shot—once we fire a missile, the Malor will know we're here."

"We've got only one chance to use our computer access before they shut us out," said Anhur. "We'll proceed as discussed. This is a good plan. Vindhu, assemble your crews. Let's get this underway immediately."

"Yes, sir," said Vindhu.

Everyone got up and left the battle room. Anhur refused to allow Sydney, Brian or Carl to join the mission. So they wished the others luck, and Melissa, Jaden, and Malia followed Nadia down to the shuttle bay.

Madu was their pilot once again. They boarded the shuttle, and Jaden watched Vindhu climb into the adjacent ship with a woman he didn't recognize.

Nadia accessed the bridge's viewscreen. Jaden watched as the entire ship moved closer to Earth. Like earlier, they descended somewhere over the Pacific Ocean, near the coast of Mexico. It was night time here. Jaden guessed that avoiding detection would be significantly more difficult in a vessel so large than it had been in the shuttle. And sure enough, flames engulfed the image on the viewscreen as soon as they entered the atmosphere.

Before long, Jaden saw land beneath them, passing by unfathomably fast. They entered daylight, and twenty minutes later, reached water again.

"This is it," said Madu. "Time to fly."

They detached from their berth and followed the first shuttle out of the docking bay. It became invisible the moment they left the ship. Nadia did something on the console, and the outline of the other shuttle showed up on the viewscreen.

Flying low over the water, they soon came within sight of the Malor ship. Madu took them uncomfortably close. Jaden peered out the windows, and it seemed the ship was almost directly over them.

"All right, you two," said Madu. "If you can take them down, now's your chance."

"Commander, we're ready here," Nadia said into a microphone on the console. "The children are going to make their attempt."

"I hear you," Anhur's voice said over the speaker.

Jaden took a deep breath, focusing on the enormous ship.

"Ready?" he asked Malia telepathically.

"Jaden, I don't know about this. We're talking about destroying an entire civilization here."

"Have you lost your mind? Of course, that's what we're talking about! But that's what they're trying to do to us!"

"If we do this... we're just like them."

"No, Malia, we're not. We wouldn't choose to do this if they went away and left us alone. But we don't have a choice—they do!"

"Yeah, but we're still killing—"

"I'm not playing this game with you! They're gonna kill everybody on Earth if we don't stop them. Now stop your crying, and let's do this!"

Malia let out a long sigh. Furrowing her brow, she focused on the Malor ship. And together, Jaden and Malia used the full extent of their powers to force the vessel down.

"It's working," said Nadia. "I don't believe this—both of your brainwaves are resonating with the magnetic field. You've each grown more powerful since we first found you."

Jaden continued to concentrate as hard as he could. He imagined the Malor ship crashing into the ocean. But he could feel it pushing back.

"It's having a definite effect," said a voice over the

speaker. "Their engine output is rising. They've stopped all forward motion and diverted full power to stay airborne."

Jaden kept pushing. But it didn't feel like the ship was moving. He didn't know how much longer he could sustain the effort.

"The Malor are panicking," said the man on the speaker. "They don't know what's happening—they think it's a malfunction."

"Good," said Nadia. "Let's hope they don't detect the children's brainwaves."

"I can't do this much longer," Jaden said inside Malia's thoughts.

"Me neither," she replied. "Is it working?" she asked out loud.

"Their position isn't changing," said Madu.

"Engine output has increased significantly," said the voice on the speaker. "But it's not going to be enough."

"We should fire quantum bombs now," Madu suggested. "Coupled with the children's powers, it may be enough!"

"Negative," said a different voice on the speaker. "It's too close to call. The shockwave may not last long enough to overload their engines." Jaden realized it was Anhur. "And firing our weapons would enable them to locate us. It's too risky."

Jaden gave up. "I couldn't hold it anymore!"

Malia sat back in her chair, heaving a sigh. "Neither could I."

"They're resuming course," Madu told them.

"They couldn't sustain the effort," Nadia reported to the

warship. "It was too much. We'll have to move forward with phase two."

"Acknowledged," said Anhur.

"I'm sorry," said Malia. "We weren't strong enough."

"You did everything you could," Melissa told her. "You both did. But it's not over yet. Gather your energy—they're going to need you again."

Jaden was tired and frustrated. It would have been so much better if they'd succeeded here. The thought of going inside this vessel filled him with fear.

Madu moved them closer to the Malor ship. Saucers came and went from the docking bay like wasps from a hive. Madu approached the portal from an angle to stay out of the ships' paths. A sheet of red energy covered the opening, although it allowed the saucers to pass unhindered.

"We're in position," Nadia said into the microphone. "Disable the energy field."

"Entering the command… now," said the voice. "You should be free to enter the docking bay."

Several seconds went by. Jaden worried it wasn't going to work. But the red glow disappeared from the opening. The other shuttle, visible only as an outline on the viewscreen, passed inside. Madu followed.

"They're aware of us now," the man said over the radio. "The Malor have initiated an attack against our network."

"Will they succeed?" Melissa asked apprehensively.

"I doubt it," said Nadia. "We've strengthened our computer security tenfold since the attack on Othal."

Jaden stared in awe at the sheer size of the Malor docking

bay. It stretched the length of a dozen football fields and rose as high as a skyscraper. The space hosted hundreds upon hundreds of saucers docked along the walls.

The two shuttles moved across the expanse. In the far corner, they came to a section of empty berths. Madu moved them close to one of these but didn't dock.

"This is as close as we can get," he told the others. "Physical contact with the berth may alert them to our presence."

"Understood," said Nadia, rising from her seat. She moved to the rear of the cabin. From inside a large compartment, she withdrew several strips of fabric and three pairs of goggles.

"Put these on," she said, handing one set of equipment to each of the twins.

"What are they?" Jaden asked, putting on the goggles. He didn't notice any change in his vision.

"The belts will make you invisible and provide some protection from energy weapons," said Nadia. "But, the glasses will let us see each other."

Malia fastened the belt around her waist. Suddenly Jaden could see nothing more than her outline, visible only in green lines. He lifted the goggles from his face, and she disappeared entirely.

"This is cool," he said, replacing the goggles and putting on the belt.

"What about me?" said Melissa. "I'm going too, aren't I?"

"No," Nadia replied. "The more people we take, the more likely the Malor will run into one of us. You should stay here with Madu. He'll keep the shuttle ready so we can depart as soon as we return."

Melissa didn't look happy, but she accepted the decision. She gave Malia and Jaden a big hug.

"Be safe out there," she said, sounding extremely worried.

"We will, Mom," said Malia. "I promise."

"This is it," said Nadia. "When I open the hatch, we've got to jump onto the berth immediately. The opening will be visible until we close it again."

"Let's do this," Jaden said, trying to seem brave. But his voice squeaked.

Nadia smiled at him, then popped the hatch.

A sudden change in air pressure made Jaden's ears pop. Odd smells assaulted his nose—it reminded him of vomit.

Nadia jumped out. Jaden looked down—only a few feet separated the shuttle from the berth, but it afforded him a view down into the chasm. The curvature of the wall prevented him from seeing the bottom.

"Let's go!" Nadia said in his mind.

Jaden leaped; Malia was right behind him. The hatch closed with a pop, and Nadia led them away from the shuttle.

27

DEATH

The corridor was wide enough for several people to walk abreast, but only dimly lit. The walls were dark; it felt like a cave. There was a faint buzzing sound coming from somewhere deeper inside the ship. Vindhu joined them from the other berth. He pointed down the corridor and started walking. Nadia motioned for Jaden and Malia to follow him; she took up the rear.

They crept along, staying close to the wall. Vindhu's outline glowed against the eerie darkness. A loud clanking noise somewhere up ahead made Jaden jump.

A minute later, they came to an intersection. Vindhu peered around the corner. But suddenly, he jumped back, pressing Jaden into the wall. Nadia did the same to Malia. A moment later, three Malor dashed around the corner. They were somewhat shorter than Jaden. Their heads appeared much too big for their bodies, with lidless, protuberant eyes.

Jaden stayed flat against the wall, his heart hammering wildly, and watched until the Malor moved out of sight.

"You don't think they found the shuttles, do you?" he asked Vindhu.

"I doubt it," he replied. "They're invisible. And they'll move away from the berths if there's any trouble. Don't worry."

But despite his words, Vindhu sounded concerned. Jaden thought of his mom.

They moved on. Beyond the intersection, the passage was much narrower. It made Jaden feel claustrophobic. They continued for a few minutes before Vindhu came to a stop. He pulled a device from his pocket and examined the ship's schematics.

"This is it," he said, indicating a narrow tunnel to their right. "We've got to go through there."

Jaden gazed inside the opening. It was small enough that they'd have to crawl. And it sloped upward at a fairly steep angle.

"Isn't there an elevator?" he asked sardonically.

"There is, but going this way will help us avoid running into any more Malor," Vindhu explained.

He climbed into the tunnel. Jaden followed, Malia and Nadia behind him. The air grew warmer as they climbed. Jaden's feeling of claustrophobia increased; he became intensely uncomfortable. The smell of vomit he'd noticed earlier was much stronger here. After a few minutes, he started feeling nauseous. But finally, they reached the end of the tunnel. Jaden crawled out behind Vindhu.

They were standing in a narrow passage, identical to the one below. Vindhu scanned the schematics again as Malia and Nadia emerged from the tunnel.

Vindhu set off. They passed several intersecting passages. A minute later, the wall to their right disappeared. Only a railing separated them from a vast expanse beyond. This area was nearly as large as the docking port; six enormous, domed structures filled the space beneath them. Jaden could make out a few Malor walking on the floor between them far below. Rectangular objects sat at the top of each dome; thick cables protruded from them, crisscrossing each other up to the ceiling like giant spaghetti.

"This is it," said Vindhu, staring at the device in his hand. "It's a good thing you came with us—the transformers are shielded. Our weapons won't have any effect on them."

"What do we have to do?" asked Malia.

"See if you can rip the transformers off the tops of those domes," said Vindhu.

"You mean the boxes with the cables coming out of them?" Jaden asked.

Vindhu nodded.

Jaden focused on the one closest to them. In his mind, he grasped the transformer and pulled it away from the dome. It was attached very firmly. He tried his hardest, at last feeling the transformer shudder against his effort. Finally, it ripped away in a cascade of fire and sparks.

Malia went to work on the next one, and Jaden the one beyond that. Within a few minutes, they'd removed all six transformers.

"That's good," said Nadia. "Let's get out of here."

But, no sooner had she spoken than a shrieking sound filled the cavernous space. It sounded like some sort of alarm. Jaden looked around in fear. Suddenly a dozen Malor came running out of a passage toward them, carrying weapons. As they approached, Jaden and Malia used their powers to pitch them over the railing. The aliens flailed and twisted in the air, hitting the floor far below.

"Go!" shouted Vindhu.

Jaden ran with Nadia, Malia, and Vindhu close behind. He went as fast as he could, pulling ahead of the others. But a minute later, Vindhu yelled, "Wait! That's the passage we want!"

Jaden stopped short. "This one?" he called back. Nadia caught up to him, but an instant later, an energy field erupted across the passage. A solid sheet of glowing red light now separated Jaden and Nadia from Malia and Vindhu.

"Damn!" Vindhu shouted as he and Malia reached the barrier. "I don't see a way to disable it. We'll have to go around. Go down that passage and head back to the shuttles. We'll meet you there."

"Be careful," said Nadia.

Vindhu disappeared into the next passage. Malia cast one last fearful glance at Jaden, climbed in behind him, and moved out of sight.

"Let's go," said Nadia. Jaden followed her into the tunnel. They clambered down for several minutes, finally emerging in the passage below.

"This way," said Nadia, dashing off toward the docking

port. Soon they reached the wider passage, but several Malor came running up the intersecting corridor. Jaden guessed they must have heard their footsteps because the aliens began firing beams of red energy.

One of the lasers struck Jaden, knocking him into the wall. Another hit Nadia. Their shields had protected them, but Nadia had become fully visible. With a thought, Jaden propelled the Malor far down the passage before they had a chance to fire on them again.

"We've got to hurry!" said Nadia. "They can see us now!"

They charged down the corridor, quickly arriving at the docking port. But as they reached the shuttle, three more Malor ran toward them. Jaden tossed them through the opening of an empty berth.

The shuttle's hatch opened, and Nadia and Jaden jumped on board. Melissa pulled Jaden into a hug as Nadia closed the hatch again.

But suddenly something hit the shuttle. It shook violently, knocking Jaden and Melissa into the seats.

"What was that?" Nadia yelled, moving into the cockpit with Madu.

"We're taking fire!" he said. "They must have seen us when you boarded."

"Move us away from the berth," said Nadia.

"No—what about Malia and Vindhu?" asked Melissa.

"The other shuttle will wait for them," said Madu. "The Malor have no way of knowing we've got a second ship here."

They pulled away, setting out across the docking port.

"We can't just leave them behind!" Melissa shouted, losing her composure.

"There's no choice," Nadia told her. "Those saucers are coming for us!"

Jaden stared out the cockpit window. Sure enough, more than a dozen ships were headed directly toward them.

"I could use some help, Jaden," said Madu. "If I fire weapons, they'll locate us again."

"I'm on it," Jaden told him. With the force of his mind, he knocked the saucers into the outer wall. They fell into the chasm below.

"Good work," Madu said appreciatively.

But now Jaden saw dozens of other saucers flying around the bay.

"They must be looking for us," he said.

"I agree," said Nadia. "And the trouble is they might find the other shuttle, too. Vindhu, can you hear me?" she asked into the microphone. "Vindhu, are you there?"

There was no reply.

"They're jamming our radio frequencies," said Madu.

"*Malia!*" Jaden called out to his sister telepathically. "*Where are you?*"

"*Jaden! I'm scared! We ran into a whole group of Malor. I think they heard us because they started shooting. They hit Vindhu, and his shield stopped working—now they can see him!*"

"*Is he hurt?*"

"*No—but we're having trouble getting out. We run into aliens everywhere we go!*"

"They're okay," Jaden said to Nadia. "I talked to Malia."

"Tell her we're leaving," she replied.

"What?!" said Melissa.

"It's the only way," Nadia told her. "The Malor will know we've left when we fire on the field generator protecting the entrance. But they don't know about the second shuttle. This should allow it to wait for the others undetected."

Melissa started to protest but closed her eyes and nodded instead. "You're right."

Jaden explained the situation to his sister.

"The other shuttle's definitely waiting for us?" she asked. He could feel the panic in her thoughts.

"Yes, I promise," he assured her. "They know the plan," he said out loud. But he feared he might never see Malia again. What if she and Vindhu failed to make it back to the shuttle? He tried to banish this thought from his mind.

Madu piloted the ship across the bay, weaving around Malor saucers. Finally, they reached the entrance.

"That's it," said Nadia, pointing to a large cylindrical protrusion next to the opening. "That's the field generator."

"Hold on back there," Madu said to Jaden and Melissa. "Things may get a little wild when they detect our weapons."

He fired a laser at the field generator, but nothing happened—the sheet of energy still covered the portal. He fired again, this time sustaining the energy beam for several seconds.

"It's shielded!" shouted Madu.

"Now what?" asked Melissa.

Madu didn't answer. At that moment, hundreds of saucers left their berths and raced across the bay toward them. He moved the shuttle high above the portal. Looking down, Jaden saw the saucers firing energy weapons at their previous position. The lasers caused explosions where they came in contact with the energy field.

"We're in trouble," said Madu.

The saucers spread out around the end of the bay, firing indiscriminately—and they were coming closer. Jaden concentrated and knocked them out of the air. Widening his gaze, he smashed every saucer he could find into the berths, destroying many others that were docked. A towering inferno consumed much of the interior wall.

Jaden turned his attention to the hull. Gathering his full strength, he imagined punching his fist through the wall. Suddenly an enormous gaping hole appeared as if someone had thrust a giant battering ram through it.

"I assume that was you?" Madu asked appreciatively, steering them toward the breach.

"Sure was," Jaden said, failing to suppress a grin.

They flew out the hole. Within seconds, the air was thick with Malor saucers. Madu had difficulty steering around them. The Malor fired their weapons aimlessly as if searching for them.

"Can they see us?" asked Jaden.

"No," said Nadia. "But they'll be able to tell if their weapons make contact with our hull. One direct hit will allow the others to target us."

"They've concentrated their fighters in the area surrounding the docking port," said Madu. "Once we get farther away, we should be safe. They won't have any way of knowing which way we're headed."

He weaved in and out of the saucers' paths, doing his best to avoid the red beams of energy they were shooting everywhere. Some came uncomfortably close; Jaden cringed every time. But the saucers thinned out as they traveled farther away. Before long, it seemed like they'd escaped.

"Malia," Jaden called out in his mind. *"Did you make it to the shuttle yet?"*

"We're almost there! Right now, we're hiding in an equipment room or something. There are a ton of Malor going by in the passage."

"Well, hurry! We just left the mother ship. I punched a hole in the hull so you can use that to get out."

"I'll tell Vindhu... Jaden, I'm so afraid. What if we don't make it?"

Her fear washed over his own mind. *"Don't say that—you're gonna make it. You just told me you're almost there!"*

"We are..."

"Then do whatever you've gotta do to get to that shuttle! You beat a mountain lion—these stupid aliens are nothing compared to that. Don't give up!"

"I won't. Thank you, Jaden."

"Malia and Vindhu are almost to the shuttle," he reported to the others. "They should make it out soon." He knew that wasn't the whole story, but he refused to accept the possibility that they wouldn't make it.

Melissa put her arm around Jaden, hugging him. He could sense the desperation she felt for Malia.

"She'll make it, Mom," he told her. "Malia's gotten tough. She can do this."

Melissa only sobbed in reply.

"This is Shuttle Two, returning to base," Nadia said into her microphone. "Shuttle One has been delayed but should be following shortly."

"Acknowledged, Shuttle Two," a voice said over the radio.

Madu accelerated, and they returned to the Othali warship within minutes. Once they'd docked, they ran up to the bridge. Sydney, Brian, and Carl greeted Jaden and Melissa.

"We're running out of time," Anhur told them. "If we don't launch the quantum bombs in the next three minutes, we're in trouble."

"What—why?!" Melissa demanded, panic in her voice.

"The Malor are almost over land," said the commander. "When they reach the capital city, they'll fire their primary weapon. But we've got to take them down over water, or everyone in or near the city will die anyway."

"There are more than five million people in the greater metropolitan area," Brian added. "It's imperative that we crash that thing into the ocean."

"Have you had contact from Shuttle One?" asked Nadia.

"Negative," said Anhur.

"*Malia! Get your ass outta there!*" Jaden shouted in his mind. "*They've gotta blow up that ship in the next three minutes!*"

There was no reply.

"*MALIA! Answer me!*"

Nothing. Jaden thought his heart might have stopped, judging by the hollow feeling in his chest.

"Mom, I can't talk to Malia! Something's wrong!"

Melissa said nothing but looked stricken.

"You've been in contact with her since leaving the ship?" asked Brian.

"Yeah, but now she's not answering!" Jaden felt panic overtaking him. "*MALIA!*" he cried out telepathically. Still, there was no response. "I don't understand…" His eyes burned with tears.

"Try communicating with Vindhu," Nadia suggested.

"I don't think I can," said Jaden. "I've never talked to him that way before."

"Try," Nadia pleaded.

Jaden focused on the Malor ship in the viewscreen and called out Vindhu's name in his mind. It was futile. He looked at Nadia, shaking his head apologetically.

The next two minutes went by alarmingly fast. Jaden tried over and over again to touch Malia's mind or to call out to Vindhu. Every attempt met with failure.

"Lieutenant, arm missiles," said the commander.

"NO!" Melissa screamed, grabbing Anhur by the shoulder. "My daughter is on that ship! You can't do this! Give them more time!"

"Melissa, there's no other way," said Brian, coaxing her away from the commander. "There's nothing more we can do."

"She's your *niece*!" Melissa yelled. "You're going to stand by and let them kill her?!"

"If they haven't made it out by now, they're probably already dead," he replied bluntly. "Otherwise, Jaden would be able to hear her."

Melissa dropped to her knees, sobbing into her hands. Jaden was crying freely now.

"Malia, please," he begged, focusing on the memory of her thoughts in his mind. *"You have to answer me... You can't be dead... you can't be..."*

Sydney sat on the floor, putting her arms around Melissa.

"Fire missiles, Lieutenant," the commander ordered.

"Yes, sir," he replied. "Missiles fired," he added a few seconds later.

Jaden watched the viewscreen in horror as the warheads sped toward the ship. Even if Malia had survived this long, she was about to die. He couldn't imagine his life without his twin sister. Grief consumed him. A low moan escaped his throat, and he trembled, still unable to tear his gaze from the viewscreen.

But as the bombs approached their target, the Malor shot them with energy beams. The weapons exploded prematurely in a blinding flash of light. The shock wave buffeted the warship, and Jaden nearly fell over. He grabbed Anhur's chair to steady himself.

"Report!" shouted the commander.

"Quantum bombs failed to reach optimum zone," said a woman from the nearest bank of consoles.

The image of the Malor vessel reappeared on the screen. It looked utterly unaffected. Jaden breathed a sigh of relief, but immediately felt a stab of guilt. Their plan had failed, but this might give Malia more time to escape if she was still alive. But he also knew this probably meant that millions of people were about to die.

"Change course!" shouted Anhur. "Move!"

"Yes, sir!" said the lieutenant. "The Malor are firing on our previous position… that was close."

"I don't understand," said Jaden. "What just happened?"

"The Malor targeted the location of our missile launch," said Nadia.

"Try to reconnect to their network," said Anhur. "See if you can get control of their navigational system."

"We can't, Commander," the woman replied. "We've been unable to reestablish access since we issued the command to open their docking bay for our shuttles. They've closed the security hole we were using."

"Sir, they're continuing to the city," said the lieutenant. "The Malor are charging their primary weapon."

"Then fire on the damn thing!" shouted Sydney.

"Negative," said Anhur. "They'll be ready for us now. If we fire again, they'll hit us with everything they've got."

"Sydney, think about it," said Brian. "This ship is the only chance we've got to stop the Malor from annihilating the entire planet. If they expose themselves now, it's likely going to be over. We have to find another way."

"There are *five million* people down there!" Sydney yelled.

"Those five million are going to die to allow us to save *billions* more," Brian told her.

Jaden thought about his last trip to Washington, recalling the Capitol and the White House, the Lincoln Memorial and the Washington Monument… And then he remembered the devastation the Malor had caused in Miami. It was hard to imagine the capital city of the United States meeting the same fate.

"Sir, I'm reading a signal… from inside the city!" said the lieutenant.

"What kind of signal?" Anhur demanded.

"Automatic distress beacon," he replied. "One of our shuttles!"

"What? Where?!"

"It's a park of some sort," said the lieutenant. "Coming up on screen now."

Suddenly the image on the viewscreen changed to a sight Jaden knew well: the Jefferson Memorial. Only sitting on the lawn in front of it was an Othali shuttle, perfectly visible.

"No shields?" asked Nadia.

"The shuttle's taken damage," said the lieutenant. "I can't raise anyone on the radio, but that's Vindhu's ship. Its engines are disabled. It looks like a crash landing."

"Lieutenant Bashandi, launch a rescue mission—but hurry!" said the commander. "You've got *no* time!"

"Yes, sir!" said Nadia. "Jaden, with me!"

Melissa rose to her feet, ready to follow.

"You should stay behind," Anhur told her.

"Malia might be down there!" said Melissa. "And you're sending my son into harm's way. I will not sit here and watch them die!"

"You're overly emotional right now and might hinder the mission," the commander replied. "Stay put."

"He's right," said Brian. "Let them do their jobs. Jaden will make sure they come back safely."

Melissa gave in. She grabbed Jaden in a hug, pulling him tight.

"Mom! Let me go—we have to *hurry*!"

He pulled away and ran out of the bridge with Nadia. They met Madu in the shuttle. Nadia sat in the cockpit, Jaden right behind her.

As they left the docking bay, Jaden wondered apprehensively what they would find down there. Was Malia on the shuttle? Was she alive? He called out to her in his mind, but still, there was no reply.

Madu took them under the Malor ship. A sense of dread came over Jaden. He could see the red glow of their primary weapon. They sped over the city, and Jaden saw the endless lines of cars trying to flee on the highways. But none of them were moving—it was a colossal traffic jam. For these people, death was inevitable.

"There it is," said Nadia as the Jefferson Memorial came into view. Once they'd cleared the trees, Jaden spotted the shuttle in the grass. Madu set them down close by. The moment they hit the ground, Jaden popped the hatch and ran to the other ship.

"How the hell do I open this thing?!" he yelled, pounding on the door.

Madu and Nadia ran up next to him. Nadia touched her hand to the hatch.

"Something's wrong; it should open," she said.

"Move!" Jaden shouted. The other two backed away. He

reached out with his thoughts and ripped the hatch away from the opening. But in the same instant, there was a noise like the biggest motor Jaden had ever heard. As he looked over the top of the shuttle, his eyes widened in terror.

Beyond the memorial stood the Washington Monument, and behind that, a thick red beam extended to the ground from the center of the Malor ship—right where the White House should be. Liquid fire began oozing down the beam.

"Jaden! Get in here!" yelled Nadia. She and Madu had gone inside.

Jaden climbed into the shuttle. Malia was lying on the floor, unconscious. One of the cockpit seats had detached from its base and fallen on top of her, covering her from the waist down. Madu was trying to dislodge it. Vindhu was sprawled out across the second row of seats; blood was spurting from the side of his neck.

"The other two are dead!" Nadia called from the cockpit. "Malia's alive, but she's trapped—the seat is stuck!"

"Get out of the way," said Jaden. Madu and Nadia crawled out of the shuttle behind him. Jaden concentrated on the broken seat, ripping it away from Malia with his mind. It smashed through the cockpit window, landing outside on the grass.

"Malia!" Jaden shouted, moving to her side.

She made no reply. He scooped her up in his arms and carried her off the shuttle.

"Jaden, run!" shouted Nadia, staring beyond him in terror.

He glanced over his shoulder in time to see the Washington Monument explode in flames as a wall of fire moved toward them. Dashing to the other shuttle, he climbed aboard, and Nadia closed the hatch behind him.

Madu took off before Jaden had a chance to put Malia down. They toppled to the floor as the ship accelerated. Jaden scrambled to his feet and looked out the window as the flames consumed the Jefferson Memorial. But the shuttle had climbed high and far enough to escape the destruction.

Jaden returned his attention to Malia. Nadia squatted down to examine her.

"What's wrong with her?" Jaden asked.

"I'm not sure," she said. "She's breathing, and her pulse is strong."

She went to the rear of the cabin and returned with a strip of fabric. Placing it on Malia's forehead, she tapped some buttons on a small device in her hand.

Malia gasped and opened her eyes.

"Jaden," she said weakly, fixing her attention on him. She tried to sit up but seemed too weak to manage it. Jaden cried tears of relief. He helped her into a sitting position. Malia flung her arms around him, hugging him tight and sobbing on his shoulder. Jaden held her, overcome with joy that she was alive.

28

CAT AND MOUSE

"What happened?" Jaden asked. "How did you get off that ship?"

"I don't know," said Malia, taking a steadying breath. "We were hiding, and we thought… they'd all gone by. But when we came out… there were Malor there. One of them shot me… and that's the last thing I remember." She let go of Jaden, and looked around the shuttle, taking in her surroundings for the first time. "Where are we? What happened to Vindhu?"

"He must have gotten you back to the shuttle," Nadia told her. "But it crash-landed. He and the pilot are both dead. I'm sorry."

Malia stared at her in shock for a moment, then grabbed Jaden again, sobbing harder than ever. Jaden said a silent thank you to Vindhu for saving his sister.

A few minutes later, they docked onboard the Othali

warship. Nadia took Jaden and Malia back to the bridge. Melissa saw them and gathered her children into a big hug, totally incapable of speech.

"I thought I was going to lose both of you," she said with her thoughts.

"Ease us away from the Malor, Lieutenant," said Anhur. "Take us higher."

Jaden pulled away from his mother. He watched the Malor on the viewscreen as they began moving away, but it seemed like the enormous ship was following them.

"We've changed course, but they're pursuing us," said the lieutenant.

"How is that possible?" asked Brian. "I thought your shields rendered this ship invisible?"

"They do," said Nadia. "But a ship this large inside an atmosphere leaves telltale signs that the Malor can track. The shuttles aren't big enough to produce the effect. But once we fired our missiles, they must have started scanning for us."

"Take us out of the atmosphere," said Anhur. "Full speed."

"Yes, sir."

As Jaden watched the viewscreen, they pulled away from the Malor ship. But the Malor fired energy beams at them. One of the shots hit them, violently rocking the warship. Jaden fell to the floor along with Malia, Sydney, and Carl.

"Direct hit," shouted the lieutenant.

"Return fire!" said Anhur. "Target their weapons."

Red beams shot from the warship, hitting the Malor vessel

and exploding on contact. Jaden couldn't tell if they'd had any effect.

"We're pulling out of range now," said the lieutenant.

"Can't they catch us?" asked Jaden.

"Not inside the atmosphere," said Nadia. "We're faster and more agile here. In open space, it's a different story. But they won't be able to track us there."

The air around them grew darker and darker until finally, it became black. They'd left the Earth's atmosphere once again.

"New course, Lieutenant," said Anhur. "Move us to geosynchronous orbit above the equator."

"Yes, sir."

"Commander, we may have a problem," said a man from the rear of the bridge. He was watching a display at a workstation there. "The Malor damaged our shields in the exchange. Our starboard flank may be partially exposed."

"Acknowledged, Ensign," said Anhur. "Lieutenant, change our orientation to make sure we're not showing the Malor our flank. Ensign, try to realign the adjacent generators to compensate."

Jaden watched the Malor ship on the viewscreen. They weren't coming any closer.

"Can they see us?" asked Malia.

"I don't think so," said Nadia. "They've entered a low orbit."

"They're looking for us," said the Lieutenant. "They're actively scanning the area."

"Hold this position," said Anhur.

Several tense minutes went by. The lieutenant made regular reports of Malor activity. They were blanketing the area with radiation but failed to detect the Othali warship.

"Commander, the damaged shield generator has failed," said the ensign from the rear of the bridge. "Adjacent shields aren't strong enough to compensate."

"Sir, they've found us," said the lieutenant. "They've changed course to intercept."

"Move us out," said Anhur. "Plot a course to the Moon. Full speed."

"Yes, sir."

"I never thought I'd go to the Moon," Sydney muttered.

The image on the viewscreen split into two frames, one showing the Moon and the other displaying the Malor ship. Jaden wasn't sure, but it looked like the Malor were getting closer.

"Time to lunar orbit?" asked Anhur.

"Ninety minutes at maximum acceleration," said the lieutenant.

"And how long till the Malor reach weapons range?"

"Sir... we'll arrive at the Moon before they catch us."

"Excellent," said Anhur. "Lieutenant, plot a course to enter lunar orbit. Once we're there, adjust our trajectory to keep us on the opposite side of the Moon from the Malor."

"That's brilliant," said Nadia. "It should buy us enough time to repair the shields."

"We're not out of trouble yet," said Anhur. "With or without shields, they can still track the heat from our engines when we're at full power. And we need a new plan.

"Lieutenant, alert the department heads. I want a briefing in five minutes."

"Yes, sir."

Jaden, Malia, and Melissa accompanied Nadia, Carl, Sydney, and Brian into the battle room. Anhur arrived a few minutes later, and the rest of his staff trickled in.

"Ladies and gentlemen, we've got a problem," said Anhur. "Entering lunar orbit will give us time to repair our shields. But we still don't have a plan to eliminate the Malor. Ideas?"

"We've lost the advantage," said Captain Patel. "The failed attack alerted them to our presence. We've been unable to reestablish computer access, and now they'll be expecting further attempts to destroy them."

"The power stations on Earth may be the only way," said Nadia. "Pulling from the energy grid there, those weapons are much stronger than ours."

"We can't access them," said Anhur. "The Malor damaged the communication systems when they shut down the beacon."

"However, we could send a team on a shuttle," said Melissa. "I was able to access the weapons on the Miami station. Someone with more knowledge of the system would be able to activate the shields as well."

"We could lure them there by disabling our starboard flanking shield," said Captain Patel. "Make them believe our repairs didn't hold."

"When was the last time someone visited those other stations?" asked Brian. "Ten thousand years ago?"

"At least," said Melissa.

"Geological activity had sealed off the entrance to the Miami station," said Brian. "It took me a long time to get inside. This may not work if the same thing has happened to the other two."

"That's a good point," Captain Patel conceded. "But our shuttles are submersible. There's a good chance we'd be able to use our weapons to cut our way in should it be necessary."

"We also don't know if the station's weapons will be strong enough to destroy the Malor ship," Anhur pointed out. "Based on the exchange over Miami, I'd guess not. Perhaps together with our own, we can damage their weapons and engines. But it may not be enough to eliminate them. They'd still have their saucer fleet, which gives them more than enough firepower to destroy this ship. Once we're gone, they'll have all the time they need to make repairs."

"I've got another idea," said Brian. "There's an asteroid belt between the orbits of Mars and Jupiter."

"Yes, we had to navigate around it on our way here," said Captain Patel. "How does that help?"

"The children," said Brian. "Take us to the asteroid belt, and they can hit the Malor with thousands of rocky bodies."

"That might work," said Nadia. "Now that we've left the Earth's magnetic field, the children won't be able to move the larger ones. But some of the smaller ones may still be massive enough to penetrate their shields and their hull. It may not destroy them…"

"But it might weaken them enough for our weapons to finish them off," Anhur finished for her. "I like this plan. If it fails, we can still return to Earth and try to use the power stations."

"I'm not sure I understand this," said Sydney. "A *nuclear explosion* wasn't enough to hurt them. But now you're going to throw *rocks* at them?!"

"That nuke our boys shot at them back there was two megatons," said Carl. "The asteroid that killed the dinosaurs was only seven miles across, but the impact was equivalent to *one hundred million* megatons."

"The trouble will be accelerating those rocks to sufficient velocity," added Brian.

"Most of them have orbital velocities between eighty and ninety thousand kilometers per hour," said Nadia. "All the children have to do is change their course."

"Oh," said Sydney, still looking dumbfounded. Jaden couldn't blame her; he also found the whole thing difficult to comprehend.

Anhur adjourned the meeting. The staff returned to their posts, and Jaden and Malia went back to the conference room with Melissa. They reached the Moon shortly after that. Jaden watched the cratered surface race by below, unable to believe where he was. Only a handful of humans had ever visited this world, and none had done so for decades.

After they passed around the far side of the Moon, Jaden watched the Earth rise above the horizon. It looked so small from this vantage point. He wondered how much smaller it would seem from the asteroid belt.

Nadia came to get them after they'd completed three orbits. They headed back to the bridge.

"The shields are repaired," she said. "Now comes the dangerous part."

"You mean going to the asteroid belt?" asked Jaden.

"No, leaving orbit."

The atmosphere on the bridge was different now. It felt much more tense than it had earlier.

"What's going on?" asked Jaden.

"There are a couple of problems with this plan," said Nadia. "The Malor ship is faster than ours in open space. We've kept ourselves on the opposite side of the Moon from them. But if we break orbit now, they'll catch us before we reach the asteroid belt. So we're going to stop here and wait. Once they've gone by us, we'll head out. It'll take them too long to reverse course, so they'll complete one more orbit before pursuing us. That should give us enough time to reach the asteroid belt before them."

"So what's the dangerous part?" asked Malia.

"Shields have to be calibrated very precisely to work correctly. We've done the calibration, but there's no way of knowing for certain if it's perfect."

"And if it's not…" said Jaden.

"They'll detect us when they pass, and probably destroy us."

"Oh. Great," he said sarcastically.

They waited as Anhur barked out orders to his people. The bridge was a flurry of nervous chatter and activity. But when the commander finally said, "Do it, Lieutenant. Take us to synchronous orbit and hold position," everyone grew quiet and still.

Half of the viewscreen showed the Moon. As they moved into position, it grew steadily smaller. The other half displayed a diagram showing the relative locations of the Othali and Malor ships. Jaden watched apprehensively as the Malor vessel came closer.

The tension on the bridge grew as everyone watched and waited. Several minutes went by. Finally, Jaden spotted the Malor ship emerge above the lunar horizon. It drew steadily nearer, growing larger in the viewscreen. He didn't know how far away they were, but the ship appeared massive. Before long, a small portion of it filled the viewscreen. Jaden could see every detail of its surface. Enormous protrusions and valleys covered the structure. The center of the ship went by, the primary weapon glowing with energy.

"Report," said Anhur.

"The Malor are holding course. They're actively scanning, but there's no sign that they've detected us."

A cheer went up around the bridge. Jaden let out a sigh of relief. Once the Malor ship had gone by, Anhur said, "That's it, Lieutenant. Take us out to the asteroid belt, full speed."

"Yes sir," he replied, excitement in his voice.

The diagram on the viewscreen now showed the Othali warship racing away from the Moon. The Malor continued their orbit.

"They've detected our engine output and are accelerating," said the lieutenant. "Their velocity isn't increasing as quickly as we anticipated. We should reach the asteroid belt in plenty of time."

"The damage to their engines must be greater than we

realized," Anhur replied. "I'll take every advantage we can get."

"Commander," said the ensign from the rear of the bridge. "I'm detecting a signal from Earth. Sir, it's one of the power stations. Off the coast of Bermuda. It's coming online."

"Verify that, Ensign," said Anhur. "There's nobody down there to activate that thing."

"Confirmed, sir. It's broadcasting a distress call on all frequencies."

"A *distress call*?" demanded Anhur.

"Someone from the military must have found the station," said Melissa. "Even with communications disabled, those stations can still emit distress signals. It's a separate system."

"How did they access the control system?" asked Brian. "I worked on it for years and couldn't crack the code."

"Probably those bastards from Dreamland," said Carl. "The Malor gained enough control to shut down the beacon. Those boys from Area 51 have been playing with technology from the Malor saucers for decades now. You saw that wedge aircraft they developed!"

"What are the Malor doing?" demanded Anhur. "Following us or diverting to Earth?"

"Impossible to tell yet," said the lieutenant. "It depends when they break orbit."

"Monitor that," said Anhur.

The diagram on the viewscreen changed. A line segment appeared, extending from the surface of the Moon.

"If they break orbit at that point, it means they're

pursuing us," said the lieutenant. "Otherwise, they're heading to Earth."

"Very well," Anhur growled. "Maintain course. If the Malor break off their pursuit, then plot a course to Earth."

"Yes, sir."

Minutes went by. Jaden watched their position on the diagram move farther from the Moon, while the Malor's grew closer to the line. But the ship reached the point the lieutenant had marked and kept going around the Moon.

"They're going to Earth!" shouted Jaden.

Anhur turned to gaze at him, surprised that he'd spoken out.

"That they are," he said. "Lieutenant, change course! Take us to Earth."

The diagram disappeared from the viewscreen. Now it showed only the Earth and the Malor ship.

"They've got a good lead," said the lieutenant. "And they're accelerating. We'll never catch them."

"Fools," Anhur grumbled. "Those Earthlings don't know how to operate that thing. And if the Malor destroy it, we may lose our only means of defeating them."

Nadia offered to take Jaden and Malia back to the conference room, but Jaden didn't want to leave. They had well over an hour before they'd reach Earth, but he didn't want to risk missing any further developments. He stayed where he was, his eyes glued to the viewscreen.

The Malor reached Earth, and their ship turned into a fireball as it entered the atmosphere. The Othali arrived five minutes later. Jaden saw only flames as they plummeted through the air.

A new diagram appeared; it showed the Malor ship approaching Bermuda from the south. Anhur ordered the lieutenant to move in from the north. By the time they reached the ocean, the Malor had arrived over Bermuda.

The Othali warship raced toward the island. On the viewscreen, Jaden saw their passage churning up giant waves. As Bermuda came into view, he could see that the Malor were engaged in an intense firefight with the power station. Beams of energy shot out of the water, exploding where they contacted the Malor ship. The Malor shot balls of fire at the power station.

The Othali came to rest directly north of Bermuda. The Malor ship was due south, across the island.

"Someone's activated the station's shields," said the lieutenant.

"Gotta hand it to those bastards," Carl muttered. "They're good!"

"Sir, the power station has damaged the Malor's primary weapon," said the lieutenant. "It's offline. But they're outgunned. The Malor will overpower the station's shields in a matter of minutes."

"Open fire," said the commander. "Target the Malor weapons."

"Yes, sir."

Jaden watched dozens of energy beams hit the Malor ship. Most exploded near the source of the Malor cannons.

"Something's happening, Commander," said the ensign. "The station's power output is approaching maximum."

Jaden noticed a bright glow under the water. And as he watched, the ocean itself began to boil.

"The Malor ship is losing altitude," said the lieutenant.

"It's the power station!" said Melissa. "The magnetic field from the collection grid must be pulling them down!"

"What magnetic field?" demanded Anhur.

"Byproduct of the energy production," said Brian. "It releases methane hydrates and generates a strong magnetic field."

At that moment, a Malor energy beam hit the source of the underwater glow. Something exploded.

"They've destroyed the power station's weapons," said the lieutenant. "The Malor are fighting to gain altitude. But the station's reactor is going into meltdown. It'll be offline soon."

"Jaden, Malia," said Melissa. "This is your chance. The field is weakening them—try to take them down!"

"You must act fast," the lieutenant told them. "The reactor is going to shut down in two minutes—you'll lose this advantage!"

"We should go to the conference room," said Jaden. "It might not work from the viewscreens—we need to see it for real!"

"Let's go!" said Nadia. She ran out of the bridge, Jaden, Malia, and Melissa right behind her. They bolted down the three flights of stairs and through the corridor to the conference room.

Jaden and Malia crossed to the windows. The Malor ship was in plain view.

"You've only got one minute left," Nadia told them.

"Can you do this?" Jaden asked, remembering Malia's initial reluctance to destroy the Malor the last time they tried.

"Yes," she said in his mind. "I'm ready."

Together, they focused on the ship. Jaden imagined reaching out and pushing down with all his might. He felt the vessel vibrating, fighting against his will.

Before long, the vibration penetrated the hull of the Othali warship. The conference room itself began to shake, resonating with the Malor engines.

Slowly, the giant ship approached the sea. Jaden could feel the power of Malia's mind, also straining against the vessel. He pushed ever harder.

The Malor fired on the Othali warship. It bucked violently. Jaden lost his focus for a moment, and the Malor ship stopped its descent.

"Thirty more seconds!" Nadia yelled. "They'll regain full power when that reactor shuts down!"

"JADEN!" Malia screamed in his mind. "I need you! I can't do this alone!"

Jaden concentrated. He reached out once again with his thoughts, gathering all of his strength, and pushing as hard as he could against the ship.

The Malor resumed sinking, a little at a time. They fired on the Othali again, and although Jaden crashed into the window, he maintained his focus. Suddenly jets of fire exploded from the edge of the Malor ship. One whole side of it listed toward the sea, making contact with the water.

This started a chain reaction. Fireballs exploded at several points where the ship had met the ocean. More explosions erupted from the opposite side of the vessel. With one final effort, Jaden and Malia exerted the full power of their will against the Malor. The leading edge of the ship disappeared under the water. The Othali fired on the vessel over and over again, their energy beams causing giant explosions everywhere they impacted. Jaden guessed the Malor shields must have stopped functioning.

Jaden felt the strain taking its toll. The edges of his vision went black, and it was as if he were staring at the Malor ship through a tunnel. He didn't know how much longer he could keep it up.

"Time's up!" Nadia told them. "The reactor is offline!"

"*Hold on*!" Malia commanded. "*We're almost there!*"

Jaden pushed. A maelstrom of fire had engulfed the enemy vessel.

And then suddenly, something broke. Jaden could feel it in his mind. The Malor ship shattered, exploding now from within. All that remained above water crashed into the sea. Steam and smoke billowed out from the wreck, overtaking the Othali warship and blinding them.

Jaden was spent; he withdrew his mind back into himself. Malia had done the same. She gazed at him with a weak smile, leaning against the window. But Jaden's vision continued going black. His legs felt rubbery, and he was nauseous. He fell to the floor and passed out.

29

FOREVER

Jaden woke up to find himself lying flat on his back on the floor of the conference room. Malia and Melissa were there, kneeling beside him. Nadia, Sydney, Carl, and Brian were gathered behind them, looking at him with concern.

"How do you feel?" asked Melissa.

"I'm all right," said Jaden, sitting up. Looking out the window, he saw a gigantic pillar of fire growing from the Malor ship, reaching to the sky. "We did it?" he asked. "The ship is destroyed?"

"Yes," Nadia told him with a smile. "You and Malia saved your world."

"How long was I out?"

"Only a couple of minutes," said Malia. "The strain must've been too much. I almost blacked out too."

"We've got one last mystery to solve," said Nadia. "We'd like your help if you feel up to it."

"What mystery?" asked Jaden.

"We don't know who was operating the power station," she told him.

"I thought it was the people from Area 51," said Jaden.

"So we assumed. But there are no naval vessels or military aircraft in the area," Nadia explained.

"At the very least, there'd be an Air Force helicopter somewhere nearby," said Carl. "Dreamland's a joint venture of the Air Force and the CIA."

"But there is a civilian submarine off the southern coast of the island," said Nadia. "It's submerged near the power station and seems to be disabled. I'm betting whoever operated the station is on board."

Jaden looked at Malia. She shrugged her shoulders.

"Yeah, sure. Why not," said Jaden.

"Madu's got the shuttle ready," said Nadia. "We're ready whenever you are."

Jaden, Malia, and Melissa followed her to the docking bay. They met Madu there and boarded the shuttle. After leaving the berth, he steered them out of the bay. He flew them across the main island of Bermuda, and partway around the Malor ship, keeping them far from the inferno.

Jaden spotted a small island directly ahead. But before they reached it, Madu took them down to the surface of the ocean and plunged under the water.

"Whoa!" said Jaden.

Nadia turned on spotlights at the front of the shuttle to

illuminate their way. They soared past an enormous coral reef.

Before long, they came to a ridge. And as they moved along its edge, a submarine came into view. It was no bigger than their shuttle. The vessel was sitting on the sea bottom at an odd angle.

"Do you two think you can lift that?" asked Madu.

"Psh," replied Malia. "Piece of cake." She focused on the submarine, and it floated off the ocean floor. "Where do you want it?"

"Just keep it with us," said Madu with a grin. "I'm going to surface. We'll touch down on that island up ahead."

Malia nodded, her brow furrowed in concentration.

Madu moved them to the surface. Malia kept the submarine directly ahead of them. As they rose into the air again, Jaden chuckled.

"What's so funny?" asked Melissa.

"Nothing," he replied. "I just never thought I'd see a flying submarine."

They reached the island. Malia lowered the submarine onto the beach. It wouldn't stay upright in the sand, so she eased it onto its side. Madu landed nearby. Nadia popped the hatch, and they climbed out of the shuttle.

As they approached the submarine, the portal opened. A lanky Black man with locs clambered out. He jumped down to the sand and moved toward them.

Melissa stopped in her tracks.

"I don't believe it," she said, staring at the man wide-eyed.

"Tessa!" the man yelled, running toward them. He grabbed Melissa in a big hug, lifting her right off her feet. "I knew you'd be on board that ship!"

"Bomani!" Melissa said, tears sliding down her cheeks. "You're alive!"

"Bomani," said Malia. "The other colonist who survived with you?"

"At your service," Bomani said, bowing to her dramatically.

"I thought you died at Buchenwald!" said Melissa.

Bomani started to reply, but Nadia interrupted him.

"I'm eager to hear your story, too," she said. "But we should get underway. We don't want to be waylaid here by the local authorities."

They boarded the shuttle, and Nadia closed the hatch. Madu took the controls, and they lifted off.

"Well, let's hear it," said Nadia. "Melissa told us much of your story, but we're surprised to discover you're alive."

"It's Melissa now, huh?" said Bomani.

"Melissa Kwan," she said. "For more than twenty years now."

Bomani nodded. "I was close to death at Buchenwald, that much is true. The soldiers shot me when I surrendered."

"I remember," said Melissa. "They thought you were the only escapee. That's the only reason I got away."

"Yes. The bullet hit me in the shoulder. I lost a lot of blood. But I managed to survive, no thanks to the Nazis. There was an old man in the camp who helped me. I would have died if it weren't for him."

"How did you finally get out of Buchenwald?" asked Melissa.

"I was there until the Allies liberated the camp. For many years I tried to find you, but of course, I had no way of knowing where you might have gone, or what name you'd assumed.

"When I heard about the crash of the extraterrestrial spacecraft in Roswell, I started paying attention to the rumors of other visits. It became apparent that some were legitimate. From the pictures, it was clear these beings were not Othali. I feared an attack and decided to relocate close to one of the power stations.

"I went to Miami first. By going scuba diving, I discovered the hidden entrance to the docking port there had caved in. So I came to Bermuda instead. The station here was still accessible. I've lived here ever since."

"And how did you come to possess a submarine?" Melissa asked incredulously.

"Ah, a good friend of mine used to use it to give under-water tours of the coral reefs. But he retired, and I bought the submarine. When that ship fired on the pyramid, the reactor went into meltdown. I tried to escape, but falling rocks hit the sub on the way out of the port. They damaged the thing somehow, and I was stuck where you found me. I probably would have died down there if you hadn't rescued me!"

"Don't mention it," said Melissa. "You saved us all. If you hadn't joined the fight, the Malor probably would have destroyed us—and Earth."

"Malor, eh?" he said with a scowl. "Tell me about them."

Nadia related everything she knew about them as they returned to the warship. Madu docked the shuttle, and they disembarked. Nadia led the whole group to the bridge and introduced Bomani to Commander Anhur.

"We owe you one," said the commander, shaking his hand.

"Commander, can I have a word with you?" asked Melissa. "In private?"

"Of course," said Anhur, looking surprised. "We can use the battle room."

She followed him out of the bridge.

"What's that about?" Jaden asked Malia telepathically; she only shrugged. But they didn't have to wait long. Melissa returned a few minutes later and asked them to join her.

"Brian, Carl, and Sydney, you should come too," she said. "And you, Bomani."

They followed her into the battle room, taking seats around the table.

"We need to decide where we go from here," said Anhur. "All of us. This ship contains every remaining Othali in the universe. We've been searching for a habitable planet ever since the Malor destroyed our world. But Melissa has suggested that the people of this planet aren't ready to accept beings from other star systems. I'd have to agree with her.

"On our way here, we discovered another planet hospitable to life. Unfortunately, we used the last of our refined fuel coming here, so we can't make any more delta-shifts. Running on our hydrogen engines, it'll take us about one hundred years to reach the other planet. Spectroscopy indicates the presence of the raw materials we need to produce more fuel. So once we get there, we'll be able to return to Earth very quickly and see how society has progressed. When the time is right, we'll make contact again.

"But for now, each of you must decide what you want to do."

"Jaden and Malia, I've spoken to the commander, and he's willing to take us along," said Melissa. "I think it's the right thing to do, but I won't make this decision without you."

"I agree," said Brian. "You know Babcock will never stop pursuing the two of you if you remain here. I'll be sorry to see you go, but it will most likely work out for the best."

"Leave Earth?" asked Malia. "But… we'd live our whole lives… here? On a spaceship?"

Jaden found the idea shocking. In a way, it was impossible to grasp the concept of leaving the only planet he'd ever known. But it made sense—for the first time since he fell off the high school, *everything* made sense. This solution seemed drastic, but he understood the necessity.

"Whatever," he said. "It's better than moving in with the polar bears or wherever we'd have to hide on Earth."

"And you heard the commander. In time, you may be able to return to Earth," said Melissa.

"Mom, what are you talking about?" said Jaden. "He said it'd take *a hundred years* to get to that other planet." But suddenly it hit him, and he was surprised he hadn't put it together sooner. "Oh—I get it… we'll still be alive, won't we?"

"That's correct," she replied, smiling at him. "You and

your sister will live forever. Once you mature into full adult-hood, you'll stop aging."

Jaden couldn't believe his ears. He remembered her telling them that they'd found a way to counteract the rapid aging her first set of twins had suffered. But he'd failed to understand that they wouldn't experience normal aging, either.

"Will you come with us?" asked Malia.

"Of course I will," said Melissa. "I'll go wherever you go."

"Let's do it," said Jaden. "We've got nothing to lose."

Malia nodded. "As long as we're together, I agree."

"Bomani?" asked Anhur. "What about you?"

"Count me in, Commander," he said. "I'm just happy to be back with my own people finally."

"That settles it," said Anhur. "We'll send a shuttle to take the rest of you back to Earth, and then we'll get underway."

"Uh, hold on just a minute," said Carl. "How would you feel about taking on one extra passenger?"

"Who?" asked Anhur, puzzled.

"Me, of course," said Carl. "This is an incredible opportunity! I always wished I could visit the stars. Now's my chance!"

"Carl, forgive me, but you're not a young man," said Brian. "You realize you'd live out the rest of your years on this ship. If I understand correctly, you won't make it to another star system."

"I know that," said Carl, waving him off. "It was a figure of speech. But think of it, Brian—I'd be the first human to travel beyond the solar system. There's nothing here for me anyway. Those bastards took everything I owned, remember?"

"You're welcome to join us," said Anhur, "so long as you're fully cognizant of the decision you're making. If you change your mind in a few weeks, there's no going back."

"I know," said Carl. "My mind's made up. I'm yours if you'll have me."

"Very well," Anhur replied with an amused grin. "What about the two of you?"

"My place is here, on Earth," said Brian.

But Sydney looked uncertain. "I don't know... Melissa, I've got you back after all these years, I don't want to say goodbye again. And reconnecting with Jaden and Malia... meant a lot to me. But... leaving Earth?" She let out a long sigh. "Maybe. I don't exactly have a lot tying me down here—just my cat. And my mom, I guess... I'm not crazy about my job, that's for sure!"

"You could work for me," suggested Brian.

Sydney snorted. "Doing what?"

"Whatever you want," Brian said with a shrug. "You're clever and resourceful—you proved that in getting these two safely across the country. I'm sure I'll find something useful for you to do."

Sydney chuckled. "If you say so—but I accept!"

"Consider yourself hired," said Brian.

Anhur ended the meeting. Jaden, Malia, Melissa, and Carl accompanied Brian and Sydney to the shuttle bay.

"The commander tells me I've got two passengers," said Madu, meeting them at his shuttle. "Where are we headed?"

"That's a great question," said Brian. "Back to Crater Lake, I guess—if my helicopter's still there."

"If not, I'll take you wherever you need to go," said Madu. "We can depart as soon as you're ready." He ducked inside the shuttle.

"I guess this is goodbye," said Melissa, pulling Brian into a hug. "Thank you so much for everything you've done."

"My pleasure," said Brian. "I'm glad Stephen's dream was finally realized."

He let go of Melissa and gathered Jaden and Malia into a hug.

"I'm gonna miss you," said Malia.

"And I you," said Brian. "Make sure you two take care of your mom."

Melissa hugged Sydney next. "I'm sorry I allowed us to drift apart. I wish I could have told you the truth."

"It worked out in the end," said Sydney, fighting back tears. "I understand everything now."

"Sydney, there's something I have to tell you," said Malia, suddenly grave.

"What is it?"

"Well, it's Jaden. He's madly in love with you—"

"Hey!" Jaden yelled, trying to smack Malia in the head. She ducked out of his reach, giggling uncontrollably.

"Aw, that's sweet," said Sydney. "The truth is I'm madly in love with both of you. Now get over here." She gave them both a hug as Carl shook hands with Brian.

It was time to go. Sydney and Brian boarded the shuttle, and Melissa closed the hatch behind them. They watched the shuttle leave the bay before returning to the bridge. Nadia met them there and offered to show them to their new living quarters.

"Not yet," said Jaden. "Do you mind if I go back to the conference room?"

"Go ahead," Nadia replied.

Jaden left the bridge, and Malia accompanied him. They ran down the stairs and sat down in front of the windows.

"I can't believe we're leaving," Jaden said in Malia's mind.

"I know," she replied. *"When we ran into the woods that night, I never imagined it'd end up like this."*

They sat there staring out at the ocean, and talking about everything that had happened. Thirty minutes later, the Othali warship rose into the sky. They left the atmosphere once again and looked down on the Earth as it rotated below them. But this time they didn't stop in orbit. The ship kept going, and the planet grew smaller in the window. Jaden and Malia stayed to watch until it was no more than a tiny pinprick of light.

"Do you think we'll ever go back?" Malia asked in his mind.

Jaden paused for a moment before replying.

"We will," he said. *"Someday."*

EPILOGUE

Christopher Babcock poured himself a glass of whiskey. He drank half, topped it off, then sat down on his couch, setting the glass down on the coffee table. Once he'd removed his tie, he took another gulp of whiskey and sat back with a sigh.

He'd spent most of his adult life working for the CIA, and while there had been good days and bad, today had been one of the worst. Of course, the invasion had been bad for everybody, but he had skin in the game. The Kwan twins were gone, and he had no idea where.

Preliminary reports he'd seen seemed to indicate that they'd been on board the *second* alien ship that had shown up. But where had that gone?

"Officer Babcock," a voice drawled from behind him.

Babcock stumbled to his feet, knocking his whiskey all

over the floor, and turned to see a man standing there. A man wearing a black suit and tie and dark sunglasses.

"What do *you* want?" he asked, trying to sound calm, despite his heart now beating a mile a minute.

He'd known the man in black would be showing up at some point but hadn't expected to see him so soon.

"We have a problem, you and I," the man told him.

"The Kwan twins—I know."

"You lost them."

"Hey, we did everything we could—"

"We had a deal."

Babcock thought his heart might have stopped, now.

"And I've honored it—I've given you all the information you wanted!"

"You were responsible for our project."

"We'll get them back... somehow..."

The man in black smirked at him.

"You don't even know where they are right now."

Babcock gulped. He didn't know what to say. His only thoughts now were for his family.

"Don't worry; we've got an asset in place. I'll be in touch again soon."

"What asset? You know where they are?"

The man ignored him and strode out the front door, closing it behind him. Babcock ran across the room and followed him out, but he'd vanished.

"Shit," he muttered, going back inside.

Retrieving his glass from the floor, he poured himself more whiskey.

To be continued…